Judgment's Shadow

Judgment's Shadow

This is a work of fiction. Names, characters, places, and incidents either are the product of the author's imagination or are used fictitiously. Any resemblance to actual persons, living or dead, events, or locales is entirely coincidental

Copyright © 2025 Tyler H. Jolley

Cover Design by Lisa Amowitz

Interior Typesetting by Melissa Williams Design

All rights reserved.

Published in the United States by Tyler H. Jolley

ISBN: 978-1-958734-38-4 (paperback)
ISBN: 978-1-958734-39-1 (hardcover)
ISBN: 978-1-958734-40-7 (eBook)

Judgment's Shadow

Tyler H. Jolley
Gentry Scott

"Every angel is terror"

—Duino Elegies, Rainer Maria Rilke

CHAPTER 1

Welcome to Hell, all ye damned and demented.
Please keep moving. Welcome to Hell, all ye
damned and demented. Please keep moving . . .

The repeating message began seconds after I reached the top of the red stone platform, hammering the morning air and making me jump even though I'd known it was coming. The tips of my fingers tingled as razor-sharp talons began to poke through the skin, and I tasted blood as fangs momentarily slid over my teeth.

Cinder laughed. "Exciting, huh?"

Her voice was nearly drowned out by the blaring announcement and the expectant chatter of the Arrival Day crowd packed into the streets below us. But I could read her lips easily enough. Even if I hadn't, her body language made clear how pumped up she was. The way her tail, light blue now to match her aqua mane and horns, flicked back and forth, her fingers caressing the shiny black handle of her souljab.

"Sure," I said, rubbing my hands up and down my arms. In another hour, the cavern roof high overhead would be flaming red, heating the air to a comfortable level. Now though, the stone was barely pink—the temperature cold enough that I shivered in my tight leather uniform. Why weren't the guys' uniforms as skimpy as the girls'?

Cinder's eyes roamed over the other demon spawns waiting with us—no doubt targeting the helpless guy who would fall under the spell of her feminine charms at the after-arrival parties that night.

"*Fire* and *brimstone*," she said, spotting her victim. A year or two older than us, he was a Dae' Ceal like Cinder. His skin was bright yellow, and the mane of fur running from his forehead to the tip of his tail was striped in a showy orange and black. Exactly her kind of guy. Not mine.

"See anything you like?" she asked.

I rolled my eyes, but she was insistent. "I'm serious, Blaze. If you don't make your move soon, all the interesting guys will be taken."

Cinder and I had been roommates at the Demon Training Center for all of three days, and already I could tell she was not going to be good for my self-esteem. I'd known her years before this, but over the last six months, she'd blossomed in ways I could only dream of. Guys flocked to her like fire worms to lava.

Part of it was genetics. Dae' Ceal girls were naturally sexier than Dae' Ungus. Where she was petite and curvy in all the places guys liked, I was tall and angular. She could change the color of her skin and fur to match whatever she wore that day, while my skin and hair were always both bright red. Dae' Ungus were mostly known for our quick tempers and deadly teeth and talons that appeared whenever we were angry or scared. Great for battle. Not so great for picking up guys.

"I don't know." I sighed. "Maybe I'll just stay home and study tonight. Training starts for real next week." Even as I said the words, I could hear how pathetic they sounded. Fortunately, I didn't have to hear Cinder's snarky retort because she was already stalking her prey. Thinking of training reminded me why we were here, and I began studying everything around me, hoping I didn't screw up my first Arrival.

To my right, the imposing Immigration Station rose like a stern stone finger pointing high into the air. As a little girl, the arched entryways had always reminded me of a pair of brooding eyes. I'd been terrified of the grimy stained-glass windows depicting figures being dipped into burning oil and hanging from their feet above bubbling lava until my mother explained that the figures in the pictures were evil humes being punished for the terrible things they'd done in life.

At the other end of the platform, two blackened spots marked the area where the Stygian Transit would deliver its cargo of condemned prisoners. A tall metal fence ran along both sides of the platform, its spikes topped with heads of the disobedient damned. Faded black circles and yellow arrows marked where we would stand, herding the clueless humes into the entrance of the station.

"Hey, don't I know you?" a familiar deep voice boomed, and an arm as big as my thigh draped across my shoulder.

"I don't think so," I said, pretending to study his large dark eyes and the broad cheekbones that always made him look like he was about to set off on some amazing adventure. "You're not the guy who cleans the food stalls, are you?"

Effortlessly, he lifted me off my hooves and spun me around. "I'll show you food stalls."

"Put me down before one of the trainers sees us," I squealed, trying to break out of his grip. It was like trying to bend forged steel.

He set me down with a laugh. "Stop worrying. Most of the trainers are barely awake yet."

Onyx was one of the few guys I was comfortable

around. We'd known each other since we were spawnlings. A Dae' Lorica, he had broad shoulders, thick horns that would one day curl completely around two or three times on the sides of his bald head, and glistening black skin that formed an almost impenetrable armor of thick scales when he got angry. At least two hands taller than me, he looked imposing. But he was actually a sweetheart.

Unlike Cinder and I, who were primies beginning our first year of training, Onyx was a tert, two years ahead of us. To him, Arrival Days were no big deal.

"Nervous?" he asked, tugging on the sleeve of my uni to straighten it out and adjusting my souljab holster.

"Terrified," I admitted. Of course, I'd seen Arrivals before—it was a holiday event all demons showed up for starting when they were little. But I'd always watched it from the streets below.

This would be my first time seeing a hume close up. Even though they hadn't arrived, the air here was heavy with the smell of their sweat and fear, as if the stone itself was permanently embedded with the rancid odor. "What if I mess up?"

"You won't," Onyx said. "The humes are so scared and confused when they arrive, all you have to do is point them in the right direction and then run like spark ants to a flame."

Easy for him to say. Despite the fact that he carried a simple leather whip instead of a souljab like Cinder and me, he looked more terrifying than the two of us combined. One glance at his bulging muscles and any hume would run in the opposite direction.

"Is it really true that they can't remember why they've been sent here?" I asked. It was one of the first things you learned about the humes sent to Hell. But I couldn't imagine how a bunch of murderers, pervs, and sickos could ever forget the horrible crimes they'd committed.

"They're mindless cattle," Cinder said, strutting back over and twining her tail seductively around one leg as she eyed my friend.

"It doesn't matter what they remember," Onyx said, ignoring her flirtations. "Just herd them off the train and into the immigration building." Unlike most guys she came on to, he didn't seem affected by Cinder's looks in any way. I almost got the feeling he didn't like her, although they'd only met a couple of times, and there was no reason he shouldn't.

"Just stay away from the seraphs," he said, his face serious. "If a hume struggles at all, stand back. Let the seraphs handle it. Halos are nothing to mess around with."

I swallowed, remembering all the stories I'd heard about seraphs and their angel-fire. How it could engulf you in an instant, snuffing you out of existence—or worse, sending you to the horror of an eternity spent in Absolute Zero, a place so vile, even tortured humes were terrified by the thought of being sent there.

"What do they look like?" I asked.

"Like flying pigs with enormous egos and less compassion than a pile of ashes." Onyx unhooked a pair of shaders from his uni, snapping them open and resting them on his forehead like he'd done it a thousand times.

I checked my waist pocket to make sure I'd remembered to bring mine. We'd been given the wraparound eye protection on our first day of training along with our uniforms and souljabs. In the past, I hadn't been able to see past the blindingly white flames that surrounded the seraphs. I was curious to find out if they were really as terrifying as the stories said.

"Never look directly at them," Onyx warned. "Halos

don't like us to make direct eye contact with them. And even with these on, their glare can temporarily blind you."

"What if—" I started to ask another question, but my words were cut off as the stone platform began trembling under our hooves.

"Everyone to your places!" called one of the quartuses who had led us here.

In the distance, the roaring of a Stygian train filled the air, and the voices of the crowd below grew louder. My pulse spiked and fangs filled my mouth as my mind went blank. Every instruction I'd been going over a moment before was gone. Where was I supposed to go? What should I be doing?

Onyx gently squeezed my shoulder and pointed to a black circle a few steps away. "You've got this."

At his touch, my pulse evened out and my fangs disappeared. "Right."

When he was sure I was going to be okay, Onyx started toward his own spot, but he looked back briefly. "Be careful."

As I hurried to my circle, going over the instructions in my head, the message seemed to get louder, if that was even possible. In the streets below, demons young and old crowded forward for a better view. A spawnling—horns barely poking out of her curly black hair—waved at me, her eyes wide with anticipation. I wiped my damp palms on my uni and waved back.

A cold breeze of air so clean it burned my lungs came from the direction of the mountains of Judgment. I pushed my long red hair out of my face, trying to catch a glimpse of motion out beyond the edges of the desert. Everyone craned their necks looking across the River Styx and over the Outer Circles.

"Eye protection on!" the quartus yelled. I took out my shaders and pulled them over my eyes.

"Ready?" Cinder yelled, her words jerked away by the wind from the approaching vehicle.

"I hope so," I said, my voice shaking a little.

"Weapons out!"

I unclipped my souljab and pulled it from the holster on my belt. Only a stride or two from where the Stygian would stop, Onyx nodded, uncoiling his whip and cracking it above his head.

"Prepare for arrival!"

A thunderous roar filled the air. The wind increased until I had to lean into it to stay upright. Even with the shaders on, bits of dust, sand, and trash battered my eyes.

"There it is!" someone screamed. I squinted toward the mountains. For a moment I couldn't make out anything. Then I spotted a long blur of white racing toward us at an impossible speed.

An audible *ahhh* came from the crowd as the train flew through the air on shining silver tracks that appeared magically before it. I braced my hooves, expecting to be shaken by the contact as the Stygian approached, but the first car linked with the edge of the stone platform so gently, I wouldn't have known it had happened if I hadn't been watching.

From this vantage point, it looked much bigger—at least twenty hands tall and wide enough that eight full-grown demons could stand side-by-side before it. The train gleamed a spotless white that looked out of place in Hell—without a trace of sulfur dust or the black ash that filled the air here.

I'd been told it could hold over two thousand humes, but normally the number was more like one or two hundred. There were no windows. I imagined they didn't want the passengers to see where they were going until they were already here.

The train's roar dropped to a low purr, and cut out completely as the front bumped against the platform. I took a deep breath to steady myself. For a moment, the Stygian Transit sat unmoving. Everyone grew silent—even the message stopped blasting temporarily. The entire front slid open like the mouth of some huge beast, and a burst of light flared from inside, so intense I could feel its heat from all the way back where Cinder and I were standing.

I dropped my eyes at once, dazzling afterimages floating across my vision. As the seraphs stepped onto the platform, the message started up again. I sneaked a brief glance at the other demon spawns. All of them had their heads lowered like mine. None of them looked directly at the shimmering figures who positioned themselves around the Stygian.

Squinting, I peeked toward the nearest of the seraphs. I could only stand to look for a second or two before my eyes began to water. Even in those two seconds, I couldn't make out much. It was like trying to stare straight into a pool of boiling lava, only ten times brighter.

They were broad-shouldered and taller than Onyx. Brilliant white light flowed up and down their luminescent bodies and circled around their heads like liquid fire. Their faces were so bright, it was impossible to make out any features. Golden wings rose from their backs, and each of them held a long, curved angel-fire sword before them in both hands.

It felt like I was in the presence of living jewels, and it was all I could do to keep from kneeling before them. Even Cinder—who claimed she couldn't care less about Halos— seemed in awe of the powerful figures. They looked so regal, so majestic. A sense of authority radiated from them.

If one of them commanded me to jump off the platform, I would probably do it without hesitation.

As soon as the seraphs took up their positions, a line of shambling creatures began making its way out of the Stygian. After the glory of the seraphs, the humes made my stomach curdle. Even through the dark lenses of the shaders, I could tell they were dismal things, weak and soft-looking.

Dressed in dull gray coveralls, they exited the train with shuffling, awkward steps and stared dumbly around. Like a flock of ignorant sheep, they muddled about the end of the platform and would probably have fallen off the edge if the nearest demon spawns hadn't begun driving them forward with lashes and shocks from their souljabs.

"Follow the arrows!" Onyx shouted at a man with stringy yellow hair. The man looked up, his eyes lost and afraid, but one crack of Onyx's whip and he quickly ran toward the next arrow.

"Get going!" A tert I thought I recognized prodded his souljab at a woman with wrinkly tan skin the color of old potatoes. She yelped and stumbled forward as blue fire ran up one leg.

"Damned ones, damned ones, damned ones," chanted the demons in the street below. A few of them hurled rocks or pieces of brick over the fence. Slowly, the humes began getting the idea, queuing up behind each other as we forced them toward the Immigration Station.

"Women on the right! Men on the left!" I called out, trying to make myself heard over the noise of the crowd. I waved my souljab at the humes while not getting close enough to let any of them touch me.

"Move it! Move it!" Cinder shouted, shocking anyone who didn't walk fast enough. She seemed to be enjoying herself, but now that I'd seen the humes close up, I couldn't wait for this to be over. They disgusted me. Most looked old, like dried-up fruit. Their skin and hair were different colors, but they all had a kind of frail, chalky appearance to them, as if they might crumble to dust at any minute.

I tried to imagine what each had done as they walked past. The man with the dark eyes and crooked nose looked like a murderer. The fat one with the brown teeth, a rapist. I saw a woman with big ears and a scar beneath her lower lip who looked like she probably hurt children.

I was so revolted by the sight and smell of them that I didn't notice the man and woman holding hands until they were almost directly across from me. They were younger than most, walking close together as if they didn't want to be separated. She rested her head on his shoulder, and he leaned protectively over her.

"You two!" Cinder shouted. "Move apart! Men on the left. Women on the right."

The woman gave Cinder a terrified look, backing away from her glowing souljab. As the couple stepped forward, I realized there was someone between them. A female child who didn't look any older than five or six. I'd thought the couple were holding each other's hands, but they were actually gripping the girl's.

My throat tightened. This had to be some kind of mistake. What could a child do bad enough to be sent to Hell? I looked around, waiting for someone to realize their error. No one did. I opened my mouth to say something. But what would I say and to whom? Shouldn't the seraphs have noticed a child had mistakenly entered the Stygian Transit?

Cinder leaped forward and struck the male hume on the shoulder with her souljab—fire snapped his head backward. "Keep them going!" she yelled, motioning for me to raise my weapon.

I tried to move, but felt frozen by shock. The hume

was as young as the spawnling who'd waved at me from the crowd.

"I said, break it up!" Cinder growled, trying to yank the three humes apart.

Finally, I managed to pull myself out of the daze that had been holding me. It wasn't my place to question. Regardless of their ages, these humes had all been judged.

"Keep walking!" I shouted, my mouth dry. As I stepped forward, the girl's blue eyes gaped in horror. She looked from me to the Immigration Station and jerked her hands free from the two adults. With a terrified wail, she turned and ran back toward the Stygian.

"Stop!" I grabbed for her and missed.

The woman screamed. She pulled away from the man, who tried to hold her back, and chased the girl.

This was my fault. I should have been paying better attention. Several demon spawns started forward, but I could see that none of them would get there in time. "Come back!" I shouted, racing after the humes to correct my mistake.

It was too late. A seraph stepped out of the formation and raised his sword. Angel-fire crackled from the tip.

I was trying to avoid the falling blade when something knocked me sideways, and a black shape stopped between me and the seraph.

The sword whistled through the air. White light flashed, showering everyone in blinding sparks. Onyx collapsed to the platform in a heap.

I heard someone screaming—and realized it was me.

CHAPTER 2

"Stop it!" I howled, fighting and kicking. "Leave him alone."

Someone tried to roll me over, and I slashed out with both hands, sure the Halos were going to finish me off the same way they'd killed Onyx. The figure standing above me leaped backward, barely avoiding the razor-sharp talons that had emerged from the tips of my fingers.

"Get away," I snarled, baring my fangs. The world had taken on a red haze, but everything looked incredibly sharp and clear. My skin felt tight and cold, my muscles wires of taut energy waiting to uncoil on whatever got in my way.

"Blaze, it's over."

Even as I recognized Cinder, my body wanted to attack, to rip and shred. I was an arrow nocked, drawn, and ready to fire. Though I knew she was a friend, my Dae' Ungu instincts made my arms quiver with rage.

"They. Are. Gone," Cinder said, keeping her distance.

I rose to one knee and saw she was right. The seraphs and the Stygian Transit were both gone, along with the humes and most of the other demon spawns, except for a few who were watching from the other side of the platform, whispering to each other and staring at us.

No, not us. *Me.*

My red eyelids flipped up, and I saw deep furrows gouged in the stone platform. "Did I . . .?"

"Oh yeah." Cinder nodded. "You are one crazy-bad demon spawn. All that growling and clawing. I thought you were going to rip my head off for a minute."

I nodded, not wanting to tell her how close I'd come to doing just that.

"Onyx?" I asked. A pool of black ichor marked the spot where he'd fallen. I'd never seen my friend bleed before, but I knew it had to be his. He'd been struck by angel-fire. The only question was whether he'd died or been sent to Absolute Zero. I prayed for the former.

"He's okay," Cinder said, breaking into a grin.

"Okay?" I spun around. "The Halo hit him. I saw it."

"Barely." Cinder drew a line with her finger across the top of one shoulder. "He bled a lot, but the efreets burned the wound shut. He's going to be okay."

"Are you sure?" I knew the Dae' Lorica were strong, but no one survived angel-fire.

Cinder nodded. "They took him to the infirmary while you were going berserk." She had such a polite way of putting things.

"I have to go see him." I grabbed my shaders from the platform and turned toward the stairs.

"Take it easy," Cinder laughed. "The way you're acting, I'd almost think you liked that big lump of lava stone."

A hand dropped onto my shoulder. Thinking it was Cinder, I spun around to tell her where she could put her lava stone. The words evaporated from my lips as I looked into a pale, perfectly chiseled face. The nose was strong but narrow, the red lips full, the eyes deep as forever. Tiny black horns rose just above his slick black hair.

"I'm afraid I shall require a moment of your time first," the incubus said.

* * *

Incubi and succubae were Inquisitors, some of the most powerful demons in Hell, judging disputes and handing down punishments. No one dared to refuse their requests.

But this one would have to wait. "I have to . . . check on . . . my friend," I gasped. Getting the words out was like walking up a steep, sandy hill.

"Of course you do, my child." The incubus spoke in a deep, syrupy voice. Even with my eyes averted from his face, the pull of his will was nearly irresistible.

He took my hand in his cold fingers, leading me through the doors of the Immigration Station. As we walked up the spiraling stone stairs, I tried to remember where I needed to go, but all I could think about was climbing one age-darkened step after another.

The incubus looked back at me. "This won't take but a moment."

I nodded mindlessly. "Yes. A moment."

Light shining through the stained-glass windows painted the marble hallway at the top of the staircase with a wash of muted colors. I'd never been to the station before. I'd always assumed it was as dark and foreboding on the inside as it looked from the street below. The lower section where the humes entered was stark and fetid. But here on the top floor, it was more lavish than any building I'd ever seen.

Rich tapestries depicting powerful demons hunting and killing lined the walls. Hume women dressed in rags scrubbed the marble floor—dipping their long hair in soapy buckets and polishing the tiles with it. At our approach, they scurried to the walls, trembling until we passed.

"Inside, please." The incubus opened a heavy wooden

door halfway down the hall and ushered me inside. At the front of the room was an intricately carved altar with a stack of papers on top. Behind it, a pair of stone masks—one grinning, the other sneering—hung from opposite sides of the wall.

"Would you care to take a seat?" the incubus asked, pointing toward a bench. He worded it as a request, but I couldn't have refused if I'd tried. All the way up, I'd been so mesmerized by his aura and the inside of the building that I hadn't thought to question what he wanted with me. Now I realized this had to be about what happened on the platform.

"This is your first day of training?" he asked, walking to the other side of the altar.

I nodded. Was I in trouble? Had I committed some crime?

"There's no need to be afraid," the incubus said, as though reading my thoughts. He settled into a polished black chair, steepled his long fingers beneath his chin, and smiled pleasantly.

All the anger and adrenaline from before left my body. I felt strangely weak and tired. Was it the excitement of the action wearing off, or was he doing this to me somehow? I'd never spoken to an incubus in person, but I'd heard of their skills in interrogating both humes and demons. "W-what do you want?" I stuttered.

"How are you enjoying your training?" he asked, ignoring my question.

"Fine, I guess. It's all still pretty new."

"And your accommodations are acceptable?"

Why was he asking me about the DTC? I tried to look away from his gaze, but his dark eyes kept pulling me back. "Yes. Of course."

He leaned forward. "I'd like you to tell me about what happened outside the station this morning."

I *was* in trouble. I swallowed, knowing it was useless to play down my actions in any way. He'd see through any lies instantly. Carefully, trying to remember every detail, I explained how I'd been surprised by the hume child and lost my focus. "I should have been in a better position to keep the hume from running," I said.

"I see." His eyes studied my face, but his hands never left his chin. "And why did you chase the hume?"

I could see my future ruined before it ever began. It was rare for a demon spawn to be kicked out of the DTC. But it did happen. And those who were rejected spent the rest of their lives performing the worst jobs imaginable. Supervising the humes working in the fields and factories or patrolling the slums where they were housed. It was the ultimate humiliation.

"It's my job," I whispered. "To herd them into the station."

"Of course it is." His lips curved into a smile, and I felt my heart lift ever so slightly. With one finger, he tapped a stack of papers on the center of the altar. "I don't think I need to pursue this with academy administration."

"Thank you," I said. "It won't happen again."

"I'm sure it won't." He put his hands on the arms of his chair as if to rise, then paused. "There's just one other thing."

"Yes?" I nodded, eager to please him and get back outside.

"Your friend . . ."

"Cinder?"

"No." His eyes narrowed. "The one who was injured by the seraph."

"Onyx?" What did he want with him?

The incubus ran a fingertip across his dark red lips,

and the air around us seemed to thicken. "How exactly did *Onyx* end up in a position to be struck?"

I held my breath. He wasn't done with me after all. "It was my fault," I admitted. "I got too close to the Hal—I mean the seraph. It raised its sword, and Onyx ran in to protect me."

"You're quite positive of that?" As he leaned across the altar, his eyes glowed, and I felt my mind bared before him.

"Y-yes," I murmured, barely able to get the words out. "We've been friends since we were little. He's always looked out for me. Why else would he have stepped in front of the seraph's blade?"

He shook his head. "Several witnesses gave conflicting stories."

"What kind of stories?" I asked.

He stared at me a moment longer, then leaned back and began reading through his papers. "You may see yourself out."

Instantly my muscles relaxed. I collapsed into my chair with a sigh. "That's it?" I asked. "I'm not in trouble?"

"Is there a reason you should be?" The incubus looked up from his work, and I could feel the power of his gaze drilling back into me.

"No." I got up quickly and stumbled across the room. My legs were still a little wobbly. But I knew I'd be better once I made sure Onyx was okay. As I walked toward the door, a question occurred to me.

"Why was she here?"

"Hmm?" The incubus had gone back to looking through his papers.

I swallowed. "The reason I wasn't doing my job was that I was surprised by the hume girl who walked out of the Stygian Transit. I'd never seen one that young, and I was just wondering what she did to get sent here."

The incubus looked slowly up. His mouth curled down, and his bottomless eyes went cold. "I'm sure I have no idea."

CHAPTER 3

By the time I reached the ground floor of the station, I could almost breathe normally, and my heart didn't feel like it was going to leap into my throat and suffocate me. The humes had all been processed, leaving the big lobby empty. Staring up at the windows, I thought about the hume girl again.

The colored images above the station entrance weren't just art, they were a reminder that what we did here was important. Once they were dead, humes had no way to make up for the evil things they'd done when they were alive. By forcing them to spend eternity suffering, we gave them a way to pay for their evil actions. To be sent here so young, the child must have been some sort of terror.

Outside on the platform, it looked like someone had tried to scrub away most of Onyx's blood. But a dark circle still stained the light red stone. I tried to picture the last seconds before he pushed me to the ground. I'd been stupid—shocked into inaction by a moment of doubt. But it wouldn't happen again.

I pushed the image out of my mind as I walked down the stairs and into the third Circle of Hell. The slums of Humeville were empty with all the demons back home celebrating and the humes either working or being tortured. Bits of uneaten food, wrappers, chunks of rock and brick, and even a few pennants littered the ground. Signs of another Arrival Day come and gone.

In the two Inner Circles, humes would be cleaning up the mess. But here at the outer edge of the city, the humes would scavenge what they could, and the rest would stay until it blew away or was carried off by the vermin that plagued this area.

As I watched, a greasy black rat darted out of the shadows and dragged a piece of gnawed bone into the sewer. I decided not to tell Onyx about my meeting with the Inquisitor. He'd risked his life for me. There was no reason to add to what had already been a horrible day for both of us.

The infirmary was in the second ring of Hell, not far from the academy. Because demons seldom got injured or sick, the building was mostly empty. A gold Dae' Ceal nurse, who seemed to be the only demon on duty, told me that Onyx had been admitted briefly, but once they determined his injuries weren't serious, they'd let him go back to the training center.

"Is he a friend of yours?" she asked.

I nodded, hoping he hadn't decided I was too much trouble to hang around with anymore.

"*Boyfriend?*"

I blushed. "No. Just a friend."

Her yellow eyes flickered as her tail swished, S-like, through the air. "Tell him if he comes back, I can give him a more thorough examination."

"I'll be sure to let him know," I said, turning away before she could see the fangs erupting out between my lips. Just because he wasn't my boyfriend didn't mean I wanted him hooking up with a predator like her. It wasn't jealousy that made me press the tips of my talons into my palms. It was protectiveness.

The DTC was built into a set of caverns and narrow

passageways drilled deep into a tall bluff. The barracks were located on the outermost layer so that most rooms had windows. I looked up at the window to Onyx's room, hoping he wouldn't be too angry, and decided I'd offer to give him my desserts for a month to make up for all the trouble I'd caused.

But when I knocked on the door, his roommate, Nightshade, answered. He hadn't seen Onyx since early that morning and hadn't heard about what had happened at the station.

"I was just heading out to hit a few parties," he said, eyeing me like he was trying to decide whether I was worth hitting on or not. Third years had this absurd notion that primies should be honored to date them. "Want to come with me? Stoneface isn't much of a partier, but we'll probably run into him sooner or later."

I shook my head. "I think I'll just wait. Is it okay if I hang out in your room?"

He grunted. "Okay. But don't touch any of my stuff."

I rolled my eyes. Like I'd make any more contact with his belongings than I had to. School had barely started, and already their room had died, exploded, and then died again—the messiness was almost impressive.

Moving a pile of dirty clothes from a granite bench, I sat and tried not to worry. The lovestruck nurse said they'd sent Onyx back to school, so where was he? What if his wound was more serious than they thought? What if it reopened on the way back? He could be lying in an alley somewhere, bleeding to death.

I looked out the window to see if I could spot him in the street below, and another thought occurred to me. What if the Inquisitor didn't believe me? What if he thought the whole thing was Onyx's fault? And what had he meant by conflicting stories? They couldn't think that Onyx was trying to attack the Halo. No one who knew Onyx would believe he was capable of doing something like that in a million years.

Classes hadn't started yet, and even if they had, today was a holiday. So where was he? Didn't he know I'd be looking for him?

What if he'd gone looking for me? After the kind of injury he'd received, he should be resting. Or what if he really had gone to one of the parties? If he was out partying while I was worrying in his room, I'd send him to the infirmary a second time.

I considered going to look for him. But if he came to the room and no one was here, who would take care of him?

His side of the room wasn't nearly as messy as Nightshade's, and I dropped onto the pallet where he slept. The hay on it was fairly clean, with just a hint of his scent and a few food wrappers and crumpled papers spread around the floor. As I collected the trash and shoved the hay into a slightly more presentable pile, something fell to the floor with a thump.

Picking it up, I saw it was a puzzle box. I hadn't seen one of those in years. When we were little, we used to make them for each other from polished stone. If you didn't know the pattern, it was nearly impossible to get one open. But if you turned and twisted the pieces the right way, you could get to the contents in seconds.

This box was bigger than the ones we used to make—five fingers wide and taller than the length of my hand. It was more complicated too. Carved into the top was a symbol I'd never seen before. It looked like a flame encircled by a loop of small links.

Trying to keep my mind from worrying, I sat on his pallet and moved the pieces around, trying one combination after another. It wasn't until the box fell apart in my hands that I realized I'd solved it. Inside the box were nearly a dozen pieces of extremely thin notes, folded like the ones we used to pass each other at school—usually about who liked who and who didn't like who.

With my heart pounding, I looked at the door and realized what I'd just done. What if Onyx came in right now and found me going through his things? It wasn't like I'd been intentionally snooping. The puzzle boxes we made for each other usually contained treats or little prizes. It was a game we played. But he hadn't given this box to me, and the pieces of folded paper were definitely not my prize.

With my hands sweating, I tried to put the box back together. But I'd always been better at solving the puzzles than building them. As I tried to slide one section of stone into another, a piece of paper unfolded enough for me to see part of a note inside. There was something about a basket and shiny metal. But it wasn't Onyx's writing. His letters were bold and straight, like soldiers lining up for battle. The letters on the note were spiky and crooked, like the hand that had written them had been shaking.

Glancing at the door again, I carefully unfolded the paper until I could read the whole message.

Six steps and a door with a handle made of shiny metal. A basket with something sweet in it.

I stared at the note, gently turning it over. What was this? It made absolutely no sense. Was it some kind of code?

Too curious to stop myself, I unfolded the next note. It looked like an equation: *.05% GPE/12 x ½ GRW pop = damnation.*

That was even more confusing than the first note. The writing on this strip wasn't Onyx's either. But it was different than the first—neat clean lines with looping script. It looked like it might have been written by a girl. I was surprised an 'I' wasn't dotted with a heart.

Unable to stop my curiosity, I began opening the rest of the notes. I couldn't understand any of them, and each seemed to be written by a different hand.

The one with the yellow one comes twice weekly.

A green clearing with an opening in the ground.

Something about drawings.

Nine rings. 2 DTR. Airborne. Ground-based. Stay under cover of . . .?

Promises. PROMISES. PROMISES!!!! Broken?

They were all gibberish.

I was so caught up in trying to understand what I was reading that I never heard the door open. I didn't realize anyone was in the room with me until the box and papers were snatched from my hands.

I looked up into Onyx's face. My cheeks burned. "I didn't mean to pry . . I was waiting because I was worried and . . . I found the puzzle box and started . . . only I—"

My words cut off as I saw his expression. I'd never seen him so angry before. His eyes were narrowed to slits, his jaw clenched.

Dark, rough flesh ridged his left shoulder, and his arm was held in a sling. He reached out and cupped the notes in his enormous palms. I jumped up and reached for his wound, but he jerked away.

"I'm so sorry," I said. "This is all my fault. I went to the infirmary to check on you, but the nurse said you'd gone back to the academy. So I came here. When I couldn't find you, I started to worry, and I . . ."

He turned away so all I could see was his back. When he spoke, his voice was so quiet I could barely hear him. "Get out." He pointed a thick finger toward the door.

CHAPTER 4

"Not talking to you yet?" Cinder asked as we walked to Hume Anatomy.

It had been three days since the accident, and Onyx was still ignoring me. When I tried bringing him my dessert at dinner, he moved to another table. When I apologized, he pretended he didn't hear. "He won't even look at me."

"Maybe you haven't given him a good enough reason to look." Cinder eyed me up and down. No longer on duty, I was wearing a dark red top and a wraparound skirt that stopped just below my knees. "You need to hike that up a little." She tilted her head, pinching her chin between thumb and forefinger. "On second thought, hike it up a lot. And unbutton your blouse more."

I snorted. "You think sex is the answer to everything."

"Guys are dogs," she said. "And we're the bones they're chasing."

I didn't want to believe her. I couldn't. Onyx wasn't like that. "You're saying that if I want to get Onyx to forgive me, I have to wear a shorter skirt and drop books in front of him?"

She shrugged. "Hey, it's always worked for me."

Cinder was fun to be around, but sometimes I wanted to smack her upside the head. If the only thing guys cared about was looks, I'd rather get a cat. At least they were easier to clean up after.

"We've been friends since we were spawnlings." I felt my face burn and was glad for the darkness. "I don't like him that way."

"*Ri-ight.*" We squeezed aside for a group of Dae' Ungu girls carrying a bubbling pot of something that squirmed and hissed. I hoped it wasn't on the dinner menu. "If you don't like him, why do you care whether he talks to you or not?"

"I just told you why. He's my friend." Except he wasn't anymore.

"Whatever you say." Cinder rolled her eyes as we walked into class. The Hume Anatomy room was round and bigger than most of our other classes. Tall granite tables scarred by countless experiments formed three rings of concentric circles. The tables had a permanent chemical smell to them that made me avoid touching the surfaces if I could help it. At the center of the room, our teacher, Mr. Pyreet, was setting things up for class.

A thin sheet of flames danced across the blue skin of his arms and face as he poured thick red liquid into a row of glass beakers.

"You still have no idea who the notes are from?" Cinder asked as we dropped our books and slid onto a pair of stools behind one of the tables in the back circle.

"No, they were weird. Like sections torn out of some-one's notes or copied from a book." I shook my head.

"What if he's cheating on tests? Maybe he's afraid you'll turn him in."

"He knows I'd never do that. Besides, if those were answers to tests, gargoyles are serving dinner in the cafete-ria." I still had no idea what the pieces of paper had been, but they weren't love notes, and they weren't answers to any questions I'd ever seen or heard of.

"I'm sure your conversation is fascinating," a sardonic male voice said. I turned from Cinder to find Mr. Pyreet staring at us from the center of the room, his arms folded across his chest. "Would you care to share your discussion with the rest of us? Or did you want to join today's lesson?" At their tables, the other primies grinned.

I swallowed, wondering if they'd heard what we were talking about. But Cinder beamed at the attention. "We'll join you."

"In that case, come get a beaker."

Cinder strolled seductively to the front of the class—every male eye glued to her and almost every female eye glaring at her jealously. "What is this stuff?" she asked, picking up a beaker and swirling a thick dark liquid in it.

"Glad you asked," the teacher said. "Each flask contains recently drawn hume blood."

"Nasty!" No longer swaying her hips, Cinder hurried back to our table and pushed the flask as far away from her side as she could. Around the room, several other students were doing the same.

"Today we will be studying the effect of heat on humes," Mr. Pyreet said. "Unlike demons, hume bodies are easily overwhelmed by high temperature. If overheated long enough, their internal cooling systems become overwhelmed. They stop sweating and may become confused or dizzy or even pass out."

"How could you tell? Humes always look confused." A boy behind me laughed, and several other students joined him.

"You better learn to tell," Mr. Pyreet said. "Subjected to high enough heat or for a long enough period of time, the hume body ceases to function, and you've got a corpse on your hands."

I raised my hand. "What does it matter? They're already dead. If their bodies stop working, they just come back again."

The teacher nodded. "You're speaking of *potestas renata*—energy reborn. While it's true that humes regenerate new bodies, they don't return until the next Arrival Day, which could be as long as thirty days away. During that time, we lose a valuable worker, and they lose the opportunity to suffer. It will be your job to make sure that happens as seldom as possible."

"Look who's here." Cinder elbowed me and nodded toward the door.

The last thing I wanted was to get in more trouble, but when I followed her gaze, I couldn't keep from giving a small gasp of surprise. Onyx stood in the hallway along with several other older students. He met my eyes for a second, then grimaced and turned away.

Mr. Pyreet nodded at the students and waved them in. "You will all be heating your blood to different temperatures and measuring the resulting change. To assist you in learning proper heating and testing procedures, I asked a group of terts to join us today."

"Don't do anything stupid," I started to whisper to Cinder, before realizing she was already out of her chair, waving.

"We'll take the hunk."

Onyx scowled even harder. "I'll work with a table in the front."

"I understand your lack of enthusiasm," Mr. Pyreet said to him. "But perhaps your presence might keep Miss Cinder and Miss Blaze on task. You certainly couldn't have any less luck than I've had today."

Onyx blew out a deep breath. As he shuffled toward us, Cinder reached under the table and tugged up the edge of my skirt. "Trust me."

"First, light your flames," Mr. Pyreet said as the rest of the terts spread out around the room.

"Thanks for volunteering to light our fires," Cinder said to Onyx, her eyes bright with amusement. "Especially Blaze's."

"I didn't volunteer," he said. His left arm was still in a sling. With his right hand, he uncapped a small opening in the top of the table and struck a spark as the gas hissed out. A flame burst into life. By twisting the opening, he decreased the gas until it reached the right temperature.

At first, I'd felt guilty for going through Onyx's things. Then I'd felt sorry for whatever pain or embarrassment I caused him—though I still didn't know exactly what it was I'd seen. But now I was just angry that he still refused to talk about it.

"Don't you think this has gone on long enough?" I said, placing the beaker above the flame and clamping it in place.

Onyx stared at the center of the room as though I hadn't even spoken.

"So, you'll talk to Cinder but not me?"

"The thing to remember about flames," he said, looking only at Cinder, "is that it's fine to heat your own test tube. But if you experiment on things that aren't yours, someone might get burned."

I ran my tongue over my teeth, feeling the fangs trying to pierce through my gums. If he wanted to be a jerk, I'd let him. "If you're stupid enough to leave your experiments where anyone can find them, maybe you deserve whatever happens to them."

Onyx snorted, increasing the size of the flame. Cinder

folded her arms and beamed as the blood in the beaker churned. "This looks to be the most interesting class ever."

"Please drop your first stone into the blood and record the time it takes to reach the bottom of the beaker," Mr. Pyreet said. "You're looking for density."

"There's something dense at *this* table," I said, dropping a stone into the beaker. "But it's not blood."

Cinder grinned as the stone sank and clanked to the bottom of the beaker with a soft thunk.

"Are you going to write the time down?" I asked her. She was supposed to be recording our results.

She crossed her legs and leaned back on her stool. "Are you kidding? This discussion is way better than any experiment."

Gritting my teeth, I scribbled down the time. Now I was mad at her too.

Onyx increased the flame. "Newbies shouldn't mess with things they don't understand." He spoke to Cinder, but clearly his words were meant for me.

I threw another stone into the beaker that was now starting to bubble. "Just because these rocks have been in the academy for years doesn't mean they've learned anything." Not even bothering to time the stone's descent, I cranked the flame higher. "They're still just stupid, stubborn rocks."

Onyx turned the flame high enough that pink steam rose from the top of the beaker and small drops of hume blood popped out of the container, sizzling. "There's something stubborn and inflexible here all right. But it's only been here for a few weeks, and it has the temper of a child."

Ignoring the heat, I slammed the rest of the pebbles into the beaker. One of them cracked the glass, and a small trickle of blood leaked out onto the page in the lab book we were supposed to be writing our results on.

"Look who's acting like a child!" I shouted, my vision going red.

"Maybe we need to turn that flame down just a little," Cinder said. But I was beyond listening. I shoved Onyx in the chest, taking a perverse pleasure from the ripple of thickened skin that rose on the backs of his arms. One way or another, I was going to get him to pay attention to me.

"What's going on there?" the teacher asked, scurrying toward us.

"I apologized!" I screamed, shoving Onyx again. "I said I was sorry. But that wasn't good enough for you." I could sense the rest of the students turning from their experiments to stare at me, but I didn't care. "Well, I'm sick of apologizing. Because whatever was in that puzzle box is your problem, not mine. So grow up and deal with it!"

Onyx stepped away, his eyes wide. I shoved him one last time. My adrenaline was racing, and he was off balance, or I couldn't have budged him even with all my strength. But as I slammed my fists into his chest, he stumbled backward. The forms on the table slipped into the flame. At that moment, the cracked beaker finally burst, sending shards of glass and scalding blood everywhere.

Propelled by the explosion, the burning paper flew across the room. One of the sheets landed on the head of a Dae' Ceal girl with flowing white tresses. Another seesawed onto a shelf of dusty texts that immediately caught fire.

"Everyone calm down!" Mr. Pyreet shouted as the Dae' Ceal rolled across the floor, knocking students right and left. But no one was listening to him. The entire class had broken into pandemonium. I dropped my head into my hands. This was so not how I wanted to start my first year.

CHAPTER 5

"Well, that was, um, what's the word I'm looking for?" Cinder said as we walked out of the tunnel and into the light, where the cavern ceiling was fading from bright orange to pale pink.

"Embarrassing? Humiliating?"

"I was thinking of something more like . . . *explosive.*"

I ducked my head, brushing bits of burned paper from my shoulders. All around us, students who weren't even in the class were staring and whispering. Apparently, word of my outburst was getting around fast. "None of it would have happened if it weren't for you."

"Me?" Cinder fluffed her aqua hair, which looked like she'd just brushed it. Somehow, she'd managed to avoid the blood, glass, and flames. "I'm not the one who exploded a blood bomb in the middle of class."

"No, you just started it." I waved my hand, popping my hips back and forth. "*We'll take the hunk.*"

"I was trying to help you." Cinder pouted. "Can I help it that instead of seducing your boyfriend, you nearly lit him on fire?"

She was absolutely impossible. But she was also right. If I'd thought Onyx was mad before, now he probably hated me. He'd managed to disappear while Cinder and I got stuck putting out the flames and cleaning up the mess.

I finally had to face reality. I guess I'd always assumed Onyx and I would end up together once we grew up. Now that we were grown? Yeah, it was clear I had misread the situation. But I'd rather have him as a friend than nothing. I could accept that. In fact, it was for the best. How I was going to fix things was another story.

"Where are we going, anyway?" I asked when Cinder turned the opposite direction from our barracks and ducked into an alley between a line of old, rusty storage buildings. The first week of training had finally come to an end, and I was looking forward to a couple of days off to recover. Maybe if I slept on it, I could come up with some way to get back in Onyx's good graces.

"Follow me," she said with a mysterious smile. "You've never seen anything like this."

Glancing around, I realized we weren't the only ones heading this direction. Dozens of other demon spawns were going the same way. Leaving the academy grounds, we wound past a pair of bubbling sulfur pools and toward an eroded and mostly dormant volcano.

A flock of Charun circled above the mouth of the volcano, snapping their hooked beaks. The sound of their snake beards hissing filled the air as they flapped and glided around and around.

"What are they doing here?" I asked.

Charun were scavengers that preyed on sick or injured humes.

"Just wait."

I followed Cinder up a narrow winding trail, wondering where we could possibly be going. At least thirty or forty other demon spawns were hiking the trail along with us. And now that we were closer to the top, I could see at least a hundred or so more gathered around the edge of the crater. By the time we reached the top, it was nearly dark, and I was getting annoyed. I was also dying of curiosity. "Are you going to tell me what this is about?"

Cinder made her way to a group of boys. "Scoot over," she said. Looking up, the boys immediately made room for her to slide between them. I sat down beside her and peered into the volcano. But it was so dark, I couldn't see a thing.

"What—" I started to ask again, but Cinder put her finger to her lips.

"Just wait."

Around the edge of the crater, the crowd grew silent as the last bit of red light faded from the sky. Everyone moved forward and stared down. For several minutes, nothing happened. Then, one by one, a series of gas vents burst into flames, lighting the inside of the volcano and revealing twenty or so figures standing at the bottom.

A pair of demon spawns, so broad-shouldered they could only be Dae' Lorica, rolled aside a huge rock, and a stream of glowing lava began flowing across the bottom of the pit.

"Culdine?" I whispered. I'd heard of this game, but never seen it played in person.

Cinder nodded. Her dark eyes reflected the red of the hot magma that pooled below us. As the molten rock filled the floor of the volcano, each of the demon spawns climbed onto raised rock platforms in the middle of the circle or around its edges. I could see now that half of the figures were Dae' Lorica, the other half Dae' Ungu like me.

When the magma had reached to within an arm's length of the top of the platforms, the two Dae' Lorica pushed the rock back into place, blocking the flow. A Dae' Ungu girl standing on a ledge above the burning pool suddenly leaped from the side. I gasped and leaned forward. The heat wouldn't kill or even seriously injure her. But it would sting for sure.

Just before she plunged into the bubbling morass, she spread her arms and, with a snap of fluttering cloth, soared into the air.

"Ohhh," I whispered as her artificial wings caught the updraft of hot air, allowing her to glide and circle above the other demon spawns.

"Show-off!" someone yelled from the other side of the ledge. A Dae' Lorica standing near the center of the pit reached into the lava—his thick skin protecting him from the heat completely—and hurled a glowing blob at the flier. The Dae' Ungu managed to dodge the throw, but a few of the fiery drops singed the edge of her wings.

The flier returned to her perch on the rocky wall, waving a mocking finger back and forth.

"The Dae' Lorica have wings too, but they're so big they can barely make it from platform to platform," Cinder whispered. "They have to rely on their strength and their ability to withstand the heat."

"Do the Dae' Ceal ever play?" I whispered back.

"Of course. Our strength is camouflage and speed." She grinned. "Plus, the fact that we're smarter than the Dae' Lorica and Dae' Ungu combined."

Down below, one of the figures on each side of the pit disappeared into a small cavern.

"The goal is to get the other team's grail and return it to your side," she said.

"What's the grail?" Each of the demon spawns was returning from the opening, carrying something in their arms. I cupped my hands to my eyes, trying to see more.

"Normally, it's a flag or a statue or something. But that's what makes tonight special." Cinder bit her lower lip and smiled in anticipation.

The two players stepped back into the light, and there was a murmur of excitement from the crowd. Whatever they were holding looked too big to be a statue. I squinted, but still couldn't make out exactly what it was.

"Tonight's game features the currently undefeated Dae' Lorica," shouted a figure at the center of the magma pool to a series of cheers and boos, "against the Dae' Ungu, who have one victory and one loss." Again, more shouts.

"Tonight," the demon spawn continued, "is a special surprise. In honor of the first Arrival Day of the year, we are using live grails."

As the crowd around the top of the crater roared, the demon spawns on each side of the ledge set down what they were holding. In the flickering red light, I suddenly realized what it was, and my heart skipped in my chest. On each side of the pool, a bound figure stared down at the lava, then up at us in obvious terror.

"Humes?" I breathed. "They're using humes as grails?"

Cinder nodded. "Isn't it great? I couldn't believe it when I heard. It'll make it much more exciting—especially if they struggle."

"What if they . . ."

"Die? It's against the rules. If one team kills the other team's grail, they automatically lose. I was flirting with a player on the Dae' Ungu team, and he told me that's actually one of their tactics. If a player captures your team's hume and you force them to drop it into the lava, you win. Injuries don't count, of course."

Staring down at the pale, frightened faces of the bound humes reminded me of what happened on the platform. I could feel my breath speeding up. "Why would they do that?"

"Loosen up." Cinder laughed. "They're only humes. Are you worried about them? Remember what Pyreet said. If they die, they'll end up in Judgment and get sent back here anyway. They probably hope to get killed as a vacation from work for a few days."

"I'm not worried about the humes," I growled. "It's just . . . we torture them because it's our job. And because it's the only way they can pay for what they did. But that doesn't mean we have to make a game out of it."

For some reason, I kept remembering the girl at the Immigration Station. How terrified she'd looked, and how close I'd come to being killed by the seraph. If it hadn't been for Onyx . . . At the thought of what he'd done for me, I felt terrible all over again. First, I nearly got him killed for my stupidity. Then I went through his private things. Then I shoved him into an open flame. It was no wonder he wasn't talking to me.

"This is gonna be good," Cinder said. She snuggled against the boy on her left, and he wrapped an arm around her contentedly.

Down below, the game began. Two Dae' Ungu took to the air and soared toward the Dae' Lorica's side. A Dae' Lorica leaped from the wall and knocked one of them spinning. With a hiss of shared pain, the crowd watched him spiral into the magma. He quickly climbed back out, his skin a brilliant red, his wings shredded and useless for the rest of the game.

Instead of watching the players, I found myself looking at the crowd, wondering if Onyx was up here somewhere. I'd come to school excited to see my friend—now it seemed I'd lost him. I was determined to fix this. Most of the faces were riveted on the figures below, but I noticed several couples slip off into the darkness.

"Don't I know you?" asked a second year Dae' Ungu I recognized from my hand-to-hand combat class.

"We have a class together," I said.

"It's getting kind of cold out," he said, squeezing

between me and Cinder. "I can put my arm around you to keep both of us warm if you'd like."

Cinder winked, and I realized the boy was flirting with me. I glanced over at him. He was good-looking, a few fingers taller than me, with clear red skin and sharp horns that poked up through his wavy hair. Maybe Cinder was right. Maybe I needed to start thinking about other guys.

"Okay, why not?"

"Great." The boy put his arm around my shoulder. "I'm Coal."

Cinder caught my eyes and mouthed, "Go for it."

"Blaze," I said, resting my head against his shoulder. He tightened his arm around me, his muscles flexing beneath my cheek. Maybe this week wouldn't turn out so bad after all.

I was just starting to relax when a figure stood up on the other side of the crater. At first, I thought it was another couple sneaking away to make out. The figure stood for a moment, seemed to look around, and then disappeared into the darkness by himself. I couldn't see his face, but I instantly recognized the sling on his left arm.

"I have to go," I said, jumping up.

Cinder cocked a questioning eyebrow as the boy by my side looked up in surprise.

"I'm sorry." I backed away. "I'm, um, tired."

"Do you want me to walk you back to your room?" Coal asked.

"No." I glanced across the crater. Onyx was nowhere in sight. "I'll see you later," I called, and disappeared into the darkness.

I made my way back to where I thought the trail was, trying not to step on anyone. I didn't have Onyx's night vision, and it took me a few minutes to get my bearings. When I finally found the trail, I could see him nearly halfway down the side of the volcano. He was moving quickly. Had the humes reminded him of what happened with the seraph as well? I considered calling out to him, but I was afraid that if he knew I was here, he'd just keep going and lose me before I could catch up. By the time I reached the bottom of the trail, he was just ducking between the pair of storage buildings.

As I raced after him, I considered what I would say once I caught up. Apologizing was something I'd always struggled with, so I'd need to formulate something now. And it would be different this time. The more I thought about it, the more I knew I was wrong about the fantasy we'd be together. It would never work. He is my friend, or *was* my friend, plain and simple.

I stepped out of the alley and turned toward the academy. He had to be heading back to the barracks. But he was nowhere in sight. For a second, I thought I'd lost him, and I began to panic. Then I spotted someone disappearing around a building out by the street.

Where was he going?

At this time of night, the streets were fairly empty. Most of the demons were downtown at the clubs and taverns or heading that way. Technically, demon spawns weren't allowed off academy grounds after dark.

Was this about the notes? For some reason, I couldn't put them out of my mind. I followed him from as far back as I dared, darting from one shadow to another. Soon we'd entered an area I was unfamiliar with. Imps scurried about in the darkness, peeking out of the sewers and snarling, baring their sharp little teeth. Streetlights were fewer and farther apart, and the streets were cracked and pitted.

The farther we went, the more secretive Onyx became. It was impossible to tell where we were going, but the streets were empty, and I could swear we circled the same block at least twice. Buildings were dark and grimy, with small, barred windows or no windows at all.

Onyx cut through one narrow twisting alleyway after another before stopping abruptly to study a crumbling stone wall. He seemed to be searching for something. Then he hurried into the night. It was only a matter of time before he spotted me. Just as I was about to step into plain view and admit I was following him, he turned and disappeared through a cloud of steam rising from a crack in the ground.

With a sigh of relief, I stepped away from the wall and hurried after him. When I reached the crack, I paused, listening. I thought I heard hoof steps, then a clunk. After that, nothing. Cautiously, I eased through the smoke. The street beyond was empty. For a moment, I thought I'd lost him. Then something clattered in the darkness, and I turned to see someone slip around the corner.

I sprinted to the intersection just in time to see the figure slide down the far side of a pile of rubble. Three quick leaps got me to the top of the pile. As I climbed down the other side, the figure turned into a narrow alley.

Reaching the corner, I saw the alley stopped abruptly in a narrow V. The figure paused near the end of the street, but something was wrong. The dim shape was too short, the shoulders too narrow. As I stood watching it, the figure opened a door built into the wall. They glanced in my direction, and I stumbled backward.

It wasn't Onyx. It wasn't even a demon. Staring at me from beneath a dark cloak was a hume. Something had happened to its face. Long jagged scars had turned the hume's eyes and nose into unrecognizable lumps. The mouth twisted up on one side and hung open on the other. It looked like some horrible nightmare. The figure opened its crooked mouth and made a repulsive cawing sound before hurrying through the door.

As I turned away in terror, a hand dropped onto my shoulder. The dark eyes of a succubus burned into mine as a voice purred, "What are you doing here?"

CHAPTER 6

Waiting in the dark hallway outside the inquisition chamber, I clenched and released my fists, trying to restore some feeling to my fingers. I couldn't tell whether it was actually that cold in the damp corridor, or if the icy numbness that ran from my hooves clear into my brain came from my own fear. From somewhere in the distance, a steady *drip-drip-drip* of water made it impossible to think clearly.

Was that intentional? Did they want to drive me crazy before I was even called in to answer their questions? If that was it, they were wasting their time. I was already so terrified out of my mind that I didn't need any outside stimulus to finish the job. What happened at the station was bad, but it could be written off as the mistake of a newbie. The scene in class the day before wouldn't look good on my record, but I could survive that.

This was the real thing. I'd left the academy grounds without permission. That alone could get a primie expelled. But what made it inexcusable was that I'd been discovered deep in Humeville at night. That was a violation, even for a full-grown demon. Losing my spot at the academy could end up being the least of my problems.

I had no idea what time it was. Although it felt like hours since I'd been brought here, there were no windows to tell me if it was morning yet. I tried to keep from shivering, and wondered if they'd discovered Onyx as well. I quickly dismissed the idea. If they'd found him, he would be here too. For now, he wasn't a part of this. That would change, though, if I was questioned and mentioned his name.

Not that I wanted to give him up. But how could I help it if an incubus or succubus took control of my will? If only I knew what he'd been up to. They might go easier on me if Onyx had a legitimate reason for being outside the academy. Except for the fact that he'd been as deep in Humeville as I was at a time of night when the only demons allowed there were on guard duty. It made no sense at all. Why did he go there? What was he hiding? Did it have something to do with the notes I'd found in his room?

My body began to shake as I realized that no matter what I said or did, my meddling was going to pull Onyx into the middle of this. And once they discovered I'd been following him, all of their scrutiny would switch to what *he'd* been doing there. Because of me, his life could be ruined. Panic pounded through my brain like the roaring arrival of the Stygian Transit, and I found myself jumping to my hooves.

I had to get out of here—had to run. But where? Hell was only so big. I might be able to disappear for a while, but there weren't that many places to hide. And once I was found, all I would have bought myself and Onyx was a few more days at the most. Why did I follow him? Why was I always doing such stupid things?

For a second, an image flashed through my mind. Climbing to the top of the Immigration Station and throwing myself into the Styx. I couldn't swim well, so if the fall didn't kill me outright, the water would. I was so desperate, it almost seemed better to take my life than to face what was waiting for me.

The double doors at the end of the hallway opened,

and a pair of armed efreets stepped toward me. "Come this way."

Clutching my elbows with my hands to stop my shivering, I followed them into a high-ceilinged cavern with a dark floor so glossy, I could see my reflection in its bottomless surface. Sputtering torches lit the room in an uneven orange light, and a haze of smoke floated near the ceiling. Three chairs were located in the center of one end of the room. Four rows of ascending curved benches filled the other end, separated by a low wall. As I looked at who was seated in the first row, my throat squeezed shut, my breath going in and out in gravelly wheezes.

It was not just a succubus or an incubus waiting for me, but six of each. I looked toward the chairs on my side of the room, wondering if anyone else was already there. But they were empty. An entire quorum had been gathered to question me alone.

My eyes searched the shadows of the upper benches, filled with a variety of demons, and I got a shock so great, I stopped walking.

"Mother? Father?" They'd brought my parents to witness the worst day of my life. Tears welled in my eyes as I saw the stern—and frightened—looks on their faces. Sitting outside, I'd held on to at least a little hope that I might be let off easy because I was young and new to the academy. But they wouldn't have called in my parents unless this was serious.

"Keep going." One of the efreets nudged me toward the middle of the three chairs.

As soon as I sat, the succubus closest to the center of the benches stood. Unlike the incubi, who were dressed in dark suits and floor-length capes, the succubae were lightly wrapped in clouds of brightly colored diaphanous material that made Cinder's outfits look like a prudish old demon's by comparison. They were so beautiful, it almost hurt to look at them, yet as the woman with waist-length black hair approached the wall, I found my eyes glued to her every movement.

"Arise." Though her voice was soft, I leaped to my hooves as if the efreets standing beside the empty chairs to my right and left had yanked me up by the arms.

"State your name."

"Blaze of Clan Dae' Ungu," I said. My lips felt like wood.

"You were discovered last night deep in a hume compound."

I swallowed hard. Behind the succubus, I could see my father leaning forward, his shoulders hunched. My mother clasped her hands just below her chin. I nodded silently, and a low murmur went through the crowd in the upper benches.

The succubus raised both her arms. In the past, I'd admired the clans of succubus spawns I occasionally saw from a distance—jealous of their graceful bodies and perfect features. Now, looking up at the woman who might very well hold my life in her hands, I realized I was looking at a weapon—her magnificence as sharp as any blade. "We will question you," she intoned.

Behind her, the other eleven members of the quorum rose. "We will question you," they repeated.

"We will learn the truth."

"We will learn the truth."

Locking my fingers together in my lap, I knew they would, and that terrified me even more than what my punishment would be. Again, I felt the urge to run. But the efreet guards would never let me past them.

The succubus turned to her left. "Dies Diei." A succubus in red stepped away from the bench. "Noctis," she said, turning to the right. An incubus separated from the quorum. *Dies Diei* and *Noctis*, day and night. I'd heard stories of the two Inquisitors tasked with making sure all questions were answered truthfully. As the two of them circled the wall and walked toward me, my heart sank. "I'm sorry," I whispered silently to Onyx, wondering where he was and if he'd heard about my capture.

The incubus and succubus lowered themselves fluidly into the chairs to my left and right. They each took one of my hands in their cold fingers, and I felt something icy and alien burrowing into my brain. Words, somehow both my own and not my own, forced themselves from my lips. "You may proceed with your questions."

The succubus at the front of the room returned to her bench with the other members of the quorum. An incubus leaned forward, his dark eyes demanding.

"Do you deny that you left the demon spawn academy last night of your own free will?"

I tried to think of a way to answer the question that wouldn't implicate Onyx. But something was blocking me. It was as if a thick wall had been placed inside my brain. Anytime I tried to cross the wall—to think of something untrue—it forced me back.

"I do not deny it," I said.

"You knew you were breaking academy rules," said a succubus, her flawless white skin standing out against the dark bench behind her.

I tried to force my way through the wall, but it was impervious to all my efforts. "I knew it was against the rules."

"Why did you go to Humeville?"

I clenched my teeth against my lower lip, trying to oppose Dies Diei and Noctis, who held tightly to my fingers. In my mind, I rammed again and again at the wall, trying to find a way not to tell the quorum what they wanted to know. The taste of blood filled my mouth. It was no use. I couldn't lie.

For some reason, an image of Cinder came into my head. The day after we met, I asked how she managed to keep so many guys on the hook at the same time. Did she lie about seeing other boys? "I don't lie," she'd said with a wicked grin. "I tell them exactly as much as I think they need to know."

Could I do that? Tell part of the truth without giving away everything? Instead of pushing against the wall in my head, I eased away from it ever so slightly. "I . . . I d-didn't know I was in Humeville," I stammered. "I've never been there before. I got lost."

From her spot up front, the succubus looked to Dies Diei and Noctis. The wall in my head seemed to waver for just a moment, then turned solid again. The incubus and succubus nodded.

"She tells the truth," one of the incubus murmured from the upper benches.

"Surely you didn't decide to go exploring on your own?" asked an incubus with hair that had gone silver along the edges, making him look more distinguished than old.

"No!" The words were forced from my lips before I could even try to come up with another answer. There was no wiggle room with "yes" and "no" questions.

"Then I ask again," said the succubus with the pale skin, "why did you leave the academy grounds?"

I tried to step away from the wall in my mind, but there was no room this time. The frigid finger squirming around in my brain pulled up the image of Onyx disappearing around the side of the academy. No matter how hard I fought against them, the words forced themselves from my mouth. "I was . . . following someone."

Behind the quorum, I saw my mother lean forward,

gripping my father's hand. *Don't ask me,* I begged. *Let me take the blame. This is completely my fault.* But the same wall that kept me from lying kept me from speaking unless I was asked a direct question.

The succubus raised her dark red lips in triumph. "Who did you follow into Humeville?"

Forgive me, Onyx. I pushed as hard as I could against the wall in my mind. Against my will, I opened my mouth. But to my surprise, instead of Onyx's name, my lips formed the words, "I don't know."

"What?" The succubus rose halfway up—clearly not getting the response she wanted—before forcing herself back onto the bench. "How can you not know who you followed?"

How could I not know? I asked myself. I'd seen Onyx leave the game. I followed him down the trail. I lost him for a moment, cutting between the storage buildings before seeing him leave the academy grounds. Except *had* I seen him leave? I'd seen a figure that looked like him. But I'd never actually seen his face. As I followed him farther and farther from the academy, I'd assumed it was him I'd been following. The only time I'd actually been close enough to get a good look was . . .

"It was a hume," I blurted. In the benches, the demons' voices rose to an excited pitch.

"Silence!" the succubus said, turning around.

"I followed someone from the academy," I said. I was able to push myself much farther away from the wall in my mind than I expected—telling the truth without directly lying about the question I'd been asked. "I was curious to see what they were up to and where they were going. I wasn't familiar with the city. And I got so disoriented, I didn't realize we had crossed into Humeville. Once or twice, I nearly lost whoever I was following. When they finally realized I was there and turned back to look at me, I saw a hume with a scarred face."

"She speaks the truth," Dies Diei and Noctis said in unison.

The ten members of the quorum conferred silently with one another. There seemed to be some disagreement between the different members of the covens. Finally, an incubus rose from the bench. "Blaze of the Clan Dae' Ungu, have you ever openly or in private conspired against the leadership of Hell?"

"No," I said, truthfully.

"Have you fraternized with any demons or humes who conspired against the leadership of Hell?"

"Never."

The incubus and succubus holding my hands nodded that I was telling the truth.

"Did you enter Humeville with the intention of attending a secret meeting of any kind?"

"Absolutely not."

The incubus standing before the bench looked back at the rest of the quorum, then turned to face me again. "You have broken academy rules. But that is not a matter for the covens. We will let the academy administration deal with this matter privately."

Dies Diei and Noctis released my hands, and I collapsed against the back of my chair.

In the upper benches, my mother hugged my father, tears running down her cheeks. She raced down to where I was sitting and wrapped her arms around me. My father was right behind her. Engulfed in their arms and sobbing, I promised myself I would never again do anything that might get me in trouble.

CHAPTER 7

"You're back!" Cinder squealed when I walked through the door of our room.

"Sure," I said, trying to look like I hadn't just returned from the most terrifying experience of my life. "What did you think I was—" My words were cut off as a pair of rock-hard arms lifted me into the air.

"Onyx?" I asked, twisting around to make sure it was really him—and that he wasn't picking me up to throw me out the window.

"When I heard you'd been taken to the Inquisitors, I was so . . . I mean, *we* were so worried about you. But you're here, and you're okay." He spun me around and around until the whole room was a blur. I didn't care though. He was smiling, and he was talking to me again.

"Put her down, or she's going to barf," Cinder said, shaking her head. "You'll crush her before she has a chance to tell us all the juicy details."

Onyx set me gently back on the ground, but kept a protective hand on my shoulder. It felt good. I looked up at him, making sure he really wasn't mad at me anymore. He was grinning like a spawnling tasting its first brimstone sweet. "You are okay, aren't you? I mean, they didn't . . ."

"I'm fine," I said, unable to stop smiling.

"Stop stalling," Cinder complained, "and tell us what happened."

"I kind of got in trouble," I said, still more than a little amazed I hadn't been kicked out of the academy—or worse.

"Thanks for the insightful update." Cinder lashed her tail back and forth impatiently. "Of course you got in trouble. Everyone's talking about it."

"Everyone?" What did they know? How did they know?

"*Everyone.* Trust me, last night's Culdine match was exciting. At least, the part of it I saw," she added with a sly grin. "But all anyone can talk about this morning is you. Is it true? Did you really sneak into the city?"

Cinder's words stunned me. How had the news gotten out so quickly? I nodded. "Yes."

"Are you serious?" She clapped her hands. "Who knew my roommate was such a rebel? If you tell me you had a rendezvous with an incubus spawn, I will die of jealousy right now."

"Yes, that's totally what I did. Two, in fact. And we got into a drunken fight with a pack of efreets." Leave it to Cinder to turn one of the worst nights of my life into a romp with a hot guy. "I'm so glad my stupidity brings you such joy."

Onyx shared none of her excitement. His eyes met mine as he squeezed my shoulder. "Are you . . .? Did they . . .? What's your punishment?"

"Well, I can't leave the academy until next Arrival Day. And even then, I have to take someone with me until I'm off probation. I have to serve thirty hours scrubbing barracks walls, and ten hours in the kitchen. And I have to write a formal letter of apology to Mr. Pyreet for nearly burning down his class."

"That's *it*?" Cinder asked, clearly expecting more.

"You were hoping for execution?"

"No." She blinked. "It's just . . . everyone thinks you've been kicked out of training at the very least. Your parents must have some crazy good connections with the higher-ups."

"Why *did* you go?" Onyx asked. I searched his eyes, looking for some sign of recognition. What I'd told the quorum about not knowing who I'd followed the night before was true. I didn't know for a fact that the figure I'd seen leaving the academy was Onyx. But I couldn't imagine a hume coming this far from Humeville—at the risk of torture I couldn't begin to fathom. It seemed much more likely I'd followed a demon out of the academy and stumbled onto the hume with the scarred face by accident.

If Onyx did leave the academy, he'd have to be suspicious. Despite my close scrutiny, he gave nothing away. His eyes held the same open curiosity as Cinder's.

"I just had to get away for a while," I said, glad I was no longer forced into telling the truth. "It's been a rough first week."

Shockingly, Onyx leaned down and took me in his arms. "This is all my fault. I totally overreacted to you reading my ideas."

"No," I said, hugging him back. "I knew your box was private, and I shouldn't have opened it. Please, Onyx, can we move past this? I can't lose you. You've been my friend for as long as I can remember."

He nodded.

"Ohhhh, this is so cute." Cinder beamed, resting her hands on her hips. "Would you like me to leave for a while so you two can . . . *make up?*" She was relentless.

"Very funny," I said, smacking her on the shoulder. "What I want is breakfast. And then a really long nap."

"I could go for some food too," Onyx said. As if to second the point, his stomach gave a thunderous rumble.

Cinder grabbed the end of her tail and flicked it back and forth as though fanning herself. "You hopeless romantics just get me all heated up."

"Is that what they were?" I asked Onyx as we left my room and started toward the cafeteria. "Those pieces of paper in your box were *ideas*?"

He hesitated for a fraction of a second before nodding. "I know it's weird, but sometimes I like to daydream. Every once in a while, something sticks, and I write it down."

I'd never considered that. But it made sense. He'd always been a little strange—in all the best ways. "What do they mean?"

"No clue." He laughed awkwardly. "That's the problem. They don't mean anything at all, which is why I keep them hidden. That's why I was embarrassed when you found them."

It sounded exactly like something he would do. So why was I so sure he was lying?

He studied my face as though waiting to see if I would accept his story. I nodded and forced myself to smile. "That's totally okay. And I'm sorry for reading them." We walked in silence for a few minutes before I glanced at him out of the corner of my eye and asked, "Where did you go last night?"

This time the pause was longer. "What do you mean?" I could hear the tension in his voice, but I had to know.

"Just after the beginning of Culdine, you got up and left. I started to follow you, to apologize. But you were too quick. When I lost you, I started wandering and . . ."

"So it *was* my fault you got in trouble." His big shoulders sank, and I felt like a total jerk.

"No, not at all." I wrapped my left arm around his waist and gave him a squeeze. "I should never have left the academy grounds."

I spent the rest of the walk to the cafeteria trying to cheer him up. I finally managed it by reminding him of the time he'd discovered me getting picked on by three bullies when I was about five and he was seven. Although he was younger than the bullies, he'd grabbed all three by the arms and ducked their heads in a barrel of fresh paving tar. They'd all ended up having to have their heads shaved to get the gunk off.

"I had to apologize to each of them, and their mothers," he said with a grin. "And I couldn't leave my house for a month. But those punks never laid a hand on you again."

"No, they didn't," I agreed.

It wasn't until we were nearly finished eating that I realized Onyx hadn't answered my question. He'd never told me where he was going the night before. And the pieces of paper in his box couldn't be what he'd said they were. He claimed he'd written them himself, but the handwriting wasn't his. Clearly, he was still keeping secrets. The question was, how much did I want to find out about what he was hiding?

* * *

Over the next few weeks, I kept my head down—focusing on training and working off my punishment. On the surface, everything was fine with Onyx. We sat together at lunch. He helped me with my science, and I helped him with his writing. But I could still sense a distance between us that hadn't been there before I found his puzzle box. Now and then, I turned from something I was doing to find him watching me with a guarded expression that disappeared as soon as I caught his eye.

Cinder and I usually came to the cafeteria right after it opened to beat the crowds. As we'd talked, it had filled up until every table was taken. Walking through the crowd, I searched for Onyx—maybe we could squish in by him. I spotted his bulk bent over a table in the far corner of the room with some other students. The entire group was made up of tert and quartus guys—nine of them altogether. They were crowded around one end of the table, shoulder to shoulder. The nearest demon spawns were at the far end of the table, as though the boys had reserved the space around them somehow.

Not wanting to bother Onyx if he was in the middle of something with his friends, I hovered a short distance away, waiting for their gathering to break up. The longer I waited, though, the more curious I became. Every so often, one of them would throw his hands up in the air or shake his head vigorously. But unlike most guy conversations that usually involved loud laughing and the occasional wall-shaking burp, this one seemed completely serious. Clearly, they were involved in some sort of animated discussion. But despite the obvious weight of whatever they were discussing, all of them kept their voices low. That was another *off* thing. Since when did guys keep their voices down? I'd heard boys talk about everything from who they made out with the night before to their most recent bodily functions, and not once did they seem to worry about being overheard.

Still unnoticed, I took a few more steps toward the table until I could just make out some words.

"...if it doesn't work?" a Dae' Ceal asked, his eyes wide.

"Who cares?" a Dae' Lorica growled.

Onyx nodded, his hands planted flat on the table. "It's not about whether it works or not. It's . . ." As the noise in the cafeteria picked up around me, I lost the rest of his words. The only thing I thought I might have heard was the word *statement*.

I eased close enough that I could have reached out and touched the nearest of them on the back.

"That's easy for you," the Dae' Ceal whispered. He opened his mouth to say something else, when the demon spawn next to him looked up from the group and saw me.

"Sssss," he hissed, his eyes wide, almost as if he were in pain.

All heads turned in my direction. The Dae' Ceal jerked backward, nearly tumbling off his bench.

Onyx met my eyes. His forehead wrinkled, and his mouth drew down in a snarl. The only other time I'd seen him like this was when . . . when he'd found me looking through his box. "What are you doing here?" he growled.

I stumbled back a step.

"She's spying," said a Dae' Ungu nearly as tall as Onyx. As he got up, his lips pulled back, revealing a mouthful of curved fangs. He lunged toward me, and I ran.

CHAPTER 8

"Wait!" Onyx called as I darted out of the cafeteria into the night.

Without looking back, I ran toward the barracks. I almost never cried, but I felt the cooling air catch drops of salty moisture from my eyes and press them against my cheeks as I raced through it. Onyx and I had been friends nearly as long as I could remember. Even when I was a pesky little spawnling, he'd stuck by me. But now, twice in less than a month, I'd seen a side of him I didn't know existed—a side I didn't want to believe he had.

Behind me, the sound of hooves echoed off the darkened classrooms. Onyx was bigger than me, but he wasn't as fast. Surprised he'd kept up for this long, I put on a burst of speed. Instead of falling behind, though, the sound of pursuit closed in. Just as I reached the entrance to the girls' barracks, a hand closed roughly around my shoulder and spun me backward.

"Leave me alone!" I screamed. Instead of looking up into Onyx's face, I found myself staring into the red-filmed eyes of the Dae' Ungu.

"Who sent you to spy on us?" he snarled. "What did you hear?" In the light of a nearby gas lamp, his fangs gleamed.

"Let go!" I tried to twist out of his grip, and his talons clamped down painfully, cutting into my skin.

Around me, everything turned red. Fangs burst from my gum tissue, pushing my lips up and back as a howl tore from my throat. Slashing out at him, I cut five deep gouges in his chest with the talons that emerged from my fingertips.

He gasped as rills of dark blood ran down the front of his torn shirt. Shaking me so my head snapped left and right, he drew back his hand, talons shining. I tried to get away from him, but his grip was too tight. It felt like his fingers had carved all the way through my shoulder to the bone. As his arm started forward and down, a hand closed around his wrist.

For a second, the bright red muscles in the Dae' Ungu's bicep bulged as he tried to get at me, then his body was spun around.

"Let go of her, Flare," Onyx said, his voice low.

Flare tried to rip his arm free, but Onyx was too strong. The demon spawn raised the hand he'd been holding me with to strike. Onyx shook his head. "Not a good idea."

For a moment, the two squared off, trying to stare each other down. Onyx's eyes hadn't gone from yellow to red yet, but his skin had taken on a thick pebble-like texture, and his hand still held Flare's pinned high in the air. Onyx looked at the Dae' Ungu's talons still impaled in my shoulder and growled. His fingers tightened around Flare's wrist until I was sure something was going to break. "Get your hand off her before I tear your arm from its socket."

"She's a spy," the demon spawn groaned. "That's why they let her off so easy after they caught her sneaking out of the school."

Onyx's eyes went from the Dae' Ungu to me. He raised his arm until Flare's hooves swung several inches above the ground.

"Fine." Flare released my arm with a snort of disgust. "But I'm telling you, she knows."

"Be quiet," Onyx muttered to him. "You've said too much already. Go back and tell the others I'm dealing with it."

I touched my shoulder. My fingers came away warm with my own blood. What were they talking about? What reason did they have to think I'd been spying on them? Spying on *what* exactly?

Flare held his hand to his chest with a wince of pain. "I know how you feel about her, but we can't take the risk. Not this close."

Onyx gave me a look I couldn't read. "I said I'll take care of things."

As the Dae' Ungu spun away and stalked back toward the cafeteria, a chill ran through my body. How was Onyx going to take care of things? I never would have believed he might hurt me.

Onyx sighed and ran his palms across the front of his shirt. "Do you have any idea how much danger you've placed yourself in?"

"No." I shivered both from the cold and what had just happened. As I began to calm down, waves of pain seared through my shoulder.

"You need to get that looked at." Onyx reached toward me, but I stepped away. Now that I was fairly certain he wasn't going to hurt me, I felt my anger returning.

"What have you been doing? Why did you lie to me?"

"Were you spying on us?" He swallowed, the thick muscles in his throat bunching and releasing. "Did you make a deal to find out?"

I clenched my fists, struggling to keep my temper under control. "No. I wasn't spying on you, and I didn't promise anyone anything. But I'm going to keep following you now unless you tell me what you're doing."

Onyx pounded a fist against his thigh. The sound was

like two rocks crashing together in the silence of the night. "Why can't you just stay out of this? Don't you see I'm trying to protect you?"

"Protect me from *what*?" It was like we were repeating the same scene over and over. "What are you hiding from me? Has it ever occurred to you that maybe I want to protect you as well?" I wanted to pound on him until he told me about whatever he'd gotten mixed up in. But when he looked at me, his eyes were filled with so much pain it hurt my heart. My anger disappeared at once.

Onyx's laughter echoed hollowly off the walls. He shook his head. "It's too late for that."

Another shudder racked my body, and I stepped forward, taking his hands in mine. His skin felt icy beneath my palms. "Whatever it is, it's not too late. Flare said something was close. That means whatever you're thinking about doing hasn't happened yet. You still have time to back out. Let me help you."

He closed his fingers around mine, engulfing my hands. "I believe in what I'm doing. That's all I can tell you. I believe in it, and I'm willing to suffer the consequences of it. But I won't let you get hurt. You have to promise to stay away from me until this is over."

"No." I stepped toward him and wrapped my arms around him—his back so broad my hands didn't touch. My shoulder groaned with pain, but I didn't care. "You're big and strong, but sometimes you can be as dumb as a rock. If you want to keep me out of this, you need to get out too. Because I won't stay away. I won't watch you put yourself in danger."

Onyx hugged me briefly before taking my shoulders and gently pushing me away. His face took on the hard look I'd seen in his room and back at the cafeteria table, but this time I recognized it for what it was. He wasn't angry at me. He was frightened for me. "Until this is over, I'm through talking with you. I'm done being seen with you. If you try to follow me, I'll see that you get thrown out of the academy. I swear it. If this goes right, things will change for the better. If it goes wrong . . ." He pressed his hands to his temples. "I won't let you be tied to my actions."

I stared into his eyes, wanting to go to him and make everything okay. But I couldn't. If he wouldn't tell me what he was planning, and I couldn't get him to change his mind, all I could do was stay out of the way. I'd already been questioned twice. If I were brought in again, there wouldn't be any leniency.

He leaned toward me, but I pulled away, closed my eyes, and took a deep breath. I had to talk some sense into him.

When I opened my eyes, he was gone.

* * *

For the rest of the month, Onyx kept his word. I didn't see him once, even though I looked for him. The group at the back of the cafeteria no longer gathered together for dinner. I didn't know if Onyx was having his food brought to his room or just making sure he ate at a different time than me, but I never saw him at any of the meals.

I didn't tell Cinder what had happened. She assumed Onyx and I ended our friendship. I let her think that. It was easier than answering questions. She tried to set me up with guys as a "good distraction," but I wasn't interested. I went through day after day of training in a blur, waiting to hear something truly awful had occurred. I didn't know what Onyx and his friends were planning, but I was sure I'd hear about it when it happened.

It wasn't until the night before the next Arrival Day

that I finally pulled out of my daze. The thought of facing the seraphs again tied my stomach in knots.

"Did you eat at all?" Cinder asked when she came back to the room to find me lying curled on my pallet.

"I can't."

She walked over and sat beside me. "It's going to be fine, you know."

I swallowed. "It's just the memory of that angel-fire blade coming toward me . . ."

"Have you talked to him?"

I looked up. "Who?"

Cinder laughed. "Don't you think I've seen how you and Onyx are avoiding each other? How you both make sure not to meet? You're going to have to see him tomorrow, and it's got you freaked out."

I *was* freaked out about Onyx, all right, but not in the way she thought. And while he was part of my worries, the idea of standing on the platform tomorrow scared me almost as much.

Cinder began turning out the gas lamps one by one until the room was in nearly complete darkness, the only faint illumination coming through the window from the street below. "Get some sleep. Onyx will come around."

I wished I could believe her. I closed my eyes, but I kept thinking about how Flare said something was going to happen soon. With the school closed, and the packed streets making it easy to go anywhere in the city, Arrival Day would be the perfect time to do whatever they were planning.

Cinder purred softly on her pallet, and I rolled over, telling myself there was no reason to worry, when a soft crackling sound came from the direction of our door.

Tiptoeing across the room so I wouldn't disturb Cinder, I found a note on the floor. I quickly opened the door, but whoever had left it was gone. Hoping it was from Onyx, I hurried to the light coming through the window to see what it said. But when I read the brief message, my hands began to shake.

Blaze,

Please stay home tomorrow. Say you're sick or still messed up from what happened last time. Can't tell you more, but it's IMPORTANT. Tell Cinder to stay away too. Everything will be better soon. I promise.

There was no signature, but I recognized Onyx's handwriting. I was right. Whatever they had planned was happening tomorrow.

Maybe it wasn't as big a deal as they'd made it seem. A prank or some dumb little stunt to impress the girls they liked. It wasn't like guys never blew things out of proportion. Only I knew Onyx would never act the way he had over a joke. And why would he warn me to stay away if it was something minor?

I thought back to what the quorum had asked. *Have you ever conspired against the leadership of Hell? Did you enter Humeville with the intention of attending a secret meeting of any kind?* The questions had seemed crazy at the time, but now a terrible certainty hit me. They were asking about whatever Onyx was up to. That's why he'd left campus the night I followed him—to attend some kind of meeting.

I'd never told Onyx about the questions they'd asked me, and if the Inquisitors already knew about what he and his friends were planning, they could all be walking into a trap. I had to warn him.

As I raced out of the girls' barracks, my teeth chattered. It had been an especially ash-filled day, with several smaller volcanoes acting up. The frigid air was still hazy with dancing black flakes, and drifts of dust piled against the walls. I wished I'd thought to put on something warmer, but that was the least of my worries.

As I hurried toward the boys' barracks, something scuffled across the path ahead of me, and I froze, staring into the darkness, listening. For several long moments there was nothing. Then I heard it again—the sound of hooves scraping across dirt.

Imps out night scavenging? No. Imps were stealthier than that—quick and light on their hooves. This sounded bigger. It was coming my way. Spotting a nearby doorway, I darted into it and pressed myself deep into the recess.

Only a second or two later, a figure approached. It stuck close to the walls, skulking in the shadows. It was Onyx— sneaking off to whatever he had planned. I was so sure it was him that I nearly stepped out of my hiding place and whispered his name as he came near. It wasn't until I saw the smaller horns—only slightly curved—and the tall, lithe body that I realized it was Flare, the quartus Dae' Ungu who'd chased me out of the cafeteria. The one who wanted to silence me.

As he passed by, my first instinct was to continue to Onyx's room. But what if he'd already left too? Following Flare would eventually lead me to Onyx, and I could tell him that the Inquisitors knew what he was up to. If Flare discovered I was tracking him, I had no doubt he would try to kill me. But if I didn't, and Onyx went ahead with his plan, it would be suicide.

Holding to that thought, I quietly stepped out of the

doorway and began to trail Flare. He had a lead on me, but unlike Onyx, he didn't have any better night vision than I did, which forced him to move more slowly. I was also smaller and lighter than him, needing less space to stay hidden. This time, though, I kept one eye on him and another watching out for anyone following me.

A hundred yards or so from the edge of the academy grounds, he stopped abruptly and knelt by a pile of rocks. Hiding forty paces behind him, I looked around, wondering if I'd been spotted. He glanced over his shoulder and dropped flat to the earth. What was he doing? The mound of charred scree provided enough cover to hide his presence, but if someone came looking for him, there was nowhere to escape.

I studied the pile of pocked lava rocks, expecting him to rise and continue any second. When he hadn't moved for several minutes, I edged a little closer. What was he waiting for? I scrubbed at my eyes, trying to make them pierce the darkness. Something was wrong. Had he heard me, or seen something I'd missed?

The longer I waited, the harder my heart thudded, until it seemed so loud, I was surprised the quartus couldn't hear it too. The only thing that kept me from running back to my room was Onyx.

I edged cautiously forward, expecting the Dae' Ungu to jump out at any moment. Halfway there, I realized I could make out the outlines of fist-sized black rocks, but I couldn't see the demon spawn anywhere. I scurried forward to the spot where I'd last seen him. He was gone. I circled the entire pile. How was that possible? I scanned the terrain ahead. There was nowhere to hide for at least a hundred paces.

Talons poked through my fingertips as my pulse raced. Dropping to my hands and knees, I crawled across the ground, looking for his tracks. In the fresh ash, it was easy to see where he approached, knelt like I was, and . . . what? There were no hoof prints leaving. Flare had been here. He hadn't walked away. He certainly hadn't flown away. He couldn't have left this spot without me seeing him. But he *had* vanished—and with him, any chance I had of finding Onyx.

CHAPTER 9

"Don't lose it," I whispered, fighting against the panic gnawing at my insides. "He's got to be here somewhere."

Turning my head sideways, my left cheek nearly touching the ground, I studied the tracks and the pile of rocks beside them. A spot a little to my right caught my eye. It was the same rocky surface as the dirt around it, only something about it was slightly different. I rubbed my finger over the ground and realized what it was. The ash was missing.

Now that I was looking for it, I could see a square roughly five hands on each side that was free of the soot layer covering everything else. I ran a nail along a line of fine black powder piled at one edge. It looked as if someone had swept away the ashes with the side of their hand or—

The tip of my nail caught on something in the dirt. Moving my finger to one side, I discovered an almost perfectly hidden hairline crack in the ground. It went completely around the square. It was a door—to a tunnel! Of course, why hadn't I thought of it before? He hadn't gone forward or back, and he hadn't gone up. The only other alternative was down.

I'd heard of underground tunnels before—even explored a few of the ones beneath our building as a child. They let maintenance workers fix pipes and sulfur steam vents.

Every once in a while, we'd discover one with a broken lock and sneak inside.

Fumbling around the edges for a handle of some kind, it occurred to me this couldn't be the door to a service tunnel. But the location in the middle of nowhere made no sense at all, and the entrance had been carefully camouflaged. It seemed to be a secret entrance. Made by whom, and for what purpose?

At last, my fingers discovered a smooth knuckle-sized stone that moved beneath my touch. I pushed it forward with an audible click. The door sprang upward just enough to let me slip my hand under its edge.

I didn't know what I'd been expecting to find inside—maybe smooth floors and well-lit walls like I'd seen in the tunnels under our building? Instead, I discovered a burnt dirt-walled passageway that looked like it had been burrowed by an animal. It was barely tall enough for me to climb into on my hands and knees. As I stared into the black entrance, realizing I would be completely blind once I crawled inside, my hands closed into fists.

It wasn't the tight space, or even the dark, that made me hesitate as I knelt before the opening. It was the thought that if I ran into something I couldn't handle, there wasn't enough room to turn around. I considered going back, but the thought of Onyx kept me moving forward.

"You better listen to me," I whispered as I slithered into the entrance. As soon as I was inside, the door dropped closed with a clunk, and total darkness engulfed me. Somewhere ahead, I thought I could hear Flare grunting and banging around. I hoped he couldn't hear me.

Pulling myself forward, I felt the passageway angle down. The ceiling wasn't wide enough for me to fully extend my arms and legs, so I had to slide along on my elbows and knees in a kind of shuffling motion. Dirt coated the insides of my nose and mouth as I gasped for air, and my limbs ached. My only consolation was that it had to be even worse for the bigger demon spawn in front of me. I couldn't imagine Onyx fitting in here.

With no idea how far I'd gone or how far I had to go, my mind began to imagine things—creatures brushing against my skin or lights in the distance. At one point, I thought I could hear voices. Farther along, the dirt walls thrummed with a steady vibration I was almost sure wasn't my imagination.

The longer I crawled, the harder it became to fight against a growing dread that the tunnel would suddenly end, and I'd find myself facing Flare, who had somehow managed to turn around. Or worse, that the dirt over my head would collapse, leaving me trapped and dying where no one would ever know to look for me. Caught up in these thoughts, and worse, I didn't realize the surface I was crawling on had changed until I fell on my face.

One minute I was reaching my hand blindly forward like I'd done hundreds of times before. The next minute I was tumbling down a steep, narrow staircase. With no sense of balance or direction, I somersaulted forward. My legs smashed against a wall. My chin slammed to the ground, crunching my teeth so hard, it felt like they could turn into powder. The jolt shot all the way to the back of my skull. At last, I came to a stop on a smooth, cool surface that felt like stone.

"Uhh," I groaned, rubbing my jaw and standing cautiously.

After so much time in the tight confines of the tunnel, I ducked my head and probed above me with my hand. I needn't have worried. The passage I'd dropped into was tall enough that I could barely reach the ceiling. By moving to the left and right with my hands extended, I discovered it was easily wide enough for five demons to walk side by side. The walls and ceiling seemed to be made of the same smooth stone as the floor.

Feeling around in the dark, I discovered the stairs I'd fallen down entered from the side of the larger tunnel, which extended in both directions. I had no idea which way Flare had gone. I stood silently, pressing my hands against a wall and listening for the clank of his hooves. But all I could hear was a steady *thum-thum-thum* that seemed to be coming from my left. With no better choice, I started in that direction.

I hadn't gone far when the tunnel curved, and I spotted a tiny circle of light bobbing a few hundred paces ahead of me. It had to be Flare. As I hurried to catch up with him, the noise turned from a *thum* to a *bang-bang-bang* that I felt rattling through the ground up into my legs. At the same time, the tunnel floor changed from stone to something that clanged against my hooves. I ran my fingers across the ground and discovered I was standing on a metal grate.

The floor wasn't the only thing that had changed. The tunnel that had been cool—even cold at some points—now felt warm. A stream of hot, damp gases flowed up through the grate. The banging was different too. Not just louder, but echoing, as though I'd entered an enormous cavern. It seemed to be coming from my right, but the sound bounced above and below, giving me the odd feeling that I was floating.

Beneath the steady *clang-clang-clang* that sounded like a giant hammer pounding over and over against an anvil, I could swear I heard voices too. I strained to make out the words, but Flare's light was moving rapidly away from me, his hooves clanging across the metal grate. With no time to explore, I ripped two strips of cloth from the bottom of my shirt, wrapped them around my hooves to deaden the noise, and raced toward him. I could still hear my hooves thudding against the floor as I ran, but with all the noise he was making, I didn't think he'd notice.

After several more minutes, we seemed to enter another tunnel. Flare slowed, moving with obvious caution. Every so often, he stopped, seeming to study something on the walls before taking unexpected turns. Eventually he led me up a staircase that spiraled hundreds of steps into the air. If he needed to backtrack, I'd be caught with no way out. Where were we? I couldn't imagine service tunnels this extensive. I heard the odd banging sound several more times, and once a rapid *chit-chit, chit-chit* that sounded like thousands of tiny night-fliers fluttering their wings.

As I was beginning to wonder if he'd ever stop, the light in front of me suddenly snuffed out. I froze, waiting for it to come back on. Instead, I heard the click of hooves and a heavy thud, like a door closing. I counted slowly. When I reached fifty and still hadn't heard another sound, I began walking forward. The sound had come from the right of the passage, so I moved to that side and ran my hand along the wall. After twenty or thirty paces, my fingers brushed against a rough metal surface that flaked away under my touch.

Running my hands up and down, I discovered a cold metal knob. I pressed my ear to the door and listened for the sound of voices or movement. When I couldn't hear anything, I turned the knob and eased open the door. Cool air blew across my face. But with it came a smell that set my fangs pressing against my lips.

I stepped through the doorway and climbed a crumbling set of stairs to find myself on a narrow street set with cracked, uneven stones and lined by tumble-down buildings dimly lit and pressed close together. The stench of sweat and raw sewage was so thick, I had to press my hand over my nose to keep from gagging.

"Humeville," I whispered. Back here again. But why gather here in this filth and trash for their meetings? Why not use the academy, or one of the clubs in the first or second Circles?

To my left, the street ended in a soot-stained brick wall. To my right, it teed in an intersection lit by a gas lamp flickering inside a rusty metal cage. Knowing I couldn't afford to lose the Dae' Ungu in this filthy hume warren, I jogged toward the light and nearly into the back of a Dae' Lorica guard—no way was I getting lost in this disgusting place again.

He was looking the other way, his eyes fixed on an orange imp just across the street. Freezing only a few steps behind the guard, I watched as the imp—who appeared to have injured one of its legs—limped forward to grab a sliver of meat. As it reached for the morsel, the guard flicked a pebble in its direction, sending it scurrying backward.

"Stupid creature." The guard chuckled, shaking his head. "You'll try this all night, won't you?"

Was him being here just a coincidence, or had the Inquisitors specifically had the guards patrol this area looking for Onyx and his friends?

I covered my face with my hand again. This time it wasn't to keep out the stench, but to cover the ragged sound of my breathing, which seemed to echo loudly in my ears. Step by step, I backed down the alley.

I was trapped. There was no way to get over the wall, which was at least three or four times my height. Finding my way back through the tunnels without a light was impossible, and I knew Onyx had to be around here somewhere. But I had no idea how long the guard would remain on the corner. Or worse, what if he decided to step into the intersection and look my way?

I glanced toward the few ragged buildings lining the street, but quickly gave up the idea of trying to get inside one. All of the doors were barred or secured with crude locks. And even if I could get past them, the only thing inside was humes. At the sight of me, they were sure to let out a howl that would bring the guard.

Sweat beaded on my forehead as I looked up and down the narrow alley. Where had Flare gone? The guard looked like he'd been there for a while. There was no way anyone could have passed by without him noticing. Having learned my lesson before, I squatted in the middle of the street to study the layer of ash. I spotted Flare's hoofprints right away, but something was wrong with them. Instead of going in a straight line, they went up and down the street— stopping in front of buildings, circling around, and looping on themselves almost as if he knew someone might try tracking him.

It was impossible to make any sense of where he'd gone. One set of tracks even went straight to the brick wall, as though he'd somehow managed to scale it. Once again, it was as if he really had vanished.

It wasn't until my third time passing the brick wall that I noticed the small symbol scratched into the soot. A flame surrounded by a circle of links—the image I'd seen engraved into the top of Onyx's puzzle box.

Without the symbol, I would never have found the door hidden in the side of the wall. The wood had been textured and painted to match the grimy brick around it so well that it was almost undetectable. Like the trapdoor above the tunnel, the tiny crack around the door was hidden in the mortar of the brick. I could only tell it was there by the slight break in the soot. I pressed my ear against the door, but couldn't hear a thing.

The idea of going through a hidden Humeville door I knew nothing about made my skin crawl, but I knew Flare must have gone through it. Scuffling sounds came from the roofs of the buildings, and I wondered if someone was watching me from above. Steam billowed from a pipe sticking out of the ground as though some huge creature slept just below my hooves. Around the corner, the guard gave a string of dry coughs.

Onyx would be furious when he found out I was here, but I had to warn him and get both of us away. Pressing my fingertips into the tiniest of crevices between the door and the wall, I got just enough of a grip to pull it. I expected the door to open with a grind and a creak—it looked as though it hadn't been used in years. But it swung outward silently, revealing a narrow wooden staircase that went down four steps before turning a corner. I quietly slid the door closed and followed the steps down, running a hand along the wall. Pausing at the corner, I heard the voices more clearly. One of them sounded like Onyx, but I couldn't be sure. Around the corner, the stairs continued down.

I was almost to the bottom when a step creaked loudly under my hoof. I froze, but it was too late. The voices stopped. I heard the sound of steps coming toward me. My heart thudded into my throat. Without warning, a dark curtain yanked open. Bright light nearly blinded me.

"Blaze?"

I blinked my eyes. Onyx stood framed in the doorway. Shock filled his face. He tried to pull the curtain shut, but it was too late. Behind him, I could see the group of demon spawns he'd been hanging with. They were sitting on benches around a table covered with silver material of some kind. Several of them were shoving gray balls into cloth packs. One held a metal tube with one end sealed off.

Flare was standing a few steps behind Onyx. At the sight of me, his eyes went red. Fangs sprang from between his lips as he snarled and started toward me. It wasn't him who shocked me though. Not him, or the small grungy room covered with maps and charts. Or the other demon spawns who stood, eyes fixed on me.

What sent me reeling back, eyes wide with horror, was that along with them—sitting side by side at the table like equals—were more than a dozen repulsive humes.

CHAPTER 10

"I told you to stay inside!" Onyx pulled me through a maze of dark, empty streets, his hand clamped tightly across my mouth. He'd dragged me out of their secret hideout before things could escalate further. I worried the guard might hear us, but after seeing the look on Flare's face, I'd guessed the guard would show me more mercy.

I struggled in his grip and managed to get my head free. "You were meeting with . . . with . . ." I couldn't force myself to say it. The thought of what he'd been doing made me sick.

He looked both ways before swinging open what appeared to be a locked door and pushing me into a hallway filled with stinky trash. "You don't understand."

"What's to understand?" I shouted. "You were sitting with humes. *Talking* to them."

He threw me up against a wall, knocking the air out of my lungs. His eyes flashed red. "Be quiet!"

"Or what?" I asked, my fangs cutting into my lips. "Afraid the guards will discover what you and your disgusting friends have been up to?"

Onyx clenched his fist as though he was going to hit me, before releasing my arm and pushing me to the floor. "Guards are the least of my worries at the moment. The demons in that room are putting their lives at stake. I managed to get you out before they could organize. But I promise you that right now, every one of them is looking for you. If they find us, I won't be able to stop them from killing you."

I opened my mouth, but nothing came out.

"Why did you come here?" He groaned, grinding his fists against his thighs.

"Because I was worried about you," I said softly, looking up at him from where I sat on the floor. "The day I snuck out of the school, the covens asked me questions about you. And they grilled me about your meetings."

He snorted. "I know all about that."

"How could you?" I asked. "I never told anyone."

"I . . ." He looked away. "*We* have sources inside the government. Not just with the incubi and succubae, but all the way up to the devils."

"That's impossible," I said. "They never let anyone—" Suddenly I remembered the women scrubbing the floors of the Immigration Station with their hair. "The humes are spying for you!"

His silence was all the answer I needed. "Then you must be aware that the covens know about your meetings."

His broad shoulders slumped. "Of course. I'm not stupid."

"You could have fooled me." The idea of what would happen to him if anyone discovered what he was doing terrified me.

"They've been watching me and the others for months," he said. "Maybe years. I accept that. But I can't let them tie the two of us together." He took my arm and lifted me up. "I'll show you how to get back to the barracks without being seen."

"I'm not going anywhere," I said, yanking my wrist from his grasp. "Not unless you come with me."

Onyx scowled. "I can pick you up and carry you."

"Great." I held out my arms. "Carry me back to the school. As long as you stay there with me, I won't say a word about what I saw tonight. But if you try to leave, I'll follow you, screaming the entire way."

He reared his head back, neck muscles bulging as though he were going to ram his horns straight through the wall. "Why are you acting this way?"

"Because I care about you," I said, realizing for the first time how true those words were. "I care about you, and I don't want to see you get hurt."

Slowly, the muscles in his neck and shoulders relaxed. His eyes went from red to yellow, and finally, a soft gold I couldn't remember seeing before. "I care about you too," he said, taking my hand. "What I'm doing is for you as much as anyone else. Maybe more."

I squeezed his fingers. "Then tell me. Make me understand what you're doing and why it's so important."

Onyx gazed at me, and I could tell there was a struggle going on behind those golden eyes. His jaw clenched and relaxed, clenched and relaxed. I didn't think he'd give up whatever he'd been hiding, so I was surprised when he exhaled slowly and said, "What if I told you that Hell was going to change tomorrow?"

"Change how?"

"For the better." His lips pulled up into a smile I hadn't seen for weeks. His eyes stared at something over my shoulder. But I knew if I turned around, I wouldn't be able to see whatever he was looking at. "What if I told you that in a few months, you'd be happier than you could ever imagine?"

"No." My voice seemed to snap him out of whatever fantastical thing he was imagining. His eyes looked hurt, but I didn't care. "No." I shook my head, gripping his hand tightly enough to make him listen. "I'm happy now. Here, with you, the way things are. Nothing else could make me any happier, especially not if it comes with the risk of something happening to you.”

“Come on,” he said. “I want to show you something.” He opened the door a few inches and peeked out.

“Where are we going?”

“You’ll see. Stay close behind me. And if you care about what happens to either of us, be quiet.” He glanced down at the cloth wrapped around my hooves and grinned. “With all the sneaking around I’ve done, why didn’t I think of that?”

“Because I’m smarter than you,” I said, nudging him with my elbow.

For the next few minutes, I followed him through a dizzying array of streets and passageways, through barred doors, out broken windows, and up narrow staircases that seemed endless.

At last, we were finally there. Wherever *there* was, before the leaning metal frame of what had once been a three- or four-story building. All that was left now were a few blackened beams that looked like they were only being held together by corrosion. When Onyx began to climb up, I grabbed his leg. “Are you trying to kill us before the guards do?”

“Just step where I step, and grab where I grab,” he whispered. “It’s stronger than it looks.”

It would have to be. It didn’t look sturdy enough to hold a spawnling, much less a pair of teenage demon spawns. But I followed him up—mostly because the curiosity was killing me. As we climbed, I began noticing the places we stepped looked almost like they’d been put there on purpose—holes cut at just the right place to grab, chunks of rusted beam twisted out to make a perfect step.

“Did you—” I began to ask, but he looked down and put a finger to his lips.

"Quiet," he breathed. "Sound carries a lot farther up here than it does on the ground."

I glanced down, which was a mistake. I'd been higher than this, but never while clinging to a rickety metal strut.

"Keep climbing," he whispered from above me. "We're nearly there."

Trying to keep my eyes on the handholds and not the ground far below, I followed after him until he finally halted near the top of the structure. "Okay," he said, reaching down to take my hand, "this last part isn't nearly as tricky as it looks."

"Tricky?" I turned to see where he was pointing, and every muscle in my body seemed to contract at the same time. "No. No, I am not going out on that."

He pulled me up to stand on a rusty brace beside him. "I'll hold your hand the whole way. I won't let you fall."

I stared at the narrow metal beam angled precariously into thin air. It looked as though it had finally broken off from the rest of the building and was waiting for the right gust of wind to send it tumbling to the ground below. "You've got to be kidding. It won't hold my weight, and it definitely can't hold yours."

"Trust me," Onyx said, "I've done it dozens of times." To prove his point, he took several steps onto the beam.

I grimaced, waiting for the ancient metal to groan under his weight and break into a hundred pieces. Somehow, it held up. "Okay, so maybe it won't fall," I said, still dubious. "But what's the point? Once we get out there, what are we supposed to do? Jump?" The nearest building to the end of the beam was a good twenty paces away. And even if we could jump that far, the only place to land was on a narrow ledge.

"I'll show you when we get there. It's actually really a lot of fun."

Walking on a rusty beam over a drop that would undoubtedly kill me was not my idea of fun, but I let him lead me forward anyway.

"Look straight at me," Onyx whispered, guiding me step by step.

"Oh, I am," I said, drawing a shaky breath. "Because the last thing I want you to see before we both die is me saying, 'I told you so.'"

"We're not going to die." He laughed softly. A gust of air made the beam sway, and suddenly, I was sure this was it. I braced my legs, waiting for the moment we would both tumble over the side.

"Easy," he said. "Easy. We're almost there."

With a promise that if we somehow managed to survive this, I would personally strangle him, I followed his steps until we finally reached the end of the beam. "Now what?" I asked, unable to keep my sharp molars from chattering.

"Sit down and hold tight." Together, we lowered ourselves to the cool metal. As soon as I was able to, I wrapped my arms tightly around the beam.

Onyx reached beneath the beam and lifted a chain I hadn't seen before. "This is the fun part." He pulled the chain, and suddenly, the beam seemed to break away from the corroded frame. I gasped as we swung sideways through the air. Wind blew through my hair, and I was so scared, I couldn't even scream. A moment later, the beam bumped up against the side of a nearby building. "What do you think?" he asked with a wide grin.

"I . . ." I gasped for air, amazed I was still alive. "I . . . I think I'm going to rip you limb from limb and dance on your guts if you don't get me down from here now."

Onyx looked slightly crestfallen, but I didn't care. "It's not nearly as exciting the second time around," he said. "When you know what's coming."

I glared at him. "There won't be a second time."

He boosted me onto a metal ladder that rose from the ledge to the roof and kicked the beam, so it swung back to the other building. I had no idea where we were. I paused, catching my breath, and finally realized where he'd led me. "We're on . . ."

He nodded. "The Immigration Station."

I turned slowly around. This high up, at the outer edge of the city, the view was incredible. Even better than the top of the volcano. I could see everything, but . . . "Isn't this the last place you should be, considering who's looking for you?"

Onyx shrugged, apparently not as impressed with the view as me, but still enjoying my reaction. "They haven't found me yet."

"How many times have you been here?"

He gave an odd little laugh. "Once or twice."

Something about that laugh gave me an uncomfortable feeling. "This is what you wanted me to see?"

"Yes." He held his arms wide. "All of Hell is below you. Take a look."

"It's amazing. But what does this have to do with your . . . *secret?*"

"No. *Really* look. Try to see it with new eyes."

I studied his face, hoping to read his expression, and couldn't. Instead, I looked down on the place I'd known all my life. Far away, at the center of the city, were the demon clan buildings where I'd lived until a month ago. Closer was the academy—still mostly dark at this time of night. To the left and right of the academy were rows of shops, clubs I wouldn't be able to enter for another two years, and a few private houses belonging to clave members—devils, incubi, and succubae. Past that were the factories and hume housing, then fields of yellow and brown crops that would soon be harvested. The River Styx, of course. And beyond that, the open desert of the Outer Circles.

Try to see it with new eyes. What did Onyx mean? I glanced toward him, and he nodded encouragingly. "Pretend you're seeing it all for the first time."

I tried. But it was hard. Obviously, I didn't know Hell as well as he did, but after sixteen years, it was impossible to pretend I'd never seen it before. "It's beautiful, of course."

He snorted, and I could see I'd disappointed him somehow. "Look at the river."

I glanced down. The Styx looked just like it always had.

"It stinks," Onyx said. "And it's full of trash. The water is so dark it might as well be ink. Look." He pointed to the left. "There's a dead hume floating near the bank."

"What do you expect? It runs along Humeville. So yes, it reeks. Humeville stinks, too, in case you hadn't noticed that in all of your adventures."

"Over there," he said, turning me to the right. "Look at the third building, the one you grew up in. What do you see?"

"What do you mean, what do I see?" I asked, frustrated that I wasn't getting whatever it was he was trying to show me. "It's just a building. Four stories high. Forty windows on each side. I've seen it all my life."

"Exactly." He squeezed my shoulders as if I'd said something right. "You've seen it all your life, so you never noticed how ugly it is. It's square and black and filthy. It's coated with years and years of thick, fuzzy soot. You can barely see through the windows, even in the middle of the day, and as far as I know, it's never been painted once."

"Painted?" Maybe he really was crazy. "Why would you paint it? It would only get dirty again a few days later."

He ignored my remark, and instead looked up toward

the cavern ceiling that was still black and cold. "Did you know lots of humes get sick and even die from the air here?"

What was he talking about?

"Their lungs can't handle the soot and the sulfur. They cough and cough until their throats finally close off. Some of them don't die, but wheeze all the time. Others get blisters and boils on their skin from the water. They ooze into pus-filled sores."

"They're just humes," I said, completely confused. "What do you care what happens to them?"

"Right." He nodded. "Just humes. But did it ever occur to you that we're breathing the same filthy air they are? Drinking the same water? This whole city is disgusting. You just don't realize it because it's the only place you've ever known."

"It's the only place you've known too," I said, bristling at how he talked down to me.

"That's true. It *is* the only place I've ever known. But it's not the only place I've ever known *of*. What if I told you there are colors we don't have here?"

There was definitely something wrong with him. "Let's go," I said. "Let's get back to the barracks, and we can talk about colors and water and air all you want."

"Where the humes come from, there's a plant called *roze*," he said. "It's covered with cups that are pink, and yellow, and purple—that's one of the colors we don't have here—and they smell amazing. And something called grass that has a stalk nearly as thin as a strand of hair. It might be edible, or it might just be for looks—I'm not completely sure. But it's soft, and it blows in the wind. When you walk through it, it tickles your legs. And in the morning, it's covered with drops of cold clear water called *roo*."

"Listen to yourself." I grabbed his hand. "You're sick. But if you come back with me, I can get you help."

86

"And honey," he recited, as if remembering a lesson from training. "It's like the candy spawnlings eat. Only much sweeter. But it's a liquid. A clear red liquid, I think, that you can pour straight into your mouth. And this might be wrong—not all the things I've learned about make sense, I think some of them are a little confused. But it's possible the honey liquid comes from tiny creatures—no bigger than your thumb—called *bards* that fly around and collect it."

"Why are you making these things up?" I asked, now truly frightened for him. "You can't know anything about where the humes came from. Even *they* don't remember."

Onyx met my eyes. He didn't *look* sick. "That's the thing," he said, squeezing my hand until it hurt. "Most of the humes don't have memories. But a few do. Just bits and pieces. A lot of the pieces don't make sense. But if you put them together, you can sometimes figure things out. Like a puzzle."

A *puzzle*. Suddenly it made sense. "The box in your room. That's what the papers were."

He nodded. "Memories. I collect them. Me and the other demon spawns. The humes write them down. Then we compare the notes and see what we can figure out. It's hard work, but we've learned a lot."

I stared at my hands with a low moan. The papers I sorted through—touched with my own fingers. They'd been written by humes. Hume fingers had held them, sweat on them. Onyx had been keeping them in his pallet, and I had touched them. The thought made me physically ill. "Why would you do that?" I gasped.

It was his turn to look at me as if I were the sick one. "To learn, of course. To learn what they're hiding from us. The devils, the seraphs. They don't want us to know how bad it is here, so we'll be satisfied with what we have. But they can't hide the truth if we won't let them."

"So what?" I laughed, even though I could see it hurt him. I couldn't help myself. "All this planning and plotting is so you can paint the buildings green?"

He shook his head. "You don't understand at all. I want everything. Everything we've been denied. Why shouldn't we have it?"

It was like I was talking to a child. "Because this is Hell. Who cares what the humes had before they came? Maybe it's all true. Maybe they dressed in fancy clothes and drank grass and sniffed honey until it came out their ears. But in case you've forgotten, they're here because they're being punished. They are nasty creatures who have done horrible, foul things, and they deserve whatever they get."

"Do they?" Onyx's eyes glowed with a fever that made me want to run back to the academy and forget I'd ever met him. He looked worse than sick; he looked insane. "How do we know they did all those terrible things? Because the same people who've been hiding things told us that?"

I tried to speak, but nothing came out.

"Remember that little girl?" he asked.

I nodded, remembering the questions the incubus had asked. I hadn't understood them then, but now I was starting to. "Were you protecting me from the seraph or her?"

"Both of you." He clenched his fists. "What did she do to get sent here? She was only a child. Did she look like a murderer to you? A robber? Do you think she ran around beating up other humes and stealing from them?"

My heart pounded, and I couldn't seem to get enough air. "I don't know what she did. But I know she wouldn't have been sent here if it wasn't bad. That's what Judgment is for—to identify the good for their eternal reward and the evil for eternal punishment. Anything else is . . . is . . . blasphemy."

A coarse stone gargoyle squawked noisily at the other

end of the building and flapped into the night. The fever seemed to leave Onyx's eyes. He gulped and nodded. "Let's say you're right. Let's say they all did terrible things. They've been sent here as punishment. What did *we* do to deserve Hell? Aren't we just as damned as they are?"

He pointed to the mountains of Judgment far in the distance. "Who decided we have to live here, and the Halos get to live there?"

I shook my head. "Nobody *decided* it. That's just the way things are."

"Some of us think we all deserve better."

I flapped my hands in the air. "Even if you're right, what can you do about it?"

"I can learn the truth," he said, staring out across the desert. "All I want is the truth."

I opened my mouth. I had a hundred questions. How he would discover the truth. What he would do once he'd learned it. How he'd come to find out the humes had memories in the first place. But at that moment, the message shook the air. *Welcome to Hell, all ye damned and demented. Please keep moving. Welcome to Hell, all ye damned and demented. Please keep moving.*

"Oh no!" I cried, looking around. I'd completely forgotten it was Arrival Day. The Stygian would be coming soon, and I was going to miss it.

CHAPTER 11

I spun around and around, gripped by panic. I couldn't believe it was this late. "I'm going to miss the humes' arrival. Cinder will be awake by now. She must have freaked out when she saw I wasn't there."

Onyx grabbed my shoulders. "Don't go. It's not safe."

"Why not?" I asked. "What are you going to do?"

He paced back and forth across the roof. "I can't tell you. But you have to promise me you'll stay in your room until it's over."

He pointed to a door I hadn't noticed at the corner of the roof. "Take that and go down all the staircases until you reach the first floor. You'd never make it past security trying to come in. But once you're inside the building, everyone assumes you're supposed to be there. Walk until you get to the bottom of the Stygian platform. Then run straight back to the barracks. If anyone stops you on the way, just tell them you were so nervous, you forgot to put on your uniform."

"I'm not skipping Arrival Day," I said. "After what happened last time, I have to prove I can do my job."

Onyx pressed his hands to his head. "It's not safe."

"Fine." I folded my arms. "Then we can both stay here together and watch what happens."

"No!" He gasped, his eyes wide. "You can't stay here either."

"I give up," I said, spinning around and walking toward the door. "I'm getting my uni and doing my job." It was still dark out. I might have just enough time if I ran.

He nodded. "You're not going to listen to me, are you?"

I smiled.

"Okay, but stay in your position this time." He pushed me toward the door, and I took several steps before turning back.

"You didn't tell me what you're going to do."

He pressed his lips together, his eyes flickering between yellow and red so quickly that they looked orange. "You'll find out soon enough."

"Be careful," I whispered.

He nodded mutely. Then I turned and ran for the door.

I raced all the way back to the academy and crashed into my room to see Cinder pacing the floor.

"Where have you been?" she shouted as I tore off my clothes and began pulling on the pieces of my leather uniform.

"Woke. Up. Early," I puffed, searching for my souljab. "Thought I'd . . . go to . . . the station . . . for an . . . early start. Forgot my uni."

Cinder tilted her head. I could tell she didn't buy my story, but there was no time to talk any further. Outside, the sky was already beginning to glow faintly. "There you are," I said, squeezing the souljab, and shoving it into my holster. "Come on, let's go."

"And they say *I'm* the irresponsible one," she said as we raced out the door.

All the way to the station, I searched for Onyx. But I didn't see him anywhere. When I found his roommate, Nightshade, on the platform, he said Onyx had left a note that he wasn't feeling well and had gone to the infirmary.

"All squared away?" asked the quartus leading today's operation.

"Absolutely," I said, touching my souljab and feeling for my shaders.

He studied me for a minute. "You look pale. Are you sure you can handle this?"

"I'm good." If Onyx was going to try something, I wanted to be here to look out for him.

He nodded and turned away. Cinder gave me a thumbs-up from her circle. Just like last time, a gust of cold air preceded the silver tracks that raced across the barren desert. I set my hooves, determined not to make a single mistake.

"Eye protection on!" the quartus shouted. "Weapons out!"

I squinted toward the mountains through my dark goggles, searching for the first sign of the Stygian. *Just a bunch of Halos,* I thought. *Nothing to be scared of.*

But when I finally spotted the train racing across the desert, my heart rate sped up. I wiped my palms on my uni and tightened my grip on the souljab.

Just a bunch of Halos. Nothing to worry about.

The train glided to the edge of the platform. The door swung open. This time, it was just a train, not a monster. The seraphs stepped out of the Stygian Transit and formed into a guard—three on one side of the platform, three on the other. I tried to remember they were nothing to be afraid of, but something about the way they stood, the way they looked—regal, and shining with power and authority—made my legs tremble. How could anyone question why they lived in Judgment and we lived here?

"Women on the right! Men on the left!" someone shouted.

I turned my attention to the confused-looking humes

staggering off the train. "Move it!" I shouted, sending a flick of blue flame at anyone who hesitated in the least. "Get inside! Go!"

My heart didn't stop pounding until the last hume was off the train and heading into the Immigration Station.

I did it, I thought, with a smile as the seraphs formed ranks and started back into the Stygian. *I didn't mess up.*

I was still congratulating myself when something bounced across the platform, landing at the feet of the blindingly white figures on the right side of the Stygian. A half-second later, an entire section of the platform exploded, throwing me to the ground.

"Look out!" someone screamed, as two more fireballs detonated inside the door of the train. Lying on the ground, I looked up toward the roof of the Immigration Station. Dozens of figures hidden beneath silvery-looking cloaks were hurling objects and firing on the seraphs.

Through the dust and debris, what looked like huge silver birds glided down from the roof. As soon as they hit the ground, they started racing toward the train.

"We're under attack!" the quartus screamed. A long cut ran from his left eye all the way to his chin, and blood dripped down his face.

I looked for my souljab, but couldn't find it beneath the piles of rubble. One of the silver figures came straight toward me. Instantly, the world went red, and I felt talons snap out from my fingers and the sharp tips of fangs against my tongue. With a howl, I raced toward the figure. Timing my jump with perfect precision, I leaped on its back and gouged at it with my talons. My fingers skidded harmlessly off its cloak.

The figure wrapped its arms around me and pushed toward the Immigration Station. "Get inside," a deep voice growled.

"Onyx?" He released his grip on me, and I stumbled backward, my legs suddenly weak.

Turning my head, I saw Cinder walking dazedly across the platform. Blood dripped from one side of her nose. As I watched, she turned and walked straight into the battle.

"No!" I screamed, running toward her. "Cinder, watch out!"

She was heading straight toward a seraph. It raised its sword, angel-fire splitting the cloud of dust and debris. Just before it brought down its blade, the silver-cloaked figure who had pushed me aside dropped its shoulder and rammed the Halo off the side of the platform. Without breaking stride, the figure raced toward the Stygian. He was trying to get inside. Onyx and his friends were trying to steal the Stygian train.

Blinding white light cut through the clouds of dust as three of the seraphs rose into the air on golden wings. "Kneel!" a voice blasted through the air, and I felt myself forced to my knees. A bolt of white shot over my head, covering the roof of the Immigration Station in sheets of flame. Huge chunks of stone crashed to the platform. One of the pillars in front of the building wobbled before tumbling to the ground and shattering.

"Stop where you are!" a seraph commanded. At the sound of its words, I found myself unable to move. It was like being near an incubus, but ten times more powerful.

Several of the silver-covered figures fell to the ground. But the one I thought was Onyx actually made it through the door of the Stygian. Before he could take another step, though, a seraph lifted him into the air like a child and threw him, spinning, to the streets of Humeville far below.

No one else moved. The attack was over. Demon spawns and silver-cloaked figures lay scattered across the ground. The stench of fire and blood filled my nostrils.

Without a word, the seraphs reentered the Stygian Transit. The door slid shut, and the train disappeared back toward Judgment.

"Onyx," I whispered, tears running down my cheeks. "Please, no."

* * *

"Girl, if you don't sit down, I'm going to tie you to a chair." Cinder lay stretched on her pallet, the right side of her face bruised and swollen.

I knew I didn't look much better, with a black eye and a gash in my chin, but I couldn't rest. "He might be in prison right now or . . . or dead." The memory of the silver-cloaked figure spinning through the air and crashing to the street below played over and over in my mind like a recurring nightmare.

"Or he could be in his room, taking a nap while you freak out."

"No." I ran my fingers through my hair. "I checked with Nightshade. Onyx wasn't there when he got back." I couldn't tell her what I knew in case anyone questioned her.

Cinder sat up, crossed her legs, and propped her chin in her hands. "That was more than five hours ago, before we were all confined to our rooms. He probably heard all the commotion and went outside to see what was happening. I'm sure he's back and safe by now."

I wanted to believe she was right, but she didn't know what I knew.

"Are you even sure that was him under the cloak?"

"What?" I spun around. "I didn't say—"

"You didn't have to." She waved her hand.

I rubbed the back of my hand across my mouth. "If the Inquisitors question you . . ."

"I don't know anything for sure," she said. "What you need to worry about is them questioning you. Now, answer my question. Are you sure he's the one they threw off the platform?"

Was I? I'd been confused and dizzy, my ears ringing from the explosion. Maybe it had just sounded like him. The Dae' Lorica all tended to have deep growling voices. "No, not completely," I admitted.

I walked to the window and stared down at the street below. For the first few hours after the attack, incubi and succubae had been everywhere. Now, the streets were almost completely deserted. The academy had been locked down, and all demons ordered to return to their homes. Down below, I could see teachers and administrators making sure no one came in or out of the grounds.

"I'm going to check on him," I said, spinning away from the window.

"That's a great idea." Cinder scowled. "Get yourself kicked out of training. You'll enjoy watching humes make charcoal bricks for the rest of your life."

I clenched my fists. "I can't just wait."

"They've got to let us out sooner or later. We have to eat sometime." She stretched her arms above her head. "I'm starving."

"Food!" I snapped my fingers. "Even better idea. If anyone stops me, I'll tell them I was too nervous for breakfast this morning and have to eat before I pass out."

"That's a terrible plan," Cinder said as I started for the door. "But if you're determined to get in trouble, I guess I can come with you."

"No. Stay here." I opened the door and peeked out. The hallway was empty.

"If you get kicked out, I might end up with some roomie

even more obnoxious than you," she called as I slipped into the hallway.

I was worried that the academy might have placed guards at the ends of the passages like they had at the entrances, but I didn't see anyone as I snuck down the stairs and out the door. The rest of the grounds seemed just as deserted. I stuck close to the cliff wall so no one in the barracks could look out their window and see me as I made my way to the boys' rooms.

No one stopped me as I entered the building, and I took a winding tunnel to the third floor. When I reached Onyx's room, I paused outside. No point in barging right into a questioning by an incubus. After several minutes with no one coming in or out, I couldn't stand to wait anymore.

I took a deep breath—*please let him be there, please*—and knocked.

Nightshade got up from his pallet. "Blaze? What are you doing here? Have you seen Onyx?"

I shook my head. "You haven't either."

"No." He looked exhausted. "This one super-annoyed succubus has been in here, like, ten times asking me questions."

If the Inquisitors were still looking for Onyx, it meant they hadn't captured him—or found his body.

"I told her he was sick," Nightshade said. He dropped his head. "She asked if I'd actually seen him go to the infirmary this morning, but . . ."

I nodded sympathetically. "You can't lie to them. It's not your fault."

He shrugged and dropped back onto his pallet. "You don't think he was involved in the attack, do you?"

"No," I lied. "He wasn't. I'm sure they're just keeping him in the infirmary until things clear up." I dropped to my knees and started to dig through the hay of Onyx's pallet.

"If you're looking for his box, it's not here either. I had to tell the succubus about it when she questioned me, and a bunch of them turned the place inside out looking for it."

Oh, Onyx, I thought, my heart aching. *Why did you do it?*

I left the boys' barracks, expecting to head back to my room. There was nothing left to do but wait and hope that Onyx returned. The idea of him dead or locked up for life was impossible to even consider. Instead, I found myself taking the same path I'd followed that morning to the Immigration Station.

As I reached the edge of the grounds, a voice called out, "Stop!"

I looked up to see Mr. Pyreet running toward me. "Where do you think you're going?" he asked, stopping in front of me.

Where was I going? Did I really think there was anything back at the station? I didn't know what I expected to find there. Some proof that I'd been wrong about hearing Onyx? Or maybe him wandering hurt and delirious through the streets? It was crazy, but all I could think about was him saying what he was doing was as much for me as anyone else.

I rubbed my hand across the gash on my chin, smearing blood across my face, and tried to look weak. "I need to go to the infirmary. I think I might have cracked my jaw."

He hesitated for a moment before nodding. "All right. But hurry there and back."

"Thank you," I said, darting away before he could change his mind. The platform and the streets surrounding it were a mess. Piles of rubble and slabs of rock were everywhere. It was all blocked off by wooden barricades. Three of the thirteen pillars had fallen, and a fourth looked like it wouldn't remain standing for long. Close to the docking point, a third of the platform had been completely blown off. It was a wonder the Stygian had been able to run at all.

Someone had started to clear it out, but whoever was working on it seemed to have left for the night. As I climbed the platform stairs, I searched for any sign of a silver cloak, but they were all gone.

Kicking at a pile of debris, I thought about Onyx's words from that morning. *Some demons think we deserve better.* Had he really believed they could steal the Stygian and ride it back to Judgment? What did they think would happen once they got there? Did they think the rest of the seraphs would welcome them? Or did they plan on fighting all of them too?

"How could you be so stupid?" Hot tears washed over my face as I looked at the ichor stains marking the spots where demons had fallen. Fallen for nothing. Because they had the crazy idea that we deserved something better than Hell.

There were no answers here for me. I wiped tears with the back of my hand and started down the stairs. If Onyx had been a part of this, there was nothing I could do for him now. He'd have to take his punishment, and I'd have to get on with my life.

I was almost to the bottom of the stairs when I heard the sound. It was a low groan. At first, I thought part of the platform was starting to come down, and I jumped off the stairs to get clear. It came again—a long, drawn-out sigh. It sounded like a person, hurt.

"Onyx?"

I ran toward where I thought the sound had come from. Piles of rubble were everywhere. I looked around for some sign of life. There was nothing but rocks, broken beams, and dirt.

"Is someone there?" I asked.

"H-help m-m-e-e-e."

The voice came from my right. I ran toward a mound of boards and stone and began digging through it. "Hold on!" I shouted. "I'm here."

Throwing anything I could lift left and right, I dug through the mound. My mind created horrible images of Onyx crushed and bleeding to death. Finally, I stopped to catch my breath. "Where are you? Can you hear me?"

There was no answer. I was too late. Then I heard it again—a soft moan coming from under a huge rock to my left. Ramming a bent metal rod under the rock, I pried at it with all my strength. My vision went red, and I could feel my talons gouging at the metal. "Come on," I gasped. "Move!"

With agonizing slowness, I lifted the rock. I threw my whole weight onto the rod. The metal squealed in protest and started to bend. "No!" I dove at the rock, flinging my body against it. For a second, it balanced perfectly. Then it rolled down the side of the mound, knocking me down.

From the hole where it had been, a blast of white light shot up into the quickly darkening night.

"Onyx?" I stood up and edged toward the hole. Something moved under the pile, and an avalanche of rocks fell away. The light got brighter. Suddenly, I felt very alone and defenseless. I glanced up and down the street. No one was in sight.

The rocks shifted again, and a hand reached out of the opening. But it wasn't a demon hand. It glowed so brightly, I could barely look at it.

"Help me." The command was so overpowering, I walked forward despite my terror. It was like a hand pushing me in the back. "Get . . . me . . . out," the voice strained to say. With no control over my body, I bent and began ripping away chunks of rock. The more I pulled away, the more the glow increased, until I had to squeeze my eyes to slits. I had uncovered both of the arms and most of the chest when the light flickered for a second, like a flame sputtering.

The force that had been holding me released, and I jerked backward, horrified. As I turned and ran, I could hear more of the rocks moving.

"Come back!" the voice called weakly. I stumbled for a moment, but farther away, the energy wasn't as strong. The image of an angel-fire sword rising and falling—of white fire tearing the roof off the Immigration Station—played before my eyes. I ran through the night. Behind me, I thought I heard steps. Was the seraph following me? I was too scared to look.

Racing through the streets, I caught glimpses of white light illuminating the buildings behind me, but I didn't dare turn back. When I reached the academy, I went straight to my room and slammed the door closed behind me.

I ran to the window and looked out, sure I would see a fiery figure staring up. The street was empty. I opened the window and leaned out, looking in both directions. There was nothing but a few scampering imps and a bit of trash blowing in the wind.

I was walking back to my bed when I heard a sound in the passageway. I rushed to the door and listened. Something was out there, moving. I could hear the sound of steps echoing. They sounded like they were coming closer. My talons shot out at the ready. As the red lenses dropped over my eyes, my hearing increased. The steps moved closer and closer. It sounded like one person, alone.

The sound reached the door and stopped. I bunched my legs, preparing to spring. My breathing stopped as the doorknob slowly turned. As it stopped, I grabbed the door, yanked it open, and dove through, my talons raised to attack.

Cinder jumped backward, food flying everywhere as the tray she was holding flipped through the air. "Demons and devils, girl!" she screamed, raising her hands in front of her. "What is wrong with you?"

I checked the passage in both directions. It was just her. Puffing out a breath of hot air, I let myself relax. "Sorry, I thought it was someone else."

"What has gotten into you? You must've thought it was the devil himself, scaring me like that." She looked at the food and drink covering the floor and shook her head. "Just for that, you can get your own dinner."

"I am sorry," I said. The red lifted from my eyes, and my muscles relaxed. "It's just that I went back to the Immigration Station, and I thought—"

"The station?" Cinder's eyes widened. "You really are crazy. You keep this kind of stuff up and I guess I *will* have to start looking for a new—" As she started through the door, her words cut off. Her face dropped into a slack mask of terror.

Behind me, the room lit up like someone had filled it with a thousand gas lamps. My hands went ice cold, and my lips refused to move. As if pulled by a string, I turned to see what Cinder was staring at.

A seraph was lying on my pallet.

CHAPTER 12

"Come inside and close the door," the seraph commanded. Almost before my mind could process the words, my body obeyed, pushing the door shut as Cinder stepped into the room with the same urgent obedience I felt.

How had the seraph gotten into my room? A glance at the open window answered that question. Why was he here? I had no idea. Inside, I was screaming over and over. On the outside, I stood perfectly still, my eyes avoiding the burning figure that lit the whole room brighter than a hundred gas flames.

I couldn't move. I tried sliding a hoof across the floor to see if I had any control over my body at all. Nothing happened. It was as if the signal had been cut off after it left my brain, but before it reached my leg. Cinder's eyes met mine. Her skin and hair had gone the same dusky gray as the walls and floor of our room, and her tail wrapped hidden between her legs.

The seraph shifted on the hay of my pallet, flapped one golden wing, and groaned. I stole a brief glimpse at him, squinting. Was he hurt? As far as I knew, seraphs couldn't be injured. "Red, come here."

I hurried to his side, twining my fingers together in front of me. "My name is—"

He cut off my words with a chop of his hand. "I don't

care what your name is. The only thing that matters is that you do exactly what I tell you."

Maybe it was his tone of voice, like a demon talking down to an ignorant spawnling. Or maybe it was just terror coming out. "Do I have a choice?" The words left my mouth before I realized I was going to say them, and I knew at once that I'd made a terrible mistake.

Behind me, Cinder gasped.

The seraph's angel-fire sword lay on the floor beside him. He moved his hand just enough toward it to catch my eye. I stood, trembling, waiting for him to strike me down for my insolence. "No, you don't. I could command you to jump out that window and flap your arms like a bird, and you'd do it. Right up until you splattered on the street below."

I had no idea what a bird was, but I understood his meaning perfectly and I couldn't stand the way he was looking at me like I was a bug trying to climb onto his plate of food.

"Do . . . it . . . then," I growled, forcing the words out through my clenched jaw. "You killed the others. Kill me too."

For an instant, the seraph seemed to see me as a person and not just part of whatever his plan was. Then he turned to glare at Cinder. "You."

At his glance, she squeaked, a glistening sheen of oil coating her skin.

"Get away from the door and sit down."

Cinder rushed to her pallet and dropped obediently onto it, hay pluming around her.

He turned back to me, the aura around his body increasing, and the defiance I'd felt before drained away like soup from a cracked bowl. I couldn't keep from trembling. Even the covens didn't inspire this kind of holy terror. "How long have I been unconscious?"

My mouth went dry. Was the question designed to trip me up? Seraphs were immune to pain or damage. How could they be knocked unconscious? The idea seemed blasphemous. I glanced quickly at his face, making my eyes water, but the fire emanating from him was too bright to read any kind of expression.

"Speak up!" he roared, and my knees shook.

"This morning," I blurted. "Since the attack." I dropped my head, expecting to be struck down.

"We were attacked?" he mused, as though remembering.

Unsure of whether it was a question or not, I stared at the ground mutely.

"The Stygian returned to Judgment?" he said in the same quiet voice—different from the voice he'd used when commanding us.

I nodded.

"And it hasn't returned?"

"No."

"It will," he said. But there was something in his voice. It couldn't have been a trace of doubt, because seraphs knew everything. But if they did . . . why was he bothering to ask us? Was this all some kind of test? I glanced toward Cinder, but she was still on her pallet—body shaking, eyes locked on the floor.

"Water!" the seraph commanded, his voice strong and undeniable again.

I hurried to the stone basin at the side of the room and filled a metal cup from the pump. Looking away from his glow, I felt a tiny bit of his control over me weaken. Was that something I could use?

"Well?" he asked from behind me. "What are you waiting for? Bring it here."

Invisible hands grabbed my body, trying to turn me around, but this time I fought against it, talons forcing themselves from the tips of my fingers as everything turned red.

"Say please," I muttered.

Cinder looked up at me in shock, shaking her head.

"What did you say?" the seraph asked, his voice icy.

It was all I could do not to drop to my knees and beg his forgiveness, but I pressed my eyes shut, fighting his force with everything in me. "Don't they teach you manners in Judgment?" I whispered, my voice shaking.

Instantly my body was spun around like a puppet. My legs marched me across the room and my hand jerked forward, offering him the cup.

He took it and sniffed it. "Foul."

Cinder squeaked again.

"Is there something wrong with the water?" I asked, unable to resist his power. "I can get you another."

"Don't bother." He closed his hand around the cup. Peeking through my lowered eyelashes, I saw the water glow for a moment. Then he downed it in three quick swallows.

"Are you hungry?" I asked, the words spilling out of my mouth with no way to stop them. "I could go to the cafeteria." I looked to Cinder, and she nodded slightly, her expression torn between hope and dread.

The seraph barked a harsh laugh. "Somehow, I don't think that's a good idea. I'm sure I wouldn't see you again, with or without food."

I dropped my head, shame filling my body. "What do you wish of me?"

"For the moment, I—" The seraph's words were interrupted by a knock on the door. His hand closed around his sword. "Who is that?" he hissed.

"I don't know."

"Don't answer it." He backed up to the wall, sword held out before him.

The knock came again, hard and insistent. From the edge of my sight, I saw Cinder shake her head ever so slightly.

"Open your door now," a voice shouted, and my breath caught in my throat. There was no mistaking the throaty roar of an ancient.

"Oh no," Cinder moaned, her hands pressed to her mouth.

"What is it?" the seraph asked, his fiery eyes darting from her to me to the closed door.

"A devil," Cinder whispered. Her skin was so close in color and texture to the hay of her pallet that she was nearly invisible.

"If we don't open it, he'll come in," I said, not sure whether having a devil or a seraph in my room terrified me more.

The seraph jerked his head toward the door. "Answer it. Both of you. But do *not* let him in or I'll kill you both."

Walking on numb legs, I crossed to the door. Beside me, I could feel Cinder shaking. I closed my fingers around the knob and pulled it open. In the hallway, a devil towered so tall, he had to stoop to look through the door. His skin was covered in thick yellowing scales that looked as old as the horns that stuck straight out from the sides of his completely bald head.

"How dare you keep an Elder waiting?" he demanded, wisps of smoke issuing from his mouth and nostrils.

I shot a quick look at Cinder. When it became clear she wouldn't—or couldn't—answer, I met the devil's blood-red eyes. "I'm sorry. We were . . . sleeping."

He peered over my shoulder. "Your lights are still on."

My mouth dropped open, my mind too frozen with terror to come up with a response.

"We were too scared to turn them off," Cinder said, finally pulling herself together. "After everything that happened today."

"Yes." The devil scowled. His breath smelled so strongly of sulfur, it made my eyes water. "I understand you have a special interest in *everything that happened today.*"

Special interest. Cinder grabbed my hand, her fingers slippery. "I don't know what . . ." I began, before realizing he had to be playing with us. Someone must have seen the seraph enter our room.

"Don't think you can fool me, child," he snarled, leaning so close, I could see the tiny bristled gray hairs sprouting from his nose and ears. "I know all about your Dae' Lorica friend. I know he was part of the band of traitors who joined a handful of humes in an act of treason."

He wasn't talking about the seraph. He was talking about *Onyx.* They knew he was part of the group. Had they captured him?

Cinder clenched my hand tight. "We don't know anything about that," she said. "He's two years older than us. We barely ever see him."

"Is that right?" The devil grinned, revealing a mouthful of crooked yellow-brown fangs, like broken stained glass. "Then you won't mind knowing he was executed less than an hour ago."

"No," I whispered, unable to help myself. Onyx was dead. My vision began to blur, and my legs wobbled. The floor tilted sickeningly beneath my hooves. In the room behind me, something clanged to the floor.

The devil jerked his head up. "What was that?" He ducked his head and started through the door.

"You can't come in here," Cinder cried. Still under the command of the seraph, we both tried to stop him from entering the room, but he shoved past us as easily as a storm blowing a pile of ashes.

I spun around, terrified by what was about to happen. My eyes went straight to my pallet. It was empty. The metal cup lay sideways on the floor. Quickly, I scanned the rest of the room. The seraph was gone. With smoke billowing from his mouth, the devil raised his long nose and sniffed the air. He raced to the open window and plunged his head outside.

Cinder and I shared a horror-filled glance. I still couldn't believe Onyx was dead. And with everything that had happened over the last few days, we might be next if they discovered the seraph had been in our room.

"Where is he?" the devil snarled, pulling his head back inside and spinning around.

"Where's who?" I asked.

The devil held out his long, clawed fingers, as if he wanted to rip Cinder to pieces. "I know you're hiding your friend here. I heard him." He ripped Cinder's pallet apart, throwing blankets and hay across the room, then tore through mine.

Our friend? Was he still talking about Onyx? If he was looking for him, that meant Onyx wasn't really dead.

I picked the cup up off the ground. "Could this be what you heard?" I asked, trying to look as innocent as possible. "It must have fallen off the windowsill."

Realizing we couldn't possibly be hiding anyone, the ancient turned and stood, panting. A cloud of gray smoke swirled just above his head. "Don't pretend you don't know him. A dozen students will testify that the two of you were friends of his. The Dae' Ungu in particular."

Cinder met my eyes, and I could practically hear her thoughts. *Be careful.* I nodded to the devil, trying to look young and scared—not all that hard at the moment. "I do know him, Your Ancientness. We grew up near one another. But I swear I haven't seen him since—" *Yesterday,* I nearly finished, before realizing what a mistake that would be. I couldn't have seen him yesterday. Not unless I was part of his group. "Since a week or two," I finished lamely.

His bloodshot eyes studied me, and I tried to hold his gaze without flinching. "You knew what he was planning."

"Planning?" I asked. "I don't know anything about what happened out there. Are you sure he was part of it?" I had no idea what he'd heard. But he obviously didn't know much, or we'd already be locked in the demon prison.

"I suppose you knew nothing about the box in his room either?" he asked almost casually. The devil didn't have the ability to force me to tell the truth, but he could get a succubus or incubus if he needed to. And even without them, he seemed more dangerous—more cunning.

How much did he actually know, and how much was he guessing at? They'd interviewed Onyx's roommate. But Nightshade hadn't actually seen me open the box. And as far as I was aware, no one but me had seen what was inside. If they *did* know what was inside or that I had opened it, I could be in far worse trouble. But it felt like another bluff.

"You mean his journal?" I asked.

The devil blinked.

In an act of incredible bravery, Cinder stepped up by my side. "What would you want with that old thing? It's just a bunch of mush about who he wanted to go out with and how hot all the girls thought he was."

"So you've read it?" the devil asked, his dry gray tongue flicking over his blackened, cracked lips.

No, I thought, *don't say you read what was in his puzzle box,* but I didn't dare meet Cinder's eyes. I didn't need to worry. She was a practiced liar.

"Of course not," she said with a sneer, sounding almost

like her old self. "I've got better things to do than sniff around some lovesick tert's diary. But he couldn't stop telling me about it. To tell you the truth, I think he had the hots for Blaze. Not that he stood a chance, of course."

I knew how much courage it was taking to lie straight out to an ancient, but she handled it like a pro.

The Elder glared at Cinder, seeming to search for holes in her story. When it became clear we weren't going to melt under his gaze, he snorted. "Most of those involved in the attack have been captured or killed. Before they died, his followers identified your friend as one of the leaders of the group. We *will* catch him. And when we do, he will not have the option of a clean death. After we have finished torturing him, he will be sent to Absolute Zero to spend an eternity in continual pain and torment."

Unable to help myself, I gasped.

My response seemed to please the devil. "But," he said, holding up a long, gnarled claw, "if he turns himself in, and names all of the other demon spawns and humes involved in the plot, leniency *could* be granted."

From the corner of my eye, I saw Cinder's warning look, but I had to know. "What sort of leniency?"

The devil puffed out a cloud of smoke and scratched his scaled chin. "I could have him locked in prison for life."

Being locked up in a tiny cell would kill Onyx. But it was far better than Absolute Zero. Again, I asked myself why he'd done it. Why he couldn't have been satisfied with what he had.

"If you see him," the devil said, looking around the room, "if he comes to you, you will tell him that giving himself up is the only choice."

"Of course," Cinder and I said in unison.

He looked back toward the window one more time and frowned. "You haven't seen anything else . . . *unusual*?"

Outside, some small creature screamed in the night. "What do you mean, *unusual*?" I asked.

The devil shook his bald head impatiently. "Out of the ordinary. Strange sounds. Odd lights."

"No," Cinder nearly shouted. The devil stared at her. "We haven't seen anything," she added in a more normal tone of voice. "We've been in our room all day."

"Very well," he said, walking to the door. "If you see your friend, tell him he has one chance. The window of opportunity for that chance is shrinking rapidly. And if you see anything strange at all, leave at once and tell the nearest coven member. There have been reports of a creature, a *dangerous* creature, on the loose."

I knew exactly what he was talking about, and the fact that a devil was referring to the seraph as a *dangerous creature* did nothing to calm my nerves.

"Close the window," Cinder whispered as soon as the devil was out the door. I raced across the room. Before I could get there, a gust of wind buffeted me backward, and a blaze of light soared into the room.

"Put a blanket over the window," the seraph commanded. He turned to Cinder. "Turn out all the lamps. *Please.*"

I couldn't help feeling a slight sense of satisfaction at his concession—small as it was. But that didn't keep me from attaching a blanket to the top of the window frame, arranging it so no light could escape. The seraph might have his reasons for not wanting to be discovered. But I had my own. It was bad enough that the devil thought we were hiding Onyx. I couldn't imagine what he'd do if he discovered what we really had in our room.

In the darkness, the seraph's searing white glow was even more blinding.

"I will stay here until the Stygian Transit returns for me," he said.

Cinder licked her lips. "Why not just go to the council and tell them what happened?"

The seraph shook his head. "I'm not telling anyone I'm here, and neither will the two of you."

None of this made sense. Why would a seraph be hiding when he could command anyone in Hell to do his bidding? And why had the devil referred to him as a dangerous creature? "Do you realize how dumb it is to stay here?"

He raised an eyebrow. "Dumb?"

My muscles tensed as I realized I'd just insulted a celestial being. "You saw how closely they're watching us. It's just a matter of time before someone discovers you."

"You lied well enough to that devil. And you seem to have more spirit than the average demon, so listen closely." His brightness increased until I had to shut my eyes. Even then, dazzling images of his form floated in front of my closed lids. "You will make sure they do not."

I opened my mouth to argue, but the words that came out of my mouth instead sent an icy dagger through my heart. "We will do as you wish."

CHAPTER 13

"This is *so* bad," Cinder said as we carried our food to a table. It was the morning after the attack, and the seraph was still in our room.

"Keep your voice down," I hissed. "Do you want someone to overhear?"

"Like anyone's listening to us."

Looking around the cafeteria, I realized she was right. All across the room, groups of students huddled together in tight little knots of conversation, discussing what had happened and passing on rumors.

In the few minutes since we'd left the barracks, I'd overheard stories claiming that the rest of the group involved in the attack had been captured and executed, that they'd tried to swim across the Styx and were swallowed by two-headed fish with huge teeth, and that they were hiding in Humeville with enough food and weapons to hold out for a month. None of it sounded even remotely true, and none of it made me feel the least bit better.

"We have to find a way to make him leave," I whispered, leading Cinder to the most isolated part of the cafeteria we could find.

"We can't *make* him do anything," she said, her eyes wide. "He's an immortal being."

I looked at my food and discovered that, although I hadn't eaten in over twenty-four hours, I had no appetite. I thought my first week at the academy was bad, but now

I would give anything to go back to the "problems" I'd had then.

Cinder and I had shared her pallet, but I was pretty sure she hadn't slept. I knew I hadn't, tossing and turning all night, worrying about Onyx and terrified the seraph would snap his fingers and send me to Absolute Zero. I could barely keep my eyes open, but my heart raced and fangs filled my mouth at any sudden noise.

I shoved a heaping spoonful of sowya into my mouth and forced myself to gulp it down. "So you'll just keep him in our room as a pet?"

Cinder choked on her food. "He's not our pet. We're *his*. He can make us do anything he wants, and the minute he decides he doesn't need us anymore, he can kill us—or worse."

I shook my head. I might be naive about guys, but now she was the one without a clue. "If we can't make him do what we want, then we have to make him want to leave himself. Can't you use some of the charms you use on the rest of the guys around here?"

"He's not one of the guys," she said. "I can't even imagine trying to flirt with him." She set down her spoon, her face losing most of its color. "Maybe we could find a teacher and—"

Her words cut off instantly, her throat muscles straining.

"Don't bother," I muttered. I'd already tried telling someone what was happening twice. And we'd both tried running away. But the Halo's instructions were clear. We could eat, go to class—all the normal things that would keep people from asking questions. But the moment we started to think about escaping, turning him in, or doing anything that might lead to his discovery, it was like a switch turned off the connection between our brains and our bodies.

Cinder shut her mouth and rubbed her throat.

At a nearby table, several tert girls glanced in our direction, and I dropped my voice even lower. "Until we find a way to force him out and convince him to leave on his own, all we can do is keep him hidden until the Stygian comes back for him. How long can that take?"

"What if it doesn't?"

I snapped my eyes back to hers. "What if *what* doesn't?"

She pushed her tray away, apparently no hungrier than I was. "You said all we have to do is keep the Halo hidden until the others come back for him. But a lot of demons are saying the Halos aren't coming back."

"Are you kidding?" I asked a little too loudly, and the girls at the other table looked toward us again with more interest than I would have liked. I leaned closer to Cinder and dropped my voice to a whisper. "Who's saying that?"

She waved her hands. "I don't know. Everyone. There are rumors that the platform was so badly damaged that the Stygian *can't* come back. At least not for a long time. Or that they're never returning as a punishment for what we did."

I rubbed a hand across my face. "They're seraphs. Why would they leave one of their own in Hell?"

"I don't know," Cinder said. "But if they were going to come for him, wouldn't they have done it already?"

I hadn't thought of that. The idea of the seraphs abandoning one of their own here didn't make any more sense than Onyx's ridiculous plan to steal the Stygian and go to Judgment.

"The Halo doesn't know if they're coming for him either," she whispered. "Didn't you hear it in his voice?"

I shook my head. I'd been so focused on trying to defy him that all I'd heard were his commands, but Cinder knew boys a lot better than I did.

I jerked my hand, splashing half the grain out of my bowl onto the tray. Had I just thought of an immortal being as a boy? This was never going to work. We could hide him for a day. Maybe a week if we were lucky. But eventually, someone would realize that the two of us were acting weird, or there would be a surprise room inspection or—

"Maybe we can convince him to speak with the devils," I said. "They're rebuilding the part of the Immigration Station that was damaged. He could stay there until the Stygian comes back. Even if it's not until next Arrival Day. I don't know why he didn't go there. Unless . . ."

"Unless what?" Cinder looked up from the table.

A thought was spinning inside my head, an idea so big—so completely wrong—that I pushed it away before it could completely come together. Seraphs were immortal, perfect beings. I was sure there was a valid reason for him hiding with us, I just didn't understand what it was. "I'm sure the others will come for him," I said. "For all we know, they already have. He'll probably be gone by the time we go back to our room."

"That would be nice," Cinder said. But she didn't seem any more convinced than I was.

I realized the group of terts was watching us again. They seemed to be staring straight at me with an expression that seemed half sadness and half—*envy*? "What's with them?"

Cinder coughed. "You're kind of a hero at the moment."

"A *what*?"

"A few days ago, word got out that you and Onyx were a thing. Now, after what's happened, a lot of them view you as a martyr. You know, the girl who lost her true love."

I glared at the terts, and they turned away quickly, whispering. "Why would they think Onyx and I were—" I balled my hands into fists. "You didn't."

Cinder's face went from blue to pinkish brown. "I might have said something about it."

"How could you?"

"If I'd known what was going to happen, I never would have said anything." She licked her lips. "It's just that after Onyx rescued you from Flare that night, and the two of you hugged, I—"

I slammed my fists on the table. "You were *spying* on us?"

"No," she yelped, leaning backward. "I didn't see what happened. I found out the next day."

"He told you?" I asked, my voice dry and papery.

Cinder swallowed.

I couldn't believe it. "You were seeing him after he refused to even talk to me?"

"It wasn't like that."

"Then how was it?" I rubbed my face. He'd been talking to her. And she'd been telling everyone else. Everyone except me. "I thought you were my friend."

"I am your friend. That's why he came to me. There were things he wanted you to know. Things he couldn't tell you himself. At the time, I thought he was afraid he was going to lose you to some other guy. I had no idea he was telling me what he wanted you to know in case he . . . in case the attack didn't work out."

My head felt empty. My heart felt even emptier. None of this made sense with the way he'd been acting toward me lately. "What kind of things did he tell you?"

Before Cinder could answer, there was a commotion at the front of the cafeteria. I turned to see a squadron of efreets following a pair of stern-looking incubi.

"They know," Cinder whispered, her eyes wide with terror.

The group marched straight toward us, students scattering out of their path. I spun around, looking for a way to escape, but the seraph's orders blocked me from running.

Efreets spread out, blocking all of the doors. How had they discovered it so quickly?

Cinder gripped my fingers. "I don't want to go to Absolute Zero. I can't. I'd rather die."

I tried to answer, but my throat was too tight. Red lids dropped over my eyes. My talons gouged furrows in the tabletop. We were outnumbered, but I couldn't let them take me without a battle. The closest incubus looked down at me with his depthless eyes, and I felt my will begin to weaken. *No,* I told myself. *Look away.* Using all my strength, I managed to tear my eyes from his.

The incubi strode up to our table, paused, and miraculously continued on past. I turned, fangs pressing against the sides of my tongue. Was it a trick? I stared at the talon marks I had dug into the tabletop.

They stopped two tables away, and the guards charged forward. "No!" a fourth-year screamed as the efreets lunged at him.

They yanked him from the table in their fiery grasps as he struggled to break away. "Leave me alone. I wasn't involved. I swear!" It was one of the Dae' Ceal boys I'd overheard talking with Onyx and his friends in the back of the cafeteria. The one who was afraid their plan wouldn't work.

"I'm sorry!" he howled as they clamped iron bands around his hands and feet. One of the guards swung a flaming blue fist, and the boy's head snapped backward. "I'll tell you anything. Anything you want! Just don't hurt me."

As they dragged him past the rows of tables—now filled with students stunned into complete silence—his terrified eyes met mine. "Help!" he wailed, bloody drool running down his chin. "Help me, help me, he-elll-p!"

"Take it easy." Cinder squeezed my forearm, trying to calm me down. Sweat coated my forehead in an icy sheen, and I couldn't stop my hands from shaking.

"He'll tell them," I whispered, looking at the door through which the Dae' Ceal boy had been dragged.

"Tell them what?"

"Everything." I took a deep breath, but kept shivering. "He was one of the boys at the table on the night Onyx and his friends were talking. He knows I overheard them. He knows Flare chased me. He knows that I—"

I stopped short, realizing I'd nearly told Cinder about following Flare into the city. It was one of the few secrets I'd kept from her. If the Dae' Ceal had seen me barge into the meeting with the humes, I'd be the next one dragged away.

Had he been there?

I knew I'd seen him in the cafeteria, but hard as I tried, I couldn't recall whether or not his face had been one of the ones staring at me with the humes in the second or two before Onyx dragged me out of the underground room. The fact that he was here suggested that maybe he'd backed out of the attack at the last minute.

Cinder watched me closely, curiosity clear in her dark eyes. "I'll ask around and see what I can find out from his friends. If he knows anything, he probably told someone close to him. You go back to the room and see if our *guest* is still there."

The last thing I wanted to do was go back to the seraph. But Cinder was right. If anyone on campus had talked to the Dae' Ceal, she was the one to find out. And with classes canceled for a second straight day, someone had to be at the room to make sure no one stumbled onto our secret.

"Take this with you." Cinder pushed her tray of untouched food across the table. "If he's still there, he'll probably be hungry. Not that I have a clue what Halos eat."

Standing outside our room with one hand balancing Cinder's food tray and the other on the doorknob, I closed my eyes and made a silent wish that the seraph would be gone when I stepped inside. Then all I'd have to worry about was where Onyx had been taken and whether or not I would be next.

The seraph's aura nearly blinded me as I stepped into the room and quickly pulled the door shut behind me. So much for him being gone.

When he saw it was only me, he let his light fade.

"I brought you food," I said, realizing I didn't know if Halos even needed to eat.

The seraph sniffed the air from where he was sprawled on my pallet, but didn't get up. "Bring it to me."

I hurried across the room with my face averted and set the tray on the floor beside him.

He glanced into the bowl. "What *is* this?"

I peeked over at him. "Sowya, your, um, immortalness." He frowned. "Grain with goat's milk."

The seraph stuck his finger in the sowya, put it to his lips, and grimaced. "Tastes like bat dung."

I turned to a small cupboard where Cinder and I kept our snacks, but my muscles locked up.

"Where are you going?" the Halo demanded.

"Grabbing a knife to stick through your heart," I snapped. Instant pain surged through my body, and I raised my hands in surrender. "I'm getting salt. It tastes better that way."

The force locking my muscles released and he watched me carefully as I carried the container to him. "Just add a pinch."

"Thank you," he said, adding the seasoning and wrinkling his nose as he tried a bite. "It's better. Not much. But a little. I don't understand how you eat this slop."

How could he sit here in my room complaining about the food while every minute he stayed put Cinder and me in real danger of imprisonment, or worse? If all immortal beings were like this, then it was a good thing we lived so far apart.

"If you don't like it, don't eat it," I muttered, stomping off to the other corner of the room. "It's not like anyone's forcing *you*."

I waited for him to strike me down with his angel-fire or command me to do something terrible. Instead, he began coughing, but that quickly changed to something else.

I risked a look. Was he . . . *laughing*? He tried a few more spoonfuls of the sowya, but had to spit it out because he was laughing so hard that his body rocked back and forth. I didn't know seraphs did that.

I stared at the floor. "You find our food funny?"

"Not the food," he said with a final chuckle. "I find *you* funny, Red. You walk around all pious, with your head bowed and your eyes averted, trying to pretend you're a humble servant. But I can tell you don't mean any of it. You'd slit my throat in a second if I let you, wouldn't you?"

I gasped, wondering if he could read my thoughts. Attacking a celestial being was the worst sin imaginable. More terrible than anything even the worst of the humes had done when they were alive. But yes, I had been trying to figure out a way to kill him. "No demon would dare harm a seraph."

"Sure," he said, his tone changing from amusement to the belittling sarcasm I'd become used to from him. "Tell that to your friends in the silver cloaks."

Something banged on the floor behind me, and I couldn't keep from jumping. When I looked up, I saw that it was just the bowl—wiped clean of all food.

"I'll return that to the cafeteria," I said, anxious to get away. Even when he wasn't commanding me, I could feel his seraph's presence radiating through my brain like a fire that continued to throw off waves of stifling heat even after it was banked to coals.

"No," he said. "Stay."

Did he want to keep toying with me until I gave him a reason to send my soul to eternal torment? For a brief instant, I wondered if this was how the humes felt. Only they'd been sent here for a reason. I'd done nothing to deserve this kind of treatment.

"Tell me about your friend," he said.

"Cinder?" I whispered, stealing a glance toward him. Had she managed to affect even a seraph?

He rolled his eyes. "Not the *girl*. The one the devil was looking for."

I exhaled. "Onyx."

"Why did he and the others attack us? What were they trying to accomplish?"

I felt my face burn. "Onyx had this idea that—that demons shouldn't be stuck in Hell." I said the words quickly, sure he would strike me down for my blasphemy. But he only studied me.

"Go on."

I licked my lips. "He wanted to see where you come from. He said that before the humes died, they lived in a place with colors we don't have here, and something called grass and candy you could drink."

My throat locked as I remembered my last few minutes with Onyx on the roof of the Immigration Station. How happy he'd looked.

"He wanted to show me Judgment. He wanted the truth. He thought it would change my life. How stupid is that?" It was my turn to laugh. But what forced its way out of my mouth was a dry sob, without any trace of humor.

For a moment, as I vented my anger and pain, I forgot the seraph was still there. But as I got myself under control again, I realized how my words must have sounded to him. The silence drew out, and I dropped my head and turned to the door. "I'll go."

"Do you demons have names?" he asked, his voice laced with something I couldn't understand.

"Blaze," I whispered.

"That's appropriate. You're definitely fiery, Red." He pushed the tray across the floor to me and lay back on my pallet, closing his eyes. "I'm Visala."

CHAPTER 14

For the next two days, Cinder and I roamed the school, returning to our room only at night to bring the seraph food or anything else he requested. Every time someone called my name, I jumped, certain our secret had been discovered. Every time we opened our door, I hoped the seraph would be gone. But he didn't seem to be in a hurry to leave, and whatever his plans were, he wasn't sharing them with us.

I listened and watched for any word about Onyx's fate, or the return of the Stygian. Rumors were flying about where the missing demon spawns were and what had happened to them. Most of the students seemed to believe they'd all been killed.

Nearly as ominous was the story being passed around in hushed tones that incubi and succubae were quietly searching the city for something besides the humes and students involved in the attack. No one knew exactly what they were hunting for, only that it was considered highly dangerous, and that the troops of efreet guards were heavily armed and jumpy enough to keep everyone at a distance.

The longer we waited, the edgier I became.

On the third day after the attack, classes finally started again—although neither the teachers nor the students seemed to be paying much attention to the lessons.

On the way to our last class before lunch, Cinder suddenly grabbed my arm. "I can't take it anymore," she said, her eyes dark-circled and bloodshot from lack of sleep.

"Be quiet," I said, looking around. "Someone will hear you."

"I don't care." She squeezed my bicep in near panic. "I can't stand lying there at night with his glow filling the room. I can't stand waiting for someone to realize that we always keep our door locked, or to notice us sneaking him food. But most of all, I can't stand the way he watches us. He's even more stressed out than we are. You can hear it in his voice. Sooner or later, he's going to snap, and who do you think he's going for first?"

She was terrified, and I couldn't blame her. I was too. There were so many things I didn't understand. Why hadn't the other seraphs come back for Visala? And why was he so determined to stay hidden? The idea I'd been pushing out of my head since the seraph first hid in our room was becoming harder and harder to dismiss.

"What if the rumors about the incubi and succubae searching the city for a dangerous creature are true? I think it's pretty obvious the dangerous creature they're looking for is the seraph."

Cinder narrowed her eyes. "If they know a Halo got left behind, why wouldn't they just send for someone to come and pick him up or something?"

I sighed. "I don't know."

Other than on Arrival Day, no one really talked about the seraphs. I'd never heard anything about there being any issues between our kind and theirs. But the efreet troops were much more heavily armed than normal, and Visala was definitely worried about being discovered.

"What if he was hiding in our room because he knew the authorities would attack him?" The idea made my head spin. Seraphs were immortal celestial beings. They couldn't be killed. They couldn't even be injured. Except clearly Visala *had* been injured—was still injured, if the way he constantly rubbed his right shoulder and carefully flexed his wings was any indication.

Only why would the leaders of Hell attack a seraph when we were hunting down Onyx and his friends for attempting that very thing?

I looked at Cinder, who stared at me with dark, haunted eyes, and knew what she wanted. "I can't talk to him," I said. "And he wouldn't listen to me even if I did."

She grabbed my hand. "He likes you. He told you his name."

Okay, it was true that after I'd brought Visala his first meal, the seraph had opened up a little. Since then, though, he'd become surlier with each day, barely saying enough words to communicate what he wanted and snarling when we didn't obey him fast enough. "What could I say?"

"Tell him he has to go," Cinder begged. "Tell him that things are getting back to normal, and it's only a matter of time before the school does a room inspection."

Chills ran up my neck just thinking about it, but I nodded. "Okay."

"Really?" Cinder sounded childlike in her gratitude. She squeezed my hand in hers so hard, it felt like my fingers were going to pop. "Thank you. I'd do it myself, only . . . every time I get anywhere near him, my brain freezes up."

I knew exactly what she meant. There was something about the seraphs that made you want to drop to your knees and grovel before them while, at the same time, wishing you could run as far and fast as possible. Adoration and terror were so closely entwined, you couldn't tell them apart.

It had been bad enough on the immigration platform from a distance. Close up, it was all but unbearable. The last thing I wanted to do was say something that might upset the seraph. But Cinder was right. He had to go.

"Yeah," I nodded, trying to swallow the taste of the terror that filled my mouth. "I'll do it right after I take him his lunch."

"You're the best," Cinder said, hugging me so tightly, I could hardly breathe.

The best. That wouldn't be much consolation if the seraph took offense and struck me with angel-fire.

As we walked into class, there was a buzz of conversation filling the room. "Did you hear?" a Dae' Ungu girl asked, her eyes shining with a mixture of excitement and horror. "They found two more of the students involved in the attack."

My jaw muscles tightened, and I could feel fangs trying to push through my gums.

Cinder saw my reaction and grabbed the girl by the shoulders. "Is it . . .?"

"Oh no. It wasn't . . . *him*." The girl looked from Cinder to me and shook her head. I felt my muscles relax a little. "They didn't find the boys who were part of the attack. They found two more who were involved in the planning, but backed out at the last minute. But the council must have learned something, because all morning they've been pulling students out of class for questioning."

Cinder glanced at me, her message clear. If they were questioning students, it was only a matter of time before they came to our room again. I barely heard anything our teacher said during class. My brain swirled with thoughts of Onyx and what I would say to the seraph hiding in our room. Why did I have to be caught up in the center of all of this? My brain kept going back to the faces of my parents the day I'd been questioned by the council. I couldn't put them through that again.

"Blaze," a voice called, and I realized Cinder was shaking me. "Come on let's go."

Looking around, I saw that class was over and the room was nearly empty.

"You're still going to talk to the Halo, right?" she asked as I gathered my books and papers.

"Yes. But I don't think he'll listen to me."

"You have to make him," Cinder said. "Tell him that—"

Her voice cut off as though it had been sliced with a knife. Her face went from blue to a pale gray faster than I'd ever seen it before.

I followed her stare, looking into the hallway, and my temperature plummeted. A group of armed efreets bracketed both sides of the door, and a succubus in a flowing yellow gown stood directly in front of us.

"Cinder of Clan Dae' Ceal and Blaze of Clan Dae' Ungu," the succubus said, her voice liquid sweetness, but her eyes flakes of burning ice, "you are hereby remanded into the custody of the covens for immediate questioning before the council."

* * *

The passage outside the administration chamber was just as cold and damp as I remembered. Beside me, Cinder shivered, her arms wrapped around her body as if she were trying to keep from exploding into a thousand pieces.

I patted her back, and she jumped at my touch. "It's going to be okay," I whispered.

"No." She swung her head back and forth, her eyes sick with fright. All traces of the cocky demon spawn who led boys around by the tail were gone. She glanced toward the guards and dropped her voice. "It's not going to be okay.

We'll get kicked out of arrival training. They'll lock us up for the rest of our lives, if we're lucky."

"You can get through this," I said, hoping I was right. "*We* can get through it. I've been questioned by the council before. It's impossible to lie directly to them, but there is a way." I reached for her hand, but she jerked it out of my grip, glaring at me.

"What's wrong with you?" I asked.

"What's wrong with *me*?" Cinder barked a laugh that quickly turned into a sob. The guards looked briefly in our direction, eyes bored as if they'd seen this kind of thing far too many times for it to hold much interest.

Cinder drew back her lips, her face hard and tight. I'd never seen her like this before. "This is all your fault. You're the one who left the grounds. You're the one who kept going after Onyx, even after it was clear he wanted you to mind your own business. You're the one who brought back the Halo."

I pulled away, scalded by her look as much as her words. She couldn't think I brought Visala back on purpose. "You're upset." I swallowed, my eyes starting to burn.

"I am." Her tail flicked back and forth, snapping against the floor. She bit her lip until a thin trail of blood leaked down the front of her chin. "I'm sorry, Blaze, but I won't lie for you."

I rubbed my palms across my knees. "What are you saying?"

"My whole life, I've always been the adventurous one—the one who wasn't afraid to cross a line or two. But this . . ." She licked the blood from her lips and looked down, refusing to meet my eyes. "This is so far past sneaking out with a boy or going into a club we aren't supposed to. You can ruin your life if you want. But I won't destroy mine too. Not because you've got a crush on a traitor."

I slumped against the wall. Was that really what she thought this was all about?

"I've covered for you all I can," she said, her words like nails in my heart. "I won't do it anymore. I won't lie for you. When they call me in there, I'm going to tell them everything."

I tried to catch my breath. I'd never meant for any of this to happen. The last thing I wanted was to get Cinder or myself in trouble. But she was right. If I'd taken her advice and started dating some other guy instead of following Onyx, none of this would have happened. If I hadn't left the school after the attack, Visala couldn't have followed me back. That night up on the roof, Onyx said he wanted a better world for me. So in a way, wasn't I even at least partly responsible for that too?

"You're right," I whispered. "It *is* my fault."

Cinder peeked briefly over as though checking to see if I was telling the truth.

I blew out a long breath, knowing I was heading down a course with no way back, but realizing it was the only choice I had left—the only choice that had a chance of clearing Cinder, even if it meant destroying my own future. "You don't have to tell them. I will. I'll admit everything."

Cinder's eyes went wide. "I didn't . . . I don't want . . ."

"There's no point in both of us getting in trouble. I'll tell them they can do whatever they want to me, but you had nothing to do with it." I reached for her hand, and this time she let me take it.

I tried to smile and found I couldn't. "Who knows? Maybe they'll take pity on me and realize I'm a hopeless moron. Maybe instead of throwing me in prison, they'll just send me to . . ." I tried to get rid of the knot in my throat and couldn't. ". . . to work with the humes."

"I'm so sorry." Cinder squeezed my fingers. "If there were any other way . . ."

Up the hallway, the door opened and a pair of flaming blue efreets stepped through. Before they could speak, I dropped Cinder's hand and stood.

"I'll never forget this," she called as I walked to the administration chamber, wondering if I'd ever see any of my friends again.

Without looking back, I followed the guards into the large circular room. Like last time, the full council filled the front row of benches. Unlike the last time, my parents were not in the stands. I didn't know whether to be sad that I wouldn't have their support, or grateful they wouldn't have to see me break down. Because I knew I would. With no one to protect any longer—not even myself—I could tell the whole truth. But if I was this close to crying now, what would I be like after they were done with me?

Dies Diei and Noctis were already seated as the guards led me to a spot between the succubus and incubus. The stone seat felt warm as I dropped onto it, and I remembered I wasn't the first person to be questioned that day. I suspected I might be the last though. After I told them about Visala, I couldn't imagine them doing any more interrogations.

For a moment, I wondered what would happen to the seraph once they found him. But that was the least of my concerns now.

"Arise," said the same succubus who had led the proceedings before, and the same unseen force lifted me out of my chair.

"State your name." Her eyes burned as though she regretted letting me go the first time she'd had me here.

"Blaze of Clan Dae' Ungu," I answered, trying not to think about what was coming.

"We will question you."

"We will question you," the quorum echoed. At least Cinder wouldn't have to go through this. Who knew, maybe Onyx and I would end up in cells close enough to talk.

"We will learn the truth."

"We will learn the truth."

The force of their wills pulled me down onto the hard stone chair. Dies Diei and Noctis took my hands in their cold fingers. Their presence inside my head made my stomach churn, but I was determined not to throw up. "You may proceed with your questions," my lips and tongue said.

The succubus took her seat along with the rest of the quorum, and another succubus—I thought she might have been the one who met Cinder and me outside the classroom—took her place.

"The last time you came before the covens, you admitted you had gone to Humeville," she said, tucking her hands behind the back of her billowy gown.

"Yes."

"You said at that time that you did not know who you followed."

"That's right." Inside my head, I could feel Dies Diei and Noctis forcing me down the path of complete truth. The wiggle room I'd sensed before was nearly nonexistent.

"Do you still claim not to know who it was that led you there?" Now that I'd decided to give myself up completely, the fear I'd felt before wasn't nearly as strong. But still the idea of telling them about Onyx—even if they already knew he was part of the attack—made my chest ache.

"I . . . I'm not sure," I whispered.

"But you do admit to being friends with a tert named Onyx from Clan Dae' Lorica?"

This was just a formality. They already knew everything. I could see it in her face. The words stuck in my paper-dry mouth, and hot bile burned the back of my throat. "Yes," I gasped.

"You are aware this student is part of the radical group that attacked the Stygian?"

Tears burned in my eyes as I nodded silently.

"Speak up, please," she said, taking obvious joy in my pain.

"Yes." The word forced itself from my lips. "I know."

"You went to his room on the Arrival Day before the attack. Did you discover a box there?"

"Yes." I tried to tell myself it didn't matter. I wasn't betraying Onyx. I was only confirming what they already knew.

"Did you open the box?"

"Yes."

The other members of the council leaned forward in their seats as she smiled slowly. "Tell the council what you discovered inside of the box belonging to the student named Onyx."

It wasn't fair. Why couldn't they just let me admit I knew everything—that I might as well have been part of the group myself—and hand down my sentence? Why did they have to ask me about Onyx? I tried to find a way to evade the question, to edge away from the wall. But this time, I was pressed firmly against it by the invaders in my mind. There was no way to avoid them. No way to answer with anything but the truth.

I tried to clench my teeth. My jaw refused to obey. "Papers," I said. "Strips of paper with sentences I couldn't understand. At first, I didn't know what they were. But later Onyx told me." I couldn't stop myself. The words were like a river forcing themselves out of my lips.

"What did Onyx tell you the words meant?" the succubus asked.

I tried to fight, but it was hopeless. They were too strong. "He said they were—"

At the side of the room, the doors I'd entered through slammed open, bouncing against the walls with an echoing clang. All heads spun around to look as a dozen or more blazing efreet guards stormed inside.

"What is this?!" the succubus shouted, raising her voice for the first time. "You are interrupting council proceedings."

"We found them," the lead guard said. "We discovered the traitors' hiding place and destroyed it."

My head began to spin.

"Where?" the succubus asked.

"In a tunnel below Humeville." The guards were covered with dirt and grime. Several of them looked injured, and all of them were splashed in a dark substance that could only be blood.

"Prisoners?" the succubus asked.

The lead guard dropped his head. "Only one. They put up a strong resistance. The rest . . . are dead."

"Who?" I cried, unable to help myself. "Who survived?"

For the first time, the succubus appeared to remember I was still there. "Get her back to her room," she commanded. "Along with her friend."

The force holding me in place let go all at once, and I leaped from the chair. "Onyx!" I shouted, running forward. "Tell me Onyx is all right."

Four of the guards grabbed me. I tried to fight my way out of their grasp, twisting and clawing, but they pinned my arms behind my back until it felt like they were going to snap, and shoved me into the hallway.

"What happened?" Cinder called as I was pushed past her. One of the guards holding me grabbed her arm and yanked her along.

At the end of the hall, another group of guards appeared, holding a long chain. A hunched-over figure stumbled behind them. He was wrapped in a dirty cloak, and something was wrong with one of his legs. But even bent beneath the cloak, he was clearly a tall, broad-shouldered demon spawn.

"Onyx!" I screamed.

At my words, the demon spawn jerked his head around with a spastic twist. The cloak's cowl fell away, and I found myself staring into a face I knew well. His eyes met mine, but there was something wrong with them. They stared in different directions—neither of them focused.

"Flare?" I whispered.

The right side of his mouth dropped open as he began to sob in a series of hitching grunts and moans.

"What happened to you?" I cried. "Where's Onyx?"

His eyes twitched and his limbs started to shudder.

"What did you do to him?" I demanded, yanking one of the guards by the arm. "Where are the others? There have to be others."

The guard pulled away from me, but even he seemed disgusted with himself as Flare's arms and legs rattled in the chains. Flare stumbled and dropped to the ground. As he thudded to the floor, his body turned, and I fell back in horror. The entire left side of his head was smashed in—collapsed into a large, blood-soaked crater.

CHAPTER 15

"I'll take her inside," Cinder said, stepping between the efreets and the door as they approached our room. "Blaze is going to lie down. Aren't you?"

"No," I said, trying to pull free from the guards pinning my arms and legs. I'd fought them all the way back to the barracks, demanding to know what happened to Onyx. The last thing I wanted to do was rest. "Not until they tell me who—"

"You need to rest!" Cinder caught my eye, and I remembered what was inside our room.

"Oh right." I stopped struggling, letting my body slump and trying to look exhausted. It wasn't hard after everything I'd been through. "I am very tired."

The efreets appeared afraid to let go of me. I didn't blame them. They'd arrived at the administration chamber bloody and battered, and I'd added at least a few more cuts and bruises on the way here.

"It's all right," Cinder said, answering their dubious looks with a smile. I didn't know how she could do it. I couldn't have forced a smile on my face if they'd put a blade to my throat. But Cinder coiled her tail around one leg and blinked her eyes at the guard nearest to the door, resting a hand on his arm. "You deserve a break too. You must be exhausted."

I knew what Cinder was doing. But I couldn't help gritting my teeth at her words. One of these efreets might have been the guard who smashed in the side of Flare's head, or even killed . . .

I pushed the thought away. I couldn't let myself believe that Onyx was dead.

Cinder's words, and the way she blatantly flirted with the guards, had an effect, though, just like they always did. The efreet holding my wrist loosened his fingers ever so slightly. "Maybe we should wait here. Just in case the council wants you back for questioning."

"Please," I said, opening my fists to show I had withdrawn my talons. "I'm sorry for the way I acted. I was upset about my friend. If you can give me a little quiet and leave me alone for a while, I'll be okay."

"Besides," Cinder said, brushing up against the two efreets locking my legs together, "it's not like you don't know where to find us."

"Neither of you may leave the building until this is cleared up." The guard who appeared to be the leader of the group placed his hand on the curved blade at his waist.

"Of course not." Cinder opened her eyelids so wide, I was surprised her eyeballs didn't roll out of their sockets. She batted her lashes again.

"Get inside," the guard said. Before Cinder and I could stop him, he stepped forward, turned the knob, and opened the door to our room. Cinder gasped and I stepped back, terrified of what would happen when the guards saw the seraph's dazzling white aura. But the only light came from the open window—no longer covered by my blanket.

"Well?" the guard asked, frowning suspiciously at our reactions.

Cinder gave me a questioning look, and I raised my shoulders ever so slightly. Could Visala really be gone?

"Thank you." Cinder flashed the efreet a tight smile and walked into the room, her eyes darting every which way. I followed behind her and pushed the door shut before the guards could say anything else.

Cinder looked quickly around the room, stopping at the window. "You don't think—" Her voice cut off in mid-sentence as Visala threw off the blanket he'd been hiding under and wriggled out from the hay of my pallet.

"Tell me what's happening out there."

Cinder backed away as he strode across the room, grabbed her chin, and forced her to look up at him. "Guards have been running back and forth in the street below," the seraph said, holding his glowing sword in one hand as though he expected the efreets to charge back in any second.

Cinder closed her eyes, and I had to look away from the glare that would have been clearly visible outside if it hadn't been the middle of the day. "They found the group that attacked the Stygian," she said.

"Hmph." Visala sniffed and spun away, pacing. "I'm surprised it took them this long. The attackers were amateurs."

"At least they didn't hide behind a couple of primies," I snarled.

The seraph turned slowly at my words. The light around him increased until I had to press my hand to my eyes. Even then, his image burned through my lids. "Kneel," he commanded.

Unable to help myself, I dropped to my knees before him. My head was forced down, as though a hand was pushing against me, until my chin touched my chest.

"What did you say?" His voice was low, but I could almost feel the walls vibrate with its authority.

I knew I would be punished for my blasphemy, but I

didn't care anymore. I was sick of this celestial creature forcing us to obey his every command in our own room. I was sick of worrying about Onyx. I was sick of being afraid. Sick of everything. "They fought," I said, struggling to speak through my clenched jaw. "They fought for what they believed in. They fought against you and your angel-fire. And when the covens found them, they fought the guards until . . ." I swallowed.

Beside me, Cinder moaned.

"Why are you here?" I said, my neck screaming in pain. "You're a seraph. What are you doing, holed up in the room of a couple of teenaged demon spawns like a—a coward?"

His response was immediate, and far more intense than I'd expected. "Grovel." One minute I was kneeling, and the next I was thrown face down on the ground with a force that set my head spinning. Blood trickled from my nose. "You think I *want* to be here?" he roared.

Pressed to the ground and caught beneath a weight like a boulder on my back, I could barely expand my chest enough to breathe, let alone speak. Even if I could suck in more than a gasp, I wouldn't have dared to say a word. I had mocked a seraph.

I heard his footsteps cross the room and stop just above me. This was it. I'd finally gone too far. I clenched my fists, hoping whatever he did to me would be quick.

"What do you think the guards out there would do if they found me here?"

Holding my breath, waiting for his blade to fall, it took me a moment to realize the pressure on my chest had eased a little. I could inhale without feeling like my ribs would crack. Was he actually waiting for me to answer?

"I—I don't know," I squeaked. What could they do? He was a celestial being.

"You heard that devil call me dangerous?"

I nodded, my eyes still pressed tightly shut. "Yes, but you're a—a seraph." I stumbled over my words. His question made no sense. "I guess they'd take you back to the Immigration Station until the other seraphs return for you."

His laughter, when it came, sounded so much like the way Cinder's laughter had sounded outside the administration chamber, it was eerie. "Do you see that Stygian Transit rushing back for me? Do you see Judgment sending a search party?"

Although the weight had completely lifted from my back, I kept my face pressed to the cool stone floor. This was all so far beyond me, I had absolutely no idea how to respond.

I could hear him pacing again. "I *am* dangerous," he said so quietly, he might have been talking to himself. "Dangerous in ways you can't possibly understand. Hell and Judgment would be happiest if I just quietly disappeared. They were probably hoping to find me crushed beneath the rubble. But I survived. Lucky me."

I risked a quick peek up. He was looking outside, standing to one side so he couldn't be seen. His back was toward me. His aura had lessened significantly, but it was still brighter than the red afternoon ceiling of the cavern shining into the room.

I licked my lips. "Why don't you go back to Judgment on your own?"

He spun around, his face liquid fire. "Just like that, hmm? Cross the Outer Circles of Hell and fly home. Why didn't I think of that?"

I turned away, embarrassed. Clearly, I'd said something wrong.

"Why didn't your friend Onyx do that? Why attack a train full of seraphs when he could have just hiked to Judgment? And why hole up and wait for the guards to find them when no creature of Hell would dare follow them across the Styx?"

It was a stupid question. Crossing the Styx was death. Not even the humes were foolish enough to try it. "You know they couldn't," I said. "They'd be killed. But you're immortal."

He grunted. "Immortal doesn't mean immune. Although I wouldn't expect you to know anything about that. Even then, if I weren't injured, I might try it. Better to die at the hands of whatever stands between Hell and Heaven than to waste away in here or turn myself over to the creatures who run this forsaken hole. But with my wing the way it is, I wouldn't last a day out there."

How was that possible? The Outer Circles of Hell were designed to keep both humes and demons alike from leaving. No one knew exactly what was in them, except that it was terrible. The last time anyone had tried entering the Outer Circles, back when my father was a spawnling, a group of humes had managed to escape across the river.

Two dozen guards followed. What remained of both groups was found the next morning. Body parts of humes and demons alike were mingled together along the edge of the river. My father refused to tell me much about it except to say that their deaths appeared to have been slow and excruciatingly painful. It was both an insult and a warning. No one had tried to cross since.

But it had never occurred to me that the same rules might apply to creatures of Judgment as well. I'd always just assumed they were invulnerable to that kind of thing. The Creator fashioned both Judgment and Hell from matter unformed. Was it possible He had never considered that one of His seraphs might become trapped here? Or were the Circles designed to keep celestial beings from crossing to Hell as well as keeping us in? Why would they want to cross? The idea made my head ache.

Cinder coughed, and I remembered for the first time that she was still there. "So . . ." She paused, as though afraid to go on. "What are you going to do? You can't stay here forever."

"Really? I've been enjoying your charming company so much; I'd never given it much thought."

It took me a minute to realize he was joking.

"At the moment, my options seem a bit limited," he continued. "So if you've got any ideas, I'd certainly love to hear them."

Was he, a celestial being of unfathomable power and knowledge, really asking our opinions? He had to be joking again. Toying with us. Yet as the seconds ticked by, and the silence grew, it became clear he really was waiting to hear what we had to offer. I had no clue what to tell him. I'd assumed he had all the answers. And like so many of my assumptions over the last few days, it appeared this one was wrong as well.

I was opening my mouth to tell him there had to be someone who could give him better advice than a couple of primies, when something moved outside the door. I turned my head and got to my hands and knees. Visala heard it too. He backed toward the wall, raising his sword.

I held up one hand and whispered, "Maybe they'll go away." But what if they didn't? What if they'd been waiting out there the whole time, listening? I looked toward the window.

"There's no time," Visala hissed.

He was right. Even as I watched, the knob began to turn. Cinder knelt on her pallet, holding her blanket up like a shield. I knelt in place, locked to my spot in front of the door by fear.

The knob finished turning. Visala held his angel-fire sword high above his head, eyes fixed on the door as it swung slowly open. An inch. Then another. Then the door slammed open with a bang, and a guard stepped inside. Only its skin wasn't blue, and it was too tall to be an efreet. Instead of a uniform, it was covered from head to foot in filthy rags.

It stumbled into the room and looked down at me.

"Blaze." At the sound of the voice, my heart—which had stopped beating with terror—raced to life.

The figure pushed back its hood. It was *Onyx*. He was alive!

I jumped to my feet and reached out to wrap my arms around his neck. As I did, his eyes looked past me, and instantly went from yellow to red.

Visala had been standing perfectly still in the corner of the room. Now he stepped forward, sword gleaming above his head.

Onyx snarled. He threw off the rags covering him; underneath, he was in one of the silver cloaks the group had worn while attacking the Stygian. With a roar, he charged toward the seraph.

"No!" I screamed. It was too late.

Setting his feet, Visala swung his sword around and down. Onyx dropped his head. The two collided at the center of the room.

CHAPTER 16

Dazzling sparks exploded off of Visala as Onyx plowed into him. They crashed through a chair, shattering it, and rolled to the floor. What was Onyx doing? The seraph would kill him.

I raised my hands, expecting to see Onyx's skin burst into flames at any second. Even getting close to a Halo was suicide. Everyone knew if their swords didn't kill you, the celestial energy flowing around and through them would. But as the two rolled around the floor, punching and kicking, I realized Onyx wasn't being injured by the light that had gone so bright, it was nearly blue. Somehow, the silver material covering his hands and body was protecting him.

Visala tried to drive his sword into Onyx's back, but Onyx managed to climb on top of the seraph, pinning one of his arms to the floor with his left hand and kneeling on the other. His right hand was clamped over the seraph's mouth.

"What are you doing?" I yelled. Visala kicked out a leg, trying to topple Onyx, and I barely managed to jump out of the way in time to avoid being struck. Onyx's cloak might protect him from the seraph's aura, but it wouldn't help me.

"Hey, what's going on in there?" a Dae' Ungu girl called from across the hallway.

Cinder ran to the door, which was still open, and said

something that sounded like, "Boyfriend problems," before pushing it shut.

"Find a weapon," Onyx said, his muscles straining as he fought to keep the seraph down. "Something sharp."

Cinder picked up a splintered chair leg.

"No," he gasped. "It has to be stronger."

"This isn't an armory," she said, frantically searching around the room.

Visala thrashed under Onyx, nearly bucking him off. Onyx slammed the seraph's head against the floor, cracking the stone.

Cinder darted around, opening desk drawers and looking under clothes as though a sharpened spear might magically appear.

"Stop it!" I shouted, squinting against the glare. It was only a matter of time before Visala managed to break free and kill us all.

"This is the missing seraph," Onyx growled, as though that explained everything.

"Thanks for the information," I said. "Here I thought we'd trapped a pet gargoyle." It was only two minutes since he'd returned, and Onyx had already managed to swing my emotions from euphoria to complete aggravation. What was it about him that made that seem so easy?

Sweat beaded on his smooth, bald head, and I could see his muscles were beginning to tremble. I couldn't imagine the kind of strength it must be taking to keep the seraph down. "Then help me kill it," he growled.

"*He's* a seraph." I clapped my hands to my head, running my fingers through my hair in utter frustration. "You *can't* kill *him*."

"You only believe that because it's what they tell you." Onyx slammed Visala's head to the floor again. The seraph grunted and his eyes rolled in my direction. "I'm going to see for myself."

"I can't find any weapon," Cinder said.

"Of course you can't," I said. "There are no weapons in our room. Onyx, let him up before someone opens the door to see what's going on."

Visala grunted something from beneath Onyx's hand.

Onyx tightened his grip. "If I release his mouth, he'll command us to jump out the window, or worse." He looked around the room. "See if you can pry the sword from his hand with that chair leg."

Visala bucked again, this time coming within a hair of knocking Onyx completely off. Cinder started for the broken chair, but I grabbed her arm. "He is an immortal being. *Immortal.* Do either of you understand what that means? All you're going to do is make him angry. If he'd wanted us dead, he could have killed us anytime over the last three days."

Onyx's head spun left to look up at me. "What did you say?"

"He could have killed us while he was hiding here. But he didn't."

Something changed in Onyx's face. "He's been here, with you, for three days?"

I swallowed. "I . . . We didn't . . ."

"Since the day of the attack?" He stared at me with a hard, cold expression I'd never seen. "All the time we've been running and fighting to stay alive, you've let *this* hide in your room?"

"It wasn't like that," I said. How could he look at me that way? "I was trying to find you. I was afraid you might be hurt or—or dead."

"We've been living in holes in the ground, drinking water so foul even the imps wouldn't touch it, and eating any scraps of food we could find. And he's been here all this time." He looked at my blanket that Visala had been wrapped in a few minutes earlier, puddled on the floor. "Where did he sleep?"

I shook my head, wilting under the force of his gaze. "It's not how it looks. We didn't have any choice. He followed me back from the Immigration Station and—"

Visala chose that moment to arch his body up and to the side, creating just enough space for him to raise one knee. Before Onyx could regain his balance, the seraph kicked out, sending Onyx flying into the wall with a sickening crunch.

"Down!" the seraph shouted before anyone could respond. All three of us dropped face first to the floor as though slapped by a giant hand.

With my nose glued to the floor, I couldn't see Visala, but I could hear him gasping in and out, trying to catch his breath. "Don't hurt Onyx," I said. "It's not his fault."

"Silence!" the seraph roared, and my jaws slammed closed, my tongue stuck to the roof of my mouth.

His footsteps crossed the room. I could hear voices outside in the hall. "Did anyone follow you here?" he asked. From where he stood, I knew he was talking to Onyx.

"Answer me, demon scum," he demanded.

"I don't know," Onyx said in a voice that sounded nothing like his own. I could tell he was fighting against it, but the seraph's power was impossible to resist. "They found our hiding place and ambushed us. Flare and I were the only two to survive. When they captured him, I ran. I didn't want to come back here, but it was the only place I had left."

Something connected with a heavy thud, and Onyx grunted. I grimaced. Maybe I should have helped him get Visala's sword. Maybe he was right, and Halos really could be killed. Had he returned here, only to have me cost him his life? I wanted to tell him I was sorry, but I couldn't open my mouth.

"Where did you get this cloak?" Visala asked.

"I. Have. No. Idea." Onyx's words came out one by one, strained and deliberate. "It was given to me."

"By whom?"

Before Onyx could answer, footsteps pounded down the hallway. The sound of raised voices came from outside. Visala walked across the room in the direction of the window. "You idiot," he whispered. "The guards are coming. They must have tracked you. There are at least a dozen of them."

"Let me up," Onyx growled. "We have to get out of here before they arrive."

"How do you suggest we do that?" Visala asked. "They're waiting just outside the building doors, and more are on the way."

Amazingly, it was Cinder who answered. "The steam vents in the basement. If you crawl through them, you come out in a building on the other side of the street. They might be a tight fit for you two, but I've taken guys nearly as big through."

"Us *two*?" Visala asked. "Why would I go anywhere with him? How about if I leave the three of you here to attract the guards, while I escape."

Realizing the seraph's will was no longer stopping my tongue—although I still couldn't move my body—I spoke up. "Onyx knows Hell and you don't. Besides, the guards want both of you, so that puts you on the same side."

"We're not on the same side," Onyx snarled.

"Definitely not," Visala said.

"Fine, then. We'll all stay here and get caught."

"Let us up and I'll show you the way," Cinder said.

"You're not doing anything of the kind," Onyx said. "You two stay here."

"And what?" she asked. "Wait for the guards to arrest us?"

I wished I could move my head to look at her. This was not the same girl who'd been crying outside the administration chamber.

"It's okay," I said. "I told you, I'll take all the blame."

Cinder actually laughed. "That might have worked an hour ago. But somehow, I don't think your words are going to carry much weight when they discover both the traitor and the monster hiding in our room. Now let us up, Halo, so we can get out of here."

For a second nothing happened, then the weight on my back released, and I was able to look around. Onyx was already up, rewrapping himself in the rags he'd been wearing. Outside, voices shouted orders. It sounded like quite a crowd had gathered. Cinder eyed Visala up and down. "You stand out a little too much, big boy. Let's see what we can do about that."

Less than a minute later, I peeked out—no guards yet. Our floor-mates, who had been milling around outside, looked up as I threw open the door to our room and Cinder rushed through, shouting, "Get out of the way, get out of the way! This is an emergency. Get out of the building!"

Close on her hooves came a hulking figure wrapped in torn, filthy rags, and the biggest woman I had ever seen, cloaked in a blanket, various scarves, coats, blouses, and skirts—all wrapped and tucked into a patchwork mess that was nearly as terrifying as what was hidden beneath it. Only a few telltale spots of light glowed through.

The girls had already been frightened and unsure about what was going on outside. All it took was our explosive exit to send them into a panic. Screaming and fighting one another to get out, they broke for the stairs.

"This way," Cinder called. It was easy to lose ourselves in the group of demon spawns, but when they turned left toward the exits, she turned right. Near the end of the passage, she yanked open a narrow door I'd never noticed.

Onyx and Visala followed Cinder down a narrow staircase. As I pulled the door closed behind us, the sound of the guards shouting rose above the voices of screaming girls. "How do you even know about this place?" I asked.

Cinder looked back and rolled her eyes. All right, dumb question.

At the bottom of the stairs, she climbed onto a stack of crates and pulled an ancient-looking mesh cover off the wall.

"I'll never fit in there," Visala said as Cinder boosted herself inside.

"You will if you don't want to get caught." She looked back at Onyx and grinned. "I've taken bigger guys through, although none quite as big as you, ox boy."

With a skeptical expression, Visala started toward the crates, but Onyx stepped in front of him. "Blaze goes next. Then you. I'll go last to keep an eye on you, Halo."

"Suit yourself," Visala said, stepping back to let me climb onto the crates. "Maybe I'll be lucky, and the guards will arrive before you get inside. It will save me the trouble of killing you once we get out of here."

"No guard is keeping me from ramming that sword of yours into your big mouth," Onyx said.

By then, I was already inside the vent. The surface was warm and slightly furry. It had a damp smell to it, even though the surface was dry. It was unpleasant, like small dirty animals lived there. I couldn't believe Cinder would go through this just to meet a guy. Of course, knowing her, she probably made them climb through it to meet her.

"Keep going straight," she called back, her voice echoing off the walls and ceiling. The space was narrow, and in the pitch-black darkness, it felt even smaller. I didn't blame Visala for not wanting to climb in. Of course, Onyx was even wider. I didn't want to think about what would happen if he couldn't fit inside.

As I crawled, I listened for any sign of the guards. Ahead, I could hear Cinder humming, and behind, I could clearly make out Visala's grunts and complaints. It didn't sound like the guards had discovered us yet. But what if they figured out where we were going, and instead of following us, sent guards across the street? How terrible would it be to reach the other side, only to find them waiting?

"Hold it," Cinder called back. I heard the sound of what I assumed was her lifting out the grate on the other side. A moment later, a flickering light lit the inside of the vent. "Okay. Come on out."

I climbed down from the vent onto another conveniently arranged stack of boxes and found myself in a small room with a couch on one side, a table, and a pallet leaned up against the wall. "Cozy."

Cinder raised an eyebrow and shrugged. "It serves its purpose."

I was sure it did.

A few minutes later, Visala slid awkwardly out of the vent. He stretched his good wing and brushed off his hands. "It stinks in there."

Cinder rolled her eyes. "I'll notify the next hume cleaning crew that comes through."

"Where are we?" he asked, eyeing the couch and the candle she had lit.

"This building used to be classrooms. Now it's just used for storage. Almost no one comes in here."

I noticed a sheen across the seraph's forehead. Sweat?

Which was strange because I was comfortable, maybe even a little chilled. "Wait, are you *hot*?"

"Do you honestly care about my comfort level?"

I paused, then shrugged. I guess I didn't. Just an observation.

"I didn't think so." Visala nodded. "Can we leave without the guards noticing?" He started to pull off the clothes we'd wrapped around him, but Cinder held out a hand.

"It might be better to keep you under wraps for now. In less than an hour, it will start to get dark. That will make it easier to escape. Hopefully, the guards will think we left before they got there, or somehow slipped out in the crowd."

Visala grunted, tugged at a leather skirt wrapped around one arm like a piece of odd but trendy armor, and plopped onto the couch.

I'd been watching the vent, waiting for Onyx to show up. I was starting to get worried. "How far behind you was he?"

"I have no idea," Visala said, reclining his head and closing his eyes. "The cow probably got stuck."

I had no idea what a cow was, but it didn't sound like a compliment. Climbing back onto the crates, I put my head back in the vent. I thought I could hear Onyx, but I wasn't sure. I considered calling to him, but remembered how Cinder's voice had carried and that the guards might be searching for us on the other side, and decided it wasn't a good idea.

"He'll be fine," she said.

I hoped so. Just as I was about to crawl in and look for him, I heard definite sounds of movement. A moment later, he appeared. But instead of his head, which I expected, he came hooves first, then legs, then tail. Finally, he dropped completely out of the opening without needing the crates to reach the ground.

"You backed all the way through the vent?" Cinder asked, her face incredulous.

"I wanted to put the grate back in case the efreets came looking."

Visala sat up and opened his eyes. "Maybe there's a brain somewhere behind that thick skull after all."

Onyx's eyes flashed red, but I put a hand to his chest. "You two can beat on each other all you want once we're free."

He grunted. "So what now?" he asked, replacing the grate.

"Once it gets dark, we sneak out," Cinder said.

"And then?"

She tilted her head. "What do you mean?'

"I mean where do we go once we're outside?"

"I was hoping you knew," she said. "You're the one with all the hiding places."

"And look how well that worked out for me." Onyx frowned. "Trust me, there's no place in Hell you can hide for long. Once the efreet started searching for us, we were constantly on the run."

I looked at Onyx, realizing we hadn't thought this through.

He folded his arms. "The two of you have to go back and come up with a story. Tell them you were scared by all the commotion and ran outside. They were looking for me. They may not even question you."

Visala looked up from his spot on the couch, crossing his ankles on the low chipped table in front of him. "It'll never work."

Onyx spun around, his hands closing into fists. "Shut

up, gargoyle face. You've lived in Hell for all of three days. What do you know?"

Visala turned his sword in his hands. With the constant glow flickering over his face, it was impossible to read his eyes, but his voice was implacable. "I know they had crouchers with them."

Cinder giggled. "The blind vendors?"

I couldn't help smiling as well. Crouchers were small, wrinkled, dog-like creatures with long snouts and a single horn in the middle of their heads who sold sweets and trinkets. Slightly smarter than imps, they could barely see anything even in the brightest light. The only time you saw crouchers out of their shops and homes was when they set up food stalls on Arrival Day.

Visala flexed his wings. The good one reached almost to the wall, the injured one less than half of that. "Those *vendors,* as you call them, are the best hunters in Hell. I'm sure they're what the guards used to track you down. And unfortunately, along with being good hunters, they can smell celestial beings. It was only a matter of time before they found me as well. By now, they have all of our scents, and they know I was staying in the girls' room. If they are captured, their fate will be as bad as ours."

"And you just thought to tell us that now?" I asked, jaw clenched.

"How do we get away?" Cinder asked, no longer looking amused.

I didn't blame her. I was terrified.

"We don't." Onyx slumped to the floor, his face a mask of misery. "I should never have come back. If those crouchers can track you as well as he claims, they'll realize any minute where we went. There's no way to escape."

Visala grimaced. "I guess Blaze was right all along."

Onyx looked at me suspiciously. "Right about what?"

"How should I know?" I asked, feeling trapped between the two of them. "As far as I know, I haven't been right about anything."

Visala chuckled. "Our only option is to go somewhere we know the guards won't follow."

All of us turned toward him. "Didn't you listen to anything I've been saying?" Onyx was fuming. "They'll follow us anywhere."

The seraph stood up and tucked his sword into the scabbard at his waist. "They won't follow us across the Styx."

CHAPTER 17

For a moment, there was complete silence. I had no idea how to respond to such a ludicrous idea.

Onyx finally spoke. "I said *you* could cross the Styx to get away. If the rest of us take even a step into the Outer Circles, we'll be dead even faster than if we stayed."

"Maybe not," the seraph said.

Onyx threw up his hands. "I should have killed him back in the room. We can't believe a word he says. I'll bet the crouchers aren't even hunters. He's just lying to get us to do what he says."

Visala put his hands behind his head and leaned back with a wince. "Brilliant deduction, boulder brain. You've got me all figured out. Except that if I wanted you to obey me, all I'd have to do is command you."

It took a moment for his words to sink in. He was right. He didn't have to lie to us. He didn't have to trick us. All he had to do was command us to follow him across the River Styx if that's really what he was planning, and we'd march like happy little soldiers to our deaths.

"Wasn't I clear enough before?" I asked. "Going into the Outer Circles is suicide."

"And staying here is any less?"

I opened my mouth, then shut it. We were long past

talking our way out of trouble if we were caught. But the Outer Circles? Just the thought filled my stomach with ice.

"If you turn me and the Halo in, it's possible they'd be lenient and just lock you two up," Onyx said, clearly trying to convince himself as much as the rest of us. But was being locked up in a tiny cell any better than death? Death at the hands of the guards would be quick. Death in the Outer Circles, from what my father had seen as a child, would not.

"They'll send us all to Absolute Zero the moment they get their hands on us," Visala said. "They don't want any witnesses to this."

"Absolute Zero." Cinder's voice was emotionless, but her words sent a distinct chill through the air.

Until this moment, I had no idea seraphs could be sent to the place of nightmares too. "What are they afraid of us talking about?"

The Halo shook his head. "It doesn't matter. Just trust me. They won't show you any leniency."

"How are the Outer Circles any better?" Onyx asked. "Even if we *could* survive for an hour. A day. Two. What kind of life would that be?"

Visala touched the hilt of his sword. "I have no intention of staying there any longer than I must."

I still had no clue what he was talking about. "The guards would be waiting for us as soon as we return."

"I have no intention of returning either." Visala's words hung in the air. If he didn't plan to stay there and he didn't plan on coming back . . .

Cinder, intuitive as always, was the first to grasp the implications of what he was saying. "You want to go to the mountains."

Onyx jerked forward. "You'd take us into Judgment?"

"No." Visala's voice was sharp. "You wouldn't be any more welcome there than I am here."

Onyx blew out a sigh of disgust. "I should have known. That's why we attacked the Stygian in the first place. You Halos will never let anyone leave Hell."

"Why should we help you get back to Judgment?" Cinder asked, her eyes shrewd. "What's in it for us?"

Visala seemed to think a moment, but even though his face was a mask of flowing fire, I had the feeling he wasn't being completely honest. I suspected he'd been planning this moment ever since he realized the other seraphs weren't returning for him. "If we make it to Judgment—and I'll be perfectly honest, the chances are small—but if we do, I'll clear all of your names." He sneered at Onyx. "Even his."

"That's impossible," I said. "Judgment and Hell don't—"

"He's lying," Onyx spat. "There's no way a Halo would ever help a demon."

Visala raised his right hand, face glowing. "I swear by my angel-fire that if you help me return to Judgment, I will make sure that all of your records will be cleared of any crimes you've committed. No one will be looking for you."

It sounded too good to be true.

I tried to think things all the way through. Onyx was right. Demons and seraphs didn't help each other. How could anything that happened in Judgment possibly affect what happened here? But why would Visala lie when he could force us to obey his will with a word? "How would you do that?" I asked.

He pursed his lips. "I have . . . *connections*." I waited for him to explain, but that's all he would say.

Cinder put words to what I'd been thinking. "Even if you *can* help us, why would you? Why promise us anything when you can make us obey you without any promises?"

"Because I need you to come willingly. I don't know

much about what stands between Hell and Judgment, but I know it's bad. To have any chance of making it across alive, I'll need all of you watching, thinking, reacting. If I have to command your every move, you're no good to me." His answer came so quickly, it was as if he'd been waiting for that very question all along. Again, I got the feeling he'd been planning this for a while—and that he wasn't telling us everything.

He raised an eyebrow. "So, what do you say?"

"I'll go with you," Onyx said abruptly. "I'd prefer an honest death to prison. I halfway expected to die trying to get to Judgment anyway. But *they* stay here. I'm not taking Blaze or Cinder into the Outer Circles."

"And what are we supposed to do in the meantime?" I asked, his attitude bugging me all over again. "A clean death is good enough for you, but we get to stay behind and suffer whatever the council decides for us?"

Onyx turned to Cinder, as if hoping she'd talk some sense into me. She shook her head, "Blaze is right. We'll probably be dead an hour after crossing the Styx, if we make it that far. It's suicide to go. But if the Halo's telling the truth, it's even worse to stay. At least by going, the decision is in my hands."

Listening to her, I had to remind myself this was Cinder. I'd never seen her like this, and I wondered what had changed her. If we lived long enough, I was determined to find out.

"Well, then." Visala stood and started for the door. "What are we waiting for?"

"Hold on. I want to talk to Blaze in private." Onyx led me to a corner of the room. "I don't trust him," he whispered.

"Neither do I," I whispered back, wondering if seraphs

had super hearing in addition to their other abilities. "But we're kind of out of options."

Onyx hesitated. I could see him weighing his words carefully. "There might be a place you could stay. At least for a couple of days. It would keep you out of the guards' hands until I make it to Judgment or . . . don't."

I checked over my shoulder. Cinder was playing with something on the table, as if she couldn't care less what we were saying, but Visala was watching us closely. "What are you talking about?" I asked, turning my attention back to Onyx. "I thought you said you came back to the barracks because you had no place else to go?"

"I did." Onyx wiped his palm across his head. "I couldn't go there myself. I've already caused them enough trouble."

"Caused who?"

His eyes darted toward Visala before he leaned close. "There's a group of humans who–"

"What?" I pulled away. "Are you kidding?"

"Just listen . . ." He tried to grab my shoulder, but I pushed his hand off.

"No."

"They're not the way you think," he said. "At least, not all of them."

"No. It's out of the question."

"Don't you understand?" he whispered, pulling me back toward him. "I'll go to the Outer Circles because I have to. But we *are* going to die out there. It will be horrible, painful. The only satisfaction I'll have is if I know you're here safe, and that Halo is the first to go. Please, at least talk to the humans."

"The whole reason you're in this mess is because of those filthy, disgusting creatures," I hissed. "I'd rather die a hundred times than spend a single minute with them."

I marched back to Visala and Cinder. "Let's go. Now. Tonight."

Onyx glared. "I'll go with you, but I want something besides clearing our names."

"Hair?" the seraph asked with a grin.

Onyx pointed at his sword. "Angel-fire. If we get you to Judgment, you give me your weapon."

"Out of the question." Visala clutched at his sword as though Onyx had already made a grab for it. "It would be of no use to you anyway. Angel-fire only harms the inhabitants of Hell. Seraphs and everyone else living in Judgment are immune."

Onyx folded his arms and set his feet—a boulder daring anyone to try and move him. "Then you can go without me. My offer is not negotiable."

Visala shook his head, as if he couldn't believe what he was hearing. "You said yourself, I can make you go whether you want to or not."

"And you said you need me to come willingly. I don't think you have the guts to go by yourself. I think it was a bluff. If you force me, I'll slow you down every chance I get."

The two of them stared at each other like opposing carved statues—one dazzling white, sword at his waist, the other deepest black, armed only with his massive muscles and curved horns. I expected Onyx to give in first. Visala appeared to have all the power. But it was the seraph who blinked. "Fine. You get me to Judgment, and I'll give you my sword. I hope you stab yourself with it the first time you try to use it."

Onyx almost smiled. "Good. Besides, I know where to find something you'll need."

"What?" Visala asked, his voice terse.

"Supplies."

* * *

"I thought you knew where you were going," Visala said, easing up beside Onyx. "This is the second time we've been down this same street."

"Third," Onyx whispered with an impatient wave of his hand. "And it will be the fourth if you don't be quiet. It's no wonder you burn all the time—you're full of more hot gas than a geyser."

"At least I don't have gravel rattling around every time I shake my head."

With Onyx leading us—his night vision picking out things none of the rest of us could see—we hadn't run into any other demons or guards. But he said they were out there, patrolling, looking for us. He also said we'd been spotted by humes at least twice. Although how that was possible, I couldn't imagine.

I didn't know a lot about humes. But I did know they were stupid and clumsy—ungainly creatures that spent all their time making messes, complaining, and avoiding work whenever they could. It was a wonder they managed to feed themselves.

"*Do* you know where we are?" I whispered as the seraph dropped back.

Onyx rolled his eyes. "I'd expect that from a Halo. Of course I do. The supplies are just around the corner. But getting them isn't like dropping into the cafeteria to get lunch." He seemed to notice something in an abandoned-looking building to our left, and waved everyone into a nearby doorway.

Together we knelt, watching and waiting—for what I had no idea. It had been dark for several hours now, and the cooling air made me realize I hadn't brought any supplies of my own. Not even a change of clothes.

I hadn't been able to say goodbye to my parents either. I was their only child, and by now they'd probably heard I'd disappeared. What did they think? Were they afraid? Disappointed? Angry? I'm sure they thought I'd let them down. And they were right to feel that way. I'd come to the academy two months earlier with so much hope. I was going to make something of myself.

Now here I was, kneeling on the dirty, rocky ground, so far into Humeville, there weren't even sidewalks or paved streets. The stink of humes filled the air and stuck in the back of my throat like river slime.

The thought of never seeing my parents again made me so sick, it was all I could do to keep from running back to the academy and throwing myself on the mercy of the authorities. If we died in the Outer Circles, they'd never know what happened to me.

"What are we waiting for?" Cinder whispered when we'd been kneeling in the cold for what felt like at least ten minutes.

Onyx pressed a finger to his lips and nodded at the rickety building across the street. Originally built of stone and brick, now many of the bricks were gone, replaced by sheets of rusty metal or nothing at all. Huge gaping holes pocked walls that leaned so far toward the street, it was a wonder they didn't collapse under their own weight. Just another sign of what happened to things when you left them to the humes.

"Second floor. Third window from the right," he breathed. "Middle-aged hume male. I didn't notice him the first time we came by until he'd already picked us out. He's good. He stays so still, he blends right into the night. He moves from one spot to another, just enough to throw you off. But this time I think we've managed to get close without being seen."

"Let me deal with him." Visala reached for his sword.

Onyx slammed him back against the wall. "You aren't going anywhere."

I searched the window Onyx was studying, but couldn't see a thing. Surely, he had to be wrong. Humes weren't that smart. Cunning, yes. And sneaky. Everyone knew they'd steal anything they could get their hands on. The demons who supervised them in the fields or factories said humes couldn't be trusted with even a single piece of bread if it was left out.

Cramped from sitting so long in the same place, I stretched my leg and accidentally kicked a pebble out into the street.

"Be still," Onyx hissed, shooting me a dark look.

I pulled my leg back, wishing we'd get on with this. I still didn't understand what we were doing in Humeville. Apparently, Onyx and his friends had hidden some kind of food or water here. Hopefully some clothes too. It was a pretty good hiding place when you thought about it. No one would ever think of searching for anything of value amongst the humes.

But how had Onyx managed to protect it from their thieving hands?

I was beginning to wonder if this wasn't all some elaborate game to make Onyx appear more important in front of Visala, when Onyx rose from his knees and whispered, "Okay, now. Across the street. *But quietly.* Go through the big hole in the left side of the building. And keep an eye out for traps. They tie strings so fine, you can barely see one. If you trip over them . . . you won't need supplies."

They? Who was he talking about? The rest of his group? It made sense that they would protect their supplies from the humes. But wouldn't he know exactly where the strings were if he and his friends had tied them?

"Careful," Onyx whispered as we ducked our heads to avoid crumbling bricks and stepped into the darkness. He pointed to something a few feet ahead. For a moment, I didn't see what he was showing us. Then I caught the faintest glimmer of light reflecting from a hair-fine strand stretched between two wooden beams.

Cinder lifted her hoof with exaggerated slowness and stepped carefully over the string. I followed, wondering what this place was.

Step by step, Onyx led us through the entrails of the building, pointing out several more strings. Once, he paused before an ordinary looking patch of ground. Leaning forward gently, he scratched at the rocky soil and nodded. "If you walk across that, we won't need to worry about the Outer Circles."

As we detoured around the spot, I glanced back, wondering what he'd seen and what would have happened if he hadn't. I didn't want to find out. We stopped before a weathered door. Onyx looked over his shoulder at Visala, whose aura flickered in the darkness through several openings in the clothing wrapped around him. "Can't you turn that thing down? Or are you *trying* to get caught?"

Visala did something, and the glow decreased a little. "Are you going to get us these supplies you talked about? Or are we going to keep skulking around until it gets light again, and we have no chance of crossing the Styx without being spotted by the guards?"

"Feel free to set out on your own anytime if you think you can do better by yourself." Onyx scowled. "The supplies are right behind this door."

"Finally," Cinder said. She reached for the knob, and Onyx yanked her hand back.

"Not that way," he said. "Not unless you want to set off about a million alarms."

Kneeling on the ground, he ran his fingers around the edges of the door, nodding and muttering. He stopped at a withered weed growing out from the dirt at the base of the wall. Dead and brown, it didn't look like anything special. But when he gently tugged at its base, it lifted a thin cord along with it. Crawling slowly across the ground, Onyx pulled the cord up from the dirt, following it as it wove around rotten-looking beams, under collapsed walls, and finally to a pile of rocks and debris.

"There we go," he whispered. He did something to the pile of rocks, and a click sounded from behind the door. "Now you can open it." How did he know all this? And what else did he know that he wasn't telling?

"Go ahead," he said, walking back to us. "Turn the knob. It's safe."

Wondering if I was about to be blown up or dropped into a pit, I twisted the knob. It was hard to see into the shadows, but a small lamp hung just inside the door. I lit it, expecting to find a couple of beat-up boxes with a few containers of food, and maybe a jug or two of water. Instead, I entered a room where every wall was lined with shelf after shelf of supplies. Food, water, clothing, tents, weapons, rope, grappling hooks, and things I didn't even recognize. In one corner, there were stacks of the wings demons used to play in Culdine matches.

"Where did you get all this?" Cinder asked, staring around the room in wonder.

Visala picked up a long spear, balanced it in one hand, and nodded.

I sorted through dozens, maybe even hundreds, of packages of food. Dried meat. Powdered sowya. "I thought you said you and your friends were living off scraps. There's enough food here to last for years."

"We couldn't risk leading the guards here," he said. "It was too dangerous."

"Dangerous to who?" Cinder asked, picking up a long cloak that looked very warm. "And how did you keep the humes from stealing it? Even with the traps?"

"Quite easily, really," a voice said from behind me. I spun around to see a female hume standing in the doorway. "Since it belongs to us."

CHAPTER 18

Shocked by the appearance of the hume, it took me a second to respond. Then adrenaline raced through my body. I charged across the room, talons tipping my fingers as I lunged to capture her before she could run off or alert the guards. Onyx got there an instant before I did. His bulk sent me reeling into the shelves.

I spun around, expecting to see him dragging the hume into the room. Instead, he was standing with an unsure look on his face.

"What are you doing?" I snarled. "Get her before she escapes."

The hume turned to look at me. Unlike most female humes who wore their hair in tangled snarls down to their waists or longer, hers was cut so short, the skin of her scalp showed through it. Her body was different too. In my limited experience, humes typically arrived in Hell all doughy and out of shape. After a few months of labor and strict diets, they took on a bony appearance, with hollow cheeks and dark circles under their eyes. This one wasn't doughy or skinny. She looked . . . hard with some muscle definition. A tight black shirt with the sleeves cut off revealed arms more muscled than I'd ever seen on a female hume before—or most males.

The strangest thing, though, was her eyes. Humes didn't

look at demons. They averted their gaze anytime they got close, glancing down or away. This one should have been terrified, encountering three demons in a deserted building at night. Instead, she stared straight at me, like she had as much right to be here as we did.

"What makes you think I want to escape?"

Cinder pulled a souljab from the rack of weapons. "You'll be begging to escape when I'm through with you," she said, shooting an arc of fire in the hume's direction.

"Put the weapon back," Onyx said.

Cinder stopped in the middle of the room, unsure. Visala was oddly silent, looking from Onyx to the hume.

I moved to stand beside Onyx. "What does she mean this belongs to the humes?" I hissed.

The hume woman snorted. "The word you're looking for is *human*. And I mean just what I said. This building, this room, everything in it is ours. I hope you weren't planning on stealing it. I hear demons are known for that kind of thing."

"How dare you?" I wheeled on her, fangs bared. No hume spoke to a demon unless she was spoken to first, and never in that manner. "Humes don't own anything. Not even themselves. You've forgotten your place, and I'm going to teach it to you."

Onyx tried to block me with his arm, but I ducked under his reach. The hume should have fallen back, terrified as I closed in on her. She smiled, though, and for a half-second, I paused, wondering if she had some sort of weapon I'd missed.

"What are you waiting for?" Cinder asked. "Kill her."

I started forward again, and the hume held out both of her arms. "Go ahead," she said. "Flay me with those sharp claws of yours. Rip me open with your fangs. You can enjoy your victory right up until you try to leave the building and find it surrounded by the guards you've been working so hard to avoid."

I checked with Onyx. She had to be bluffing.

He rubbed the back of his neck with one hand. "The guards mean death to you as much as they do us," he said. "And you'd lose your cache."

The hume quirked her lips. It was a cocky expression that made me want to rip away her grin, along with most of her face. "There are more caches. And how important could my death be?" she asked, looking directly at me. "After all, I'm just a *hume*. A little pain, and potestas renata. I'll be back on the next Stygian."

"What are you listening to this for?" Cinder demanded. "Grab her so she can't alert anyone while we get our stuff and get out of here."

Onyx shook his head. "We can't. There are bound to be more humes out of sight. She wouldn't come alone." He sighed. "And she's right. This is hers."

"What?" I turned, certain I must have misheard him. "Humes can't own anything. It's against the law. Even if they could, where would they get these kinds of supplies?"

"Your friends are as ignorant as they are arrogant," the hume said to Onyx. "Where do you think these *kinds of supplies* come from? Who do you think makes them?"

Now it all became clear. "You've been stealing from the factories where you work and hiding your loot here. That doesn't surprise me at all. Well, we're taking what we want, and if you're lucky, we'll let you live."

From somewhere deeper in the building came a long soft whistle, followed by two shorter ones. The hume glanced over her shoulder. "A group of guards just passed by in front of the building. Two efreets and an incubus. Shall I alert them to your presence? You might be able to catch me before they arrive. I'm not as fast as you. But that will be your last act before you're captured."

I looked from the woman to Onyx. Where did a hume get this kind of attitude?

"I know you," she said, nodding at him. "You were part of the group that attacked the Stygian Transit. I'm surprised you, of all people, would try to steal from us."

Onyx actually looked ashamed. I couldn't believe this. I knew he'd been spending time with humes, but I thought it was just to have more bodies for the attack. Now I wasn't so sure. "We didn't have any choice," he said. "We need gear for a . . . a trip."

"Yes." She nodded. "A trip. I'm surprised it's taken you this long to make the attempt."

"What are you talking about?" I demanded. She couldn't possibly know what we were planning. We hadn't decided ourselves until a few hours earlier.

"Isn't it obvious?" she asked in that same condescending tone that made me want to tear her head off. "A demon spawn on the run. His two wanted friends—one brave, or foolish, enough to follow him to the meeting where the attack was being prepared." I stared at her, stunned. Where was she getting this information?

She lifted her chin, trying to peer over Onyx's shoulder. "And if I'm not mistaken, the rather bulky man with the odd taste in clothing has the aura of a seraph. I believe he would be the one who the highest leaders of the covens have been searching so anxiously for."

"You appear to be quite well informed," Visala said, speaking for the first time since the hume's arrival.

She shrugged, her shoulders flexing. "I have my sources. It doesn't take a genius to put the pieces together. Three demon spawns and a seraph with no place to run. No place to stay hidden for long. All in search of supplies.

You've decided to do it. You're going to attempt to cross the Outer Circles."

Cinder stepped forward, fingering the trigger of her souljab. "We have to kill her. She knows where we're going. She could tell someone."

"If we do," Onyx said, "we're as good as dead. It was a mistake to come here. It was my fault. We'll leave the supplies."

I couldn't believe we were being denied by a hume. It was all I could do to keep from running her through with the nearest weapon. But Onyx was right. We had no choice. "Come on," I growled. "Let's go."

"Don't be so hasty," the hume said. "You won't last an hour in the Circles without supplies. And I didn't say I wouldn't share with you."

"You'll give us supplies?" Onyx asked.

She nodded. "For a price."

"Name it," he said.

I hated this. We were negotiating with a hume. A *hume*!

"Take me with you."

"No!" I shook my head, my red hair brushing against my shoulders. "We are not taking a hume with us. Never! I'd rather die."

"Oh, you will." She walked into the room, pulling things off the shelves seemingly at random. "Without food, water, shelter, and weapons, you might as well kill yourselves now."

"We'll find supplies somewhere else," I said. "Break into a warehouse and steal them if we have to."

She stopped in the center of the room. "Do you really have the time? I've already figured out where you're going. How long do you think it will take the covens? They could be placing guards around the borders of the Styx right now."

"Why?" Onyx asked. "Why do you want to go with

us? You know we're probably going to die, even if we do have all the equipment."

The hume pressed her already narrow lips together until they almost disappeared. "That's my business."

The sound of a scuffle came from outside the door to the supply room, and a tall hume stumbled inside, followed by a shorter one.

"What's he doing here?" the female hume demanded. "I told you to keep him home."

"I couldn't stop him," the short hume said. "I was afraid he'd hurt himself."

The taller hume moved so the lamp illuminated his features, and I stepped backward. I recognized him. He was the old man with the horribly scarred face. The one I'd seen the night I followed Onyx into Humeville.

"The Father," Onyx gasped. He knew him. He looked from the old man's distorted features to the female hume at the center of the room. "That means you're Sparrow."

For the first time since she'd arrived, the female hume looked like something had happened that she didn't expect. "Don't call me that." She turned to display the numbers branded onto her shoulder—the identification numbers all humes were given when they first arrived in Hell. "I'm 664082."

Standing in the doorway, the old man flapped his hands in a strange crossing motion and made a series of sharp hooting noises.

"What's wrong with him?" I asked, afraid he might have some terrible hume disease. Demons were supposed to be immune to hume illnesses, but that didn't mean I wanted to take the chance.

"There's nothing wrong with him," the female hume said, going to his side. "He doesn't have a tongue. This is how he talks."

174

"He *is* Father," Onyx said. "And you're Sparrow. You translate for him."

"Don't call me that!" she shouted. "I told you. I'm 664082."

The old man began hooting again, adding a series of odd grunts and chirps. He made a circling motion above his head with one hand, before chopping both hands straight down.

"What's he saying?" Visala asked, stepping closer.

"He's not saying anything." She tried to pull him toward the door. "Take him home," she said to the short hume. "He's tired."

The short hume pulled the old one through the door. But the hume Onyx called Father tore out of his grip. He repeated the same twirling and chopping motions as before and hooted louder than ever.

"Shut him up," Cinder said. "Before the guards hear."

Visala pushed past her, staring at the old hume's scar-twisted face. "What's he saying now?"

The female tugged at her short hair and shook her head. "He's confused. He's never been there."

"Been where?" Visala asked, now so close he was nearly touching the old hume.

The female sighed. "He gets like this sometimes when he hasn't been sleeping. It's just his mind playing tricks on him."

The old hume chopped his hands vehemently in front of her face.

"Fine," she said. "I'll tell them."

The hume raised his twisted lips, revealing a mouthful of cracked yellowing teeth. His breath was putrid.

"He claims he remembers," Sparrow said. She looked at Father and shook her head. "It's not possible. He's never left Hell. But he says he has memories of the Outer Circles."

Visala stepped forward and placed his hand on the old hume's shoulder. "You can come with us. Both of you."

* * *

"I told you this was a terrible idea," Cinder said. We stood at the edge of the Styx, just left of the damaged platform of the Immigration Station. As Sparrow had predicted, guards were monitoring the river's border. Fortunately, the river was long, and only a few guards had been assigned to patrol it. Apparently, the idea of us crossing over was still considered unlikely.

We'd watched the patrols and discovered we had more than enough time to swim across and disappear on the other side before the next guard arrived. Unfortunately, Father refused to enter the water.

"I thought he wanted to go," Onyx said.

Sparrow raised her hands to either side. "He did. But I told you, he gets confused."

The old hume held his arms, which were as scarred as the rest of him, above his head, spinning around and grunting something that sounded like "Gak, ra, ra, nak."

"What's he saying?" Visala asked. Like the rest of us, the seraph was wearing a cloak that was warm but surprisingly light over the pack strapped to his back. The only person who wasn't was Onyx, who had chosen to keep the silver cloak he'd worn during the attack. I suspected it was because he still expected to end up fighting Visala at some point.

Sparrow shook her head. "He doesn't always speak in words. It's more like images. I think he's saying something about globes of light. Or burning worlds. It doesn't make any sense."

"Tell him he can ride across on my back," Onyx said.

I grimaced at the idea of having a hume actually touch me. But the old man shook his head and babbled something that was obviously a no.

"Can you fly him over?" Onyx asked Visala.

The seraph shook his head. "Ordinarily, yes. But with only one good wing, I'll be lucky to fly myself across."

"Let's leave them," I said. "We never should have agreed to bring humes in the first place."

"Try, and I'll call the guards," Sparrow said.

Cinder bared her teeth. "You won't if we drop you in the deepest part of the Styx first." She turned to Onyx. "Make the call. Either we leave them, or we drown them."

"We aren't doing either one," Visala said. "If the old man knows something about what's out there, he could be invaluable."

"Then how are we going to get him across?" I asked, frustration and fear making me jumpy. The platform provided the ideal spot to swim across. Its shadow lent cover from the torches that illuminated most of the river. "If we don't get going in the next few minutes, we'll have to wait until after the next patrol."

Humes were nothing but problems, and I still didn't understand why Visala had agreed to bring them. The crazy old man couldn't possibly know anything that would help us. No one could. No one had ever crossed the river and returned alive.

"Maybe if I show him it's safe," Onyx said. "I can swim partway, return, and offer to put him on my back. If that doesn't work, I'll have to drag him across by force."

The old hume circled his arms above his head and began spinning again, gibbering away insanely.

Sparrow threw up her hands. "It's worth a try."

Onyx sat on the bank and lowered himself into the black river. "Keep your pack dry as much as possible,"

Sparrow said. "They're supposed to be waterproof, but I'm not sure anyone's ever tested that."

Like many of the items in the storage room, the humes claimed to have created the backpacks from parts of other things they'd scavenged. More like stolen. But I had to admit they came in handy for carrying supplies. Everyone but Father was carrying one.

"See, it's easy." Onyx paddled a few feet from the edge. I watched nervously as he stroked farther out in the dark water. As spawnlings, we'd all learned to swim at the pools in each of our building basements. It was supposed to build up our endurance and strengthen our lungs.

But those were only a few feet deep, and you could see the bottom. The Styx was slow moving but pitch black, and far too deep for my tastes. Farther across the river, something that looked suspiciously like a hume body floated slowly along the current, lodging itself against the far bank.

"See, nothing to worry about." With his ebony skin, the shadow-covered water almost swallowed Onyx up. As near as I could tell, he was about halfway across. He was so big and heavy, I'd halfway expected him to sink like a rock. But he moved surprisingly well.

If Father was impressed, he didn't show it. He was still croaking away. "Gak, ra, ra, nak. Gak, ra, ra, nak. Gak, ra, ra, nak." And spinning so violently, it looked like he'd get dizzy and fall in on his own any minute.

"Maybe you better come back!" Sparrow called out. "I think you're just going to have to take him."

As Onyx turned and started to paddle back, something began happening to the water. At first it was just a rippling, as if someone had thrown a handful of rocks into the center of the river. Then a few tiny bubbles rose to the surface and burst.

"Gak, ra, ra, nak! Gak, ra, ra, nak!" Father stopped spinning and pointed to the water.

"What is it?" Visala called.

"I'm not sure." Onyx stopped paddling, and treaded water near the middle of the river. The bubbles were getting bigger now. First the size of his fist, then his head, and finally nearly as big as Onyx himself. "It smells strange," he said.

"Get back!" I shouted.

As Onyx started to swim toward us again, the entire surface of the River Styx burst into flames.

"Gak, ra, ra, nak! Gak, ra, ra, nak! Gak, ra, ra, nak!" Father screamed, his face lit by the inferno that roared higher than our heads.

Onyx was nowhere to be seen.

CHAPTER 19

As the raging flames spread up and down the river, a sound I'd never heard before shook the early morning air—gongs clanging over and over. The fire must have set off an alarm of some kind.

"What is it? What's happening?" humes called to one another, rushing from doors or sticking sallow faces out their windows—most of them dressed in ragged gowns, tattered undergarments, or nothing at all.

"Onyx!" I screamed, searching the flaming water. All demons had some level of immunity to fire—the Dae' Lorica most of all. But this was no ordinary fire.

"Go back inside! Get in your houses!" The authoritative voices of guards converging toward the bank of the Styx overrode the humes' bleating. As the burning efreets closed in with weapons raised, the pale white figures disappeared inside their slum buildings.

"What do we do?" Cinder's blue skin had turned a reddish-orange as her body unconsciously mirrored the flames.

"We've got to get out of here!" Sparrow shouted. Beside her, Father was no longer grunting or spinning. Instead, apparently satisfied that he'd made his point, he stood facing the fire with a contented expression as sweat poured down his face.

Cinder edged to the bank and grabbed my arm with trembling fingers. "Come on, Blaze. We can make it."

I eyed the unnaturally bright flames. Who knew what other dangers they might hide? But our options were quickly disappearing. The guards were closing in on us in a blue line, shouting to one another as they searched for the cause of the alarm. They hadn't seen us yet, but it wouldn't be long before they did.

Sparrow pulled the old hume toward her. "You have to protect him," she said, every bit as arrogant as she'd been earlier, despite the fact that she now had no leverage. Visala looked from the fire to the two of them.

"Let's get out of here." Cinder cinched the tie around the waist of her robe, preparing to dive into the burning water.

I didn't care about either of the humes. Let them scald, or drown, or get captured by the guards. They deserved whatever happened to them after the way Sparrow forced us to take them. I stepped to the riverbank. "Okay, let's swim." I sucked in a mouthful of air, psyching myself up to leap into the flames that might not kill me, but were definitely going to sting.

Cinder bent her knees, took a deep breath, and lunged forward.

"Wait." I stepped in front of her.

"Get out of my way!" she howled, trying to slip past me. Her skin was slick with oily secretions, and her eyes were wild.

"Look." I pointed to where something was approaching through the drifting black smoke and dancing orange pillars.

Onyx paddled out from the flames and heaved himself halfway onto the bank. "Help," he gasped, trying to pull himself the rest of the way up. Clouds of steam rose from his back as I took his hands; Visala lowered his aura and helped. "Can't. Breathe," he choked between hacking coughs. "No . . . air."

Air. I hadn't even thought about that. "Stop!" I grabbed for Cinder, realizing she was about to dive into the river anyway.

She shoved me backward and reached for her souljab. Her face was a mask of terror. She hadn't understood anything Onyx was saying. I shook her, trying to make her listen. "We can't swim across. The fire is burning all the oxygen. We'd suffocate before we got halfway."

Slowly, my words got through to her. "Then wh-wh . . . do w-we do." She was shaking so badly, it was almost impossible to make out what she was saying.

Onyx got to his feet shakily. "We've got . . . to find . . . a place . . . to hide," he said, coughing with every breath.

"It's no good," I said. "The guards will be on us any second."

"I have an idea." Sparrow began pawing through her pack. I had no clue what she was looking for. We'd brought all manner of supplies, including several weapons, but none of them would be enough to hold off the number of guards that were so close, it was a wonder they hadn't seen us already. The hume pulled out something flat and black. It took me a moment to recognize the wings used to glide above the lava in Culdine matches.

"We can fly across," she called, shouting to be heard over the fire's roar.

It was a surprisingly good idea for a hume, but it would never work. "They're not like gargoyle wings. You can't actually fly up. We'd have to be high enough to glide across."

"There," Onyx said, still hacking and gasping. He pointed to the top of the Stygian platform. "If we can make it to the top, we can glide over."

"Too late," Cinder whispered, her voice flat and empty.

I looked up to see a pair of efreet guards less than a dozen steps away, framed by a black background of brimstone. "Stand where you are," the first shouted, raising a spear with a tip that shot out tongues of hot blue energy.

Onyx reached for the tube-shaped weapon at his waist, but Visala stepped in front of him. "Let me take care of this!" He ripped off his cloak and pulled out his sword, his aura shining brighter than even the flames behind him. "Retreat," he commanded, his voice booming. The first guard turned and ran, but the second hesitated.

"Be gone!" the seraph roared, raising his shimmering blade above his head. The second guard dropped his spear and fled in terror. I didn't blame him. It took all my will not to run from Visala, and he wasn't even talking to me.

"Take my pack." He slipped out of the straps and let the backpack drop to the ground. "The higher orders are less vulnerable to my commands. But I think I can get you enough time to reach the platform."

Still holding his sword high, he spread his wings. Even with one of them only halfway extended, it was the most magnificent thing I had ever seen. If I'd lost any faith that he was a celestial being, it all returned as he flexed his back and neck, flapping his great golden wings. Rising into the air, the brilliance of white and gold shone against red and black. He looked all-powerful, majestic. He glanced over his shoulder at me, and my heart pounded.

"Come on." Onyx shook me, and I realized everyone was leaving. He scooped up the seraph's pack as we walked by and muttered something I couldn't make out. As we passed the spot where the guards had stood, he grabbed their abandoned spear and added it to his load.

I spared a last look back as we headed for the platform stairs. Visala's bright figure flashed across the sky, leading the guards away from us. Balls of fire volleyed through the air at him, but he avoided them easily.

Within a few minutes, we reached the top of the platform. Much of the debris from the attack had been cleaned away, but blasted holes and chunks of the Immigration Station's facade that were too big to be moved in one piece made it impossible to forget what had happened here.

If the thought of what he and his friends had gone through affected Onyx at all, he didn't show it. "Make sure you strap them on tight," he said as he dropped his and Visala's packs and began pulling the wings over his thick arms and broad shoulders.

"Have you used them before?" I asked.

"A few times," he grunted without offering any more information.

In a different time and place, the thought of gliding through the air would have been exciting, but knowing that if I made a mistake I would suffocate dampened my enthusiasm.

"You're putting it on wrong," Onyx said, taking Cinder's wings from her shaking hands.

I searched the sky for Visala, but he was nowhere in sight. He must have flown in toward the center of the city. I hoped he'd be all right. I had no idea what we'd do if we managed to get across the river, only to find our whole reason for doing so had been to get captured.

"We don't have enough wings," Sparrow said, looking into her pack. "I thought I brought two, but there's only one set here."

"You think that crazy old freak would be able to use them anyway?" Cinder turned, letting Onyx pull the wings snuggly down on her back. "He'd probably fly straight into the flames or back into the hands of the guards." The gray feathers tickled the back of her neck.

Onyx scowled as he tightened Cinder's leather straps. "I'll take him."

"You can't," I said at once. "You're already so big those wings will barely hold you up. With your pack and Visala's, you'll be lucky to make it across by yourself."

Onyx stared at me. "Are you volunteering?"

"No." The thought of touching a hume—having its body touch mine—was revolting.

"I'll take him," Sparrow said. "I wouldn't trust a demon spawn with him, anyway."

I was going to point out that she'd seemed more than willing to trust us with him when the guards were closing in. Before I could, Cinder said, "You may not need to worry about who carries him. I think your passenger is about to take a dive."

All of us spun around at the same time. Father was walking straight toward part of the platform that had sheared away in the battle. Hands held out to his sides, he tilted his head up, seeming to enjoy the breeze that had blown off his hood and streamed his long gray hair out behind his back.

"Father, stop!" Sparrow screeched.

Onyx raced toward the old man, but the hume woman beat him to it. Dropping her pack and wings, she dashed across the pitted stone surface. It didn't look like she was going to get there in time. He was less than three steps from falling to his death. But right before he stepped off the edge, Father stopped and twirled back around. He watched with a bemused smile as Sparrow pulled him away from the edge.

"Hurry up," I said. "The guards could return any minute."

Cinder popped the release on her wings, letting them extend open several times the reach of her arms on either side. I did the same. The minute the frame snapped into place, I could feel the wind tugging at the stiff fabric and feathers, trying to pull me toward the river.

"Let's get you strapped in," Onyx said, picking up the hume woman's pack. I wondered again how he could stand being that close to them. "Where did you put your wings?"

Sparrow searched the platform. "I was holding them when . . . I must have dropped them. They should be right here."

A blast of air flapped Cinder's wings. Onyx ran to the edge of the platform. "The wind must have caught them." He searched the dark street below and shook his head. "We don't have time to look."

"Guess you're staying behind after all." Cinder chuckled.

Onyx turned on her, furious. "We aren't leaving anyone," he growled. "Say it one more time and you're on your own. I swear it."

Cinder backed away, turning uncertainly to me. "I was just saying there aren't enough wings now. We can't all get across. Maybe if they, I don't know, go back for more wings, they can catch up."

Onyx's face was stone. "No one's going back, and no one's getting left behind." He looked from Cinder to me, hands fisted at his sides. "Blaze, you take Father. You're stronger. If he struggles, he'll be less likely to throw off your balance. Cinder, you take Sparrow. You're lighter and she can hold on better."

He couldn't be saying what I thought he was. "You want me to . . . *carry* . . . the hume?"

"No." Cinder thrashed her tail back and forth. She pointed at Sparrow. "I won't touch that piece of trash. You can't make me."

"Let me use one of their wings," Sparrow said. "I'll carry Father, and they can decide which one will take the other."

"Their wings are the wrong size," Onyx said. "They wouldn't fit you." He walked slowly to Cinder and glared down at her. "You'll take the hume, or I'll shred your wings, and then Blaze's. I still think the Halo and I should be taking this risk alone. If *they* stay, so do the two of you."

Cinder opened her mouth, then snapped it shut. She looked at me and I shrugged. I thought Onyx might be bluffing, but if I'd learned anything over the past week, it was that I didn't know him nearly as well as I thought I did. The idea of carrying a hume across the river made me gag. But turning myself over to the guards was worse—barely. The only consolation was that I'd probably be dead before anyone ever found out what I'd done.

"All right, if we're going to do this, let's get it over with." I started toward the end of the platform, where the Stygian came to a stop on Arrival Days.

But Onyx pointed off to one side. "You'll need to angle your flight. Let the wind catch you, and then lean to the left. The heat from the fire should keep you well above the flames."

"Why not go straight off the end?" I asked. It was the most obvious launching point—a clear shot out over the water.

"It's dangerous. Didn't you ever notice they don't let anyone stand within ten steps of the Stygian?"

Of course I had. It was one of the first things they stressed in training. Don't get near the end of the platform. "But this isn't Arrival Day. The Stygian isn't—"

He cut me off with a glare. "Do you want to stand around here arguing until the guards find us, or do you want to get across the river?"

I went to the edge, wondering when he'd become so bossy. I nearly puked as Onyx led the old man to me and bound him to my back with a pair of straps. The stench of the hume's breath and sweat were beyond foul, and his body had a soft, squishy feel to it that made me think of mold.

At least he didn't struggle. He clung to my waist with arms that were wrinkled and rough like old parchment, hooting.

Sparrow laughed. "He says you smell bad."

If I could have dumped him off the edge of the platform I would have, gladly.

I was sure Cinder would balk when Onyx led the hume woman to her. But she didn't say a word as he tied Sparrow on. The only signs of how furious she was were her tail whipping left and right, and the icy disdain in her eyes. I was glad I wasn't the hume. Cinder had a bad temper and a good memory. If we survived long enough, I knew she'd find a way of getting back at her.

"Okay, let's keep this simple," Onyx said when he'd finished checking our wings and straps one last time. "I've flown before, so I'll go first. After I launch, Cinder will count to three and follow my exact movements. Blaze, you'll follow Cinder. The most important thing is keeping your balance." He demonstrated raising one arm and lowering the other ever so slightly. "Make small adjustments."

Cinder glared over her shoulder at Sparrow. The hume glared back.

I wiped my palms together, drying the moisture on them. The hume tied to my back grunted, "Gurr eeg erg."

"What'd he say?" I asked, sure I didn't want to know.

Sparrow shrugged. "He said you're going to do fine."

Just what I needed. A vote of confidence from a hume.

"Okay," Onyx called. "Here goes." He launched himself off the platform. Immediately, his weight plunged him downward, and I bit my lip. But as he banked over the river, the rising hot air lifted him up.

". . . two . . . three," Cinder whispered. "Don't knock me off balance." She snarled back at the hume.

"Wouldn't dream of it," Sparrow said.

Cinder leaped forward, and the two of them glided out over the steaming river as though they'd been doing it forever.

Now it was my turn. I walked to the edge. It looked so far down to the street below. Much farther than it had on Arrival Days. Of course, I hadn't been standing anywhere close to the edge then. "Gurr eeg erg." Father's voice came from behind my head.

"Thanks," I said, wondering if a demented hume's voice would be the last words I'd ever hear. I held my arms out to my sides, gripped the leather handles of the wings, and jumped.

Air rushed past my face, cold and then increasingly hotter as I approached the river. I tried to turn and leaned farther to the left than I should have, diving toward the fire. The old hume hooted something at me.

"Be quiet and let me do this," I yelled back. I adjusted to the right a little more gently and regained my balance. My mistake had cost us too much height, though, and the tips of the flames nearly reached my wings.

"That's the worst job of flying I've ever seen," a voice called out of the dark. I looked over to see Visala flying above me and to the right. "Relax your shoulders. You're pulling down on the front of your wings."

I did, and at once, the hot air lifted us up. Hot plumes of moist air pushed against the wings. Relieved that maybe I wasn't going to die after all, I had a chance to enjoy the feeling of flying for about two seconds before reaching the other side of the river. Without the heated air, I quickly began losing elevation.

Just ahead, I could see Onyx and Cinder on their feet. Cinder looked like she was trying to rip the straps from her chest to free herself of the hume. Onyx was waving his arms and shouting something I couldn't understand.

"How do I land?" I yelled.

I could have sworn I heard the seraph laughing as he banked his wings and dropped gently to the ground. "Like this."

I tried to follow his example, relaxing my shoulders and lowering my hooves. But instead of the smooth landing he made, I hit the ground hard, stumbled, and ended up somersaulting across the stony ground, Father being my landing pad.

"Ohff ow, wow!" he hooted. When I finally came to a stop, he patted my shoulder and grunted something that might have been, "I can't believe I lived through that."

I turned, and for the first time saw Hell from the other side of the River Styx.

I was in the Outer Circles.

CHAPTER 20

"Let's get out of here before anyone comes looking for us." Onyx shouldered his pack and began moving from person to person, checking to make sure everyone was carrying at least one weapon. "Keep an eye out for anything at all. We have no idea what we might be facing. I've got the best night vision, so I'll take the lead. Visala, you watch our backs."

I'd expected the seraph to take charge once we crossed the Styx. Instead, Onyx was running things like an efreet guard commander. Once again, a side of him I'd never seen. Even after I knew he was part of the group that attacked the Stygian, I told myself he'd been drawn into it by someone else. Now I was beginning to wonder if he'd had a more prominent role in its activities—maybe even a leader?

He walked to the edge of the Styx, where the flames were still blazing, and pulled something out of the water. It took me a moment to realize it was the remains of the hume body that had floated past earlier—now charred from head to foot. "Disgusting," I said, pulling the collar of my robe over my nose to block the stench. "What are you doing with that?"

He tugged the blackened corpse onto the bank and dropped it there, scrubbing his hands with sand and rocks afterward. "It might throw off the guards a little if they come searching for us."

Would they follow us? I wondered, walking a few steps behind Onyx as he set off away from the river at a brisk pace. "The last time a group of guards crossed the Styx . . ." My words trailed away as it occurred to me the guards weren't the only ones whose bodies had been brought back in pieces the last time anyone dared to cross into the Outer Circles.

The previous group hadn't lasted a day. What made us think we were any better? Did we have better weapons? More supplies? Other than the seraph, we were just a bunch of kids and a couple of lunatic humes. As we walked through the darkness, Onyx scanning the terrain from left to right, it all seemed real for the first time.

With every step, we were leaving the safety of Hell behind, walking into a place no demons had ever survived. A chill lanced through my bones that had nothing to do with the temperature.

"Want to turn back?" Onyx asked. "You could probably wait by the river and the guards would pick you up."

I didn't know if he was mocking my earlier bravado, or seriously offering to let me return while that was still an option. Either way, it didn't matter. My future wasn't any brighter than Onyx's if I gave myself up. "No. I'm staying to the end," I said, wishing I'd phrased it differently as soon as the words left my mouth.

I glanced over my shoulder at the rest of the group. The smell of sulfur dissipated the farther we got from the Styx. Sparrow and Father were walking ten to fifteen paces behind me. Every so often, the old hume grunted or hooted. I couldn't tell if he was talking to the woman or just making noise. Sparrow walked silently beside him, her eyes sharp and alert as she searched the horizon the same way Onyx was.

Another dozen paces back and off to the side, Cinder

eyed the humes with a concentration that would have made me extremely nervous if I'd been in their place. Stalking silently after them, her tail twitching left, right, left, right with every step, she reminded me of a sharp-toothed imp hunting a particularly tasty hell rat.

At the back of the group, Visala strolled along with an easy grace, his hands tucked into the pockets of his robe. Inside the dark shadow of his hood, his face was a silver glow. He didn't appear to be watching ahead or to the rear. If anything, he looked like he was out for a comfortable walk, interested only in stretching his legs. I hoped nothing came up from behind us.

Somewhere along the way, Father had found a long, narrow strip of scrap metal. He dragged it through the dirt and rocks behind him, first on one side then the other, leaving tracks even a spawnling could follow.

"Can't you make him quit that?" I asked.

Sparrow said something to Father, and he stopped dragging the scrap. But a few seconds later, he was back at it. So much for Onyx's plan of throwing off the guards.

"Are you going to let him do that?"

Onyx glanced over his shoulder at Father and Sparrow. "At this point, I don't think it matters. I'm pretty sure the guards won't follow us this far—if they make it across the river at all." He grunted. "If they do, we won't be hard to find. They have to know where we're going."

I shook my head. "Why did you let them come, anyway?"

"Who, the humans? Ask your best friend the Halo. He's the one who agreed to take them."

"You could have argued. It's like you *want* them with us."

Behind us, the flames appeared smaller, but I couldn't tell if that was because they were dying out or because we were leaving them farther behind. Onyx shrugged. "If

Father really does know something about the Outer Circles, he might be useful. And Sparrow has a reputation. The other humans don't talk about her much, but when they do, it's with respect."

"You don't really believe the old man has memories of anything out here, do you?" I asked. "There's no way he could ever have been here."

Onyx shrugged again, his eyes staring off into the darkness.

The more we left the flames behind, the harder it became to see. With no gas lamps, the only illumination was the faint glow that came from the cavern ceiling even at night. "He tried to warn us about the river. I wouldn't have come within seconds of suffocating if I'd listened to him."

"You think he *knew* the river was going to burst into flames?" I could barely believe he would even consider the idea.

"You heard him yourself. *Globes of light. Burning worlds.* Sounds a lot like the flaming gas bubbles that came out of the river."

I sniffed. "I heard what the hume woman *claimed* he said. For all we know, she knew about the fire all along. Maybe that was just her way of making sure we believed their story. Wasn't she the one who suggested bringing wings in the first place?"

Onyx adjusted the straps of his pack. I could tell he didn't want to believe anything bad about the humes. But it was time he considered the fact that they were all a bunch of liars, thieves, and murderers, or they wouldn't have been sent to Hell in the first place. "What I know is they provided us with supplies. Without their help, we'd still be stuck on the other side of the river."

"Supplies they stole," I said. Onyx shook his head, and I could tell I was getting under his skin. After all he'd been through, the last thing I wanted to do was cause him more pain. But if I couldn't convince him that treating humes as equals was asking for trouble, he was only going to end up getting hurt much worse. "You know why they really wanted to come?"

"I'm sure you'll tell me," he muttered, setting his jaw with the stubborn determination I knew all too well.

"To stop their eternal damnation, of course." I lowered my voice to make sure the humes couldn't overhear. "They're trying to escape from Hell."

"*Trying to escape from Hell*," Onyx said, his voice cold. "Imagine that."

I couldn't understand what he was so upset about until it occurred to me that's exactly what he and his friends had been attempting. "That's different," I said, putting a hand on his shoulder. "You weren't being punished. You only wanted to see . . ."

"Look, let's not talk about this right now," he said. "I need to keep my attention on what's around us."

I sighed, realizing I'd managed to offend him—again. Fire and brimstone, I was getting really good at saying the wrong thing. Dropping back, I tried talking to Cinder. At least she'd be open-minded enough to see things my way. But after a few one-word responses, I figured out she wasn't in a talking mood.

Fine. I'd walk by myself. Slowing down until I was about halfway between her and Visala, I contented myself with silently studying what was around me. Close to the river, the ground had been dirt and small rocks, with an occasional stunted brown bush to break up the monotony. The farther away we went, the sandier the soil became. The bushes disappeared, replaced by rock formations sticking up out of the ground. The wind and sand had carved them into twisted shapes that looked far too much like hulking creatures clawing their way out of the ground and ready to grab us at any moment.

Tugging my cloak more tightly around my shoulders, I tried to imagine what the last group to come this way had seen. What was lethal enough to rip more than twenty efreets to pieces? The thought made me shudder, and I quickly shifted my mind to something else.

What were the other demon spawns in our barracks thinking right now? It was far past curfew, and classes would start in only a few hours—if there *were* classes. I couldn't imagine anyone sleeping after the day's excitement. By now, they must know that Cinder and I had been hiding a seraph in our room. The thought would probably terrify and excite them at the same time. How many would claim to have caught a glimpse of a burning form through the doorway?

The thought of the girls laughing and giggling as they compared stories brought a smile to my lips. But a moment later, I found myself crying. I was never going to be there laughing and joking with them again. I would never go to another class or eat in the cafeteria. In a few hours, our friends and parents would learn we'd fled into the Outer Circles. Any hope that we'd been taken against our will would disappear.

My parents wouldn't attend my graduation in four years the way they'd planned. Instead, they'd be attending my funeral.

"Are you all right?"

I turned to see Visala watching me. "You better speed up or you're going to get left behind," he said.

Looking around, I saw that I'd fallen much farther back than I intended. I ran my hands across my cheeks, hoping he didn't know I'd been crying, and picked up my pace.

"Probably not what you expected to be doing a week ago," he said, walking beside me.

I choked out a laugh. "Not what I expected to be doing a day ago."

"I guess I should apologize for drawing you into this situation," he said.

I peeked at his softly glowing face, barely able to believe a seraph was apologizing to me. Ordinarily, his features were so bright, looking at him was like trying to stare into a blinding gemstone. But here, with only silvery flickers dancing across his cheeks, it was possible to make out a fine, straight nose, high forehead, and eyes that were curiously compelling.

"If you ask Cinder," I said, pulling my gaze away from his, "I don't need anyone's help to get into trouble. I seem to find plenty of *situations* on my own." When I looked over again, his lips had risen into an amused smile. "Of course, it wouldn't have bothered me a bit if you had chosen someone else's window to fly into."

"I imagine not." He chuckled. His voice was deep and almost gentle when he wasn't ordering people around. We walked for a few minutes in silence, and then he asked, "What made you go out, anyway—after the attack?"

I felt my face grow warm. Stupidity was probably the best answer. I didn't say that. I was sure he thought I was dumb enough as it was. Not that it mattered what a celestial being thought of a demon spawn. "I was looking for Onyx," I said. "When he didn't come back to the barracks, I was afraid he might have been hurt—or dead."

"That was incredibly bráve," he said. Now I *was* blushing.

"Cinder will tell you it was moronic."

"Cinder didn't go looking for a friend," he said.

I had no idea what to say to that. So I said nothing.

Visala took his hands out of the pockets of his cloak. Like his face, his fingers glowed less brightly than normal. Silver fire flowed down his palms, across his fingers, and up the backs of his hands in a constant stream, as though he were made of some fiery liquid. I was fascinated by his fingers, which were surprisingly long.

"You must care quite a bit about him."

"What?" I hadn't been paying attention, and I quickly searched my memory for what we'd been talking about.

"Onyx," he said with the same amused smile. "You must care about him a lot to have risked going out after the attack. For all you knew, there might have been armed humans around. Maybe even Halos."

I stifled a gasp at the insulting slang he used to describe himself. But if he was offended by the term, he didn't show it. "I really wasn't thinking at all, or I probably wouldn't have done it. I acted before I considered all the possibilities. I seem to be good at that."

The seraph touched a finger to his lower lip, and the silvery liquid flowed from hand to face. I knew it would kill me, but for a second, I wondered what it would be like to have that hand touch me and watch his aura flow over my skin. Then Onyx sprinted toward us.

"Get down! Get down!" he called, sprinting back through the group.

Sparrow dropped to the sandy soil, pulling Father with her. Cinder spread herself flat against the ground, her hands and face already changing to match the texture and color of the earth.

I wanted to ask what was wrong. Before I could get the question out, Onyx dragged me to the ground, his weight knocking the air from my lungs as he landed on top of me.

I gasped for breath, and Visala knelt, reaching for his sword.

"Not yet," Onyx said. "Something's coming, but I don't think it's seen us." He pointed to a twisted rock pillar about twice our height and a little less across. "Crawl over to that," he whispered. "But stay low. And Visala, get your hands and face out of sight."

Still smarting from my bruised ribs, I scooted across the sand until, crowded against the others, I reached the base of the rock.

"Where is it?" Sparrow asked, peeking around the side of the formation. "I don't see anything."

"Get back, and hopefully you won't," Onyx said. "If we stay here and don't move, I'm hoping it will pass right over us."

"Over?" Visala asked. His hand crept out of his pocket and stole toward his sword.

"Don't even think about it," Onyx growled. "And I told you to hide those hands." Easing around the edge of the rock, he peeked upward. "I never considered the possibility of something coming from the sky. If I hadn't been stretching my neck, I wouldn't have seen it."

"What did you see?" Cinder whispered. Pressed against the rough rock, she blended in so well, she might have been part of the formation. The shadow of her robe was all that gave her away.

"I'm not sure." Onyx leaned a little farther out. Only when his shoulder brushed against mine did I realize he was shivering. "It was way bigger than any creature I've ever seen. And it was coming fast. I'd guess it was halfway to the cavern ceiling. But even at that distance, it was large enough that I couldn't blot it out with my palm held out at the full length of my arm."

"What are we going to do?" I asked, shifting uncomfortably. Away from the rock, the ground had been mostly soft sand, but a pile of loose shale surrounded the base.

"Nothing." Onyx moved back carefully and rested his head against the stone. "All we can do is wait for it to go by and keep an eye out for it in the future. There's a lot of area for it to cover. Now that we know it's there, we should be able to sneak by."

Lifting myself with my hands, I tried to get more comfortable. If we were going to be stuck somewhere for a while, why couldn't it have been where the ground wasn't quite so painful? Something jabbed into the skin between my thumb and forefinger, and I pulled out a shard of sharp white rock.

I turned the stone over in my fingers. The texture was odd, rougher than I would have expected and porous against my sweat-damp palm. With a start, I realized it wasn't a stone at all. "This pile of rocks we're sitting on," I said, touching Onyx's arm. "I don't think it's rock. I think it's bone."

Onyx's mouth dropped open, but he wasn't focused on what was in my hand. He was gaping at something over my shoulder. A dark shape soared over us, growing impossibly larger and larger, until it blocked out the entire sky. The smell of sulfur and burning hair filled my lungs, and a ground-shaking scream rang out in the night.

CHAPTER 21

With the dark of night edging toward dawn, it was impossible to make out exactly what the creature was. Huge, leathery wings that looked as if they were flapping too slowly to keep it aloft blew up a storm of sand and rocks as it circled.

"Don't move. Maybe it hasn't seen us yet," Onyx whispered.

Gliding above, it twisted its flattened head to fix our location with eyes like vast pools of black tar. Lowering a wing nearly as long as the entire Stygian, it banked around.

Visala drew back the front of his robe to free the hilt of his sword. "I don't think we're going to be that lucky."

The beast opened its muzzle, gave another screech that vibrated through my skull, and plummeted out of the sky straight at us.

"Get back," Visala said. Bracing himself against the stone pillar, he raised his sword in both hands. A bolt of white angel-fire shot from its tip. At the last possible instant, the creature pulled out of its dive and snatched at him with talons that reflected the sword's light.

Visala dove to the ground, rolled, and came up swinging. His sword clashed off the creature's right leg, sending a shower of glittering sparks exploding through the air. As the monster circled around, Onyx dropped to one knee and raised the silver tube he'd been carrying to his shoulder.

He pressed something on top of the weapon, and the tube jumped in his hands with a thump. A second later, a ball of orange flame exploded against one of the creature's wings.

"You hit it," I yelled, raising a fist. Flames licked across the beast's leathery skin, but sputtered out quickly. Unhurt, the creature screamed in fury and dove for a second attack.

"Get behind the pillar," Onyx yelled, before firing another blast.

I ran to the back of the stone with Cinder just ahead of me. Sparrow and Father circled around the other side. Onyx's second fireball did even less damage than the first, bouncing harmlessly off the monster's thick pelt to the desert floor. Visala stepped forward to attack again with his sword, but the creature slapped him with one of its wings and knocked him to the ground.

"Look out!" Sparrow shouted. An instant later, a pair of talons slashed the stone formation. Chunks of rocks exploded around me, one slicing a cut across the side of my jaw. When I looked up, half the pillar was gone, V-shaped grooves marking the top.

Sparrow jumped to her feet, spinning something above her head. Several bright blue sparks whizzed through the air. Most of them went wide, but two hit the creature's wing, wrapping the metal cable between them around it. For a second, the beast hesitated in midair, screaming as it flapped its bent wing, then something snapped with a *twang,* and the blue sparks dropped away.

"It broke the cables," she cried, despair clear in her voice.

"It's too strong for us to fight," Visala said. "We have to run!"

"Where to?" Onyx waved a hand. "Everything's out in the open." He rammed two more cloth-wrapped balls into his weapon, but it was clear neither he nor Visala thought we stood a chance. I glanced down at the souljab tucked into my belt, realizing how pathetic it was against something nearly as big as the Immigration Station itself.

How had we thought we could survive out here? We weren't even going to last long enough to see morning light.

"Here it comes again!" Sparrow called.

I spun around to see the creature tuck its wings against its massive body and drop out of the sky. At the edge of my vision, something raced past me. I turned to see a blur of movement speeding back the way we'd come.

Onyx dropped his weapon. "No!"

It was Cinder. She'd panicked and was running for safety. But there *was* no safety. We'd picked the biggest formation within a thousand paces to hide behind. There was no cover of any kind in the direction she was going, only barren sand with not even a bush to hide behind. I hoped her coloring would hide her from the creature's sight, but it turned its head and screamed, as though excited by the chase.

Cinder glanced over her shoulder and squealed in terror. She cut toward a pile of rocks no higher than her knees, but even that was too far. The monster would be on top of her before she got halfway there.

Without thinking about what I was doing, I threw off my pack and sprinted after her. Everything went red as energy pumped through my body.

"You can't help her!" Visala called after me. But I was beyond stopping. Beyond thinking. Fangs drew back my lips. Barely touching the ground, I loped across the sandy soil. The muscles in my arms and legs trembled as I closed the distance between Cinder and me. I was nearly to her. But the creature got there first.

As it swooped down behind her, Cinder gave one last burst of speed. It wasn't enough. Talons longer than she was tall wrapped around her waist and lifted her off the ground. Throwing back my head with a howl of fury, I leaped at the monster. My fingers caught on its leg, slipped, and caught again. Not planning, only following a murderous desire to tear and rend, I climbed the creature's leg past Cinder and sank my teeth into the spot where scaly talon disappeared into flesh.

It was like trying to bite through stone. Screaming, I gouged and tore. Slowly, my claws sunk in, ripping out chunks of flesh. I grabbed the souljab from my belt and triggered it over and over into the open wound. With an angry caw, the monster opened its talon and released Cinder. I watched her tumble through the air and thump to the ground. Was I too late?

No. She rolled over, got up, and began running again.

I tried to let go of the creature myself, but one of my talons was jammed into its flesh. Cawing again, the beast shook its leg, trying to break me loose. I managed to pry myself free, but by now, we were too far up in the air for me to safely drop.

High overhead, the cavern ceiling was beginning to glow pink. Nearly as far below, Onyx, Visala, and the humes looked tiny. One of them shouted something, but I couldn't tell what they were saying. The beast circled, and I could see the buildings of Hell outlined in the distance.

As my fury departed, realization of what I'd done and where I was made my muscles go weak. Only my grip stood between me and a drop of thousands of feet. My arms and legs felt like jelly, shaking from what I'd just put them through. Something black and slippery dripped from the gashes I'd torn in the creature's flesh. It shook its leg again, and my fingers began to slip.

Down below, Onyx threw something to Visala. The seraph threw off his cloak, stretched out his wings, and launched himself into the air. Forgetting about me for the moment, the monster I was clinging to gave chase. What was Visala doing? It was crazy to try and fight the beast in the air.

As the creature closed in on him, Visala must have had the same thought. He turned and began flying away. The monster was much faster than him, though, and halved the distance between us in seconds. Visala saw it coming, but instead of heading for the ground, he kept climbing. What could he possibly be thinking? He had something tucked under one arm and was clutching something else against his body. It wasn't his sword, but whatever it was, it didn't matter. All of us combined had barely managed to scratch the beast's skin.

"Watch out!" I yelled as the creature opened its maw wide and dove toward Visala.

The seraph didn't seem to hear me. We were so close that I could see the look of desperation on his face, but he kept flying up, fighting for altitude. His wings strained and shook, the bad one stuttering so that he flew in a slightly zigzag pattern. The creature opened it jaws, flashing hundreds of glass-like, needle-thin teeth. I couldn't watch.

Just as the beast snapped its teeth shut, Visala tucked his wings and dropped. The creature passed so closely over him that I could almost have reached out and touched his head. Spinning in midair, Visala drew back his arm and launched what he'd been holding next to his body.

I recognized it at once—the spear Onyx had taken from the efreet guards. Flashing blue bolts of energy, the lance flew directly into the creature's right eye. Tossing back its head in rage, the monster screamed. Black smoke bellowed from its mouth. Gouts of flame shot from the spot where the spear had entered as the creature's eye exploded. The same black liquid I'd seen dripping from its leg rained out of the empty socket onto the ground below. Its wings flapped, shuddered, and went limp.

Suddenly we were falling. The ground raced up toward me.

"Jump!"

I turned to see Visala falling alongside us. He held out his arms. We were nearly to the ground, and even if he caught me, his aura would kill me. But I kicked off the creature's leg and leaped.

For a moment, I was floating. I closed my eyes, waiting for my body to splatter against the ground. Instead, a pair of strong arms closed around me. Something cold and slightly metallic brushed across my skin. I opened my eyes to see Visala holding me wrapped in Onyx's cloak.

Visala threw open his wings to halt our plunge. The force rushed blood to my head. The desert floor leaped toward us, but instead of breaking our bodies, it cushioned us as he managed to glide almost completely to a stop before we landed. Nearby, an explosion shook the earth as the creature's body plowed into it. Flames and smoke billowed through the air.

Visala knelt in the sand, still cradling me in his strong, trembling grip. "Are you all right?" he asked for the second time that day, his voice breathless.

I looked into his silver eyes and nodded. "You saved me."

"Blaze, are you . . ." Onyx came running over, panting and out of breath. His eyes took in Visala and me.

Realizing I was still lying in the seraph's arms, I got up, careful not to brush up against him. "I'm fine."

I turned to Onyx. "It was your idea to use the spear and the cloak wasn't it?" Standing on my tiptoes, I threw my arms around his neck. When he didn't hug me back, I let go and stepped away. "What's wrong?"

He looked away. "I'm just glad you're okay."

Was he angry? Scared? Embarrassed? Wishing I understood guys half as well as Cinder did, I turned and tried to
wipe off the black liquid smeared across my body.

The three of us watched the smoking crater where the
creature had landed. An inky cloud still trailed into the sky.
"What was that thing?"

Onyx frowned, as if he should somehow have been
expecting it. "I don't know. I've never seen anything
remotely close to that big or that strong. When I saw it carry
you away . . ." He shrugged and ran a palm across his head.

"How's Cinder?" I asked.

He shook his head. "Not good."

By the time we got back to the shattered pillar, Cinder
was still sitting on the ground, shaking so hard I could hear
her teeth chattering together like dice. "Hey," I said, hoping
to cheer her up. "That was quite a ride, huh?"

Her skin felt like ice, and she didn't even look up
at my words.

"What's wrong?" I whispered.

Onyx shook his head. "Shock, maybe. I think that
really messed her up."

"You're all right," I said, taking her hand. "It can't hurt
you anymore."

As Onyx and Visala gathered up the packs and weapons, the realization of what had just happened slowly
sank in. We'd survived something two dozen efreet guards
hadn't. We were all alive, and other than a few cuts and
scratches, uninjured.

Even Father seemed to be celebrating in his own odd
way. He'd drawn two parallel lines in the sand, and was
running back and forth between them, roaring at the top
of his lungs.

Cinder had taken off her cloak earlier, perhaps in an
attempt to blend in better. Sitting down beside her, I pulled

it over her shoulders and rubbed her fingers between mine. "Hey," I said, trying to catch her eyes. "It's okay now. *You're* okay. You don't have to be afraid."

It was as if she hadn't heard me at all. She continued to stare straight ahead, her body shaking. Onyx pulled a blanket out of his pack, and I wrapped it around her.

"How's she doing?" he asked, kneeling beside us.

I shook my head. "Maybe we better stop here and rest for a while."

I'd never seen Cinder like this before. Ever since the guards had taken us for questioning, she hadn't been herself. One minute, she was fearless, willing to try anything. The next minute, she was afraid of everything. Panicking had nearly cost Cinder her life.

"All right," Onyx said. "Let's camp here. It's going to get hot, and I'd like to get a couple more hours of travel in while it's still morning. But we've had a long day, and it's probably better if we all get plenty of rest. The important thing is we're okay."

Sparrow, who had been trying to calm Father down, stopped and looked out in the distance. "No," she said softly, shielding her eyes with one hand. "No. I don't think we are okay at all."

"What are you talking about?" I stood and looked in the same direction, wondering if this was some kind of hume play for attention.

Onyx was the second one to see it. He sucked in his breath and whispered, "No," in a voice that didn't sound anything like him.

Visala shook his head. "It can't be."

"What are you talking about?" I asked, staring. The sky was glowing a soft pink now, and except for assorted rocks and a few stunted bushes or two, the horizon was empty. Except . . . I squinted. Something about the horizon was wrong. It seemed to be . . . *moving*. As I realized what I was seeing, a feeling of despair struck me so completely, it was all I could do not to fall down next to Cinder and give up.

The black line I'd taken for the horizon wasn't the ground at all. It *was* moving, and quickly. Like the creature we'd miraculously fought off, it was coming straight toward us. Only this time, it wasn't one monster flying through the sky. It was hundreds.

CHAPTER 22

Frozen by terror, the three of us stood shoulder to shoulder, watching the black line draw ever closer. I was beginning to think my initial guess of hundreds had been low. It was like a black cloud—growing bigger as it got nearer.

"We can't fight that," Visala said. "We have to run." And still he stood unmoving, watching.

"Where?" Onyx asked, his voice robbed of all emotion. "There's no place to hide. We can't even make it back to the city."

I tried to think. But all I could do was stare at the approaching horror that had grown from a line to dots, and now distinct individual shapes, in less than a minute. I could clearly picture how the sky would look packed with such a horde of those monsters that the cavern ceiling would be completely blacked out.

"What if we . . ." Sparrow began, before closing her mouth and shaking her head. "No. There's no way to escape this."

For once, I agreed completely with a hume. Death was coming for us, and we had two choices. Wait for it here, or run and buy ourselves an extra five minutes of life. Ten if we were lucky. I found myself envying Cinder, who appeared to have no idea what was happening.

On the other side of the formation, Father was still running back and forth, roaring louder than ever.

"Do something to shut him up!" I yelled, clapping my hands over my ears. If I was going to die, I didn't want the last thing I heard to be a maniacal, screeching hume.

Sparrow started toward him, but Visala stopped her. "What's he doing?"

The hume woman flapped her hands. "I told you. He gets confused sometimes. He's afraid."

"Can't you talk to him?"

She looked at the old man with a depth of emotion that surprised me from a hume. "Anyone can talk to him. He's not deaf. He just doesn't always listen."

"Come on." Onyx picked up his pack. "We've got to go."

"Where?" I grabbed my pack too.

"I don't know," he said. "But I'm not going to wait here to die." He gently shook Cinder. When she didn't respond, he slung her pack over one shoulder and lifted her onto the other.

"Wait," Visala said. "The old man knew about the river. Maybe he knows something that can help us here." I couldn't believe he'd fallen for the humes' lies as well. Obviously, the old man was out of his mind. The hume woman had only used him to get us to bring her along.

Visala stepped between the lines Father had drawn on the ground and stood in front of him. "Can you hear me?'

The hume quit his growling and looked up at the seraph.

"Do you know how to stop those?" Visala pointed at the approaching creatures that were now close enough to make out their individual shapes. "Or escape from them?"

Father looked at the black shapes, and for a moment everyone was silent—listening, waiting. A tiny part of me wondered, *Could he know something? Is it possible he'd*

Then the crazy old hume stepped around Visala and started roaring again, running between the parallel lines from one end to the other and back. Over and over.

"Come on," I said. "We'll go toward the mountains. Maybe there's something we can't see from here." Clearly there was nothing—nothing that we could reach in the few minutes we had left to live.

Visala's shoulders slumped.

"It's not his fault," Sparrow said. "He's been hurt more than you can imagine. There's so much inside his head that can't get out." She crossed to the old man and held his hands. "Come on, Father."

The old hume refused to go. He pulled away from her grasp, stomped his foot, and ran to the end of the lines. Sparrow took his shoulders. "We need to leave."

The old man bared his teeth and roared, almost as if he really *was* trying to tell us something. The noise he was making sounded familiar. I got the feeling that if I listened to it a little longer, I would remember what it reminded me of.

Visala leaned over to pick up his pack, then spun around. "Wait!" He turned to the old man. "Are you trying to say . . ."

Father looked at Visala, his eyes bright. He roared and ran to the end of the lines.

Visala clapped his hand to his forehead. "Of course. Why haven't we been listening?" He flew briefly into the air, turned in a circle, and dropped back to the earth, clutching his shoulder in pain. "This way," he said pulling on his pack with his good arm and running to the right of the direction we'd been going.

As soon as the seraph began to run, Father stepped

from between his lines and followed, a wide grin on his face. Sparrow grabbed her belongings to run with them.

"Where are you going?" Onyx yelled. There wasn't much cover except for a few small bushes and rocks where we were, but there was nothing but open sand in the direction they were running for as far as I could see. It was part of the reason we'd stayed to this side. If we went that way, we'd be completely in the open.

"The creatures will see us for sure out there!" I screamed.

"There's no time to explain," Visala called over his shoulder. "Run! We may already be too late."

Onyx looked at me, and I held up my hands. Clearly Visala thought he knew something, but how could running through an empty desert protect us from a sky full of monsters? Behind us, the first screech made up our minds, and we broke into a sprint together, with Cinder still on Onyx's back.

"Do you want me to take Cinder's pack?" I called.

"No need," he yelled back. "I'll be dead long before I get tired." That wasn't a comforting thought.

"Faster!" Visala shouted, racing across the dry, hot desert.

Onyx and I picked up our pace. I was amazed at how fast the old hume could move once he put his mind to it. He ran like a spawnling, arms swinging, head thrown back, hair streaming behind him in a long, stringy, fluttering gray banner. I was running almost all out—holding back only enough to keep from leaving Onyx behind—and still Visala and the humes were threatening to pull away.

I chanced a quick peek over my shoulder and nearly fell. The monsters were much closer. It was hard to describe creatures the size of houses as a swarm. But that's what they looked like. Diving and twisting, so close together they nearly brushed wings, they filled the air with a solid wall of gray and black. It was clear they'd seen us. They were coming even more quickly than before, sensing their prey was trying to escape.

"Hurry!" Visala called. "This way!"

The creatures screeched back as though answering him.

We ran without stopping for what felt like forever, but couldn't have been more than four or five minutes. Onyx was strong. I suspected he could carry all of us on his back if he had to without breaking a sweat. But speed had never been his strong suit. He panted for breath. Sweat poured off his face and soaked the back of his robe. Without asking, I took Cinder's pack from him.

"How much farther?" I yelled.

"I don't know." Visala looked back, and even beneath his aura, I could see his eyes go wide. "Keep running!"

A welcome wind pushed against me, and for a second, I was grateful—until I peered over my shoulder and realized it was coming from the creatures. Needle-filled mouths open, they were racing each other to see who'd be the first to get a meal. They'd be on us in a minute, maybe less.

Onyx stumbled and almost went down. His chest heaved. Howls and shrieks filled the air behind us, along with an unearthly roar that could only be the beating of the creatures' wings. Everyone gasped now. Father leaned on Sparrow, looking as if he might collapse any minute. Even Visala's stride had gone ragged. Sparrow might still have had a sprint left in her, but I could tell she wouldn't leave Father behind—just as I refused to leave Onyx.

A shadow fell over us. I looked up to see three of the creatures break from the pack. They swooped down, talons outstretched. It was over. Whatever Visala thought he was looking for, he hadn't found it. Miles of open sand surrounded us. I looked at Onyx's drawn face. "I'm . . . sorry," I puffed. "I wish . . . things were . . . different."

Onyx shook his head, tongue lolling over his lower lip. "Shouldn't have . . . brought . . ." That was all he could get out.

Ahead of us, Visala spread his wings and rose into the air. I didn't blame him. Flying would only buy him an extra minute or so of life, but I couldn't begrudge him that.

It turned out it wouldn't buy him even that. Lured either by his glow or his flight, the creatures passed over our heads and went for him.

He strained to stay ahead of them, but it was too much. As they closed in, his wings gave out and he tumbled from the air. The creatures shrieked with triumph. They dove toward him, and all three burst into flames at the same time.

I was so shocked, I stumbled to a stop. One second, the three creatures had been closing with incredible speed. The next second, they were plummeting to the ground in a ball of flames. Smoke billowed from their ruined bodies.

"Come on!" Visala screamed, his voice hoarse with effort. Onyx had stopped too, apparently as stunned as I was. I grabbed his hand, and the two of us raced forward. What could have done that? What could kill three of the enormous creatures at once? Father tripped, and Sparrow caught him around the waist.

Above us, two creatures dove. Pulling Onyx, I sprinted with the last of my strength. His breathing was a high-pitched whistle, and his eyes were red. We caught up with the humes as shadows blacked out the morning light. Hot sulfur breath blew across my neck. "Dive!" I shouted, lunging for the spot where Visala waved us forward.

The four of us hit the ground, and behind us, something sizzled and popped. Bright light lit the desert floor, followed by two ground-shaking thuds. I looked back to see five monster corpses burning, two of them stacked in a leathery black pile, popping and sizzling from the flames.

But hundreds more were coming. Getting to my hands and knees, I tried to keep crawling, but Visala stopped me. "Right here, it's safe. Don't go any farther."

I still had no idea what was going on. Only Visala appeared to understand. He and Father—who, despite his exhaustion, was practically dancing with joy.

"What is it?' I gasped. Three more creatures flew at us in a line. And just as each began their dive toward us, a loud, hissing pop sent them flaming to the ground. As the third creature flew to its death, I looked up at just the right angle to see two silver bars appear, shrouded by blue, before they blinked out of sight again.

Staring up, I remembered why the sound Father had been making seemed so familiar. Onyx had seen it too. I could tell by the shocked expression on his face.

"The Stygian," I said. "He was trying to imitate the roar of the Stygian."

Onyx shook his head slowly back and forth as a ninth and tenth creature burst into flames. "How can they be running into the tracks when the tracks aren't there?"

* * *

Two hours later, we had all eaten and were resting under a single open shelter Onyx and Sparrow had erected. Cinder was sleeping soundly, though I questioned how soundly every time I saw her twitch. At least we had managed to get a little food in her, and she was no longer shivering. Father, who had eaten nearly as much as Onyx and Visala combined, snored loudly enough that I wondered if he was dreaming about the Stygian too. Lying by his side, Sparrow had her eyes closed, but I suspected she might not actually be sleeping.

"I still can't believe the tracks have been there all

along," I said, softly enough to not wake the others. "I saw them fly through the air on Arrival Day. Just before the Stygian came."

"You only thought you saw that," Onyx said. "It's what Judgment wanted you to believe. But that was an illusion. It looked like the tracks were flying across the desert because they made them appear from one end to the other. The rest of the time, they kept them invisible to keep people from trying to climb out on them." He glared at Visala.

"If they were always there, why didn't we—" I began, before looking at the smoldering remains in the sand.

"We wouldn't have gotten far," the seraph said.

Nearly two dozen creatures lay smoldering on the desert floor, having been cooked alive by some kind of protective force surrounding the tracks. Eventually the rest had realized attacking us wasn't a good idea. Now they circled lazily less than a quarter league away—waiting and watching.

Onyx growled in the back of his throat. "What else are you keeping from us that might cost our lives?"

"Might *save* your lives, you mean?" Visala lay on his blanket, resting on his side and doodling with his finger in the sand. "I told you I had no idea the tracks mattered one way or another until I realized what Father was trying to say. Even if we'd all known they were there, none of us could have guessed they could be used as a defense. I didn't. All I knew was that Father wanted us to reach them. I swear, the rest was a surprise."

I glanced over at the old figure so obviously enjoying his sleep. "How do you think *he* knew?"

Onyx rubbed his chin thoughtfully. "He's been in Hell a long time. I don't think even Sparrow knows how long. Maybe he was part of the group of humes who tried to escape. Maybe there was a survivor no one knew about."

Visala said nothing.

The seraph seemed good at keeping his thoughts to himself when he wanted to. I knew Onyx didn't trust him. And with good reason. If he knew about the tracks, what else might he know that he was holding back? I definitely didn't trust the humes. Father might be crazy, or maybe he only wanted us to think he was. The language he shared only with Sparrow allowed them to keep secrets while appearing to speak openly.

I wasn't even sure how far I trusted Onyx. He might not be hiding as much as Visala or the humes, but even when he'd taken me to the roof of the Immigration Station, it appeared he'd only told me as much as he wanted me to know. I suspected there was more to why he was helping Visala than clearing our names and getting angel-fire.

Cinder, the only person I felt like I could talk to about almost anything, seemed to be going through some kind of breakdown.

"You better get some rest," Visala said to me. "We'll probably be walking all night."

Onyx scowled and moved his blanket so he was lying between the seraph and me.

Visala caught my eye and grinned before rolling over.

One thing I knew for sure: There were secrets being kept, and I intended to find out as many of them as I could before we reached Judgment—even if it meant using the kinds of tactics Cinder was better known for. Our ability to get safely there and back might depend on it.

CHAPTER 23

I woke to the sound of Father's hooting and the smell of cooking food. "What time is it?" I asked, rubbing my hands across my eyes. The sky was still the pinkish-orange of late morning, so I couldn't have slept too long. But my muscles felt slow and sludgy, like I'd been lying in one position for hours.

"Dinnertime," Onyx said, stirring a pot over a small fire.

"Huh?" I checked the sky again. It wasn't the color of late morning turning toward noon, as I'd thought. It was late afternoon, bordering on evening. I got up and groaned as red-hot pain knifed through my arms and legs.

"The demon princess warrior finally awakens," Visala said. He was standing just outside the shelter, hands on the small of his back, gazing up at the sky.

"What's a princess?" I asked, feeling grumpy that I'd slept so long while everyone else appeared to have been up and around for a while.

"I doubt you'd take it as a compliment," he said. "I got the warrior part right though. Nice to see you showing at least *some* effects from your little flight. After you almost single-handedly rode that beast into the ground, I was beginning to think you were invulnerable."

"I didn't ride anything into the ground. If it weren't for you . . ." I left the sentence unfinished, not wanting to consider how things might have ended if Visala hadn't rescued me. And if he hadn't deciphered Father's message. He'd saved my life twice in less than an hour. "How's your wing?" I asked changing the subject.

"Not too bad." He stretched his shoulders and immediately groaned. That and the tightness in his face made it clear he wasn't nearly as well off as he was pretending. "All right," he said, noticing my skepticism. "Maybe I won't be doing any flying for a while."

I hoped he wouldn't have to. The tracks led all the way to Judgment, and the winged monsters didn't seem any more willing to try their luck with the Stygian's defenses than they had when I'd fallen asleep. Walking to his side, I looked up at the dark shapes circling and circling. "Hopefully, they won't figure out all they have to do is land and come for us on foot."

"I'm not sure they can. They're pretty tall. Besides, I've been watching them since I woke up, and not one of them has landed. Maybe those talons aren't made for walking. You'd think they'd have to come down eventually though. If only to rest."

The idea of creatures that never needed rest was not a pleasant one—especially when said creatures were big enough to eat even Onyx in one gulp. "You really didn't know about them?"

"I promise, I was as surprised as you." His face seemed sincere. I wanted to believe him. I couldn't imagine him letting us come that close to being eaten alive if he had known about the monsters. But I had to remind myself he had his own reasons for what he chose to share and what he didn't.

That reminded me of my thoughts just before I'd fallen asleep, and I looked around for Cinder. She was sitting a short distance from the fire—as far from the creatures as possible. She held a blanket wrapped around her shoulders, even though it was still warm enough to bring sweat to the faces of the humes sitting beneath the shade of the tent.

"Hey there," I said, crossing to sit beside her. "How are you doing?" She glanced up at me before dropping her gaze back to her hands folded in her lap. This was definitely not the Cinder I knew. I understood the creatures had frightened her. They'd terrified all of us. But we'd gotten over it. Why couldn't she?

"You're looking better," I lied. Her face was pale, with circles so dark, they nearly looked like a second set of eyes. And her hair was a mess. Back at the academy, she wouldn't have gone as far as the hallway looking like that.

A ghost of a smile crossed her lips. "Liar." She'd caught me. "Not that it matters. Somehow I don't think I'll be competing for the attention of either of your two boyfriends."

I had no idea what she was talking about. Clearly, she still imagined Onyx and I were more than childhood friends. But if she'd also convinced herself Visala would give a demon spawn like me a second glance, she really was out of it. I took her hands in mine and was relieved to find they weren't nearly as clammy as they'd been. "We're going to be all right. The creatures can't get at us as long as we stay beneath the tracks."

The faint smile again, as though she wanted to put on a good front, but didn't have the strength. "They'll find a way. Or something else will. We're going to die out here. I've been amusing myself by trying to decide how and when."

I looked to Onyx for support, but he appeared to be concentrating especially hard on the pieces of dried meat he was shredding before dropping them into the pot. "You've got to stop thinking that way," I said. "We've made it this far."

Cinder stared at her lap for so long, I was afraid she'd drawn back into whatever place she'd been lost in before. Then she ran her tongue across her lips. "Back at the academy, when you volunteered to take the blame for everything—"

"I *was* to blame for everything."

She held up a trembling palm. "Let me say this. I need to get it out, before . . . before anything else happens." She looked at me with such pleading, all I could do was nod. "When I watched you walk into the administration chamber, I realized two things. I was a selfish brat who thought about only herself, and you were the kind of person I wished I could be."

I opened my mouth to tell her that was nonsense, but she stopped me with a look.

"I've known you for a long time, Blaze. And I've known myself even longer. For years, I've told myself I was the brave one because I wasn't afraid to talk to any guy."

"You *were* the brave one," I said. "You still are."

Outlined against the pink of the cavern ceiling, one of the circling shapes gave an angry-sounding cry that was echoed by several of its companions. Cinder shivered and pulled her blanket more tightly around her shoulders. "No. I'm not brave. I'm selfish. That's why I can go up to any guy and have him wrapped around my pinky in minutes. It's because I don't care about his feelings. I don't care if I hurt him. As long as I get what I want, I'm fine. And if I don't get what I want from the first guy, I'll get it from the next one. That's not courage. What you did, walking in to face the council alone, that was courage."

This was so unlike Cinder, I couldn't even respond.

"But that day—can you believe it was just yesterday? It seems like a month ago. A year. That day, I swore I was done being selfish. I was going to be like you. I was going to stop thinking about myself and focus on others for once."

She shook her head and bit her lip, as though the idea seemed as far removed as the day.

"It even worked for a while. When you escaped the questioning, I thought I could make it work. I agreed to come out here." She waved her hand loosely at the empty desert. "I helped us escape the guards. I flew across the river. I really thought I was being brave."

"You *were* being brave," I said, meaning every word of it. I couldn't disagree that she was selfish at times. But wasn't everyone? "I can't imagine another girl I know doing what you did."

"No." She laughed. It was a harsh sound. A hurtful laugh—aimed directly at herself. I didn't like it at all. If a sound could cut skin, she'd be bleeding in a hundred places. "I was being selfish all over again. I was looking out for myself. I just found a new way to do it. When I found myself looking back at Hell from across the Styx—when I realized what I'd gotten myself into—all I could think of was finding a way out of this mess. No matter who it hurt. Even if it meant betraying the rest of you. If I could have crossed back over and blamed it all on you and Onyx, I would have."

"But you didn't. That's the important thing. You didn't, you kept going."

"No." She shook her head vigorously. "I kept going because I had no choice. And as soon as I saw that creature, I panicked. I ran because I hoped it would let me escape while it went after the rest of you. I was still thinking about myself. I can't be like you, Blaze. Never. It's not in me."

"Cinder . . ."

She squeezed my hands, the pain on her face so obvious, I wanted to hold her until I could make it go away. When I leaned toward her, though, she pulled back. "Let me finish. Please. I'm almost done."

I nodded, wondering what else she could possibly say. What other way she could find to injure herself.

"I'm never going to be like you, Blaze. I'll only ever care about myself, and as long as I do, I'm going to put the rest of you in danger. I've realized that if I really want to stop hurting people, there's only one way to do it. I'm staying here."

I was sure I must have misunderstood.

She scooped a handful of gravelly grayish-brown sand and let it trickle between her fingers into a pile in front of her. "I'd go back if I didn't know I'd break under questioning. We both saw how well I handled that last time. I'll stay here. If you do make it to Judgment and back, you'll know where to find me. If not . . . at least I'll know I wasn't responsible for your deaths."

Cinder was a lot of things. Silly, flirtatious to the extreme, a little self-absorbed most of the time, a lot occasionally. But she was also kind and funny. She could shake me out of my worst moods with just the right words. She could read people's feelings better than anyone I knew. And despite what she'd said, I didn't think she was a quitter.

I scooped up my own handful of sand and added to the pile she was making. "When I was a spawnling, my father used to tell me I was the most willful child he'd ever met. He said he was afraid of letting me anywhere near an active volcano for fear I'd wander into it, just to see where the lava came from."

Cinder giggled. It was short and not very loud, but it was a good sound—a Cinder sound. "That's what I mean. You're so brave."

"No." I mashed the sand pile flat with the palm of my hand and waited until she met my eyes. "I'm not brave, I'm impulsive. I do things without thinking and end up suffering because of it. I have a quick trigger, and an even quicker temper. What you said outside the administration chamber was right. I did get you into this. I'm not sure how much I'd change if I could go back and do it all over again. But one thing's for sure: I'd be positive no one was hurt by my decisions but me."

She opened her mouth, and I shook a finger at her. "I want you to come. I *need* you to come." I was pretty sure Onyx was listening in on our conversation, and maybe Visala as well. That was fine, let them hear what I had to say. "You think you're selfish? Maybe you are, but I am too. And for my own selfish purposes, I refuse to leave you behind. You're the only person whose motives are out in the open. I need you because you're the only person I can completely trust."

I expected her to argue more. But Cinder had always been the best at hearing things people didn't say out loud. She looked at me, then let her eyes move beyond me to Onyx and Visala. Finally, she glanced at the humes, who were watching us from inside the shelter. "Okay," she said, her voice low enough that only I could hear. "I can do that. For you. You saved my life. Watching your back is the least I can do."

Onyx surprised us again with dinner—this time by cooking a stew better than anything the cafeteria served—then we packed up our gear and followed the path of the tracks. I was worried it would be hard to stay directly under them. But it turned out if you looked up carefully enough, and from the right angle, you could just make out a slight distortion in the air where they ran.

"If you can't see the ripple in the air, just keep an eye on *them*," Visala said, pointing to the creatures keeping pace with us in the sky to either side. "Apparently they can tell where the tracks are too." He veered a little to the left to demonstrate his point—several of the creatures immediately broke from the rest of the formation and glided toward us. Not until he moved back under the protection of the tracks did they circle around to join the swarm again.

Personally, I could have done without the demonstration.

For the most part, the hike was uneventful. It seemed all of us were either too tired or too lost in our own thoughts to say much. Sometime around midnight, though, I saw something moving off to our right. Startled, I peered into the night and spotted a pack of dark shapes with four legs and oddly large heads loping across the desert floor. They ran just close enough that I could see them racing through the darkness, but too far to tell exactly what they were.

"They've been tailing us for about an hour," Onyx said.

"Why aren't they attacking?" I asked, trying to get a better look.

"I don't know." Onyx took out his whip and cracked it in the air. One of the creatures yelped. I thought it sounded decidedly more hungry than afraid.

About an hour later, we discovered why they were maintaining their distance. "Look," Cinder called. I turned to see one of the creatures rise up onto its hind legs and charge toward us, running with an awkward but speedy gait. Onyx pulled out his fireball launcher, and Visala withdrew his sword. But before the shape got halfway to us, one of the flying creatures swooped out of the sky and swallowed it whole.

In the brief glimpse I got before it disappeared into the monster's mouth, it looked like a mix between the body of a goat and a hume. The reason for its misshaped head was that it was almost completely mouth. I turned away, not wanting to see any more.

"Guess they'll take whatever they can get," Sparrow said in a tone that made it clear she wished she hadn't seen it either.

The pack continued to follow us, but after hours of walking through the night in a single-file line—trudging over a landscape that was mile after mile of the exact same featureless terrain—even that lost its ability to hold my interest. Eventually I fell into a kind of dozing half-awake state where my feet continued to shuffle forward while my chin drifted onto my chest, jerked up, then slowly drooped back down again.

I had no idea how long we'd been walking when Onyx came to a stop so abruptly that I ran straight into his back. It was like stepping face-first into a brick wall. "A little warning next time," I complained, rubbing my nose.

"They're gone," he said.

My first thought was that he was talking about the pack of half-goat, half-hume creatures. But he was staring into the sky. I followed his gaze. The first traces of pink were painting the cavern ceiling, but no huge, winged shapes circled above us.

"Did they land somewhere during the night?" I asked.

"I don't think so," Visala said, stopping beside us. "I think we must have passed some sort of barrier."

"The things are gone too," Sparrow said, pointing to where the pack had been.

She was right, the flying monsters and the goat-hume things were all gone. At some point during the night, they'd returned back to wherever they called home—leaving us to continue our trek alone. It should have been a relief, yet I found myself staring at the miles of desert between us and the mountains of Judgment with an even greater fear than before.

"The question is, what's going to take their place?" Cinder whispered as we began setting up camp, summing up my feelings perfectly.

CHAPTER 24

"Watch your mouth, hume."

"I knew you were low, but this is even below demon standards."

"That's it, you pasty-faced rodent. If no one else is willing to put you in your place, I will!"

"Try it, blue skin!"

I woke up groggily to the sound of an argument that seemed to be escalating quickly into all-out war.

I'd been having a horrifying dream where two unseen creatures each held one of my arms, pulling in opposite directions until I could feel my muscles and joints tearing apart. For a moment I thought I was still asleep, and this was just a continuation of the nightmare.

The unmistakable zap of a souljab, followed by a cry of pain and a pair of rapid thuds, then a scream of anger and surprise, pulled me out of the dream haze and onto my feet. Reaching for my own weapon, I saw Cinder and Sparrow facing off with one another just beyond our piled supplies.

The hume had a bright red welt on one bare shoulder. She lunged at Cinder, swinging a black metal rod nearly the length of her arm. Cinder, trying to struggle out of a silver cable wrapped around both arms and her chest, ducked beneath the attack and fired off a random burst with her souljab that nearly caught the roof of the shelter on fire.

"Stand down!" Visala's aura spiked as he commanded Cinder and Sparrow. At his words, both of them backed away from one another, their faces drawn tight in snarls that made it clear they weren't doing so by choice.

An energy that reminded me of the force protecting the tracks thickened the air until I felt like I could reach out and touch it. But a moment later, the seraph's glow flickered on and off so quickly, I might have thought I'd imagined it if the energy hadn't disappeared along with it. It was the same thing that had happened the day I'd found Visala buried beneath the rubble, and at least a couple of times since. At the time, I'd thought he was doing it on purpose for some reason. Now I wondered if it might be unintentional—related in some way to his injury.

At once, Cinder and Sparrow were back at each other. Before either could get in the next blow, Onyx stepped between them. Holding each by the soft spot between her neck and shoulder, he frowned. "Aren't the creatures out there bad enough without you two attacking one another?"

"The demon did something to our water," Sparrow said, her fingers tightening on her weapon.

"That's a lie," Cinder spat back. "I'd rather die of thirst than touch anything a hume put to her filthy mouth."

"Water?" Onyx asked, clearly concerned.

Visala picked up one of the canteens lying in the sand by the packs and put it to his mouth. He spit the water out with a grimace. "Salt."

Onyx's frown deepened. Water was the one thing we couldn't survive without here. We'd carefully rationed enough to get us to Judgment and back. "Are they all salted?"

Visala tested each of the cloth-wrapped metal bottles in Sparrow's backpack before moving on to the others. "Only the humes'. The rest seem to be fine."

"I can't believe you'd do this." Onyx glared at Cinder, his fingers tightening on her neck. "No matter how much you hate humes."

"I didn't," she yelped, trying to pry his hand away.

"What makes you so sure it was Cinder?" I asked, as Onyx released them both, watching closely in case either of them tried to get at the other.

"Who else could it be?" the hume demanded. "Father and I both drank before we went to sleep. I didn't touch our water again until *she* woke me to take my turn."

After setting up the shelter that morning, we'd all agreed the disappearance of the creatures made us nervous. Onyx came up with the idea of each of us taking two-hour turns at guard duty while the rest slept. He'd suggested the order of himself, Sparrow, Visala, and me—intentionally leaving Cinder to rest and recover.

But Cinder insisted that all five of us take a turn, volunteering for the first shift. I thought it was a good thing at the time—a sign that she was learning to at least tolerate the humes. Could it have been part of a plan to take revenge on them for forcing their way into our party?

Cinder hunched her shoulder defensively. "Anyone could have gotten to the canteens."

Sparrow smirked. "We certainly didn't tamper with our own water. Did one of you three?"

Visala, Onyx, and I looked at each other, intentionally avoiding Cinder's eyes. I knew I hadn't done it, and Visala and Onyx both seemed as surprised to discover the salt as I was.

"Can you fix it?" I asked Visala. "The way you changed the water in our room?"

He paused for a moment before shaking his head. "I don't think I better."

"Why not?" Onyx asked, his eyes flashing.

"I don't need to explain myself to you." The seraph's jaw tightened, and I wondered if a second fight was about to break out. It wasn't exactly a secret that Visala and Onyx were only cooperating because they had no other choice. "Besides, we've still got enough to reach Judgment if we're careful. Once we get there, I can get you water that makes this stuff taste like pond muck."

I had no idea what a "pond" was. But if it would help settle things down, I was all for it.

Onyx blew out through his clenched teeth. "And we're supposed to trust you again? How do we know you didn't ruin the water yourself to make us more dependent on you?"

"I guess you don't," Visala said.

The tension in the shelter was as thick as the seraph's energy had been earlier. Only Father slept soundly through all the commotion. "I'll empty the bad water and redistribute the canteens," I said, trying to ease tempers a little.

I eyed Cinder, wondering if she'd refuse to share, but she only snapped her tail and stalked to her blanket. "Do whatever you want."

"I'm keeping our water with me from now on," Sparrow said. Part of me wanted to smack her hume face for suggesting demons were the ones who couldn't be trusted. But considering I wasn't sure Cinder *hadn't* done it, I satisfied myself by throwing her canteens to her extra hard.

"I think it would be a good idea for all of us to keep our belongings close," Onyx said, targeting a meaningful stare in Visala's direction.

"You believe me, don't you?" Cinder whispered once we were both resting again.

I swallowed. "Of course. But why would anyone else want to ruin the humes' water?"

"Maybe it was the Halo, like Onyx said. Don't you think it's a little suspicious he refuses to fix it?"

I did. But I couldn't think of any reason for him to take a risk like that. He needed water as much as we did. And honestly, how could we be any more dependent on him than we already were?

Cinder slid a little closer. "What if it wasn't one of us at all? What if it was something out *there*?" She squinted toward the desert.

"Did you see anything while you were on guard duty?"

"No. But I *felt* something—watching and waiting for us. And when the wind blew the right direction, I thought I could smell something."

I didn't know what to think. Cinder was my best friend, and I wanted to believe her. But she had the strongest reason to get back at the humes, and the best chance to do it. Whether it was due to the stress of not knowing who I could trust, or Cinder's suggestion that something was watching us, I had a hard time falling back asleep. Once I did, I kept jerking awake, sure I'd heard stealthy footsteps coming toward me.

During my turn at guard duty, I found myself searching the horizon and sniffing the air. At one point, I turned to see Visala leaning on an elbow, watching me.

"You feel it too, don't you?" he asked in a hushed voice.

I stared out at the coming evening, almost wishing I could see something. I didn't think anything could be worse than the fear of not knowing. "What do you think it is?"

He shook his head. "Don't know. But I suspect we'll find out soon enough."

The wind began picking up as Onyx started cooking dinner, and by the time he was finished, it was blowing steadily, stinging our eyes and faces with flying sand.

"Not one of my better efforts," he said as we all ate silently with our backs to the gusts and our hands trying to hold our plates and keep our cloaks from blowing off of us.

I hadn't noticed. I wasn't very hungry. With the wind came the smell Cinder thought she had detected earlier. It was all too easy to pick up now—a dark, musty scent that made me imagine dust that had lain undisturbed for a hundred years, or caves where the only living things oozed from the walls, ready to plop into little wet piles if you brushed against them.

No one seemed to have much of an appetite. Even Father only picked at his food. Instead, we hunched into ourselves, saying little, peering into the darkness that closed quickly, and jumping at even the smallest noises. Taking down the shelter was an onerous chore. Even with all of us holding the pieces, one of them whipped out of our grips and disappeared into the night like a fleeing specter.

For the first time on our journey, Sparrow lit a small brass lamp, adjusting the wick to get the biggest flame possible. In the growing storm, it flickered and danced, barely illuminating more than a few steps ahead of her.

"How far can you see?" Visala asked.

"Not far enough," Onyx grunted. "I think we'd better tie ourselves together to avoid getting separated."

Looped together like a herd of goats being led to the butcher, we staggered into the night. Soon the wind blew so hard that even breathing was difficult. I pulled up the neck of my cloak until there was only a narrow slit between it and the front of my hood to peek through. Although the rope snapping stiffly in front of me told me Onyx was a few steps ahead, I could barely make out the hint of a dark shape leaning into the storm.

"Can you see where you're going?" Visala's disembodied voice rose and fell on the waves of sand-drenched air.

"Not very well." Onyx's answer was snatched away by the storm.

"Maybe we should stop and wait it out?" At first it

sounded like Visala had moved up on my left. Then on my right.

The rope went slack for a moment before pulling tight again. "We can't afford to lose a-a-a-a ni-i-i-i-ght of trav—" Strange swirls of air caught Onyx's words and twisted them, cutting some off and drawing others out. "-ve ten-n-n-n min-it-s."

"What?" Visala shouted.

"Ten more minutes!" I yelled back, feeling like Father's translator.

As we stumbled across ground we couldn't see, I tried not to imagine shapes stalking us, their movements hidden by the storm. Things like the goat-humes with heads that were all mouth or monsters soaring hungrily through the night filled my head, along with images much worse.

Just when I was about to untie myself from the rope and run screaming into the night, a voice called out of the darkness. "—op—ther." It sounded like Sparrow.

"What did she say?" Onyx shouted back.

"Something about Father, I think." Bits of stinging sand burned my throat when I opened my mouth. A minute or so later, a stooped creature appeared in front of me, changing into Onyx as it got nearer. Wrapping an arm protectively around me, he reeled in the rope until we found Cinder. Together, the three of us made our way back to two pools of light that turned out to be Visala and Sparrow, trying to provide at least a little cover for Father.

The old hume had both hands tilted together over his head like the roof of a house. Even I could translate that.

"He says we need to find shelter," Sparrow said, coughing as she tried to outshout the storm.

"Great plan," Onyx said. "Did he happen to say where we can locate this shelter?"

The hume shook her head.

"Maybe we could put up the tent again?" Cinder suggested.

"Not a chance." Onyx squinted upward, as though searching for the cause of the wind that was so strong, everyone except for him had to lean into it to stay upright.

"I've never seen a storm like this," I said, holding the cloth of my robe across my mouth. "I don't think it's natural."

Visala nodded. "Maybe we better huddle here and wait it out."

Onyx opened his mouth as though he was going to argue, then closed it and tilted his head. "Shhh. Did you hear that?"

I listened, closing my eyes to concentrate better. All I could hear was the storm growling steadily, like a living thing determined to beat us down if it couldn't make us turn back. Then a sound like a crying spawnling cut through the wind.

"What is it?" I asked, opening my eyes.

"It sounds like a child in pain," Visala said, pointing to our left.

Onyx pointed to the right. "A woman screaming."

The sound came again, a mournful howling that went on and on until I wanted to slap my hands over my ears.

"No." Cinder's eyes went wide as she put a hand to her mouth. "It's not a child or a woman." Unmindful of the storm, she let her hood blow from her head. "It's a hellhound."

Visala withdrew his sword and held it above his head like a torch. "What's a hellhound?"

"Nothing," Onyx said, his brow pulled so low, his eyes nearly disappeared. "They aren't real." I wasn't as good at reading people as Cinder, but it was easy enough to see he was worried about losing control of the group.

"He's right," I said, putting an arm around Cinder's shoulder. Visala still looked confused, so I explained. "Hellhounds are make-believe creatures. In stories, they come in the night for bad demons and carry them to Absolute Zero."

"Absolute Zero is real," Visala said, and for a moment I was shocked that he would know about something so unique to Hell. Then I remembered he could send a demon there with a swing of his angel-fire sword. Spending so much time together, I'd started to think of him as a friend and not a celestial being. That could end up being a mistake.

"Well, hellhounds *aren't* real," Onyx said.

The howl came again, cutting through the rage of the storm much more effectively than it should have. I could swear it was closer than it had been before. It seemed to be coming from behind us.

"Let's go," Visala said. "Whatever it is, I don't like the idea of facing it in this. We've either got to outrun it or find a place where the wind isn't so bad."

Onyx nodded grudgingly. "Try and stay close."

Clutching one another and hanging on to the ropes, we fled through the storm. It was impossible to tell which way we were going. I hoped we'd left the flying creatures behind, because we'd never be able to find the tracks again.

The only thing that gave me any sense of direction at all was the ghostly howling that urged us forward. Sometimes it seemed closer. Sometimes farther away. But it never disappeared completely, as though whatever was out there was playing with us, intentionally matching our pace. I knew Onyx was right; hellhounds weren't real. But every time the bone-jarring scream echoed through the night, I couldn't help imagining a broad-shouldered beast with a pelt of thick gray fur and long curved tusks to carry off its prey.

A howl split the night, this time from our right. "There." Cinder pointed. "I saw it."

"What did you see?" I asked. The sand—blowing nearly parallel with the ground—made it impossible to discern anything. At the same time, if you stared into it long enough, you could imagine seeing whatever your mind conjured up.

"Eyes." She shuddered beneath my grip. "Glowing eyes."

Onyx shook his head. If anyone could see through this mess, it would be him. "This way," he said, dragging us to the left.

A shriek came so close from our right, I could have sworn whatever made it was on top of us. A second later, it came from our left.

"There are two of them," Sparrow said, holding Father close. The old man looked terrified. He kept raising his hands over his head. I didn't blame him. The howls would have been bad enough under normal circumstances. With visibility close to zero, I felt completely helpless. I kept fighting against the claws that wanted to spring from my fingers, knowing I'd lose all control if I gave in to the panic.

Something growled from directly behind us. Onyx spun around.

"Can you see it?" I yelled, as his lips thinned.

"No. I mean . . . keep going. We've got to stay ahead." He gasped, pulling us until we were sprinting blindly through the night.

The howls came faster and closer—from both sides and behind—driving us. There had to be dozens of them out there. Maybe it was my imagination, but I began to think I could see flashes of red through the blowing curtain of sand.

"What are they waiting for?" Sparrow screamed.

As if they'd heard her question, a pair of howls sounded in front of us. Onyx skidded to a halt, his head swiveling. A chorus of howls and growls came from all sides. "We're surrounded," he shouted. "Take out your weapons and form a circle, back-to-back, with Father in the middle."

With Onyx to my left and Cinder to my right, I held my souljab in front of me. Its flame seemed all but useless against the unseen creatures whose cries were nearly as loud as the storm.

"Get ready," Visala said. "I think something's about to happen."

The howls grew louder and louder, coming from every direction, rising into a deafening crescendo before cutting off all at once. At the same time, the storm stopped. For a split second, the sand hung suspended in midair, as if just realizing the wind was no longer there to hold it aloft. Then it fell to the ground with a soft *whump*.

In the suddenly clear night, I stared dumbstruck at what stood before me, and my hands shook so hard, it was all I could do to keep from dropping my weapon. From the darkness, at least a hundred pairs of glowing red eyes stared back at me. They formed a perfect circle around us, standing not quite shoulder to shoulder. Their broad chests were nearly as tall as I was, their heads as tall as Onyx. Gleaming white tusks curved down and forward from their mouths, just like in the stories. Massive paws stood motionless, but I could see claws protruding through tufts of thick gray fur. Plumes of smoke rose from their flaring nostrils.

My voice was hoarse and strained as I whispered, "Hellhounds."

CHAPTER 25

"Don't move," Visala said, his sword swaying slowly left and right, as though he couldn't decide which of the creatures to focus on.

"Why aren't they attacking?" Sparrow whispered. A pair of softly glowing blue balls hung suspended from a silver cord in her left hand.

Now that the wind wasn't blowing, our voices sounded much too loud. I could feel trembling against my right arm, but I didn't know if it was coming from Cinder, me, or both of us. All around, the hellhounds stood perfectly still. The only signs that they were living creatures were their bright eyes, and the constant streams of smoke rising from their muzzles.

Father hooted behind me.

"It's all right," Sparrow answered.

Visala shifted his sword from one hand to the other, and I thought I saw the hounds follow him with their eyes, although their heads never moved. "Does Father have any idea how to get out of this?" he asked.

Sparrow shook her head. "He's terrified."

I looked at the dark gray muzzles, all fixed unwaveringly forward. My mouth was so dry, I could barely swallow. "It's like they're waiting for something."

"Not waiting," Cinder said. "Deciding. They're deciding which of us deserves to be taken to Absolute Zero."

"Stop it," Onyx growled, and the hellhound nearest him pricked up its ears. "Maybe they *are* hellhounds and maybe they *aren't*. But this isn't a story. They're here to stop us from getting to Judgment, not to carry us to Absolute Zero." He tucked his fireball launcher under one arm. "The rest of you stay put. I want to try something."

"Where are you going?" Cinder whimpered, as Onyx took a step toward the hellhounds.

"Just testing something."

He eased forward, and Visala whispered, "Careful."

"You don't have to tell me." Onyx swallowed, waited, and took two more steps. In the light of Sparrow's lamp, I could see sweat gleaming on the back of his head. He walked slowly toward the hellhounds, and for the first time, the creatures moved, swinging their heads to fix red stares on him.

"Stop," Cinder called, and then so softly only I could hear, she added, "Me. They're going to take *me*."

I reached over and gripped her fingers. "I won't let them." There was something in her returning look that I couldn't read.

Onyx was almost halfway to the circle when the hounds directly ahead of him closed ranks and the ones to his left and right stepped forward. "I think that's far enough," I called, my voice cracking.

"I think you're right." Onyx backed away, and the hounds returned to their original positions. "It's like they're holding us here for some reason," he said, joining the rest of us.

"For what?" I asked, pointing around. "Why hold us in the middle of nowhere?"

"*Absolute Zero*," Cinder murmured under her breath.

"What's that over there?" Visala pointed his sword to a small rise in the distance. At first it looked like nothing more than a sand dune. But as I studied it more closely, I could just make out a pair of sharp angles rising above the ground.

"Some kind of building," Onyx said, leaning forward.

He had better eyes than I did, but if it was a building, it was tiny. Sand was piled up against one wall, nearly to the top. "Whatever it is, there's no way to get to it," I said.

"What if we move as a group?" Sparrow suggested. "Maybe the hellhounds aren't trying to hold us in this exact spot, just keeping us together."

"It's worth a try," Visala said. "When I count to three, everyone take a step toward the building . . . One . . . two . . ."

On three, we all stepped in the same direction, still holding our weapons and forming a rough wheel shape with Father as its hub. As with Onyx, the hounds simply watched us until we began to get close. Then they collapsed that side of the circle, forcing us to back away.

"They're smart," Visala said, leading us to the center again. "As long as they keep in formation, there's no way to feint or draw them out. We might be able to attack one or two, but the rest would be on us in an instant."

"They could be trying to starve us," Sparrow said. "Keep us here until we run out of food and water."

"I don't think so." Onyx studied the grizzled faces watching us impassively, before looking beyond them to the empty horizon. "That storm was obviously created to blind us. But it also slowed us down until they had the numbers they needed to hold us in place. It didn't end until we were surrounded. I think they were spread out across the desert. Now I get the feeling they're waiting for . . ."

"Their leader," Visala said. "Look at the way they're

acting—moving in unison, as a team. These are soldiers. This is a pack, and they're waiting for the head to arrive to tell them what to do."

"I don't think they'll have long to wait." Onyx nodded to the left, where far out in the distance, something kicked up a cloud of dust and sand. He cupped his hands to the sides of his face and squinted. "I can't make it out. Can you?"

"No." Visala shook his head. "But whatever it is, it's big. And it's coming quickly. My estimation is they'll be here in fifteen minutes, tops."

I stared at the cloud, but all I could see was a swirl of dust and sand.

"What if we all rush at one spot?" I said, the tips of my claws pushing out of my fingers into my palms.

"No good," Onyx said. "They'd be all over us."

"Then we split up."

Visala bobbed his sword in the air, counting the hounds. "They've got us outnumbered at least ten to one. We'd never survive, even if they had half that number."

I kicked at a patch of sand in frustration. "So we're just going to do nothing?"

Staring at the approaching cloud, Onyx shook his head. "Tell me what you see out there."

It was closer now, and bigger than I'd thought. Maybe as big as the Immigration Station. But I still couldn't see anything except sand. Then something appeared out of the flying debris just long enough for me to make out a head. It disappeared as another peeked through. And another. "There are three of them."

"Three heads," Visala said. "But only one creature."

"What?" I looked again, sure he must be mistaken.

"Cerberus," Sparrow whispered.

That was crazy. Cerberus—the three-headed hound that guarded the gates of Hell—was a fable, just like . . .

the hellhounds. Around the circle, they began to whine and paw the ground.

"It's why they didn't kill us right away," Sparrow said, her face even more pale than normal. "Cerberus only eats living meat."

"That's a story. Made up to keep spawnlings in line." I turned to Onyx, but he said nothing. Holding his launcher loosely in one hand, he continued to stare at the approaching cloud. "Tell them, Cinder." I looked to her, but she wasn't there.

I turned in a circle. She'd been standing right next to me a moment before, and now she was gone. That was impossible. There was nowhere for her to go. Noticing a dark pile on the ground, I picked up her cloak, her top, her skirt—everything she'd been wearing lying loose on the sand by her pack and her weapon.

Onyx saw what I was holding and glanced around wildly. "Where is she?!"

The only thing I could think of was her whispering, *Absolute Zero.* Could she have been right? If hellhounds and Cerberus were real, could they actually have taken her to Absolute Zero? My second thought—and this one made much more sense—was Cinder telling me she thought only about herself. Somehow, she'd managed to escape, leaving the rest of us behind.

"Hey, you stupid mutts!" a voice shouted from behind me. "Can't you count?"

I spun just in time to see Cinder waving her arms wildly halfway between us and the building before blending into the background again. Camouflaging herself with the desert, she'd managed to sneak outside the circle. The hellhounds—appearing as surprised as we were—stood still for a moment, heads cocked.

"What's wrong?" Cinder's voice taunted. "Are your heads as full of smoke as your mouths?"

The four hounds closest to her broke from the circle, barking and growling as they ran toward her. The others hesitated, unsure whether to go or stay.

"A diversion!" Onyx shouted. "She's creating a diversion." He lifted the launcher to his shoulder and fired two quick fireballs at the closest hounds. "Run!"

The first fireball caught one of the hounds chasing after Cinder. The second hit the hound closest to the opening in the circle. Engulfed in a pyre of flames, the hellhound leaped jerkily to its hind legs, howled, and collapsed to the ground. The one beside it charged toward us, but an instant later, a silver cord wrapped around its legs, sending it sprawling to the dirt.

Pulling Father by the hand, Sparrow ran for the opening.

"Go!" Visala pushed me in the back, raised his sword, and lopped off the head of the nearest hound with a single swing.

Something bounded out of the dark, and I turned to see a hellhound lunge for me, its mouth a mass of smoke and teeth. Before it could snap its jaws closed, a pair of curved horns rammed into the side of its head. The hellhound collapsed to the ground. Onyx did too, but a second later, he was on his feet, shaking his head. "Wow," he said, racing for the building with Cinder's pack tucked under one arm. "They're tougher than they look."

Then I sprinted like my life depended on it because I was sure it did. The world was a blur of red as my hooves pounded through the sand.

"On your right!" Visala shouted.

Unable to find Cinder, the hellhounds had circled back. One streaked toward Father and Sparrow. Snarling, I leaped onto its back and plunged my claws into its neck. It turned to snap at me, and I rammed my fingertips into its eyes as I slashed at its legs with my hooves. With a howl of pain, it somersaulted to the ground, and I leaped free.

Visala rammed his sword through the chest of the other one. Checking over my shoulder, I saw that the rest of the pack was chasing us. They ran with odd, jerky strides that covered the ground quickly. But they weren't going to catch us before we reached the building.

I put on a burst of speed, and a voice to my right said, "Tell me you didn't leave my best skirt behind."

Unable to keep a huge grin from spreading across my face—a painful thing to do with fangs—I glanced at the blur running beside me. "You'll do anything to get the attention of a pack of guys, won't you?"

Cinder's laughter was the most beautiful sound in the world at that moment. We were both probably going to die in the next few minutes, but at least she was back.

"Beat me to the building, and I'll give you *my* skirt," I yelled.

"I'll let you win," she called back. "You have terrible taste."

We sprinted to the rise. As we rounded the white stone wall, Sparrow and Father were standing just outside the open doorway. I looked in and all of my euphoria disappeared. There was a single room, barely big enough for the six of us to squeeze inside. There was no door to close or any way to block the entry. And except for a low stone bench, the room was empty.

* * *

Visala and Onyx skidded to a halt seconds later. Their disappointment was cut short by the arrival of a pair of snarling hellhounds.

"Inside." Onyx pushed Cinder and me through the doorway. Flinging the packs after us, he turned to face the hounds with his whip in one hand and a blade about half the length of Visala's in the other.

I tried to go back outside to help him and Visala, but Cinder grabbed my shoulder. "There's no room."

"She's right," Sparrow said.

The last thing I wanted was advice from a hume. But I could see for myself Onyx and Visala fighting shoulder to shoulder in the doorway. The two of them effectively blocked the entrance, leaving no room for the hellhounds to get in, or for me to get out and help. Not that it mattered. This building had us trapped every bit as effectively as the circle of hellhounds.

Outside, the snarls and yaps of the beasts echoed around the tiny room as the hounds from hell tried to fight their way inside. It was only a matter of time. Visala and Onyx couldn't hold off all of them, and even if they could, Cerberus would be here any minute.

Still terrified, Father crawled to the back of the room and appeared to be trying to bury himself in sand. Not that I was any more use. All I could do was stand there, waiting for Visala or Onyx to fall. Once one of them did, I would take his place and go out fighting. It was small comfort.

A cool hand rested on my arm. Cinder, who had apparently found some clothes in the pack, smiled at me. "I didn't run."

"No, you didn't." I wrapped an arm around her shoulder. "Sneaking naked past a hundred hellhounds and then turning around and flashing them is the bravest thing I've heard of. If we make it back to Hell alive, you'll be the hero of every girl in the academy—and most of the guys." If I was going to die, it was good to have my best friend as her old self to spend my last moments with.

A handful of sand hit me in the face, and I glanced back to see Father on his hands and knees, robe pulled up almost to his thighs, as he tossed piles of sand between his skinny white legs. A lot of help he'd ended up being. Sparrow tried to pull him out of his hole, but he slithered away from her.

Something thudded against the outside of the building, and Onyx shouted in pain. Visala's sword flashed. I wished I could be out there helping them. Better to die clawing and gouging than cowering in a building that seemed to have absolutely no reason for being. I kicked at the low stone bench, wondering why it was even there. Who put a bench in the center of a tiny room, facing the back wall? The height was wrong too, below the entrance, almost as if . . .

I walked to the bench and brushed away the sand. It had an oddly worn look to it, especially in the center. Digging several inches down, I discovered another bench just below it. It too had the worn look, as if instead of sitting on it, people had . . .

I spun around to where Father was still digging. His head was nearly buried in the sand at the base of the oddly sloped back wall. I looked from him to the benches, and realized they weren't benches at all.

"Quick," I yelled, diving to the ground beside the old hume. "Help him dig."

"What are you doing?" Cinder asked as I flung handfuls of sand toward the entrance.

"The benches aren't benches," I shouted. Sparrow moved to the other side of Father, pushing away the sand he was piling up. "This isn't a room. It's an entrance, and those are stairs."

Once she realized what I was telling her, Cinder helped me dig. Together, the four of us managed to uncover more and more of the sloping back wall that was actually a ceiling. But would it be soon enough? The ferocious snarling and howling cut off, replaced by a roar that shook the entire building. I wanted to tell Onyx and Visala to hang on—that we might have a chance if they could last a few more minutes. But there was no time.

"Don't inhale its breath!" Visala shouted from outside, and I wondered exactly what horrors they were facing.

Thudding booms that could only be Cerberus's footsteps shook the earth beneath my hands. A tremendous bang rattled the walls, and bits of stone and dust rained down on my head. I reached for another handful of sand, and my fingers hit solid stone. I tried to dig under or around it, but it seemed to be a solid beam. The others had stopped as well. At some point in the past, a section of the roof must have collapsed.

"Push!" I shouted. I turned around and shoved with both hooves. Cinder and the humes shoved as well, but the stone wouldn't budge.

Onyx screamed a war cry, and Cerberus slammed into the building again, cracking one of the walls.

"Look out!" Visala yelled. Another crash came from above, and a heavy piece of rock slammed against my back.

As I took stock of how badly I was injured, the beam in front of me rumbled and dropped out of sight. A hole opened up before us, and Father fell through without a sound. A second later, the sand began whirling down around our feet. With a squawk of surprise, Sparrow was sucked into the opening.

"Go!" I screamed to Cinder.

She grabbed her pack and dove through the opening.

I threw the rest of the supplies after her. Outside, a pair of howls shook the air, and a blast of icy cold shot through the doorway. Visala stumbled backward. Something was wrong with his bad arm. As he started for the door again, sword clutched in his right hand, I pointed to the opening in the floor that was growing bigger every second. He gawked at it with a shocked look, then slid feet-first into it.

Now there was only Onyx.

I rushed to his side. When he saw who it was, he tried to push me back. I knew he'd never hear me above the roar of the three-headed creature biting and slashing above us, so I pointed to the room and mouthed, "Escape."

He looked over his shoulder and saw the hole that took up nearly half the floor. Cerberus raised one of its clawed feet. Onyx and I turned, and hand-in-hand, dove through the hole. Behind us, stone exploded, and the entire building collapsed as we dropped into darkness.

CHAPTER 26

Dust coated my throat and tongue, filled my nostrils, and stung my eyes. In the darkness, someone stumbled over my arm.

"Blaze?" Cinder called between hacking coughs.

"Over here." My back screamed with pain as I pushed myself into a sitting position. My right elbow stung where I'd hit it as I fell, and I thought I might have a black eye. I could hear people gagging on the fog of dirt, but there was no sign of Cerberus or the hellhounds. The collapsing building seemed to have blocked the entrance.

I tried to clear my throat, but couldn't draw enough saliva. "Does anyone have a lamp?"

Visala stepped out of the gloom, his aura doing little more than illuminating the clouds swirling around him. A few seconds later, Cinder staggered into view. Her dark eyes peered at me through a powdery gray mask. "You look like a ghost," I said.

She choked out a mouthful of grit, wiped her lips with the back of her hand, and frowned. "You don't look much better yourself, sister. Good thing you have horns, or I might mistake you for a hume."

"Speaking of humes, where are Sparrow and Father?" Onyx's voice called from off to the left.

"Over here," Sparrow answered. "The dust isn't quite

as bad this way. And you're going to want to see this. But be careful, there's a drop of about three feet. I nearly broke my ankle before getting my lamp going."

Cinder, Visala, and I found Onyx holding a sputtering lantern above his head. Between that and the seraph, there was just enough light to make our way toward the sound of the hume's voice.

"Watch out for the drop," Sparrow called.

A moment later, the floor disappeared out from under my hoof. I sat and slid down to a lower level. The original floor came nearly to my waist. Sparrow was right—the dust lessened as we moved farther away from the point of the collapse, though the air still had a musty smell to it.

Onyx stepped down beside me, and his hoof clanged against something on the floor that gave a metallic ring. "What's this?" he asked, kneeling and lowering his lamp to reveal a grimy metal bar.

Sparrow stepped forward, holding Father's arm in one hand and a lantern in the other. "That's what I was wondering. There's another one a few feet over." She lowered her lamp, illuminating a second bar parallel to the first.

Onyx ran his palm along the metal. It was wide enough that he could barely get his hand around it. He rapped his knuckles against the bar, and it gave a solid *bong*. "Tracks?" he asked.

"Why would there be tracks beneath the Outer Circles?" Cinder asked.

I knelt beside Onyx and touched the bar. It was cool beneath my fingers, pitted with age, but still solid. "Where do they go?"

"At least a hundred paces that way," Sparrow said, jerking a thumb over her shoulder. "Into a tunnel of some kind. I didn't follow it any farther than that."

This made no sense. Who would put a staircase in the

middle of the Outer Circles, or run tracks beneath it? What were they for, and why had they been buried? "Where do you think they lead?" I asked.

Onyx looked up at Visala, his eyes narrowed. "Ask *him*."

All of us turned to the Halo.

He snorted. "Why ask me? I have no idea."

"That's what you keep saying." Onyx held the lantern out toward the seraph, as though trying to get a better look at him. "You know a lot more than you're admitting, and I'm not taking you another step until you tell us what's going on."

What was Onyx talking about? What did he think Visala was holding back?

"Okay," Visala said. "You caught me. I admit it. I knew all about the flying creatures, the hellhounds, and the three-headed monster. I intentionally led us right to them. Except that you were the one leading us. But that's beside the point.

"Of course, I could only hope the rest of you would find the hidden staircase while I nearly got killed fighting Cerberus, if that's indeed what it was. And I did all that just to get you here. Obviously, my plan is working since we are here—wherever here is. Are you happy?"

Onyx growled. "I never believed you would have gone into the Outer Circles unless you knew something we didn't. You're not that stupid."

"That's not saying much for the rest of you, is it?" Visala's lips pulled up in a sardonic grin. "Now if you've finished accusing me of whatever it is you think I've done, I seem to have dislocated my shoulder. Or was that part of my plan too?"

For the first time, I noticed the lump sticking forward from the top of his robe. "Oh," I gasped. "Does it hurt?"

He nodded, biting his lip. "Quite a bit, actually. I think I'm going to need your help getting it back in place."

"I'll do it." Onyx stepped forward, but Visala held out his good hand.

"You won't blame me if I tell you that you're quite possibly the last person in the world I want pulling on my injured arm."

I swallowed. "I don't know anything about that kind of stuff. The only medical class I've taken is hume anatomy. Somehow, I don't think that applies to seraphs." I glanced at Cinder, hoping she'd offer to take my place, but she backed away.

"I'll do it," Sparrow said. "I've reset shoulders before."

Visala shook his head. "Blaze is stronger." He rolled his left sleeve up, revealing a blazing white bicep covered in liquid fire.

"I'll need Onyx's cloak to protect me from your aura," I said, unable to believe I was going to try to perform a medical procedure on a celestial being.

"Not if we're both very careful." Visala's eyes met mine, and for a moment, I had difficulty breathing. He took his left hand in his right, wincing in pain as he bent his arm at the elbow and tucked it in front of his body. "I'm going to lower my aura on my left arm as much as I can. At the same time, I want you to take hold of my wrist and elbow. It shouldn't hurt you if you move slowly."

"You don't have to do this," Onyx said, his voice tense.

"No. It's okay." Feeling the eyes of everyone else watching me, I stepped forward, took a deep breath, and reached for Visala's arm.

"Gently," he whispered. "Gently."

I was convinced I was about to be shocked at the least, or burned to death at the worst. I put the fingers of my left hand to his wrist. Pearly white flames leapt from his skin to mine, and I nearly jerked away. But it didn't hurt. It actually felt good—warm and tingly. I closed my other hand lightly around his elbow. A skin of glistening fire flowed up both of my arms.

"Oh," Cinder whispered.

"Now rotate my arm outward," Visala said.

No longer aware of the dust or the dark, all I could think about was that I was touching a seraph. As if we were the only two people in the room, I looked into his eyes. I felt almost as though I could read his thoughts through the aura that flowed between us.

"That's it," he said as I moved his arm. He gritted his teeth, muscles bulging in his neck. "Now pull down, hard. Harder!"

I pulled his limb with all my strength, and something gave a small click.

"Yes," he gasped. Beads of sweat glistened on his forehead like tiny crystals, reflecting his glory.

I'd done it. I'd helped a seraph. I'd cured his injury. Or if not cured, at least aided. I looked down at my arms, glowing like flaming torches—almost as if I were celestial myself.

"You can let go of my arm now," Visala said.

I looked around, realizing I'd lost all track of time. How long had I been holding him? As I released his arm, Cinder raised an eyebrow. I looked for Onyx, but he and the humes were at the other end of the room, making something to eat.

"Sorry," I said, licking my lips. "I guess I forgot where I was for a minute."

"It's the aura," Visala said. "It even does that to me sometimes."

"Of course." I nodded. What else could it have been? Except for a moment I felt as if . . . well, I didn't know exactly what I'd felt. My face grew hot, and I turned away. Now that more of the dust had settled, I could see we were in an open room much larger than I'd expected. The walls and floor were covered with squares of stone or brick. At one end of the room, the tracks ended abruptly. At the other, they disappeared into a high, narrow tunnel.

As Visala left to join the others, Cinder walked up beside me and whispered, "Not a good idea."

I boosted myself up from the tracks, refusing to look at her. "I don't know what you're talking about."

She chuckled and climbed up beside me. "I may not hold a flame to you when it comes to fighting. But in boy-girl stuff, I run circles around you. And trust me when I say that if you keep heading in the direction you're going, things will not end well."

She had no idea what she was talking about. So why did I feel guilty? "What direction do you think I'm headed in?"

Cinder looked at me with a smug grin that nearly made me sorry we'd brought her. "You think lover boy's going to stay in Hell to be with you?"

I turned on her, clenching my fists. "Lover boy? *Lover boy*? You're talking about a seraph."

"So then you think he's going to take you with him?"

I spun away, walking toward the opposite end of the room, but Cinder stayed right by my side, matching me step for step. "I fixed his arm," I hissed, trying to keep my temper under control. "That's all there is."

"Really?" Cinder stepped in front of me, and I could barely keep from pushing her out of the way. Instead, I folded my arms tightly across my chest. This far from Visala and the lanterns, it was too dark to read her expression, but I'd spent more than enough time around her to recognize the sarcastic tilt of her head. "You're telling me nothing happened back there? That you haven't been swooning over that Halo since he first entered our room?"

"That's right."

"Fine." Cinder put out her hands. "Maybe I was reading you wrong. But I wasn't the only one. If there isn't anything going on between you and Visala, you need to tell that to Onyx."

"Onyx?" I asked, completely bewildered. "What does he have to do with this?"

Cinder shook her head. "Either you're the most naive demon spawn I've ever met, or just the most stubborn. Probably both. But I'm telling you, candles weren't made to be lit on both ends. And remember what you said. Visala *is* a seraph. Ask yourself if your feelings for him are real or if he's controlling you."

Walking back to join the others, I thought about what Cinder had said. There was nothing between Visala and me. There never could be. I was a demon spawn, and he was a creature of glory and light. We each belonged in our own worlds. That's what got Onyx into trouble—thinking he could change who he was and where he belonged.

The truth was that I *had* felt something. More than likely it was just Visala's aura, or the natural awe that celestial beings inspired. And even if it was something more—something like what Cinder imagined—there was no future in it. In a few days, if we managed to reach Judgment, he'd be gone. I had no illusions of him returning, or if he did, that I'd be able to tell him apart from any of the other Halos.

But what had she meant by saying I needed to tell Onyx?

I knew he didn't like me spending time with Visala. It was actually kind of endearing, seeing the way he pouted when I spent more than a minute or two with the seraph. But the idea of romantic feelings for Onyx scared me—maybe scared me more than the flying monsters. We'd spent our whole childhood together. He was my best friend. I'd barely gotten his friendship back, and I wasn't going to ruin it by stupidly thinking we'd eventually end up together.

And if Onyx declared himself to me, how would I react? What would I do if he came up to me, put an arm around my shoulder, and said, "Hey, you hot demon, I've been dreaming about kissing you ever since I was a spawnling."

What was it Cinder told me back when we were in training? It seemed like ages ago. Something about Onyx talking to her after he'd started giving me the silent treatment. At the time, I'd been angry that he'd spent time with her while ignoring me. What had he confessed to her regarding his feelings about me? Why go to her instead of coming to me? Did he think I'd . . . laugh?

Standing in the shadows, I really looked at him for the first time in . . . maybe forever. On the Immigration Station, he'd told me to look at Hell through new eyes. I tried looking at him with new eyes. He was definitely handsome. I hadn't been blind enough to miss that. Even when we were spawnlings, all the other girls wanted to be around him. Half the girls in the academy would have cut off an arm to make him theirs.

What if instead of showing me Hell from the top of the Immigration Station, he'd run his fingers through my hair, pulled me close, and kissed me? I was pretty sure I wouldn't have laughed. The thought brought out feelings I'd never experienced before while thinking of Onyx. The feelings felt impossible. He'd had lots of chances to open up to me, but he hadn't done it. Would he ever tell me how he really felt?

Watching him pick up his pack and sling it easily over his shoulder—though it had to weigh nearly as much as I did—I couldn't help wondering what it would feel like to have those strong arms wrap around me, lift me from my feet, and . . .

"Come on," Cinder said, shaking me. "We're leaving."

"Right," I said, trying to erase the image from my mind.

Cinder looked from me to Onyx and back again, then laughed. "And with that oblivion at an end, you are in so much trouble."

CHAPTER 27

Following the tracks through the dark, echoing tunnel, I tried to think of a way to get Onyx to open up to me. It wasn't nearly as easy as it sounded. I couldn't exactly edge up beside him and say, "If we live, and if Visala really does figure out a way to clear our names with the covens, do you have any plans for the night after we get back?"

I wished I were as smooth with guys as Cinder. She'd have Onyx spilling his heart's secrets in no time. But Cinder was a little way back, pausing every so often to hold out her lamp while she examined the floor or the wall.

I sped up to walk beside Onyx, hoping he might start the conversation himself. He refused to even look at me.

"Do you have any idea where the tracks lead?" I asked, trying to get him talking.

"No." He didn't so much as turn his head.

Cinder was right about him being angry, then. But was he upset that Visala had chosen me to fix his arm, or was he actually jealous? He picked up his pace, as though trying to leave me behind, but I wasn't ready to give up. "What if they're taking us the wrong direction?"

This time he did look over, and his expression was so cold, I almost wished he hadn't. "It wasn't like we had a lot of options, was it? Or did you want to wait back there to see if Cerberus managed to dig us out?"

What was he so angry about? It wasn't like I had asked to help the seraph. "I'm not suggesting this was a bad idea," I said, hoping to patch things up a little. "It's just . . . someone obviously built these tracks for a reason. If we knew who and why, it might help us figure out where they go."

"What a great idea." He grimaced, as if I'd just insulted him. "Maybe I should try thinking, instead of blindly leading us from one catastrophe to the next."

It was like he *wanted* to get into a fight. He was taking everything I said in the worst possible way, baiting me. Normally, I would have thrown back some cutting response. But I held my tongue. "That's not what I meant."

"I don't know why the tracks are here," Onyx said in a tone that was slightly more civil. "Maybe . . . maybe, a long time ago this was the Stygian route."

Of course. That made such perfect sense, I wondered why I hadn't thought of it myself. Maybe at some point far in the past, the Stygian Transit had run underground. Something could have happened to it. Or maybe it just got old and was replaced. That would explain why the entrances had been buried. Only . . . "If it was the old Stygian, why would the tracks end in the middle of the desert?"

"The tracks didn't end back there," Onyx said, his voice taking on the chill it had held before. "They were buried. It looked like it was done intentionally. You might have noticed that if you'd been paying attention to anything besides him."

Ouch. So we were back to that. "Okay. Maybe I missed it. But what about the stairs? Why would the Stygian have stops between Hell and Judgment? It's not like humes would have been getting on or off in the Outer Circles."

"How should I know? Maybe Hell is bigger than I thought. Maybe the seraphs do something in the desert that we know nothing about. Go ask the Halo."

Couldn't he leave Visala out of this? "What did you want me to do? Refuse to help him?"

"Why not?" Onyx snorted. "You keep reminding everyone that he's a celestial being. Shouldn't he be able to heal himself?"

I jammed my fingertips into my palms, willing myself not to explode. If Cinder was right and Onyx was jealous, I would end it now. "I don't know what you think is going on between Visala and me. But you're wrong. He's the only hope we have of being able to go home again. That's all there is."

That should have stopped the argument, but Onyx looked away. "Why should I care about what's going on between the two of you?"

So there it was. The feelings were really all on my side only. "You shouldn't," I snapped, not sure whether I was more angry or hurt. "Cinder had this stupid idea that you did care. I told her she was crazy. Obviously, I was right."

"That went well," Cinder whispered as I dropped back, leaving Onyx muttering to himself.

I glared at her. "I guess we really are nothing more than friends."

She gave me an infuriating little smile, as if she held the key to all the world's secrets. "Give him some time."

"I'll give him lots of time," I said, kicking the tracks. "But that's all I'll give him. His ego's too big to let anyone near him anyway."

"It's not ego. It's fear. He feels like it's up to him to get us to Judgment and back safely, and he's afraid he's messing up."

I shoved my hands in the pockets of my robe. It was cooler down here, and I was tired of walking. I was also tired of trying to figure out guys. "If you know him so well, you can have him."

She tilted her head. "Don't think I haven't thought about it. But he doesn't look at me the way he looks at you."

I scoffed at that. The way Onyx had just looked at me was the way you looked at an annoying bug—trying to decide if swatting it was worth the effort, or if it would just go away on its own. At the moment, I didn't have enough patience to deal with his lack of honest communication.

Cinder paused for a second, glanced at something on the ground, then continued walking.

"What do you keep looking at?" I asked.

"I'm not sure." She held up her lantern to the wall, revealing a string of wires and pipes attached to it. "Think of the kind of effort it must have taken to build these tunnels. Why go to all that trouble when the ground above is perfectly flat? It seems like it would have been much easier to build the tracks up there."

That was one of the things about Cinder that both attracted and infuriated me. I liked how smart she was, but hated that she pretended to be dumb around guys. "I guess the tunnels are to avoid the creatures, or the storms?"

"That could be." She reached into her pocket and took out two small items. Both were made of a dark metal, and both looked very old. The first appeared to be a key, although not like any key I'd ever seen before. It was triangular, with jagged edges on three sides. The second was a circular disk. As Cinder held it to the light, I could see that something had been engraved on one side, but time, and probably sand, had worn it so smooth, it was impossible to tell what.

"Where did you get these?" I asked, taking them and turning them over in my fingers.

"On the ground. The disk was in the room with the stairs, and I found the key a few minutes ago."

I handed them back to her. They were unusual, but I

didn't see much use for either of them. "Somebody must have dropped them."

"Have you ever seen humes arrive in Hell with personal belongings? And the seraphs don't seem to bring anything but their swords."

She was right. What would a hume need with a key? "Couldn't they have been dropped by whoever shut the tunnels down?"

Cinder shrugged. "You're probably right. This whole thing just feels odd. The Outer Circles are nothing like what I expected." She glanced over her shoulder to where Visala was trailing the group. "I'll tell you what seems even stranger though. The only person who doesn't appear curious about this tunnel in the least is him."

I frowned. Cinder was right.

We continued following the tracks for what felt like days, but was probably only hours. Twice more, the tunnels opened out into large rooms like the one we'd fallen into. Both times, we discovered stairs leading up, and both times, the stairs were buried by sand and stone. As far as I could tell, the tunnel never curved right or left. It was a constant black void opening up before us as our lights uncovered league after league of tracks.

Several times, sections of the tunnel itself had collapsed. Once, it was so completely blocked that we had to dig our way through the debris. I tried to keep my thoughts on moving forward—taking step after step after step. But the longer we traveled, the more two worries plagued my mind.

"What if there's no way out?" I whispered to Cinder as we stopped for a break. "What if all the entrances are blocked, and at some point, we reach a dead end?"

She shivered. "Don't even suggest that."

She was right. There was no point in worrying about things we had no control over. But as we finished our rest and continued on, the other thought I couldn't get rid of was how we'd lost all sense of direction in the storm. If Onyx was right, and this was the old Stygian route, we had no idea which direction we were headed. For all we knew, we were on a course straight back to Hell.

If Father held any such worries, he didn't show them. Instead, he hooted and grunted happily as we walked along, pulling metal cable from the corroded brackets on the walls and wrapping it around his arm in looping coils.

"What's he doing?" Visala asked.

Sparrow raised her hands. "He likes to collect things. In his room in Hell, he has a bowl of imp teeth he found in the street. And if I didn't throw them away, his entire room would be filled with shiny rocks."

Listening to her talk about a hume that way gave me an odd feeling. Of course I'd known humes had lives too, but I'd never thought about them much. I hadn't considered that they might have personalities and hobbies, even.

"What's he saying?" I asked.

The hume woman studied me for a minute before turning back to Father. "Nothing."

Visala walked up beside Father and tried to take the cable from him. The old man grunted angrily before realizing Visala was only offering to carry his burden. Once he did, he gestured for the seraph to cut the end of the cable still attached to the wall. Visala did, slicing it smoothly with his sword. Satisfied Visala wasn't going to leave his precious cargo behind, Father returned to hooting, a smile creasing his horribly scarred cheeks.

"It sounds like he's repeating the same thing over and over," I said.

"I can't understand him," Visala said. "It might be important."

Sparrow sighed. "It isn't. He's talking about a woman who fell into a river and drowned."

"Was it a friend of his?" I asked, interested in spite of myself. Maybe that was part of the pain Sparrow had been talking about. "Did he get those scars trying to rescue her?"

"No." She rolled her eyes. "It's not even real. It's a song. He thinks he's singing."

"What's . . . singing?" I asked.

"Trust me," Sparrow said. "That's something you wouldn't understand. All that matters is it never happened. It's a kind of story. One of his favorites—'Ruby lips above the water. Blowing bubbles, soft and fine. But alas, I was no swimmer. So I lost my Clementine.'"

At her words, Father hooted excitedly, waving his hands at the hume woman.

"No," Sparrow said angrily. "I told you I won't. Stop asking."

"That's horrible," I said. "How could he like a story about a hume who drowns?"

"I know." Sparrow raised her lips into a sneer. "It sounds much more like something a demon would enjoy, doesn't it?"

The hume's words stung, and I couldn't place my finger on *why*.

* * *

By the time we reached the fourth room—with stairs as completely blocked as the others—I was sick of everyone. Onyx could sulk all he wanted. Cinder could pretend she knew more about me than I knew myself. The humes could tell all the morbid *songs* they wanted. And Visala, well, he could do whatever he wanted too.

I needed space. And time to myself. Unfortunately, in

our current circumstances, none of those were available. Carrying my dinner to the farthest corner of the room, I wrapped myself in my blanket and tried to pretend I was back at the academy. Or better yet, at home, with my parents. I'd been so anxious to get out on my own. Now I'd give anything to be a spawnling again, curled up on my pallet, with my biggest worry being who I'd play with the next day.

Onyx looked at me from where he was eating on the stairs, but I turned away. I didn't have anything to say to him, and it was clear he didn't have anything to say to me.

At least we didn't have to worry about guard duty here. Curling up and resting my head on my arms, I tried to ignore how hard and cold the floor was. I was so angry and frustrated, I was sure I would never fall asleep, but my body knew better. I was out almost as soon as I closed my eyes.

Sometime later, I jerked awake. Rolling over, I groaned at how stiff my muscles were. Cinder was sleeping soundly. Beyond her, a low lamp revealed the humes curled side by side on their blankets. Onyx was lying near the stairs, his snores echoing off the walls and ceiling. But I didn't think that was what had awakened me. As I pushed myself up on one elbow, a flash of light reflected off the wall of the tunnel ahead and disappeared. I scanned the room again, quickly. Visala wasn't here.

Where was he going? I thought about waking Onyx, but I knew he'd just make some sarcastic comment about me and Visala. Besides, what did I need him for? What did I need anyone for? It wasn't like I thought Visala would hurt me. And if I followed him carefully enough, he wouldn't even know I was there.

Leaving my pack and blanket, I tiptoed across the floor, slid silently down to the tracks, and followed his blue-white glow disappearing into the darkness.

CHAPTER 28

Slipping as silently as I could through the cold black passage, I experienced a happiness I hadn't felt in days—maybe weeks. For once, I was doing something not because I was afraid or pressured, but because I wanted to. Cinder wasn't looking over my shoulder, judging me. I didn't need to worry about what Onyx thought of me or whether he was safe. Disconnected from everyone and everything, focused only on the distant light, I felt . . . free.

I tried to keep the click of my hooves on the hard floor as quiet as possible, but Visala was moving more quickly than I expected, and soon I had to jog to keep up. Not that I was in any danger of losing him. The tunnel was arrow-straight, and there was nowhere else to go. But without the illumination of his aura, I wouldn't be able to see where I was stepping.

It occurred to me that when I turned around, I'd have no light to find my way back. But I'd worry about that later. For now, I enjoyed the thrill of the chase and the excitement of being on my own. I was so caught up in the euphoria of the moment that I didn't realize Visala had stopped until I was nearly on top of him.

Skidding to a halt, I dropped down and pressed myself against the wall. Visala stood in the middle of the tunnel. Had he heard me? He didn't look back. He stretched his arms, sat, and leaned against one of the walls. I watched from the darkness, waiting for him to do whatever he'd come here for.

An embarrassing thought occurred to me. What if he'd slipped away from the group not to do anything illicit, but to get a little privacy? What if he was just here to go to the bathroom?

"Are you going to hide there all night, or come on over?"

Visala's voice echoed through the tunnel. I looked around, wondering who he was talking to before realizing it had to be me. Sheepishly, I stepped from the shadows into the light of his aura. "Hi," I said, feeling totally stupid.

"You can keep on going if you want to be alone," he said, not seeming to be put out at all by the fact that I'd followed him. "I assume you came here for the same reason I did."

"I'm sorry." I shifted from one hoof to the other. "I shouldn't have intruded."

"Not at all." He smiled, and I was struck again by what nice features he had. Especially his eyes. "I'd be happy to have you join me if you'd like. Not the most exciting accommodations. But at least we're far enough away that we don't have to listen to Onyx snore."

I couldn't help laughing. "He *is* loud."

"I woke up sure the Stygian was bearing down on us." Visala patted a spot on the ground beside him. "Sit with me."

I wondered for a moment what Cinder would say if she knew where I was and what I was doing. It didn't take much imagination. But wasn't I just thinking about how nice it was not to have her watching my every move?

I dropped down beside him.

For a few minutes, we sat quietly. Then he turned to me. "I'll bet you wish you were back in Hell."

Just a few hours earlier, that's exactly what I had been

wishing, but when I opened my mouth, I was surprised to hear myself say, "No. I don't." I had no idea how we were going to get out of this tunnel. We were down to only a day or two of food and water at the most. It was the strangest thing, but right now, at this moment, I didn't want to be anywhere else but here. "How about you? Do you wish you were in Judgment?"

He rubbed his chin, and light danced from his fingers to his face. "Well, the food's better there. And I wouldn't have to sleep on the ground. But considering the company, I'd have to say I'm pretty happy to be where I am."

My skin went hot, and my heart began to pound. I had to change the subject. "What's it like there?"

"Judgment?" he said, and I thought I could hear disappointment in his voice. Then he smiled. "It's beautiful. Clean and sparkling. The air is so clear, it almost hurts to breathe it. The water is pure. No one goes hungry or sick."

"It sounds wonderful," I said, trying to imagine a whole world outside of Hell. It was scary, but also a little exciting. For the first time, I could see the attraction.

"You'd love it there."

"I would?" I asked, wrenched out of my vision. He couldn't be saying what I thought he was saying. I was a demon spawn, and that was . . . *Judgment.*

Visala licked his lips, seeming to realize what he'd just said. Or maybe how I'd taken it. "Of course, Hell is nice too. It's, uh, warm."

"Sure." I nodded. Cinder was right. Following Visala had been a bad idea.

"Thanks for helping me with my arm," he said.

"Oh. You're welcome. How is it?"

"Good." He flexed it.

We sat quietly again. But what had been a comfortable silence before now seemed awkward. "I better go," I said. I started to get up, but he reached out and caught my hand, lowering his aura so it flickered lightly over my fingers.

"Stay. Please," he whispered.

I sat back down, still holding his hand, and a shiver raced through my body.

"Are you cold?" he asked.

"A little," I said, not telling him my trembling had absolutely nothing to do with the temperature.

"Here." He took my other hand. Fire licked along my fingers, over my wrists, and up my arms to my shoulders. Although I could see the flames flickering across the surface of my robe, I could also feel its heat on my skin beneath the cloth. The fire inside my body meeting the fire outside banished any trace of cold.

He moved toward me, and I couldn't seem to breathe normally. My chest hitched. My hands shook. I couldn't take my eyes away from his perfect lips, only inches from mine. "Can you . . . take the aura off of your . . ."

He shook his head. "But I can do this."

He shifted slightly, and all at once I was staring through a haze of dazzling brightness. Looking down at myself, I realized I was covered from head to foot in his aura. White heat sizzled up and down my body. Every inch of my skin tingled. His hands traveled up my arms and around my back. One of them caressed my neck while the other pulled me toward him.

I leaned into him, and the light between us was so bright, I had to close my eyes. His tongue brushed across my lips. His mouth met mine. I wrapped my arms around his neck, pulling him against me. It was like I was standing in the middle of an erupting volcano. Was this as dangerous? I didn't care. I'd never wanted anything more in my entire life.

The tunnel erupted in howls and screams.

Visala jerked backward. The fire that had burned so deliciously warm a moment before now scalded my skin and threw me across the tunnel. I jumped up in pain and surprise.

"I'm sorry," he said. But I was already turning away to see what was happening.

"Run!" Cinder screamed, racing toward us. Right behind her were Father and Sparrow, their faces gray and terrified.

"What's going on?" I shouted. A blast of fire rocked the end of the tunnel, and in its light, I could see Onyx kneeling in the center of the tracks. Howls and barks shook the tunnel with their deafening thunder.

"The hellhounds got in," Cinder cried, racing past us.

"Go!" Visala pushed me after Cinder and the humes, drawing his sword as he ran toward Onyx.

With no lanterns and Visala running in the other direction, the tunnel quickly went pitch-black. Somewhere ahead of me, the clatter of Cinder's hooves and Father's hooting echoed against the walls. Behind me, the hellhounds' growls were occasionally interrupted by howls of pain and shouts that could have been either Onyx or Visala.

It sounded as if they were holding the hounds off for now, but how long could they expect to keep that up, and what would happen when they gave out? I had to go back and help them. Knowing me as well as always, even in total darkness, Cinder called out, "Don't leave us, Blaze. We need you in case any hounds get past them."

She was right. Visala and Onyx could take care of themselves. But I had to find a way out of here. Or at least a place to hold the creatures off. "Where did they come from?" I gasped.

"Don't . . . know," Cinder called back. She was smaller

and faster, but she sounded as winded as me. "Woke up and they had snuck up on us."

I bumped into something, and for a second thought it was a hellhound, before Sparrow pushed off me and yelled, "Look where you're going."

That would be a lot easier to do with a lamp, but I assumed they must have left them behind in the confusion. Racing through the darkness, I kept waiting for the hot breath of a hellhound on my back, or the growl that would warn me I was about to be attacked. I kept checking over my shoulder for the glow of red eyes.

We'd been running for what seemed like an hour when the sound of our echoing hooves changed, and I realized we must have entered another room.

"Look," Cinder called from somewhere in front of me. "Light."

I turned to see a single orange beam cutting through the darkness to my right. It was tiny, but after the total black, it seemed like a torch. Feeling my way to the edge of the track, I pulled myself up.

"Over here," Cinder yelled as I raced across the floor. I tripped on something and landed hard on a set of sand-covered stairs, but I didn't care. I crawled toward her until I reached the spot where she was clawing at the small opening. Together the two of us dug at the passage, tossing aside handfuls of dirt and pushing away rocks and debris.

A few minutes later, Father and Sparrow arrived. Even with the four of us digging, though, the hole opened far too slowly. I could hear the sounds of galloping paws drawing closer and closer, and still we hadn't expanded the opening wide enough for even Father to climb through. We weren't going to be in time. Visala and Onyx would show up, and we'd be trapped. We had to do better.

Letting rage and fear flow through me, I urged my

temper forward. I pictured Flare's crushed head. Onyx, arriving in our room dirty and battered. I imagined hellhounds filling the tunnel, overpowering Visala, tearing at him, ripping him open as his aura flashed and went out.

"Get back," I growled.

Cinder turned to look at me and dropped away. Sparrow pushed Father behind her. With a roar, I attacked the hole. Dirt flew. Rocks shredded beneath my claws. And still it wasn't enough. They were so close now that I could hear Onyx and Visala clearly.

Attacking the earth as if it were a living creature standing between us and freedom, I threw my whole body into the hole. Screaming with fury, I raked and gouged. Red flooded my brain. And then I was outside. Light blinded my eyes as I stumbled out of a small stone building like the one we'd entered the tunnels through.

Father was right behind me. Then Sparrow.

I started back for the opening, but Cinder lunged out, nearly bowling me over. "They're coming," she screamed, pushing me back.

Seconds later, Visala bolted out of the hole. Bloody fur and gore were matted to his chest. His arms and face were a mess of cuts and scratches.

Onyx's sword flew through the opening, clanging to the dirt. A second later, his pack followed. His face appeared in the hole, then one arm. He pulled himself partway out, pushed his other arm through, and stopped. "I'm stuck."

Visala and I grabbed at his silver-cloaked arms. "His shoulders are too broad," Visala said, straining with effort.

Onyx grimaced in pain, and suddenly he was sliding back down the hole. "They've got me!" he cried, his face contorted in agony. "Run before they dig their way out!"

"No!" I screamed. "Cinder, take his hand."

Diving back toward the hole, I attacked with both

hands, clawing away the dirt around Onyx's shoulders. He screamed again, and I could hear the hounds growling and barking only feet away.

Visala and Cinder pulled again, and Onyx was through.

"Get him outside!" Visala yelled. He drew his sword and attacked the nearest wall. White flames flew as a crack split the stone.

Grabbing Onyx under the arms, I saw his leg was gashed open from his calf nearly to his thigh. Blood gushed in a dark red pool as we pulled him through the doorway. We had to close the wound or he'd bleed to death in minutes. As soon as we had him through the door, I tore off my cloak and wrapped it around his leg. It soaked through immediately.

Rock and dust flew as Visala attacked the building.

I pulled the tie from my robe and tried to slow the bleeding by twisting it around Onyx's leg. But his skin had gone rock hard, and my knot did nothing. His eyes flickered and closed. His hand reached for me and dropped away.

Visala ran through the doorway just before the entire building came down with a crash. "Do something!" I screamed. "He's bleeding to death!"

The seraph dropped to the ground and raised his sword.

"No." I reached out to stop him, but he pushed me away. He pressed the side of his sword to Onyx's wound. Smoke billowed into the air, and the smell of burning flesh filled my lungs. When he took away his sword, the wound was closed.

"Come on," he said. "We have to get out of here. Those rocks won't hold the hellhounds for long."

"I don't think we're going anywhere," Cinder said.

I looked up, and for the first time heard the roar that filled the air. The mountains were close now. Maybe as close as a day away. But between us and them, a chasm cut through the desert. It looked at least a quarter of a league wide, so deep I couldn't see the bottom. The roaring was the sound of water rushing somewhere down the floor of the divide.

"The wings," I said. "We can fly across."

Sparrow shook her head. "Only Onyx managed to get his pack."

CHAPTER 29

My heart sank as I stood at the edge of the gorge. It was incredibly deep, with walls so sheer, it would be impossible to scale. A cool mountain wind blew out of the canyon, pushing my hair back from my face. Even if we could find a way down, we'd never be able to cross the river that foamed and crashed high into the air as it smashed over giant boulders.

It appeared that at one time, a bridge had spanned the divide, but it was long since gone, the only remains a few broken beams reaching out to the middle of nowhere. A tunnel that blasted into the rock on the far side was sealed closed. The one on this side must have been sealed as well, or we would have seen its light down below. If we hadn't gotten through the opening when we did, we'd have been trapped in a dead end.

"Maybe we can find a way around," I suggested, although the canyon reached as far to our right as I could see and seemed to stretch clear to the other end of the mountains on the left.

"We don't have the time, or the supplies," Visala said, staring desolately down at the river. "I can't imagine it will take more than a few hours for the hellhounds to find a way out. And with all our other backpacks gone, we're down to two canteens."

Father grunted and waved his hands. None of us needed a translation when the old man put a hand to his mouth in a drinking motion, shook his head, and pointed to where Onyx lay unconscious a short distance away. We'd managed to get almost half a canteen of water into him, but his normally lustrous black skin was chalky and gray. With his blood loss, he'd need all the liquid he could get.

Visala shaded his eyes. "We've got to make it to the mountains by midday tomorrow, or we'll all die of thirst."

"Can't we build some kind of bridge?" Cinder asked.

I shook my head. "Even if we still had all the packs, we wouldn't have enough rope."

Grunting, Father ran back to the collapsed building and returned a moment later with the coils of cable he'd pulled from the tunnel wall.

"How does he still have that?" Visala asked as Father dropped it at his feet.

"I have no idea," Sparrow said. "He must have picked it up when the hounds attacked, but I can't imagine how he carried it all that way." She pulled down the collar of the old hume's robe to reveal bloody grooves cut deep into the back of his bony neck. Tears came to her eyes as she gently touched the wounds. But Father smiled happily.

"The story he kept repeating," I said. "Didn't you say it was about a girl who fell into a river?"

"In a cavern, in a canyon," Sparrow whispered, staring at Father. "You knew, didn't you? And you brought the cable to make sure we had a way to cross."

Father gazed blithely out at the desert, as though such accolades were unbecoming of a man of his age, and nodded wildly.

Visala ran his fingers over the cable. "It's old, but still in pretty good shape. I think it could hold our weight if we're careful."

"That's it, then," Cinder said, digging through Onyx's pack. "All we've got to do is take the wings and glide to the other side. We can tie off the cable ends on the bridge struts."

Visala walked to the edge of the gorge, his hair blowing back from his forehead, and his wings fluttering in the heavy gusts. "The way that wind's coming out of the mountains into the desert, you'd never get across."

"Then we wait until it stops," I said.

An unearthly howl, muted but unmistakable, floated across the air. Visala glanced at the ruins of the stone building. "I don't think we've got time. I have to cross now."

"Can you make it?" I asked. It would have been hard enough with his bad wing, but now with his shoulder injured as well, I wasn't sure he could fight the wind.

Visala raised his hands helplessly, and I could see he wasn't sure either. "What choice do we have?"

Taking one end of the cable, he handed me the coil. "Make sure to feed it out fast enough that it doesn't slow me down, but not so fast that it tangles in the wind."

I swallowed as he tested the air one more time and spread his wings. I wanted to say something—or do something—before he flew off. But I didn't know what. Standing in the red-hot glare of the desert, our kiss in the dark tunnels seemed almost like something I'd dreamed. With just the two of us, it had felt absolutely right. But in front of the others, I was reminded that the gap between a seraph and a demon spawn was every bit as big as the canyon he was hoping to fly over. I wasn't sure either of us could find a way to cross it.

"Be careful," I finally managed, knowing it was inadequate, but finding nothing better.

"You too," he said. Did I see something in his eyes? A silent communication that he understood the feeling behind my words? It was so hard to tell behind his blazing glow, and I wished again that he could drop his aura completely so I could look directly into his eyes. I didn't even know what color they were.

As soon as he launched himself from the cliff, I realized he wasn't going to make it. The wind that buffeted him even before he began flapping his golden wings only got worse the farther he flew. The cable twanged in my hands as the wind caught it and nearly yanked it from my grip. Visala fought against the gale, trying to rise above it. I unreeled the spool, but there wasn't enough cable to give him the height he needed. He dove down, trying to muscle his way through, and nearly plunged back into the side of the chasm.

Three times he attacked the crossing, circling around and trying to build up enough momentum to carry himself over. Each time, just as he reached the halfway point, the force of the mountain winds drove him back. As he looped around for a fourth try, I could see the way his left wing trembled just to keep him aloft. He was going to end up in the river, just like the girl in Father's song, if he didn't stop.

"Come back!" I shouted, waving my arms.

"What are you doing?" Cinder frowned. "He has to keep trying."

"If he does, he'll kill himself."

"Thought Halos were immortal." She studied me, her head tilted. "Or are you just worried that if he makes it across, he might leave you?"

I knew she'd seen the two of us in the tunnel, although she hadn't said anything about it yet. I didn't care. "How's he going to help us if he ends up at the bottom of the canyon?"

Visala landed a few steps away from us, his chest heaving and his wings shaking as he panted for air. "Give me a minute. I think maybe if I dive down and let the wind pull me up farther out, I'll—"

"No," I cut him off. "You're only going to get weaker the more you try."

"You want us to wait here for the hounds?" Sparrow glared at me, her hume eyes burning. A week ago, that kind of insolence from a hume would have sent me into a rage. But the desert seemed to have taken something out of me. Or maybe it was my feelings for Visala. It was becoming harder and harder to separate us into seraphs, demons, and humes, and easier to think of us as survivors. I wondered whether I would still see things that way once, or if, we made it back to Hell.

"No." I studied a spot on the far side of the chasm to the left of where the tunnel had been sealed on the other side. A section of the canyon wall had broken away, either by time or the building of the tunnel itself, leaving a long, narrow crevice.

I turned to Visala, my heart pounding. "Every time you get almost halfway across, it's as if something doesn't want you to go any farther."

He opened his mouth to argue, but I spoke before he could. "I don't think it's accidental. I think this chasm is the last obstacle. A final way of stopping anyone who managed to make it past the creatures back there." I looked at Father. "Maybe this is what stopped the other groups."

"I'm not going to give up," Sparrow said, her hands clenched.

"Neither am I." When I'd first looked at the crevice, I wasn't sure I could go through with the idea that had come into my head. Now, I was sure. Visala's eyes narrowed, as if he sensed some of what I was thinking. "Visala can't fly more than halfway. But if he can get that far, and as high as the cable will allow while carrying me—"

"Absolutely not." He folded his arms. "If I lose it out there by myself, the worst that will happen is that I fly to the bottom. If I lose it with you, I might not be able to keep us both from falling."

"And if we stay here, we'll all die," I said. "You fly as far and high as you can and throw me toward the crack in the wall on the other side. I'll have the end of the cable tied around my waist so I can use my claws to dig into the rock and climb up the other side."

"Don't bother arguing with her," a hoarse voice croaked. We all turned to see Onyx trying to push himself up. I went to him, but he managed to reach a sitting position before I could help. His eyes went from Visala to me, and I knew at once that he'd seen the two of us, or at least realized we had been together when the hellhounds arrived.

"She's going to do whatever she wants." Onyx's face was pale. It was easy enough to read both messages behind his words. "If you argue with her, all you'll end up doing is wasting time. Get her my wings. They might help her reach the far wall. And you'll need this." He began struggling to remove his silver cloak. "I can do it myself," he said, when I knelt and helped him.

"I'm not the only stubborn one."

He looked like he might argue for a minute, but then shook his head and smiled, allowing me to help.

I grinned, gently pulling his right arm out of his sleeve. It was good to see that I could still make him smile, even if only briefly.

By the time I managed to strap on Onyx's wings and get into his cloak—which I decided was not a bad idea after feeling the power of Visala's aura earlier—the cries of the hellhounds were closer than ever.

"Don't spend too much time enjoying the scenery," Cinder said. "Or the ride." She gave me a wicked grin.

I could only laugh. "I'll try not to die, either."

"Never crossed my mind," she said. "But if you do, I'll kill you."

Onyx called me over, and I dropped to one knee at his side. "I need to go."

"I know," he said, his voice tired. "I wanted to tell you . . . all I care about is that you're happy." My throat closed and I couldn't speak. He seemed to understand, and closed his hand around my fingers. "Don't use the wings too early or the wind will throw you right back. But if you see that you're falling short, let the wind lift you on the other side."

"Okay." I turned away before he could see the moisture in my eyes.

"Are you sure you want to do this?" Visala asked as I walked to the edge of the gorge and stood beside him.

I looked down at the river below, realizing that if I didn't catch the far wall, I had no hope of surviving. "No." I licked my lips and tried to dry my hands on the front of Onyx's cloak, realizing too late that whatever material it was made from wasn't absorbent. "But let's get it over with before I can change my mind."

I tied the cable around my waist. As Cinder picked up the slack, Visala wrapped me in his strong arms, and I couldn't help flashing back to the tunnel. I closed the fangs that were filling my mouth on my tongue, using the pain to clear my head.

"Kick off of me just as I throw you," Visala said.

"My hooves are too sharp," I tried to say back. But he was already in the air, and the gusts whipped the words away. The blast of cold wind doubled in strength as soon as we were airborne, as if trying to force us back. Visala and I were tossed up and down. Although we were climbing, the river appeared far closer and far more dangerous. Invisible fingers snatched at my cloak and tore at my hair.

Visala strained for altitude as he pushed forward. Pressed against his body, I could feel his chest and arms shaking with the strain. I looked back to see that Cinder was nearly out of cable.

"Now!" she screamed.

No, I wanted to cry. We were still too far from the other side. Visala leaned forward, and his lips tickled against my cheek. With a tremendous heave, he threw me forward. At the last second, I remembered to kick off of him. Then I was flying toward the far wall. It was coming at me fast. But I was falling faster.

Amazed at how quickly the crevice seemed to be rising above me, I stretched out my hands and missed. The crack was gone. There was nothing in front of me but bare wall. My claws skidded over rock, and found nothing to grab on to. The whirling river raced toward me.

"Use the wings!" Onyx's voice screamed out behind me.

I grabbed the struts and snapped them open. As if I'd been caught in the talons of some great flying creature, I was jerked upward. My arms and back cried in outrage at the pain that shot through them. Ignoring it, I reached for the edge of the crevice. My claws slipped for a moment before gouging into the stone. As I clung to the narrow crack, the wind ripped at my wings, threatening to pull me off my narrow perch. Holding on with my right hand, I reached down with my left and unhooked the leather straps around my waist and shoulders. Instantly, the wings disappeared into the air.

Voices shouted behind me, but the pulse in my ears and the roar of the water was too loud to make out any words. Trying not to look down at what waited for me if I slipped, I worked my way up the crevice. The wind whipped and tugged, but I kept a tight hold with my claws as I inched toward the top, until at last, I reached up and my fingers found the edge of the cliff.

Looking across the chasm, I could see that the other end of the cable had been tied to a bridge strut. Visala, Onyx, Cinder, and the humes were all wearing what looked like some kind of harness they must have rigged from the rope in Onyx's pack. With arms and legs that still trembled, I ran to the metal bar on my side of the chasm and pulled the cable tight. I had no feeling in my fingers from clinging to the rock, so I rolled onto my back and heaved heavy breaths, hoping that the knot was tight and the metal bar was secure.

Onyx came across the cable first, although he seemed to be arguing against it. Cinder was close behind, in case he needed help, but obstinate as always, he managed to pull himself across. The humes came next, and I could swear Father stopped halfway across to enjoy the view down to the river. By the time Visala managed to loop his harness around the cable, the first hellhound burst from the ground, growling and barking as it raced toward the cliff.

Wearing Onyx's backpack, Visala launched himself off the cliff. The hellhound lunged at him, its claws kicking up plumes of dirt. But it was a hair too late. Snapping its jaws, it flew through the air and plunged into the river.

Watching it disappear into the foaming water, I couldn't help but think how close I'd come to doing the same thing.

But I hadn't. None of us had. We were alive . . . for the moment.

CHAPTER 30

By the time the cavern ceiling went from pink to orange the next morning, my throat felt coated with sand. Breathing and swallowing was torture. We'd been walking almost nonstop since the night before.

"They look so close," Cinder said, staring at the mountains that towered like giants. She and Sparrow were taking their turn supporting Onyx, who had refused any assistance until he literally couldn't walk any farther on his own. I wanted to offer my help, but he'd made it clear he was done with me. Last thing either of us needed was another confrontation. He kept mumbling that he didn't need their help, but his chin had dropped to his chest, his breathing was ragged, and it was clear he couldn't keep going much longer.

"Maybe we should take a rest," I said, noticing the way he dragged his injured leg.

"No," he grunted, his voice as dry as crinkling parchment. "Keep going. Gonna be hot soon." We'd forced him to drink one of the last two canteens. But he threatened to dump out the last one if we didn't share it between us. I'd appreciated the few swallows that disappeared from my dry mouth far too quickly. But I wondered if not making him drink it all hadn't been a mistake.

We were nearly to the edge of the mountains, but Onyx

was almost completely spent. And the rest of us weren't much better. We'd never be able to climb the imposing gray rock that loomed high above us if we didn't find a source of water soon.

Visala paused and pointed to a V in the mountains. "Rock Canyon. I think we can get water there, and maybe an easier way up."

"We can't make it that far." Sparrow looked at Father, who'd appeared to be in a somber mood ever since we crossed the river. I couldn't recall him hooting or grunting once since we began this leg of the journey. His face looked thoughtful, his gaze turned inward. I wondered if he knew something else we didn't, some other obstacle that fate—or whatever forces had made the Outer Circles—would throw in our way.

Cinder tilted her head. "Do you hear that?"

I listened. All I could hear was the steady grating of the desert wind that had returned to normal once we reached this side of the chasm.

Visala nodded and licked his lips. "It sounds like . . . like water."

Onyx lifted his head and put a hand above his eyes. "There," he said, pointing to the left. "A waterfall."

I followed his gaze, but I couldn't make anything out. Onyx seemed sure though. He released his arms from around Cinder and the hume and starting forward on his own.

"Hey, take it easy." I rushed to take one arm, and Visala moved to the other, sliding beneath one sleeve of the silvery cloak I had returned to Onyx.

He tried to pull away from us, but a few steps later, he stumbled and would have fallen if it hadn't been for our support.

Soon, even I could hear the rumble that was just different enough from the wind to carry across the open waste between us and the edge of the mountains. It did sound like the crash of falling water, and even though my mouth had been bone-dry for hours, I began to salivate.

"Look!" Cinder cried. "It's beautiful."

She was right. It was maybe the most beautiful thing I'd ever seen. Clear water burst from the side of a rough rock face as though it was waiting for us. The closer we approached, the louder the sound of the water became, until all I could hear was the splashing of the falls as they crashed and burbled into a clear pool big enough to swim in. A light blue mist floated in the air above the water.

If I hadn't been holding up Onyx, I would have run to it. Cinder grabbed one of the empty canteens and did just that. Her hooves kicked up puffs of dry desert soil as she raced toward the water.

Onyx barked, "Stop!" She whirled around like a spawnling denied its favorite toy.

"It could be some kind of trap," he said, sounding more exhausted than I'd ever heard.

"What?!" Cinder looked at the inviting pool less than a hundred steps away, and back at Onyx, her mouth hanging open.

"He's right," Visala said. "It's too easy."

I looked at the waterfall that seemed every bit as pure and clean as the Judgment water Visala had described and wanted to disagree. The ground between us and the pool was bare. The rock wall left no place for a creature to hide. And yet it sounded exactly like the kind of thing whoever had created this terrible place might do.

"It could be poisoned," Visala said.

Cinder rubbed her mouth with the palm of her hand. "I could try a taste, a small drop."

Onyx sighed. "A drop of the wrong thing could be enough to kill you."

"It's not fair." I stomped my hoof, knowing I sounded like a spawnling, but unable to stop myself. "What if it's *all* been a trap? From the beginning? What if there is no way out? What if we reach the mountains and discover they're not climbable, or filled with even more vile monsters?"

Visala rested a hand on my shoulder, the heat of his aura soothing. "We'll deal with that, just like we've dealt with everything else."

"What does Father think?" Onyx asked.

Sparrow turned to her left, where the old hume had walked silently since the night before, but he was gone. "Father?" she said, surprised.

I glanced around. He'd been there a moment before. He couldn't have gone far.

Sparrow turned toward the pool and her face went white. "Father, stop!"

While the rest of us had paused to discuss the situation, Father had continued walking, unnoticed. At the sound of Sparrow's voice, he broke into a shambling run toward the water's edge.

"Come back!" she screamed. "It's not safe!" Before anyone else could move, she sprinted after the old man. She was less than halfway to him, though, when he reached the water. He stopped by the edge, turned, and looked back. Then he did something I'd never be able to erase from my mind.

With the same calm, introspective look he'd been wearing all day, Father glanced down at the pool. Then he looked at Sparrow and raised one wrinkled hand.

"He's saying goodbye," Onyx whispered.

"He knows," Visala agreed.

"Knows what?" I asked. If it was a trap, why would he go to it? Why would he knowingly put himself in danger?

Still holding out his hand, the old man dropped to one knee.

He smiled at the woman who was racing to him.

She wouldn't make it in time to stop him.

He plunged his face into the water.

A creature leaped from its rippling surface and wrapped itself around his head. The air was filled with Sparrow's horrified shriek.

Father rose briefly to his feet, and his hands began to stretch toward his face. We all ran toward Father. Weapons drawn. I skidded to a stop as smoke poured from the top of the old hume's hair and a glistening blue creature writhed and twisted on his head. Father's hands fell away as he took a step backward and collapsed to the ground in front of us.

By the time Sparrow reached him, it was over. She grabbed the monster that had camouflaged itself perfectly, floating on the surface of the water, burning her hands in the process, but it slithered out of her grip and buried itself back in the sand.

"He's dead," she whispered, glaring back at us. "It was a trap, and he knew it. He died to save the rest of us."

I knelt beside her. Father's face had been burned badly. The charred flesh hung off his gaunt skull. His left cheekbone was exposed from the skin being completely seared away. Sparrow fell to him and wept on his chest as she hugged the old man.

* * *

Onyx knelt at Sparrow's side as she sat cradling Father's head in her lap and wept. The old man's face that had always been scarred was now unrecognizable. What little hair was still left on his head was singed black.

"Why's she making such a fuss?" Cinder whispered. "After potestas renata, he'll go back on the next Stygian."

"I don't know," I admitted. The more time I spent around humes, the more I realized how little I understood them. Sparrow and Father were nothing like what I'd expected. I still believed they'd done horrible things in their previous lives—things that justified eternal torment. But I couldn't help being sad at no longer having Father with us, hooting and pointing.

Was Sparrow right? Had the old hume known it was a trap? After all the pain our kind had put him through, had he really suffered so much more to save us? If it was true, didn't he deserve some kind of recognition, or less severe punishment, when he returned to Hell?

Would he remember what had happened when he came back on the next Stygian Transit? Would he remember Sparrow? Or would his memories be washed away like all the other newly arriving humes?

Why had I never considered that before? Why hadn't I thought about how terrifying it would be to have your entire life removed from your memory?

Visala handed me an ice-cold canteen. "Whatever that was in the pool seems to be gone for now. And the water tastes fine."

I took a swallow. It was delicious, and so cold it felt like fire going down my throat.

"Careful," Visala said, as Cinder filled the other canteen and began to gulp from it. "Don't drink too fast or you'll get sick."

I took a few more swallows and carried the rest to Onyx. He offered the canteen to Sparrow, but she refused it. Tears coursed down her cheeks, and I wondered how she still had enough moisture in her to cry. Was there some secret reserve the body held back for just such moments?

"I'm sorry," I said.

"I should have known," she said, rocking forward and back over and over. "He was never planning on going all the way there."

"Of course he was," I tried to reassure her. "He wouldn't have come if he didn't think he was going to make it."

"No." She wiped her nose with the back of her hand and patted the dead hume's back gently. "All he cared about was getting us safely through the Circles. Why didn't I figure that out? I would never have let him do it."

Onyx put a hand on Sparrow's shoulder, encouraging her to drink. I turned away. I didn't understand humes at all. Why would Father endure everything he did if he never intended to finish the journey? I was sure his plan was to try and escape Hell. But if Father knew the water was dangerous, why did he still try and drink it? It seemed so selfless to give us a warning that way, and I knew humes were selfish by nature. At least the ones sent here.

I felt sick to my stomach and wondered if the water was tainted after all. But when we'd all had enough to get completely refreshed, we rested against the stone cliff until we were ready to continue, and none of us got sick.

As we packed up our few belongings to leave, Onyx looked around. "Where's my cloak?"

I checked the ground. It wasn't like there were a lot of places for it to go. "Did you check your backpack?"

"Why would it be there? I took it off and set it right beside me. Now it's gone." He opened his pack and sorted through the last of his supplies. But it was clear the cloak was missing. "What did you do with it?" he growled, walking to stand nearly nose to nose with Visala.

"Me?" the seraph asked. "What would I want with your cloak?"

Onyx balled his fists. His skin took on the pebbly

armored texture it got when he was angry or afraid. "First it was clearing our names. Then it was the water. Now it's the cloak. You've been doing everything you can to keep me from standing up to you."

Visala stepped back and lowered his hand to the hilt of his sword. "Is that what you've been planning? You want me to lead you to Judgment so you can attack me like you did on Arrival Day?"

Onyx pulled his whip from his belt.

"Stop it," I said, stepping between them. "There's no reason for this. Where would he put your cloak, Onyx? Maybe it blew away and we didn't notice."

Onyx scowled, his eyes searching the seraph as though he thought Visala was somehow concealing the cloak beneath his aura. Was he? Onyx's cloak was even heavier than ours, and none of them had blown away. And the silver fabric had a sort of crackly sound to it. Wouldn't we have heard if something like that had blown across the desert floor?

Cinder eyed Visala with clear suspicion. There was no question what she thought. I didn't know if he had done something with the cloak or not. I wasn't sure I completely blamed him if he had. It was clear Onyx wasn't going to be satisfied coming this close to Judgment without trying to enter it—even if that meant attacking Visala all over again.

But it was equally clear Visala had plans of his own. What if he'd taken the cloak and salted the water so he could disappear without clearing our names or giving Onyx the angel-fire sword? All I knew was that I had to settle things down.

"We've made it this far," I said, turning to Visala. "Let's not stop ourselves after all we've been through.

"Fine." He moved back another step and let go of his

sword, raising his hands. "I swear I had nothing to do with taking your cloak. But I'll help you look for it."

For the next thirty minutes, all of us except Sparrow helped search. She continued to hold Father, whispering to him as though he were still alive. For a moment, I wondered if the hume could have taken it. They *were* thieves, after all. But what would be the point, and where would she hide it?

The search turned up empty, and Visala and Onyx both appeared on edge, watching each other warily and keeping their distance from one another. But at least they weren't fighting.

We had to move on. Onyx grumbled, but we had no choice if we wanted to reach Rock Canyon before night. As we started to leave, Sparrow picked up Father's body.

"What are you doing?" I asked.

"I'm not leaving him here." She stared, as though daring me to disagree. I didn't care what she did. But Father's body was heavy, and already the heat was beginning to affect it. Soon she would have no choice but to leave it behind.

"Let me carry him," Onyx said. But Sparrow shook her head.

"He brought me this far. I can take him the rest of the way. At least to the mountains."

I was sure she would give out. But for the next two hours, she carried Father's body in her arms, never complaining or accepting help, although sweat poured down her face, and her arms shook under the strain of weight.

As the last of the color began to drain from the sky, Visala led us out of the flat sandy soil into a series of small canyons and rolling passes where things he called brown grass and tiny yellow flowers no bigger than my fingertip hugged the ground. It wasn't much, but after nothing but day after day of sand, the change was nice.

Every so often, he stopped to examine a boulder or a canyon wall. I had no idea what he was searching for, until at last, he led us into a canyon that dead-ended in a slope too steep to climb.

"Ready to admit you're lost?" Onyx, whose limp had become more pronounced the farther we went, settled himself on a boulder.

Sparrow dropped to the ground, clearly exhausted, but still without a word of complaint. It was as if she blamed herself for Father's death and was determined to punish herself.

"Not at all," Visala said. He studied the hillside, carefully examining each rock and plant, although it didn't look any different from a dozen hills we'd passed before. Finally, he squatted down and placed his hand on a section of rough bare rock. His aura flashed, and the ground shook.

Cinder, who'd been sitting a few feet away, jumped to her feet with a squawk of surprise. Onyx grabbed his sword. I backed away, wondering if it was another trap.

Only Sparrow seemed unaffected as the side of the hill rumbled and then swung outward. Visala stepped back and pushed the rock like a door. Behind it was a dark rectangular opening, a little taller than the seraph, and wide enough for all of us to stand side by side.

The seraph stepped into the entrance and the ceiling glowed white, revealing a polished floor and walls so smooth, they gleamed like metal. Visala bowed and waved his arm as though inviting us into his house. "Welcome to Judgment."

CHAPTER 31

"I don't understand." I peered into the passage that curved up and directly into the mountain. This was nothing like what Visala had described to me.

Onyx moved close enough to look inside, but no nearer. Cinder tilted her head and lifted an eyebrow as if to say, *See, I told you that you couldn't trust him.*

Visala peered into the opening and lifted his good shoulder. "Okay, maybe not Judgment itself. But a direct passageway there. It's not the most beautiful, but I can promise no more traps or surprises from here on out."

Onyx snorted.

"Excuse me if I don't take your word for it." Cinder laughed.

"Take my word or don't," Visala said. "But we can spend the night here. And by the end of the day tomorrow, we'll reach Judgment."

"Why not go the rest of the way tonight, if we're that close?" Onyx asked, clearly suspicious that Visala was up to something.

"Because whether you like it or not," he said, "you're exhausted. And so am I. We all are. The rest of the way will be easy compared to what we've been through. But it is a hike."

Cinder edged through the doorway and tapped on a

wall. It rang like metal too. She quickly backed away. "I'm not sleeping in there," she said. "It creeps me out."

"Suit yourself." Visala walked through the doorway. "But I'm going to enjoy climate-controlled peace and quiet."

"Climate-controlled?" I asked, stepping into the tunnel. It was so smooth. So clean. Not a trace of dirt, or rust, or corrosion. I'd never seen anything like it except the Stygian.

"It senses your body heat and controls the temperature of the air," Visala bragged. "Not too hot, not too cold."

The idea was so incredible, I couldn't even fathom it. How was controlling the temperature of the air even possible? Like Cinder said, it did seem a little creepy. But it also seemed . . . I wasn't sure of the word I was looking for . . . elegant maybe?

"You'd like us all to sleep outside, wouldn't you?" Onyx stomped into the opening, jumping a little when his hooves clanged on the floor, then continuing on. "That would make it so easy for you to leave in the middle of the night."

Visala waved his hands as though that was the silliest thing he'd ever heard, but personally I thought it wasn't a far-fetched idea. I knew I had feelings for the Halo, but I still wasn't sure I could completely trust him.

"I need to take care of Father," Sparrow said. "I'll be back in a few hours."

As she stood and carried Father out of the canyon, Visala walked into the tunnel, running his hand along a gleaming wall. "Nice to be home."

Onyx followed close on his heels.

Cinder was leaning against a wall. Although we all had washed as best we could in the pool, her clothes were filthy, and her hair was a mess. I knew mine wasn't any better. But she put her hands behind her head, grinned, and sighed contentedly. "So. Have you made your choice?"

I grimaced, less than thrilled that she found me so amusing. "I'm going for a walk."

I didn't intend to follow Sparrow. What humes chose to do with the bodies of their dead was of no interest to me. When I left the mouth of the canyon, I turned left, only because it was a direction we hadn't been, and I wanted to be alone. But when I climbed a small hill and found the hume in a valley below, scraping away rocks and dirt, I couldn't help wondering what she was up to.

Demons burned their dead. It was clean and honorable. I assumed humes did the same, although now that I thought about it, I'd never seen a hume funeral pyre. Watching Sparrow claw and scrape, I realized she was digging a hole. Was she going to leave Father's body in the dirt? The thought was repugnant. His corpse would rot there. How could they view that as showing respect?

The longer she dug, the more fascinated I became. I moved back and sat down to remain out of sight. When she appeared to have dug as deeply as she could, she carefully lifted Father's body and lowered it into the hole. Was the idea to keep animals away from his body? We hadn't seen a living thing since crossing the gorge.

She leaned over him, adjusted his robe, and picked something up. Even in the dim glow of twilight, I saw it flash silver. Onyx's robe! She was the one who'd taken it. She'd hidden it under Father's robe. But why? Was she working with Visala? To what end? Or had she stolen it just because she was a thief and could?

Part of me wanted to rush down, yank Onyx's robe away, and confront her. But as she bowed her head over the hole, speaking softly enough that I couldn't make out her words, I couldn't bring myself to disrespect Father that way. He was a hume, and sticking his body in a hole was horrible, but he had saved our lives more than once.

After she finished speaking, I expected her to return the way she'd come, and I started to stand up to intercept her. Instead, she began scraping the dirt and rocks over Father's corpse. Why would she cover the body of someone she loved in filth? I didn't understand. Maybe humes couldn't come up with the fuel for a proper funeral.

By the time Sparrow finished covering Father, all but a faint glow had disappeared from the sky. I stood hidden by the darkness, waiting for her to return. Again, she paused. Lifting her head, she opened her mouth, and what came out was so shocking, so incredible, I could only stand dumbfounded.

It was like speaking, but slightly higher pitched and more melodic. But the way she said the words was . . . amazing. She raised her voice, but she wasn't yelling. She swayed back and forth, holding herself. Some of the words rhymed, but that wasn't what made them so special. It was the way they came out, in a sort of cadence or rhythm—her voice rising and dropping in a way I'd never heard.

Listening to it made me want to move in time to her words. It made me want to repeat them with her. Her voice did something to me. Something I'd never felt before. She spoke about hills and skies, friends found and lost. It touched me deeply.

When she finished, my eyes were blurred with tears and my cheeks were flushed. And when she began again, I felt my heart soar with her voice. What was this? Could all humes do it? If so, why hadn't I heard it before?

The rhythm was different this time. The words were different too. After a moment, I recognized them. This was what Father had been saying back in the tunnel. *In a cavern, in a canyon.* Some of the words were repeated, and soon I found myself saying them with her, trying to copy the way she said them and failing miserably.

Was this *singing*, then? It didn't sound like what Father had been doing, but that was probably because he had no tongue. And in a way, it was the same. I remembered how he had hooted, his body moving in time to his "words."

The third time she did it, I stood silently, letting her voice float over me like a cloud. It was without a doubt the most beautiful thing I'd ever heard. When at last she finished and started up the hill, I couldn't help myself from running toward her.

"What is that?" I called. "What you were doing. What is it?"

Startled, she stepped back. Her face went tight. "What are you doing here? Were you spying on me?"

"No." I shook my head, still enthralled by what I'd heard. "I didn't mean to follow you. I came to the same place by accident. Then I saw you with Father. And you did that thing. What is it? Can you teach me?"

She scowled and tried to push past me. "Leave me alone."

I couldn't let her. I had to know what she was doing, and if I could do it as well. As she tried to get by me, I grabbed her shoulder and spun her around. Something fell from her arms onto the ground. It glinted silver, and I remembered what I'd seen her do before. I snatched Onyx's cloak before she could get to it. "Tell me what you were doing, or I'll tell Onyx you're the one who stole this. Do you think he'll still want you along if he knows that you're a thief?"

Sparrow exhaled. "I was going to leave it for him tonight."

"Leave?" I thought I understood. "You're sneaking away, aren't you? You want to escape to Judgment."

Her shoulders slumped.

So much became clear. She was setting Onyx against Visala to create distrust. And if she'd done that . . . "You salted your own water, didn't you? And made everyone think it was Cinder." I couldn't believe even a hume would sink that low. "If it weren't for you, Onyx would have had twice the water in his pack. You could have killed everyone, including Father."

"I had no idea we'd lose the rest of the supplies," she said, "or I never would have done it. I swear. But I knew they'd be watching us closely. I needed contention. A diversion, so when the time was right, Father and I . . . only now it's just me. Please." She grabbed my hand. "Don't tell anyone till the morning. Let me slip away."

I pulled my hand from her grip, disgusted by her touch. "Why should I?"

She bit her lip, and I could see tears gleaming in her eyes. It looked strange on someone as tough as her. "If you promise to let me go, I'll tell you what I was doing. But I don't think I can teach you. I think . . . I think I might be some kind of mutant."

I considered her offer. She didn't deserve to escape a punishment she'd earned. But I did want to know more about what I'd heard. And even if she did manage to make it back to Judgment, eventually she'd be captured and returned. "Tell me."

She wiped her tears away, embarrassed. "I don't think you'll like hearing it."

I sniffed. Humes were all liars. "I'll decide for myself what I like. But if I think you're lying, the deal's off."

"I won't lie," she said, her voice softening. "It's just, the only person I've ever told this to is Father." She sighed again and stared out into the desert. "You know that humes arrive in Hell without memories?"

I nodded.

"Most of us think it happens in Judgment. But I guess it could happen on the way here, in the Stygian train.

Or maybe it's just the shock of arriving in a . . . a place like this."

That was another thing about humes. They all thought they were too good for "a place like this." Onyx had spent enough time with them that it had rubbed off on him as well.

"Anyway," Sparrow continued, "most of us arrive with no memories at all. But for a few of us, it's like they missed erasing something. Usually, it's not much. An image, or a phrase. Some people think they can remember the face of a loved one. Or a scene from a world nothing like this."

I remembered Onyx's puzzle box. "Go on."

She ran her fingers through her short hair. "There's not much more than that. I didn't arrive with the faces of any loved ones. No images of another world. Just the ability to *sing* as Father calls . . ." She swallowed. "As he *called* it. I don't know where the songs come from. Or why no one else can do it. Maybe it's part of what was erased from us. Or maybe, maybe there's just something wrong with me. It's why Father named me Sparrow. He said I reminded him of a creature that flew through the air and sang like me."

"But you don't like to be called that," I said.

She folded her arms across her chest and hunched her shoulders. There was something she wasn't telling me. "If you can do something so, so beautiful, why not do it all the time?" I asked. "Why hide it?"

She gasped for breath, and I realized she was trying not to cry again. "Why are you doing this to me?"

"Doing what?" I couldn't understand why she was acting this way. "If I could sing, I'd do it every day."

"You want to know why I don't sing?" she spat, her eyes blazing as she spun around to stare at me. "Fine. I'll tell you. I don't sing because it makes me so sick that I have to throw up. I don't sing because . . ." Her face crumpled, and her entire body trembled.

"I used to sing, all the time. I felt strange doing it because I was the only one who could. But Father encouraged me. He said it made the other humes happy. It made their pathetic lives a little more bearable. It made me happy doing it. So I sang. In the fields, in the factories. Wherever I was assigned."

I could understand that. It had made me feel happy in a way I'd never imagined before.

"And it did make them happy," she said, her voice filled with a bitterness I couldn't understand. "It made the demons happy too. The ones who drove us night and day. Who whipped us for being too slow or too fast. Who beat us for not knowing what they wanted us to do, and for making the wrong assumptions when we tried to guess." She laughed a jagged gale, and all at once, I wasn't sure I wanted to hear the rest of this story—was afraid of where it might go.

"The demons *loved* my singing," she said. "They loved it so much that they brought their friends to hear me. One of them, the one who beat us the most when we worked in the fields, loved my singing so much that he would call me over. He would grab me by the arm and . . ."

She was sobbing now, and I didn't want to hear any more. But she wouldn't stop talking.

"He forced himself on me. I would have preferred a beating than him violating me in the worst way possible. And the worst part? He made me sing. Sing while he did disgusting, vile, *inhumane* things to me!"

I pressed my hands to my ears. I didn't want to believe that a demon could do something like that, or was capable of such a thing. That was the kind of thing humes did. But I knew she wasn't lying, and somehow her voice made it through my fingers.

"I knew he would continue doing it over and over if

I didn't stop him. The other humes were too afraid to say anything. And with good reason. They could have been next. So one day, when he came to beat me, I had found a sharp rock. I kept singing as I rammed it into his ear. Then I ran. Father hid me, but other humes were punished in my place. Would you like to hear what happened to them?"

I shook my head.

"It was the last time I sang until tonight. Can you understand why I don't like to be called Sparrow now?"

"Yes," I said, my teeth chattering. I was going to be sick, but I didn't want her to see it.

"Father hoped . . . he hoped one day I could, if not forgive, at least forget, and sing again. He called me Sparrow in hopes that he would hear me sing. By the time I finally did, it was too late." She swallowed hard. "Can I go now?"

Before I could say yes, my stomach clenched, and I was violently sick against the side of the hill. When I finished throwing up, she was gone.

On my way back to the passage, I met Onyx, Visala, and Cinder searching for me. "Where have you been?" Visala asked. "We thought something happened."

"Sorry. I . . . had a lot to think about."

"Have you seen Sparrow?" Onyx asked. I shook my head.

When we reached the doorway, Onyx's cloak was folded neatly on the floor.

Sparrow was nowhere to be seen.

CHAPTER 32

Visala and Onyx argued all night over who had taken the cloak and why they'd returned it. Visala was sure Onyx had the cloak all along, and Onyx was sure the seraph had given it back to convince him to let his guard down.

I was sick of their fighting, but I didn't tell either of them that Sparrow had taken the cloak and salted the water. It didn't seem fair somehow, after what she'd confided to me.

When she hadn't returned by morning, opinions were mixed as to whether Sparrow had stayed in the desert to mourn Father or gone ahead into Judgment on her own.

Visala went outside to look for her. And since Onyx was sure the seraph was trying to abandon us, he refused to let him go alone. So the two of them stomped into the brush, arguing and growling the same kinds of threats at each other that they'd been making since they'd first met.

"What's wrong with you?" Cinder asked, sitting beside me on the smooth metal floor that somehow managed to feel both warm and cool at the same time. "Afraid your two boyfriends will kill each other out there?"

I tried to smile, but couldn't seem to remember how to make my lips form the expression. "Guess I didn't sleep very well."

"It's this place," Cinder said, wrinkling her nose. "The air tastes like metal here. And it smells weird."

I sniffed. The only scent was from the stink of our unwashed bodies. "I don't think it actually smells like anything."

"Exactly," she said, looking around like she expected the walls to close in on us at any second. "It's *unnatural*. No smoke, no sulfur. Anything could be sneaking up on you and you'd never know it. I can't wait to go home."

Visala said that something called air exchangers filtered the air to clean out all the impurities. I didn't understand that any more than I understood how they could automatically adjust the temperature. But what if this was the way air was *supposed* to smell? What if it only seemed unnatural because we'd spent our whole lives breathing air that *wasn't* clean?

The morning before he and his friends attacked the Stygian, Onyx had tried to tell me that I wasn't seeing Hell the way it really was because I'd been born there. I didn't understand what he was talking about at the time. Now I was beginning to.

"Have you ever thought about what it would be like if we *didn't* go home?" I asked.

"What?" Cinder narrowed her eyes, her skin tone shifting ever so slightly toward the color of the wall she was leaning against as though she was trying to hide. "You want to stay here? In these lifeless gray tunnels?"

"Of course not."

She pursed her lips with a knowing smile. "You think angel boy is going to take you to Judgment and buy you a set of wings so the two of you can live in a metal house that doesn't smell like anything and make little angel-demon babies together."

"I do not," I growled, digging my talons into my palms.

"Good," she snapped. "Because trust me, fire-eyes, that is not happening. But where else would you go? The only thing left is the Outer Circles, and even at your fangs-and-claws worst, you aren't tough enough to survive out there alone for long."

"I don't know," I said, running my fingers through my matted hair. "I'm just not sure I can go back to Hell."

Cinder slid closer and took my hand. "This isn't about not getting enough sleep. And it's not about having a couple of imp-eyed hot bodies fighting over you. What's really going on?"

How could I tell her what I'd been thinking? Sparrow's story had affected me so deeply, it felt like something inside me was broken forever. It was one thing to torture humes. That's what we were there for—what *they* were there for. To pay for the horrific things they'd done in life. But what had happened to her was a violation every bit as horrible as the sins the humans were being punished for. And the fact that it had been done to her by one of my own made me disgusted to be a demon.

"Sparrow was beaten a lot," I whispered, "almost to death. And they did *things* to her. The ultimate violation."

Cinder gasped. "When? Last night? Is that why she's gone?" Her hand squeezed mine until I could feel the bones in my fingers grinding together. "Was it the Halo?"

"What? No. It wasn't last night, and it wasn't by Visala. It was back when she was in Hell. She used to do something called singing that's sort of like talking in rhythm, but way more beautiful. The guard watching her group of humes heard her singing. He violated her. Repeatedly. Forcing her to sing while he did it."

"Oh." Cinder nodded. "Well, that's terrible." She glanced toward the door. "At least it wasn't one of those two. Because that would be super horrible."

"That's all you care about?" I demanded. "That she wasn't attacked by Visala or Onyx?"

Cinder frowned. "I said it was terrible. What more do you want? It's not like we can go back and fix it."

I yanked my hand from hers. "That doesn't make it right!"

Cinder shrugged. "I mean, you need to remember that the humes are here because they've done things that are at least that bad and much worse, and it continues in Humeville. I'm sure of it."

"But we're supposed to be the *good ones*!" I screamed, jumping to my feet. "We were chosen by Judgment to punish sins. Not commit them ourselves."

Before we'd left Hell, I'd been sure of so many things. Now I wasn't sure of anything. Who was good? Who was bad? Who decided? And how did I fit into any of it? *Where* did I fit in?

It was like I'd spent the first sixteen years of my life walking blindly along a seemingly solid road, completely unaware that my safe path was covered with slippery patches, sucking sand pits, and holes so deep, I couldn't see the bottom. I tried to tell myself that the road must have changed, but the more I learned, the more I realized it had always been that way, but I just never bothered to look down.

Cinder slashed her tail against her legs. "I don't understand what you're freaking out about. They're just humes. No matter what happens to them in Hell, it will never be as bad as what they did to get sent here. They're evil."

"Are they?" I ran my tongue across my lips, my mouth suddenly too dry. I'd always believed what Cinder said. But the first two humes I'd met weren't anything like what I'd expected. Sparrow was angry, arrogant, even condescending. But could I blame her after what she'd been subjected to? Would I have been any different?

And despite her stealing and selfishness, there'd been

something honorable about her. Something almost pure. The way she'd cared for Father. The way she blamed herself for his death, despite the fact that there was nothing she could have done. She was far from perfect. But was she actually evil?

"If Father was so bad, why did he sacrifice himself to keep us from dying of thirst?"

Cinder leaped up and began pacing back and forth across the hall like a caged animal. "I don't know. And I don't care. I just want to get out of here and back to my own life. Maybe it's not perfect. And maybe some of us are just as bad as the humes. But it's the only thing I have. If wanting that makes me bad too, then I guess I am."

I shook my head, all the anger draining out of me. "You're not bad, Cinder. And you're right. There's nowhere else we can go. Once Visala clears our names, we can head back."

She shrugged. "*If* he does."

"What are you talking about?" I asked. "You heard him say that he would."

"I heard him," she said. "We all did. But how do we know he wasn't lying to convince us to come with him?"

"He's a seraph. He promised."

Cinder sneered. "Maybe humes and demons aren't the only ones who do bad things."

I opened my mouth and shut it, unsure what to think. It was like the road I'd been walking wasn't just dangerous, but there was actually no road at all and never had been.

"Onyx doesn't believe the Halo has the ability to clear our names even if he wants to," Cinder said. "Think about it. If he has that kind of power, why didn't anyone come back to Hell to get him?"

"If you both believe that, then what are we even doing here?" I asked. "Why bother crossing the Outer Circles?"

Cinder sighed. "We need to know if you're with us."

I clenched my fists. "What are you talking about?"

She glanced toward the tunnel winding up into the mountain and then at the opening where Onyx and Visala had gone out searching for Sparrow.

"We're getting close to Judgment. If Visala's going to betray us, he has to do it soon. When he does, will you side with him or with us?"

"You're my friends," I said, unable to believe what she was asking. "Do you really think I'd do anything to hurt you?"

Cinder narrowed her eyes. "Onyx doesn't. I'm not so sure."

Fangs filled my mouth, and my vision turned red as I pointed a taloned finger inches from her face. "I've known Onyx my whole life. I would never do anything to hurt him. But if you ever accuse me of being a traitor again, I will shred your body and feed the pieces to the creatures in the desert."

I expected Cinder to run in terror. Instead, she burst into laughter. "Okay, I'm convinced. Put away your claws."

She reached into her pocket and handed me a pair of small hairy blobs.

"What are these?" I asked, not sure I wanted to know.

"Hellhound fur," Cinder said. "Hellhounds are immune to seraph commands. Onyx thinks that if we plug our ears with their fur, it will give us time to overpower the Halo and take his sword."

I grunted. "So that's what this is all about. You helped him cross the desert just to get the sword."

"It's the most powerful weapon in Hell or Judgment," Cinder said. "Once we have it, we can either fight our way into Judgment to take whatever's there, or use it to buy our freedom when we get back to Hell."

CHAPTER 33

After not finding any sign of Sparrow, we all agreed it was time to continue on to Judgment. The hallway flattened out after several hours of climbing. Shortly after that, we rounded a corner to find ourselves in a room with two rows of benches and a table covered with stacks of folded white robes. Despite the clean air, the cloaks had a dusty, unused look, as though no one had touched them for a long time.

"This is it." Visala turned, visibly excited. He nodded to a hallway on the other side of the room. "Judgment is right through there."

My heart raced as I looked into the hall. It didn't seem any different than the one we'd been hiking through all morning. But the idea that we'd finally reached our destination was so thrilling, I wanted to yell or jump up in the air. For a second, I wished I could sing like Sparrow, before remembering what it had cost her.

Cinder and Onyx glanced at the seraph before quickly raising their hands to their ears.

"That's it?" Visala asked, clearly disappointed by the less-than-enthusiastic response. "We crossed a desert no one's ever survived, were almost killed by too many creatures to count, and nearly died of thirst, all to get here, and you have nothing to say now that we've finally succeeded?"

Onyx and Cinder tensed, preparing to attack.

"They can't hear you," I said.

Visala frowned. "Why not?"

I shook my head. "Their ears are filled with hellhound fur to stop you from commanding them."

"Commanding?" Visala slowly grinned as realization dawned on him. "So they can't hear a word I'm saying?"

I shook my head.

"Have I ever mentioned that I can't understand why your friend thinks she's such hot stuff? Waving her tail and shaking her rear?" Visala did an eerily accurate impression of Cinder, swiveling his hips as he walked slowly across the room. "And then there's Onyx. Me strong. Me trust no one. Halo bad. Demon good."

I couldn't help laughing. By now, Onyx and Cinder had realized I must not have put the fur in my ears. Cinder shot me daggers with her eyes. Onyx simply looked disappointed.

I was sorry I'd hurt him. But I wasn't sorry I hadn't gone along with their plan.

Onyx pulled the fur from his ears. "I thought you were on our side."

"Traitor," Cinder said, throwing her fur pellets to the floor.

"Sorry," I said. "I can't talk right now. Visala commanded me to name all the guys you've ever made out with. It could take months."

Cinder sneered. "Very funny."

"I've been thinking about what you said the whole way up here. And it doesn't make sense. Visala had way too many chances to betray us if he was going to. And even though Onyx attacked the Stygian, he did it for a good reason. We only made it across the Outer Circles by trusting each other, and I'm not going to stop now."

Onyx crossed his arms. "Fine. Give me the sword and take us to Judgment."

"I'm sorry," Visala said. "I can't do that."

"What?" I felt my heart skip a beat. *Please,* I whispered to Visala inside my head, *don't prove me wrong about you.*

"You were right to trust me," he said. "I'm going to do everything that I promised. But I need to ask you to trust me just a little longer. I have to go the rest of the way alone. I'll be back in a few hours, and your names will be cleared. I swear."

"I'm not letting you go anywhere," Onyx growled. "I've never trusted you, and I still don't." He lunged forward as Visala backed away, drawing his sword.

"The very fact that I'm *not* commanding you should prove I'm telling the truth," Visala said. He looked at me, but I didn't know what to believe. All this time, he'd let us think we were going to see Judgment. And now, at the last minute and only a few steps away, he wanted us to wait in a cold gray room while he went ahead.

"It proves nothing," Onyx said, his hands out and his body tense. "If you really are telling the truth, take me with you."

"You'd be captured and thrown in prison the first time someone saw you," Visala said. "Your plan would never have worked, even if you'd managed to take control of the Stygian. Demons can't just go strolling down the streets of Judgment."

Onyx snorted. "I'm not letting a lying coward like you go alone!"

Visala looked at me again. I could read the pleading in his eyes—begging me to believe in him. I wanted to. I really did.

He turned back to Onyx. "Fine. I'll take her."

I gasped. "What?!"

Visala swallowed. "I understand that the three of you don't trust me to go into Judgment and clear your names. But it's going to be hard enough for me to get in, do what I have to do, and get out undetected alone. If I have to bring one of you, it's got to be someone I can trust to do what I ask when I ask it. Sorry, big guy, but that's not you. And it's not the scheming little demon who's been trying to stab me in the back ever since I got here. That only leaves Blaze."

"Absolutely not!" Onyx roared.

Still holding the sword, Visala edged toward me. "Come with me," he whispered. "I promise I'll keep you safe."

I shook my head, speechless. I tried to catch my breath. "You said we'd be thrown in prison as soon as anyone sees us."

"*He* would," Visala said. "Because there are things he'd refuse to accept. But if you do what I say, I can sneak you inside." He lowered his aura and reached out and touched my hand. Fire flickered and swirled between our fingers. "Once you're there, I have friends who could hide you. Protect you. I could show you my world. Who knows? Maybe you'd like it enough to stay."

Onyx shook his head silently when I glanced at him, pain clear in his eyes.

Cinder grimaced.

I turned to Visala, and he squeezed my fingers. "Please," he whispered. "Come with me, Blaze. I think . . . you're not what I expected. And I don't think I'm what you expected. Maybe, together we can show people that all of the things they believe are wrong."

For a moment, the whole room seemed to freeze. I looked at Visala, begging me to go with him. Onyx, pleading silently for me to stay. So many thoughts filled my head—so many emotions. Memories of Onyx and me growing up together. Of him showing me Hell from the top of the Immigration Station. My not-so-chaste kiss with Visala. So much I wanted to know. So much I didn't understand.

"I'm sorry," I whispered. "Hell is my home. It's not perfect, but it's where I belong."

Onyx released a pent-up breath.

Visala's shoulders slumped. He let go of my fingers. The warmth of his aura—and something else?—disappeared with his touch. "I understand," he said. "Here." He dropped the angel-fire sword to the floor and kicked it in Onyx's direction. "It won't be of any use to you for long. But I believe I already warned you of that."

As Onyx's eyes followed the path of the sword, Visala turned and ran from the room.

"Guess I lost that bet," Cinder said. "I was sure you and Halo-Boy were a done deal."

I walked to one of the benches and slumped onto it, feelingly surprisingly disappointed. Had I wanted Visala to argue more? To fight for me? To drag me kicking and screaming with him? It didn't matter. I didn't belong in Judgment any more than he belonged in Hell.

"I guess we just wait now."

"Blaze?" Onyx knelt by my side, the sword lying forgotten on the floor for the time being.

"Yeah," I said, wishing everyone would leave me alone.

"There's something I have to tell you."

I looked up. There was an expression on his face I'd never seen there. It was a little like when he'd talked about changing Hell. Only this time, it seemed to be directed at me.

"I couldn't let you go with him."

"I didn't need your permission," I said.

He swallowed. "I know. And I wouldn't have tried to stop you if you'd decided to go. But when he asked, I realized I'd waited way too long to say something I've wanted to say forever. Maybe you won't want to hear it now. And maybe it's too late. But I need to get it out."

Why was everyone telling me things that changed my life? Wasn't I already messed up enough as it was?

Onyx licked his lips, his forehead wrinkled as though whatever he had to say took immense effort. "I love you, Blaze. I always have. Even when we were little, I always knew you were the one I wanted to spend my life with."

I glanced at Cinder, who was nodding silently. I looked at Onyx. He was smiling like a spawnling, waiting for me to say something. I opened my mouth to tell him that I loved him too. To tell him I'd always known he was the one I wanted to spend my life with.

But I couldn't.

I *hadn't* known. I didn't know. Things had changed so drastically over the last few months. I did love him. But did I love him *that* way? If I did, how could I have had such intense feelings for Visala inside the tunnel? All at once, the emotions I'd been experiencing all morning seemed too overwhelming to deal with. I didn't know how I felt about humes. I didn't know how I felt about Hell. It was my home, but it seemed different now—changed in a way I couldn't explain.

I didn't know how I felt about Onyx or the way he felt about me. I didn't know how I felt about Visala, either. I was so mixed up about demons and humans and seraphs— about myself and Hell and Judgment. But all of my doubts and fears came back to one thing: accepting what I'd been told without bothering to discover the truth for myself.

If I let Visala go without finding out how I felt, I'd never be able to forgive myself.

"I'm sorry," I said, jumping to my feet.

Onyx nearly fell over backward, shock clear on his face. I didn't want to hurt him, but suddenly I knew that if I didn't follow Visala to Judgment, I'd never learn who I was or where I belonged.

"I have to go." Without looking at Onyx or Cinder—without giving either of them a chance to say something that might change my mind—I turned and ran through the door. Gray walls flew by me in a blur. My heart raced as my hooves clanged against the floor. I had to find Visala, had to catch up with him and tell him I'd changed my mind.

Ahead of me, the hallway ended. A metal ladder was attached to the wall. I was terrified the doorway to Judgment would already be closed. But overhead, I could see sparkling white light shining through a circular opening.

As I ran toward the ladder, someone stepped out of a small alcove and grabbed me. Sure that it was Onyx trying to drag me back, I turned on him with a snarl.

It was Sparrow. "Don't follow him," she said, her voice urgent. "You can't go up there."

"Why not?" I asked, trying to pull away before the door shut.

"Because I did." She squeezed my arm with surprising strength. "Blaze, you have to trust me. Don't go through that doorway. If you do, the life you know will be destroyed forever."

I stopped struggling. "What do you mean? What did you see?"

Sparrow rubbed her mouth. "I'd tell you if I could. All I can say is this: If you go through that portal, everything you've thought, everything you've believed, will be changed forever. You'll never be able to come back. Trust me when I say you are better off not knowing some things."

She stared up at me, eyes filling with tears. "You let me escape when you could have stopped me. Allow me to return the favor. Go back to your friends. You can have a happy life. Maybe not the most exciting one, but good enough. If you follow the seraph, all hope of happiness will be lost forever."

I wasn't sure if I trusted Sparrow or not. The hume's motives were still as unclear as everyone else's. The one thing I *was* sure of was that I was tired of being in the dark. Tired of having so many things I didn't understand. I couldn't imagine how having more knowledge would make me unhappy. But it was a risk I was willing to take.

I lifted her hand from my arm. "I have to know."

"I understand," she said with a sad little smile. "I'd probably do the same thing."

I walked to the end of the hallway and turned back to look at her. "What will you do?"

"What can I do? There's no turning back. Outside, a few of my memories started to return. Father thought there were others in Judgment who might be able to help me recover the rest. After what I've remembered so far, I almost wish there weren't." She shrugged. "Since we probably won't ever see each other again, I want to say I'm sorry."

With no idea what she was apologizing for, I stared up through the circular doorway into dazzling white light. Cold air—every bit as fresh as Visala had described—filled my lungs. Taking a deep breath, I put my hands on the ladder. Rung by rung, I pulled myself up until I reached the hatch.

Closing my eyes, I climbed through the opening and entered Judgment.

CHAPTER 34

The first thing I noticed when I opened my eyes was how clear everything was—brilliant, and sharp as the edge of a blade. The ground was white. The sky was white. The air itself danced and sparkled. Nothing I'd ever experienced in Hell had ever been this pristine.

As I stood, clutching my arms to my chest, my cloak began turning white too. Was this where seraphs' auras came from? If I stayed here long enough, would my skin start to burn with a white fire of its own?

The second thing I noticed was the bitter cold. I shivered, and my chest ached every time I inhaled. Each breath out produced a cloud of mist that floated from my mouth and nose before disappearing into the sky. I pursed my lips and blew out a stream of smoke, pretending I was a hellhound, then laughed at the plumes that swirled about my freezing nose and cheeks.

I was going to need some warmer clothes soon. Maybe that's what the robes below had been for. I probably should have put one on. Hopefully they weren't required. How terrible would it be to discover I'd broken a rule my first few minutes in Judgment? But it was too beautiful to worry. Instead, I twirled slowly around and around, holding out my hands and marveling at the splendor. My hooves sank into the pillowy ground, leaving glittering tracks. The air was so fresh, I could actually taste it, like candy, as it brushed across my tongue.

I looked for Visala, but the shimmering air made it hard to see. Climbing a small ridge, I discovered an ugly brown hill that curved out from the side of the mountain below in a rough dome shape, extending as far as I could see. The white ground disappeared abruptly at its edge. What few patches crossed over were dark and dirty, as though filled with corruption.

Wisps of fetid smoke rose from cracks and seams in its pebbled surface, and streams of filthy water puddled and dripped down its sides. Even the air seemed to lose its sparkle above the shell of steaming ground. It was the opposite of everything I'd just seen.

For a moment, I could only stare at the repulsive mound, wondering why Judgment would allow such an abomination to exist. Slowly, realization settled in, along with a dawning horror. "Hell?" I murmured, touching my fingers to my lips.

I was looking at the top of Hell from the outside. *Hell.* My home. Where I lived. Where I *had* lived. How could I have imagined it was beautiful? Onyx had been right all along. It was horrible, disgusting. The thought of him and Cinder returning there once Visala cleared their names made my stomach knot. I had to find the seraph and convince him to let us all stay in Judgment.

Calling his name, I ran back down the rise and across the open ground. Clouds of white crystals puffed from my hooves as my legs sank knee-deep in the soft surface. Past the hatch, I saw footprints that could only be his. The tracks led away from the opening to a maze of tall, dark pillars, and disappeared as the ground changed from white to brown.

It was a little warmer here, and dimmer. The air was no

longer glittery, but it smelled wonderful. Despite my worry, I couldn't help stopping to inhale the rich, tangy scent and run my fingers over the surface of one of the pillars. It was rough to touch. Looking up, I realized I was now standing beneath a feathery ceiling of a color I'd never seen before. It was both dark and bright at the same time.

I walked slowly between the pillars, inhaling deeply and holding the fragrant air in my lungs for as long as I could before reluctantly releasing each breath. I stretched out my hand to touch a section of the ceiling just above my head. It was soft but prickly, and when I crushed it between my fingers, it spread the wonderful scent to my hand. Something chirped just above me, and I jumped back, afraid I'd set off some kind of alarm by touching the ceiling.

But a second later, I relaxed as a brown-and-white creature small enough to fit into the palm of my hand flew from one part of the ceiling to another and chirped again. This time I stood perfectly still, listening as it repeated a series of sounds over and over. It was . . . *singing*. To me.

"Sparrow?" I whispered, careful not to disturb its song. Was this what Father had named her after? After finishing its performance, the creature tilted its head as though seeking my approval. "Wonderful." I clapped, and it flew off, perhaps to find another audience.

No wonder Visala loved it here. No wonder Onyx had fought to see this. I walked across the ground that whispered beneath my hooves with each step. If I lived here, I'd never want to leave.

Could I live here though? The thought made me halt, stiff with uncertainty. Judgment was so beautiful. So different from Hell. But *I* was from Hell. Was I any different because I'd managed to escape it? I was still a demon. What if people here looked at me the way I looked at the filthy mound that was my home? The way demons looked at damned humes?

I didn't believe that Visala viewed me like that. But just because he saw past where I'd come from—what I was—didn't mean others would. I remembered what he'd said about Onyx being thrown in prison if he were seen. Maybe that was because we didn't belong here—any of us. Maybe we weren't worthy.

I began running between the pillars, anxious to find Visala, to get his reassurance that I hadn't made a terrible mistake. They seemed to go on forever, and as the air grew darker, I wondered if I'd gone the wrong direction. While I'd been admiring Judgment, Visala could have gone anywhere. I thought about calling his name again, but worried that someone else might hear my voice and discover me. My pulse raced as I hurried through the rapidly dimming light, and I couldn't seem to get enough air.

Just as I was about to turn back, the pillars thinned out and, a few minutes later, disappeared completely. Although the ground was white again, the air had stopped sparkling; maybe because it was night. The sky overhead was a dark gray that seemed to be moving from left to right. Staring up at it, I nearly fell when the ground dropped sharply away beneath me.

I glanced down and gasped.

In the valley below, what could only be the city of Judgment glowed with a brilliance I could never have imagined. It was beyond beautiful. Buildings rose high into the air, their windows sparkling lights in the darkness. Roads were straight and neat. The houses and buildings were spotlessly clean. None appeared run-down or damaged. There were no smokestacks or factories that I could see. No dirt or grime. Everything was white and lovely. I didn't think even

Onyx could have envisioned anything this incredible when he pictured Judgment.

Silvery light glinted off the white ground, and for a moment I thought it was coming from the city lights. Then I raised my head, and all the strength went out of my legs. Dropping onto the icy ground, I gaped up at a ceiling so high, it made my mind reel. The ceiling of the cavern over Hell was high, but this was hundreds of times higher, thousands. It almost looked like it wasn't a ceiling at all—as though it went on forever. It was the deepest blue, set with chips of shimmering gems so bright and clear, I reached out my hands, almost expecting to touch them.

I could never describe something like this to Onyx and Cinder unless they saw it for themselves. The exquisiteness, the majesty. There were no words.

Again, the thought came to me that I didn't belong here. It wasn't just that I was different—unfit. I felt like my very presence here was an affront. Demons weren't made to experience this kind of beauty. But the thought of leaving it, of returning to Hell, was equally as impossible. How could I live there a single minute knowing what I was missing?

Reluctantly tearing my gaze from the lights overhead, I looked down at the lights of the city and noticed something I'd missed before. Far below me, a single bright spot was moving rapidly down the side of the mountain. I recognized the awkward way the glowing figure held its arm. Visala. He was almost to the city.

I raised my hands and cupped them to the sides of my mouth to shout his name. Just as I called out, a sound rang through the cold night air. It didn't come from the mouth of a hume—or any creature at all, as far as I could tell. But it was a song—at least I was pretty sure it was. It had a metallic sound, like a hammer clanging against steel.

The song seemed to be coming from a large building at

the center of the city. Unlike the other buildings that were rigidly straight with sharp lines and corners, this structure was filled with high, curving archways, pointed steeples, and tall windows made of colored glass. I felt like I had seen it somewhere before, although that was impossible. Near the base of the mountain, Visala paused to look up before hurrying on.

Ignoring the cold and the soft ground that collapsed beneath my hooves, I sprinted down the side of the hill after him. Icy air blew past my face as my hooves slipped and skidded. My lungs burned, and twice I tripped on something hidden by the deep white surface. The second time, my head hit the corner of a large rock, and a line of hot blood trickled across the lid of my right eye. Visala was nearly there. If he made it, I'd never be able to find him.

I was less than halfway down when he reached the nearest of the perfectly straight streets. "Visala!" I screamed, straining to make him hear me over the song. "Wait for me! I'm coming!"

Unable to hear me, he broke into a jog, running past row after row of small, perfect houses. Shivering with cold and exhaustion, I watched as he approached a brightly lit three-story building. As he started up the stairs, another seraph came out the door. The two of them appeared to exchange words, and both entered the building. It was too late. I'd waited too long to make my decision.

"Go back," I told myself. "At least you had a chance to see Judgment." Who knew? Maybe when Visala returned, having cleared our names, his offer to bring me with him would still be open.

But I didn't want to go back. I wanted to go to Visala. Tell him how I felt—how I wanted to be with him. I knew I should wait for him to return, but my hooves started down the hill again, and I didn't stop them. The night was frigid, and getting colder by the minute, but thinking of Visala—the heat of his aura, the taste of his lips—kept me warm as I picked my way down the side of the mountain, until at last, I stepped onto the streets of Judgment.

"I'm here," I whispered to myself, giddy with fear and excitement. "I'm really in Judgment."

I walked in the direction Visala had gone, passing one flawless house after another. Peering into their softly glowing windows, I tried to imagine what it must be like living every day in paradise. As I continued to walk, though, I began to get a strange, unsettled feeling. I told myself it was because I didn't belong here. But it was more than that.

None of the houses were exactly the same. And yet the differences were so minimal, they might as well have been. A window on this house was on the left instead of the right. Double doors, instead of a single. This one had rounded pillars on either side, while that one had rectangles. It was as though they'd all been made from the same set of pieces—changed just enough to trick you into thinking they weren't identical.

On my way down the mountain, I'd wondered if the city could be as perfect close up as it had appeared from above. Nothing ever was. Places, things, friends—they all had flaws when you looked closely enough. But Judgment didn't seem to. The buildings were just as straight. The streets just as clean. I tapped a hoof on the dark surface beneath me. It was completely smooth, unblemished black in counterpoint to the glittering white ground of the mountain.

How could that be? Everything broke down over time. Who kept it up? Who made sure each house was just so? And what if you wanted something different?

I couldn't see a single toy in any of these yards. A single spot of dirt. No clue to the personalities of the people who lived inside. Even the rectangles of light shining into the yards seemed to stretch exactly the same distance.

I was passing the last house on this side of the street when the clanging started up again. This time it was not a song—only the same sound, repeated over and over. Several blocks away, the doors to the building at the center of the town swung open as the lights behind the tall windows brightened, illuminating a series of vividly-colored pictures.

I sucked in a sharp breath, realizing why the building had seemed so familiar. The archways, the pillars, the tall narrow windows. It was as though someone had taken the architecture of the Immigration Station and intentionally set out to mock it. Belittling the most impressive building in Hell with a structure that was similar, but so much better, the original became a joke. Or was the Immigration Station a pitiful attempt at replicating the grandeur of this?

Either way, it didn't matter, because the images blazing in the night only served to validate all of my worst fears. Like the colored glass in the Immigration Station, these windows also showed pictures of torture and pain. But unlike the ones in Hell, it was not humes being tortured, but demons.

Imps dripped blood, sharp spears sticking through their sides. Efreets hung, impaled on tall poles. Succubae and incubi clawed at melting faces. But the demons were the worst. Fire blasted from the empty eye sockets of spawnlings. Elders choked on clouds of yellow gas. A demon spawn girl who could have been Cinder lay on the ground, arms blown off. Another who looked far too close to me appeared to have a sword plunged through her chest, its tip sticking out from her back. Flying above the carnage on golden wings, seraphs looked down with expressions ranging from pity to disgust.

This was what they thought of us. I didn't belong here.

How could Visala have asked me to come, knowing how I would be viewed? Was he sure I'd say no all along?

I turned to run back to the mountain, but the streets behind me filled up with glowing white figures leaving their houses and heading toward the building—toward me. They hadn't seen me yet, but it was only a matter of seconds before they did. And what then?

What would they do when they discovered a creature from the bowels of Hell in their midst?

CHAPTER 35

I searched for a place to hide, trying to stave off a blind panic. In this world of straight edges and open streets, there were no shadows to duck into. The city was completely encircled by houses, and from each door flowed men, women, and children—humes, dressed in robes of white, gold, silver, and red. They moved with a slow, eerie grace, but they were coming straight at me. Could I fight my way past them? None were seraphs, but they were each enveloped in a protective white aura, and as far as I knew, might possess the same power to command me.

The only chance of escape was the three-story building Visala had gone into. Sticking close to the wall, I ran to the stairs, raced up, and pushed through the double doors. I expected someone to stop me, or at the very least apprehend me once I was inside. When I went through the doorway, though, the small vestibule was empty.

With my back pressed to the cool stone wall, I glanced around the room and tried to catch my breath. It appeared to be some kind of waiting area—two sets of benches lined both of the side walls, with a pair of doorways leading deeper into the building. From where I was standing, I could see a few paces into some kind of hallway.

I could wait here, hoping to stay hidden until all the people outside went into the big building. But what if someone came out from one of the halls before then? The seraph who met Visala seemed to have known he was here. Was it possible they'd gone to the big building as well? If so, they must have exited through a different door.

Edging to my right, I peered farther down the closest hall. It was empty, but I could see several doors. Wait, or go? I thought about Cinder and Onyx back in the tunnel. Neither of them had trusted Visala. I had, but now I wasn't sure. He'd had plenty of chances to tell me how things were here. But he'd never said a word. What if he had no intention of clearing our names? What if right now, he was telling the other Halos about us?

I walked forward, ready to duck back out at the first sound of anyone coming. The building was deeper than it looked, with five metal doors on each side of the hallway, and a staircase at the end. It had a strange smell that burned the back of my throat. The crack under the first door on the right was dark. But light shined out from under the one on the left. There were no signs indicating what was behind either of them.

I tiptoed up to the door on the left and pressed my ear to its plain metal surface. At first, I couldn't hear anything at all. Then I made out a low moaning, as though whoever was behind it was in pain. What if Visala was being punished for crossing the Outer Circles?

I licked my lips. "Visala?" I hissed.

The moaning stopped.

"Help me," someone whispered back. It didn't sound like Visala, but I couldn't be sure.

Although the door had a lock, it must not have been engaged, because it swung open a crack when I pushed against it. "Is that you?"

"I'm sorry." The voice sounded hoarse, and even more scared than I was. "I didn't mean it, I swear."

It wasn't Visala. I could tell that now. It sounded like a woman. I knew I should get away, but something was so strange about this place. I had to know what was going on. I swung the door all the way open, and it swooshed shut behind me as I stepped through. Across the room, a female hume sat strapped into a reclined chair. Her hair was tied back, and colored wires hung from her head, connecting to a box with a series of lights and numbers.

The chair was turned away from the door, so she couldn't see me, but she must have heard me come in, because she immediately began sobbing. "I'm sorry. I swear. Give me another chance, please."

"Who are you?" I asked. She was dressed in a red robe like the ones I'd seen outside. But unlike the citizens of Judgment, she had no aura. A wheeled metal table beside the chair was covered with vials and tools that reminded me of something from my hume anatomy class.

She tried to turn around, but the bands holding her down were too tight. "Don't erase my memory," she begged, her voice sounding raw. "Don't send me to Hell."

A hume damned to eternal torment. She didn't look much older than me. What could she have done to deserve this? Since her memory hadn't been erased yet, she might be able to tell me. "What are you being punished for?"

"I'm sorry!" she screamed, thrashing, and I looked toward the door, afraid someone would overhear us. "Give me another chance. Tell the Deit I'm sorry. Tell them I promise to wash all the dishes perfectly and keep our yard cleaner. I'll work harder. I swear I will. I was just tired. I won't talk back. I'll eat nothing."

Wash dishes? Eat nothing? Talk back? This didn't make any sense. Humes were sent to Hell for only the most terrible and serious offenses—murder, lying, stealing, blasphemy. Not talking back or not cleaning messy dishes. Like everything else I'd seen in Judgment so far, something was completely wrong with this, but I couldn't understand what. Was this what Sparrow had been trying to warn me about? Was this what she didn't want me to see? That humes were being sent to Hell for not cleaning?

"Calm down," I said, walking around to the front of the chair. I reached for one of the straps binding her to the chair. "Tell me what's going on here and maybe I can—"

I never got to finish my sentence. As I stepped into the hume's view, her mouth dropped open, and she threw back her head. "Nooo!" she screeched. Spit flew from her mouth as she shook her head back and forth, clawing at the arms of the chair with her bound hands. "No! No! No! Don't take me! Leave me alone!"

She was terrified of me. "Please," I whispered, "be quiet. I want to help."

She snapped her teeth at my fingers, her eyes rolling back in her head. "I won't go to Hell! I won't!" She was struggling so hard, it looked like she might actually rip the chair out of its metal brackets.

My hip bumped against the table. Instruments and glass bottles crashed to the floor. I flinched.

I had to get out of here before someone heard her. As I reached for the door, it swung open. My hooves skidded on the slick floor, and I slid directly into the arms of a waiting seraph, expecting a terrible shock from its aura.

But it never came.

For a second, we were both so surprised, neither of us could move.

He tilted his head. "Blaze?"

It was Visala.

"What are you doing here?" he demanded, taking in the screaming hume and the spilled contents of the table.

"I'm sorry," I said, sounding way too much like the

crazed hume behind me. "I was trying to find you. I called, but the song was too loud. I followed you to the city. Then the lights, and sounds, the horrible pictures . . . The people came out of their houses, and . . ."

He looked from me to the chair and gritted his teeth. "Did anyone see you?"

"No. I don't think so."

He picked up something off the floor and touched the hume's arm. She stopped screaming, and her body went limp.

"What did you do to her?!"

He shook his head. "We've got to get you out before whoever was working on her comes back."

"What is this place?" I asked as he pulled me through the door, across the hall, and into the darkened room on the other side.

Visala turned on a light, slammed the door behind us, and locked it. He spun around and glared at me. "Why are you here?"

"I . . . you asked me to," I said, unsure of myself.

"I didn't ask you to sneak into the city and walk straight into the Hall of Enforcement!" I hadn't heard him this angry since he first entered our room at the barracks.

My temples began to pulse. "Because you knew what I'd find here. Did you think you could hide this from me?!"

He ran a hand through his hair. "I wasn't trying to hide anything."

I choked back a strangled laugh. "Funny, I don't remember you telling me about the pictures of demons being tortured. Or did you think I'd like the surprise of knowing everyone here wants to see me stuck on a spit?"

"They're. Just. Pictures," he said, clipping each word. "You have the same kinds of images in Hell."

I wiped sweat from my forehead, trying to keep my

fangs from pushing out of my gum tissue. "The girl in the other room said she was being sent to Hell for talking back and not cleaning."

Visala's jaw tightened. His aura flickered rapidly. "I'll explain everything, but right now isn't the time."

I shoved my hands against his chest, then stumbled as his aura knocked me back with a cracking shock. "Is it true?"

He swallowed, glancing nervously around. "There isn't time to—"

"Is it true?" I screamed.

"Judgment isn't what you think," he snarled, rubbing his hands on the front of his robe. "Neither is Hell."

"What's that supposed to mean?" I was so sick of him avoiding my questions. "Just answer this. Was that girl telling the truth? Is she being sent to Hell for not cleaning?"

He looked down. That was answer enough. Everything Onyx had suspected was true. We *were* being lied to. But how could that be? How could celestial beings lie, especially about something as important as eternal damnation? And if they lied about that, what else might they be lying about? "Were you *ever* planning on clearing our names?"

He stepped toward me, but I circled away. "I know what you're thinking," he said. "And I know you have a lot of questions. But right now, you have to trust me."

"*Trust you*?!" I shouted, fangs beginning to press against my lips. "How can I trust you? You've been lying to me since the day I found you."

"No!" he shouted back. The bright white light around him flared and dimmed, and for just a minute, his skin seemed to change somehow. "I *never* lied. I just haven't told you everything."

"You haven't told me *anything*." Talons poked up from my fingertips. If Judgment was a lie, what did that make

Hell? If the humes sent down to us hadn't committed crimes worthy of eternal damnation, *we* were the guilty ones. We were torturing them for nothing.

Visala licked his lips. His aura was blinking on and off so rapidly, it was hard to look directly at him. "You have to calm down."

"What's wrong with you?" I asked. "Why is your aura doing that?"

He began to answer, but at that moment, his aura glared blindingly bright and went out.

Blinking as my eyes tried to recover from the sudden flash, I saw something that made no sense. I backed away, my eyes wide with horror. "You . . ." I pointed, my hand trembling.

With Visala's aura gone, I could see his pale skin. His yellow hair. His chalky complexion and the wisps of fuzz growing from his cheeks. His wings, which had been so glorious and golden, turned gray and dull, and I could swear I saw a flicker of metal shining from between the feathers. It couldn't be. Of all the terrible things I'd seen, all the horrors I'd discovered here, this was the one I wanted to deny the most. But here he was, standing right in front of me.

"You're a . . . *hume.*"

"It's what I've been trying to tell you," he began. "I'm human. So are you. We all are."

"That's a lie." I tripped over something on the floor and fell.

"No, it's the truth," he said. "Let me explain." He leaned down to pick me up, and I knocked him away. Claws that I hadn't realized had come out cut into his hume flesh.

"Get away from me!" I screamed. Everything went red. I leaped to my feet and pushed him across the room. No longer protected by his aura, he slammed against a cabinet. I ran to the door and fumbled with the lock.

"Don't go out there," he warned, grabbing my shoulder.

"Get away from me!" I kicked at him with a hoof. "You're a monster!"

Finally, the lock turned. I pushed open the door and ran into the hall.

"Look what we found trying to sneak into the city," a voice called from the entryway. Before I could turn to run the other direction, a group of seraphs appeared from the entrance, pushing Onyx and Cinder in front of them. Blood ran down the front of Onyx's face. One of Cinder's eyes had swelled closed. Both of them were bound at the hands and ankles with heavy chains.

I stepped back, and a pair of metal cuffs locked shut around my wrists. "Good work," Visala said from behind me. "I caught the third."

CHAPTER 36

For three days, we sat in a windowless gray room that, until recently, had held humes waiting to be sent to Hell on the next Stygian Transit. Onyx's fists were bloody and bruised from pounding on the barred door at the front of our cell, and a large purple lump stood out just above his left eye where one of the seraphs had hit him. His slashed leg was healing surprisingly well though.

Cinder, who swung from dark humor to depression almost by the minute, sat in a corner, staring moodily out at the short section of hallway that was our only view. Her eye was no longer shut, but the puffy purple bruises surrounding it gave her a dark, dangerous look. "We could have stayed in Hell and ended up in pretty much the same place."

Onyx ran a swollen hand along the bars. "I'm sorry. This is my fault."

"No." I went to him and cupped his injured fingers in my palm. "It's *my* fault, if I hadn't trusted Visala . . . if I hadn't followed Visala, we'd be on our way back to Hell now with our names cleared."

Cinder gave a harsh laugh. "You still believe he was going to do it?"

"I guess not." I walked back to the bench and slumped against the wall. I honestly didn't know what I thought. Did I believe in the Visala who seemed genuinely afraid for me when he discovered I'd followed him—the one whose kiss I still couldn't erase from my mind? Or did I believe in the one who'd invited me into a trap, who'd put a sword to my throat when the other seraphs arrived?

I'd told Onyx and Cinder everything I'd learned. But there was still so much I didn't understand. How could humes be running Judgment? Why were they sending their own to Hell? How could Visala be a hume, and why had he lied about me being one too? "Sparrow tried to warn me just before I went through the hatch," I said. "But I didn't listen."

"Sparrow?" Onyx turned around. "She made it out? Where is she now?"

"No idea," I said. "If you two didn't see her when you followed me, she must have left the tunnel. She told me there were things I'd be better off not knowing. I couldn't imagine how knowledge could be a bad thing. Now I understand."

"Knowledge is never a bad thing," Onyx said. "Even if knowing costs us our lives, it's worth it."

Cinder grabbed her tail, tugging angrily at the tuft of fur on the tip. "That's exactly the kind of thinking that got you into trouble in the first place. You wanted to know what was outside Hell. Now you do. And what good has it done you? Are you happier? Are you better off? Most of your friends are dead. Your family's probably already disowned you. You're locked inside a cell in a world where everyone hates you. How is that worth it?"

I had to admit, I agreed with her. Before we'd left Hell, I was happy. I had a life, direction, goals. Now I had none of those. Until I'd followed Visala into Judgment, I thought I was part of a group doing the right thing—punishing murderers, rapists, and thieves—when the truth was, we were the very things we thought we were punishing. Everything

I'd spent my life believing was a lie. *I* was part of the evil. What was better about that?

Onyx's eyes flashed. "If you were back at school today—knowing what you do—could you keep going to classes? Could you keep going to the Immigration Station every Arrival Day? Could you watch another Culdine match with humans used as game pieces?"

"I wish I'd never found out," I said.

"No!" Onyx pounded his fist against the bars. I winced as drops of blood spattered on the cold, hard floor. "Don't say that—*ever*. Sparrow was wrong. Ignorance is never an excuse. Think about all the demons in Hell right now, abusing humes because they believe they've been damned for eternity. Just like Sparrow. Think of all the humes who believe they deserve whatever treatment they receive because they must have done something despicable in a life they can't remember. Just because they don't know the truth doesn't make it right. Committing atrocities isn't okay just because you don't know any better."

I'd never thought of it that way. "There is no good choice. Before, we committed unspeakable acts, but at least we didn't know we were. Now we know that acts are being committed, and we can't do anything about it. Either way, we're just as guilty."

"We're not the ones to blame." Onyx wiped his face, leaving a bloody smear across the center of his forehead. "The guilty ones are the leaders who set this all in motion— the ones who sent the humes down there in the first place."

"Make sure and tell them that," Cinder said. "Right before they execute us."

"You should be so lucky." An older hume with a thin, mournful-looking face and long gray hair combed straight back from his head appeared in the hallway. He was wearing a white tunic with silver buttons down the front and a stiff gold collar. The hem of his robe reached clear to the floor and dragged several feet behind him. In one hand, he held what looked like a small metal tray with a flickering glass surface.

Onyx lunged forward, reaching for him through the bars. Although the hume had no aura, sparks exploded off him, throwing Onyx across the cell.

"There are easier ways to kill yourself, if that's what you're trying to do," the hume said, straightening his tunic sleeves. "Although I imagine the guards would stop you. They don't want to let you off that easy."

I helped Onyx up, but his legs wobbled, and his eyes had a dazed look to them. "Who are you?"

"Who I am isn't important. *What* I am is."

Cinder scowled, her eyes tracking his every move. "Fine. *What* are you?"

"You may call me Counselor." He reached his hand holding the tray into the cell, and Cinder's tail twitched. If I hadn't seen what had happened to Onyx, I'd have grabbed for him. He moved his arm to the left, and both his hand and the tray went right through the bars.

"You're a spirit?" Cinder backed away.

The hume chuckled, though his lips showed no trace of a smile. "I'm what you might think of as a moving picture. An image sent here on my behalf. The force from touching a vid-field would have knocked a human unconscious at the very least. Possibly even stopped his heart. It's a shame I wasn't given permission to run tests on the three of you." This time he did smile, his eyes glittering. It was a hungry smile.

I didn't want to know what kind of tests he had in mind. I was reminded of how the teacher in our hume anatomy class talked about running tests on *them*. Now *we* were the specimens being studied.

"I'm here to share . . . information," he said.

"What kind of information?" I snarled. "No one's told us anything since we got here. Even the guards won't talk to us when they deliver our meals."

His dark eyes continued to study us coldly. "No, I don't imagine they would. Be that as it may, I'm here now." He tapped the glass surface.

"What is that?" I asked, trying to get a better look at the tray.

"It's called a tablet." he said. "Again, you wouldn't understand the technology, but think of it as an advanced pen and paper. I've got a few questions for you."

I helped Onyx sit. "We're not telling you anything until you answer *our* questions."

He nodded slowly. "Of course, I could *make* you answer my questions. But I did say share. *Quid pro quo.* I answer one of your questions, you answer one of mine. Fair enough?"

It wasn't like we had a lot of choice.

"Why are you sending innocent memory-wiped humes to Hell?" Onyx asked. His voice sounded hoarse and raspy.

"They're not innocent," the hume said. "They have been tried and convicted by the Deit, the ruling council here in Judgment, and sentenced to Hell."

"But how can a hume be sent to Hell for not cleaning?" I yelled, starting toward him before remembering that he wasn't real.

"You saw for yourself—Judgment is a place of order, a place of peace, a place of grace. It is not a place for those who wish to coast along while relying on others to pull their weight. Living here is a privilege. Those who don't deserve it are sent to where the value of work will be instilled in them."

My throat tightened. They were sentencing their own to

eternal damnation for not working hard enough. And *we* were carrying out the punishment.

The Counselor turned to Onyx. "I've answered one of your questions. Now it's your turn. What made you decide to attack the Stygian Transit? And please be aware that I'll know if you are lying," he said, holding up the tablet. "You will not like the consequences."

I wondered if Onyx would try giving only a partial answer or lying anyway. The hume's superior attitude made me want to claw his eyes out. But Onyx lifted his head and stared straight back at the Counselor.

"I question anyone who feels they have the right to judge anyone else. Especially when they lack the guts to enforce the punishments they hand down. You send humes to eternal damnation because you're afraid to do the tormenting yourself. I've never trusted the fact that humes' memories were erased. It made me wonder what the people behind it were scared of."

I looked at Onyx. He'd never said any of that to me. Was it because he knew I'd think he was even crazier than I already did? The idea that humes didn't deserve what they'd been sentenced to had never occurred to me before I left Hell. But he'd proven to be right on all of it.

A muscle twitched on the side of the hume's face, but he didn't accuse Onyx of lying. "You had to know the attempt was futile, right?"

"It's not your turn to ask," I told him. "Visala said we were all humes. What did he mean by that?"

The hume glared at me, the skin above his eyes furrowing. Then he smiled slowly, and the wrinkles disappeared. "Very well. It's something I've looked forward to telling you anyway. But in order to explain that, I'm afraid I'll need to fill you in on a few other things first. Please, make yourselves comfortable." He sat down in midair, although there was nothing to support him, and crossed one leg over the other.

I sat beside Onyx as Cinder paced back and forth at the back of the cell.

"You are aware that humans come from another world?"

"The world some of them claim to have memories of," I said.

Onyx gave me a sharp look, but the hume only laughed. "We know all about the memory leaks. We found the puzzle box you left in the tunnel. In fact, technicians are going over the memories you so helpfully provided us at this very moment. It should prove quite useful in improving the process."

Onyx slumped against me as the hume went on, clearly pleased that he'd gotten under our skin. "You've probably heard that some humans are violent."

I nodded. I'd also learned recently that it wasn't just humes.

"Some of them are more violent than you can probably imagine." The Counselor tapped his tablet, and the back wall of our cell seemed to disappear. It was as if we were standing at the top of a hill, looking down on a city bigger than Hell and Judgment combined.

Cinder stepped toward it, and I started to warn her to be careful. But there was no need. Without a hint of warning, the city burst into a searing ball of fire. Buildings collapsed. People ran through the streets screaming, hair and clothing in flames. I put my hands to my mouth, moving away. The image changed, and now we could see humes falling to the ground, quivering as clouds of yellow gas floated over them.

"They called it *war*," the hume said.

"Killing each other for power or land," Onyx muttered, his voice grim. "I've heard about that too."

Ever since I was a spawnling, I'd been taught most humes were born with brutal natures. But this was worse than anything I could ever have imagined. Images began flashing by: charred bodies, maimed children, trenches filled to overflowing with hume corpses. I spun away, unable to watch it a second longer. Onyx looked as if he was going to be sick. Even Cinder turned around, her mouth pulled down in disgust. For some reason, though, the hume seemed amused.

"Several hundred years ago, humans had the biggest war of all time. They killed so many of each other, and did so much damage to their world, that even many of those who survived the war died from other causes, like starvation, sickness, weather."

It was worse than horrible. Maybe it was better that they had their memories wiped away after all. If I'd lived that kind of life, I wouldn't want to remember it.

"Big surprise," Cinder said, her voice still a little unsteady.

"That doesn't explain sending someone to Hell for not cleaning well enough," Onyx said.

The hume ignored both of their comments. "After the war and the deaths and the disease, only two groups remained. At least, in that part of their world. One group had been afraid of just such an event. They'd built a city to protect themselves. The other group didn't have a protective city, but they still had many of the same weapons that had been used in the war in the first place."

Feeling chilled, I leaned against Onyx. "They didn't use them, did they? Not after everything that happened before?"

"They did. They felt that the mistake in the previous war had been not attacking soon enough or hard enough. They were determined to use force to get whatever they wanted, and while they still had weapons, they didn't have enough food or medicine. They'd heard about the city, and threatened to destroy it if they didn't get what they wanted.

"The people in the city agreed to help them, but only if they abandoned their weapons. Because while the people with the weapons believed the mistake was not attacking soon enough, the people in the city believed the mistake was attacking at all. They'd sworn an oath never to kill another human again, no matter what."

I didn't know what this story had to do with us, and I didn't like the person telling it, but I found myself interested anyway. "What happened? Did the humes destroy their weapons, or did the city break its oath?"

The hume shifted in his invisible chair. "The violent humans wouldn't destroy their weapons. When the city refused to let them in, they began to attack. The leaders of the city refused to fight back. They believed in the oath they'd made, and they held their group to it. But a subgroup inside the city disobeyed the leaders and broke their oath.

"The people who formed the city had special knowledge no other humans possessed. It was part of how they'd managed to build the city and survive so long in the first place. The oath breakers knew they didn't have the weapons to defeat the army outside their city, so they used their specialized knowledge to change themselves."

He pointed to the back wall again, where the scenes of carnage had been replaced by images of humes in long white coats working with gleaming equipment I didn't recognize. "They made their bodies immune, or at least very resistant, to the effects of the weapons. When the leaders realized what was happening, they demanded the oath breakers stop what they were doing, but by then it was too late. The group had already made their changes. The oath breakers left the city and attacked the assaulting army."

"Which group won?" I asked.

"Neither." The hume rapped his tablet against his palm. "The oath breakers defeated the attacking army. But when they returned, they discovered that during the battle, their city had been ruined. Because of their duplicitous actions—because they broke their covenant—the city was so contaminated, it was uninhabitable."

"So they were supposed to roll over and let themselves get destroyed?" Cinder sneered. "Sounds like typical hume thinking."

"You didn't answer my question," I said. "What does something that happened hundreds of years ago in the humes' world have anything to do with us?"

"I thought you'd figure that out for yourselves." The Counselor scoffed. "But then again, *your kind* isn't exactly known for their intellect, are they?"

He stood up, and I found myself standing too. Onyx was right beside me. Something was coming, and I was no longer sure I wanted to know what it was. Despite what Onyx had said, I was afraid that what I was about to learn was too much. Cinder's fur was on end from the top of her head all the way down her back. Even her tail stuck out stiff, unmoving.

The hume's lips raised in a mirthless grin. "The oath breakers modified their DNA to make themselves immune to radiation, fire, and chemical warfare. They made themselves look like nightmare creatures to frighten the invading army. When they returned to the city, they wanted to change themselves back. But the technology to do so was destroyed."

He pointed to the back wall, and I turned to see groups of figures I'd known all my life. Succubae, incubi, efreets, imps, gargoyles, devils. And hundreds of demons—Dae' Lorica, Dae' Ceal, and Dae' Ungu. All standing before the smoking ruins of a huge domed city.

Onyx's jaw dropped. "You're saying the oath breakers were . . . *us?*"

The hume chuckled darkly. "They turned themselves into the creatures that now inhabit Hell. By breaking their promise of peaceful resistance, they damned themselves to spend life looking like exactly what they were. You are their descendants."

"That's a lie," I spat. My mouth tasted like acid.

"It's not," the hume said. "And you know it. I can see it in your eyes. The oath breakers' actions despoiled the city so that those who kept their covenants could no longer live there. They were forced to rebuild in the only place left to them—the mountains. Even there, they were required to block the city with a dome and wear a protective shield—what you call an aura—to survive the polluted environment when they visited it."

He stared at us like we should understand. Like his story should answer our questions. But it didn't. What did a war on the humes' planet have to do with us? "Are you saying we were sent to Hell for breaking our oaths?"

"You still don't understand," the hume said, laughing so hard he could barely speak. "Ironically, or perhaps fittingly, the changes the oath breakers wrought upon their own bodies allowed them to survive in the ruined city. The leaders agreed to help fix the city for them, as long as the oath breakers promised to stay there and never come out."

He pointed his finger at my face, and I would have torn it off his hand if I could. "There is no Hell. No Judgment. What you call home is the ruined city—covered by a dome to keep you in your place, and to protect those who kept our promise from your filth. Judgment is the city we built in the mountains. This place—where you live, where *we* live—is the hume planet, Earth."

I tried to speak, but my tongue stuck to the roof of

my mouth. That couldn't be right. If there was no Hell or Judgment—if this was all some long-running hoax—that meant the humes sent down to us weren't damned at all. The people in Judgment sending them to us for torture were monsters. But we were the ones torturing them—killing them—which made us the biggest monsters of all.

Onyx's face was nearly white. "If we're living in some ruined Earth city, if we agreed to that, why don't we know about it? Why doesn't anyone in Hell know?"

The hume licked his lips. "*Pacis per a pretium*—peace with a price. After those who kept their covenant rebuilt the domed city, they were afraid the oath breakers might break their promise again and try to take the city in the mountains. They modified the oath breakers' memories. Made them think they were all demons living in Hell. They also modified them to respond immediately to the commands of anyone with an aura."

I tried to think, but my brain refused to process what I was hearing. Everything I knew, everything I believed, my entire world, was a lie. "Heaven and Hell," I whispered. "None of it's real."

"On the contrary," the hume said, "this is as real as it gets. Your ancestors damned themselves long before you were born. You live in Hell because of it. My forbearers, on the other hand, proved themselves worthy of exactly what we have. Utopia. Of course, Utopia isn't for everyone. Those who are worthy remain. Those who aren't are sent to you as punishment. Heaven and Hell, exactly as it was designed. Just on Earth instead of some religious concept."

"What are you going to do with us?" Onyx asked. "You never would have told us this if you planned on letting us live."

"Technically, it's my turn to ask a question," the hume said. "But I really don't think there's anything more I can learn from you since this conversation has provided me with enough information. So I'll answer yours. As you know, we do not believe in killing—even when the offending party is not precisely the same species. We leave that to your kind. We will not stain our hands with your blood. But due to the heinous nature of your crimes, allowing you to return to Hell is not an option. At exactly midnight tomorrow morning, all three of you will be summarily and immediately ported to Absolute Zero."

CHAPTER 37

"I wish I'd had a chance to say goodbye to my family and friends," Cinder said.

Sitting across from her in our new narrow cell, I nodded. "I'd like to talk to my parents one last time. Thank them for everything they did for me."

"I told my parents goodbye the day before we attacked the Stygian," Onyx said. "I was pretty sure I'd never see them again. But I couldn't tell them that, knowing they'd be questioned . . . after."

I glanced up at the red numerals on the wall. Another miracle of Judgment—clocks that kept perfect time using something called *electricity*. Apparently, electricity was the same thing that powered the Stygian and the seraphs' angel suits. They hadn't seen fit to share it with us in Hell. Just below the numbers, a shiny black circle glistened. Our guards had taken great delight in explaining that once the clock reached 12:00, a field sent from the circle would teleport us all to Absolute Zero. It read 11:45 now. As I watched, it changed to 11:46. Fourteen minutes left before we were sent to the place of our worst nightmares.

"Why make us wait?" Cinder asked, pacing the room. "Why can't they send us now and get it over with?" We'd all been forced to change into thin white jumpsuits that felt like they were made out of paper, and Cinder's tail stuck awkwardly out of a hastily cut hole.

"Maybe they can only send people to Absolute Zero at

certain times. Or maybe it just makes for better drama," Onyx said, sitting in a corner with his arms wrapped around his knees. "I'll bet they throw parties at the stroke of midnight, celebrating their salvation from the horrible monsters."

I rubbed my stomach, trying to calm it. "Why couldn't they have sent us back to Hell? With their ability to change memories, they could have erased everything we knew about Judgment—this, what'd he call it? Utopia?"

"Too risky." Onyx stretched his arms, as though he was trying to keep from falling asleep. But I knew better. He was as anxious as the rest of us, but he hid it for our benefit. "If anyone in Hell knew we'd gone into the Outer Circles and come back alive, they'd think about trying it themselves. The leaders of Judgment are terrified of that. They'd never take the chance."

"So Visala *was* lying about clearing our names," I said.

Onyx shrugged his broad shoulders. *You can figure that one out on your own,* his expression said.

I crossed the small room, sat down beside him, wrapped my arms around his neck, and buried my face against his chest. "Thank you," I whispered. "For everything. You're right. Knowing is worth it."

He shifted, and I felt his lips brush across the top of my head.

From outside our cell came the sound of slamming doors, followed by footsteps.

"You're early," said one of the guards.

"Never seen a port," answered a female voice. "But we can come back if you'd rather stay till the end of your shift."

"You kidding?" A second guard laughed noisily. "I hear things are going to be crazy out there. Can't wait to go join it."

"Sure you don't want to stick around and see the scum get what they deserve?" the female asked.

"Nope," the guard answered. "There's not much to it, from what I've been told. One minute they're here. The next . . . nothing but an empty jumpsuit."

Doors slammed again, and the footsteps came closer. Three seraphs stepped up to the bars and looked in. I turned away, not wanting to let them see how terrified I felt. The numbers on the clock read 11:52. Eight more minutes.

"All three of you get over here," the female voice said. The aura of one of the seraphs disappeared. It was Sparrow!

"What are you doing here?" I cried, running to the barred door.

"Quiet." She held a finger to her lips. "In less than a minute, the power will go out. It's been storming outside, and thanks to a few friends of mine, the power's been going on and off all day. So no one will be too surprised when it does again. The power override should take about ten seconds to kick in. The electronic locks and alarms will reset themselves. You all need to be out here with the door closed again before that happens."

"But how do we get past the other guards?" Onyx asked.

Sparrow looked at a band strapped to her wrist and counted. "Five . . . four . . . three . . . two . . . one."

At the count of one, the lights went out, leaving the cell and hallway dark except for the glow of the auras.

"Everyone to their stations!" a voice called from somewhere in the building.

Sparrow bent to the door, slid something into the lock, and there was a clicking sound. "Hurry," she said, pulling us through and pushing the door closed behind us.

At almost the same second as the door clanged shut, the lights came back on. "That was close," she muttered. "Someone can't count to ten."

"What now?" Cinder asked, glancing anxiously around. At the moment, the hall was empty, but someone could come around the corner any second.

"Guard shift happens at midnight." She stripped off the angel wings strapped to her back and handed them to Cinder. "The real ones are surgically implanted, but these should work for the brief time you'll need them. Each of you three will put on a pair. As far as the guards are concerned, you're just three seraphs escorting a group of damned humans to have their memories wiped."

"And once we get outside?" I asked. "We can't hide in Judgment forever."

The seraph to Sparrow's right handed each of us a set of wings, an angel-fire sword, and a heavy belt. "You can't hide in Judgment at all," Sparrow said. "There is a small group of us humans who feel what we're doing here is wrong. I was part of the group before Father and I were captured. He was one of the opposition leaders. Fortunately, his instructions helped me locate a safe house where they've been helping me restore most of my memories."

"But how did Father keep from losing *his* memories?" Onyx asked.

"His real name was Davah Zebraski. He was part of the Deit. His grandfather was one of the original builders of the city who designed the outer defenses. They tried to erase his memory, but he'd modified his brain to stop them. Instead, they ended up cutting out his tongue and nearly driving him insane." Sparrow swallowed. "He was also my actual father."

"I'm sorry," I said.

She shook her head, and all traces of emotion disappeared from her face. "I can stay out of sight here for a while. But you three stand out a little, if you don't mind me saying."

"Not at all." Strapping himself into his wings and belt first, Onyx began examining the contraption.

"On your belt," Sparrow said.

Onyx pressed a button, and an aura of white fire spread over him. The transformation was incredible.

"You look just like a seraph," I said.

The dark-haired hume raised his chin to look at Onyx. "A very tall seraph with shoulders like a bull, and horns."

"It will have to do," Sparrow said. "The guards going off duty will be anxious to get out, and the ones coming on will probably be too drunk to notice."

Cinder pulled on her angel suit, pushed the button, and became a slightly smaller than normal seraph. "Look at me. I'm a Halo." She turned to me and commanded, "On your knees, demon spawn." I fell to my knees. She flicked off the aura, and I was able to stand. "Oh, I could totally get used to this."

"Stop fooling around," Sparrow said. "We've only got a couple more minutes."

I pulled on my suit. The straps were too large, and I had to tighten them to fit. "If we can't hide here, where are we going?"

"Once we get you out of the building, we'll take you to another passageway back to Hell," Sparrow said. "You'll have plenty of supplies and equipment to get you back. The auras should help too. But their energy packs are only good for ten days. After that, they're little more than pretty junk."

"But we'll be arrested as soon as we enter Hell," I said.

The male hume shook his head. "The authorities there have already received a coded message informing them that the three of you crossed the Styx in pursuit of a runaway seraph. You may not be heroes when you return, but you shouldn't be thrown in prison."

Cinder tilted her head. "Why would the authorities in Hell pay any attention to a message from Judgment?"

"We don't have time to go into that now," Sparrow said. "Just trust me when I say there's more to Judgment and Hell than you know. Much more."

Onyx sighed and shook his head. "It's a great plan. And I appreciate everything you've done. But it won't work."

"Why not?" I asked. It sounded like they had everything figured out.

"The Deit will never allow us to go back. As soon as they realize we weren't ported to Absolute Zero, they'll keep searching until they find us."

"The port must take place." Sparrow's eyes flickered over my shoulder, and I realized that although three seraphs had come into the hallway, only two were still there.

I spun around, and my throat closed to a pinhole. "Visala?"

He smiled weakly and waved from inside the cell. "Guess you're probably a little surprised to see me here."

"In a cell." Onyx sneered. "Right where you belong, traitor."

"He's not a traitor," Sparrow said softly. "As soon as you were arrested, he came looking for me. It was a huge risk. If it weren't for him, we couldn't have pulled off this escape."

I looked into his deep-blue eyes—eyes I'd never wanted to see again. "But you captured me."

Visala bit his lip. "Sorry about that. I had to make sure I wasn't thrown in prison, too, if I wanted to help you escape. It was the only way I could think of at the time."

I glanced at the numbers on the wall—11:58. "You have to get out of there."

"Can't do that," he said. "A port has to take place, or the authorities will know you escaped. That can't happen unless there's someone here to get ported. As long as at least one person is sent, they'll think it was a success."

"No!" I yanked at the door. It was locked. I turned to Sparrow. "You have to open it. Let him out."

She shook her head and tossed two white jumpsuits—identical to the ones we'd been forced to wear—into the cell. They fluttered down like ash from a fire, landing haphazardly on the cold floor. "I couldn't even if I wanted to. Once the power is on, manual override keys don't work."

"We've got to find a way to stop the transfer, then." I turned back to Visala. "You can't do this."

He reached through the bars and took my hand. Without the aura, his grip was surprisingly gentle. "I'm sorry about lying to you."

"You did what you had to."

"No." He squeezed my hand and looked at all of us. "I lied because I was trying to protect myself. And because I bought into the lies I'd been told about Hell. About you. If I'd been honest from the beginning, none of this would have happened."

"Forget about that," I cried. "We have to get you out of there."

He glanced up at the clock, which now read 11:59, and winced as he lifted his injured arm to touch my face. "I meant what I said about you not being what I expected. I wish we'd had more time to get to know each other. Could I possibly ask for a favor before I go?"

"Of course," I said, tears blurring my vision. "Anything."

"Kiss me one more time. This time not as a seraph, but just me? The real me."

With no fire flowing over him, his wings were no longer gold. His face was pale and human. But somehow, I liked that better. And this time, I knew the feelings were coming from me and not from some programmed response.

Standing in the corner of the hall, Onyx watched me with the same pained expression he'd had when Visala asked me to go to Judgment. I knew I'd hurt him before. Could I do it again? After everything he'd gone through for me, was that fair?

As I turned back to the bars, unsure of what I was going to say or do, there was a flash of purple light, and Visala was gone, leaving only the white jumpsuit he'd been wearing drifting slowly to the floor.

CHAPTER 38

"Stay low," Sparrow said, as the four of us flew toward the edge of the enormous dome that glowed a soft pink in the darkness. "Most of the people in the city are celebrating your deaths, but all it takes is one person to see us flying and this will be a very short escape."

"Hell looks different," I said, grimacing at the dome through the frigid air that stung my nose and cheeks. The cold was a good distraction, because I could not emotionally process what Visala had done for me. For us. "And not just because we're seeing it from the outside."

"New eyes?" Onyx asked, scowling at the place we'd once called home.

"New eyes," I agreed.

Cinder looked from Onyx to me, not getting the reference.

"I don't know how we can go back," I said.

"Are you kidding?" Cinder swooped from left to right. I'd expected flying to be hard to control, but all I had to do was think of where I wanted to go, and the wings did the rest. "At this speed, we can fly there in a couple of hours, tops."

"Not happening," Sparrow said. "If I don't get these wings back where they belong before the next equipment count, the seraphs will be on you before you even reach the outer wall—"

"You're not coming?" I interrupted.

"But with what you know about the Circles and the supplies in your packs, you should be okay," Sparrow said, completely ignoring my question.

"I wasn't talking about crossing the desert," I said. "I was talking about returning to Hell. Now that we know what it really is—what we're doing there—how can we return to that?"

Sparrow frowned. "If you don't, Visala's sacrifice will have been for nothing."

"Why did he do it?" Cinder asked.

I'd been asking myself the same question. We'd known each other for less than a month. How could he give up everything for people who were practically strangers?

"Why do you think?" Onyx grunted, and I felt my cheeks grow warm despite the cold.

"He might have cared about Blaze," Sparrow said, "but that's not why he did it." She guided us away from a group of humans laughing and waving sticks that shot out colored sparks.

"I couldn't believe it when Visala came to me with his idea to rescue you. Just like most demons view humans beneath contempt, most of the people up here view demons as damned for who they are and what they did. He'd convinced himself that what he was doing here was the only way to prevent another war."

I felt a lump block my throat as I remembered all the self-righteous things I'd said and done, sure that I was so much better than the humans. "Maybe they're right. Maybe we *are* monsters."

"No, you're not," Sparrow said fiercely. "You can't be blamed for doing what you'd been taught any more than you can be blamed for what your ancestors did long before you were born. The monsters are the people who continue this charade because it keeps them in power. Once Visala met the three of you and my father and me—saw who we really were—he realized how wrong he'd been. I believe that allowing himself to be sent to Absolute Zero was his way of paying for the guilt."

I clenched my jaw, shivering at more than the cold. "Is there any way to get him back?"

Onyx glanced at me, but I couldn't read the expression on his chiseled face.

"I've never heard of anyone getting out," Sparrow said. "The AZ is at the center of where the war was fought. Almost nothing lives there, and the few creatures that survive have been so mutated by chemicals and radiation that . . ." She shook her head. "It's better to think of him as dead."

"What about you?" Onyx asked.

"I'm staying," she said.

"Won't they eventually figure out you've returned?" he replied.

"Probably," she admitted. "But I've learned from my past mistakes. I'll do a better job of hiding this time."

"We have to do something," I said. "We can't just let this go on."

"We're trying," Sparrow said. "There aren't enough of us to fight in the open. But I promise that we'll keep fighting until we find a way to make these atrocities stop."

Again, Onyx looked over at me. "What if we could convince the demons to join you? Together we could—"

"Convince demons to fight with humes?" Cinder asked, cutting him off. "Against seraphs? They'd never do it."

"They would if we told them the truth," I said. "If they

understood how they're being used and who the humans really are, they'd have to stop what they're doing."

"They'd never believe us," Cinder said.

"Maybe not at first. It will be hard for them to accept the truth about Judgment. But if we tell them about everything we've seen here—the sky, and the air, and the colors, and—"

"All the things I told you about?" Onyx asked.

His words stung more than the icy air, but he was right. He'd told me about almost everything I'd seen here, along with what he'd learned about humans and their memories. But even though he was my best friend, I hadn't believed a single word until I'd seen it for myself.

No one would accept what we had to say. At best, we'd be written off as troublemaking demon spawns with too much time on our hands. At worst, we'd be accused of being hume-loving traitors. Either way, the moment the devils found out what we'd been up to, we'd be locked up, executed, or sent to Absolute Zero with Visala.

"I appreciate your desire to help and how quickly your beliefs have changed," Sparrow said. "Father would, too, if he were still here. But you can't do anything that will draw attention. Even though we've cleared your names, the leaders of Hell will be watching the three of you closely."

"So what, then?" I asked. "We just go back to torturing humans? Letting them think that they deserve what we're doing to them?"

Sparrow's face went stiff. "You do what you have to do down there, just like we do what we have to do up here. Because neither of us has a choice."

She pointed down to a small group of people holding flashlights in a glittering white field in the distance. "Let's get you into that entrance."

I looked to the left and spotted something that made

every muscle in my body seize up. Less than a stone's throw away, the Stygian sat parked at its station. Maintenance equipment was spread around the gleaming cars, and there was no trace of the damage from the attack.

"The woman back in the city said she was having her memory erased. Does that mean . . .?"

"Come on," Sparrow growled, flying down toward the group below.

I shot forward to catch up to her. "They've repaired the Stygian, and they're getting ready to deliver more humans."

She refused to meet my eyes. "There's nothing you can do about it."

Suddenly I was back on the platform in front of the Immigration Station, watching what I now knew were a mother and father with their young daughter. All three had been robbed of their memories, and yet somehow, they still knew that they belonged together.

Where were they now? Being tortured by demons who could very easily be my own parents? Working in ash-covered fields, breathing toxic air and drinking poisonous water until they died of exhaustion or their injuries? Being beaten?

All at once, I understood why Visala had taken our place.

"Where are you going?" Cinder called as I swerved up and to the left.

"Come back!" Sparrow shouted.

"I can't let another innocent human be tortured," I cried, tears streaming down my face.

Onyx appeared to my left, his eyes glowing red. "You understand that if you try this, you'll probably die?"

"Yes," I said without a second of doubt.

His teeth flashed white in the darkness. "Excellent. Let's do this."

* * *

"We were *that* close to getting away," Cinder grumbled as the four of us walked along a metal path that magically moved under our feet, making it feel like we were going twice as far with each step.

"You don't have to come with us," I said. "Take the packs and go back to the tunnel."

"Oh sure." She smirked, swishing her tail. "And let you get all the guys with your amazing stories?"

Onyx opened his mouth, but she held out one hand.

"Save your breath, Hammer Head. I know she's not doing this to get dates. Although if we do manage to survive, I will have guys lined up around the block."

Sparrow, who'd given up trying to change our minds, ground her teeth. "Tell me you at least have some kind of plan."

"Not really," I admitted. "But if we steal the Stygian, they can't take any more humans to Hell."

Sparrow shook her head. "There are way too many guards protecting it. And even if you do manage to take it, they'll just send seraphs down to get it back."

"Then we'll destroy it."

"They'll build another."

I dug my talons into the flesh of my palms, realizing how much this conversation sounded like the argument I'd had with Onyx that night on the tower. But now I understood. Even when the chances of failing were enormous—when the goal seemed all but impossible and any kind of success would be temporary at best—there were times when it was worth dying for what you believed in.

"Maybe I can't permanently stop what's happening here. But if I can buy the humans waiting to be sent to Hell one more month, or one more week, or even one more day of freedom from being tortured by my people, it will be worth it."

Cinder laughed. "Righteous indignation looks good on you, girl."

Onyx wrapped one of his enormous arms around my shoulders, squeezing me until I could barely breathe. "I'm proud of you."

"I'm proud of you too. And I'm sorry I didn't believe you before. Now let go of me before I pass out."

Up ahead, a pair of seraphs turned in our direction. Cinder reached for her sword.

"Don't do it," Sparrow whispered. "Right now, they're just wondering what we're doing here. If you threaten them in any way, they'll call for backup."

She pulled me forward. "Blaze come with me. We look the most like typical seraphs. You two drop back."

As we approached the entrance, the two guards came to attention. "Identify yourselves!"

A few steps away from them, Sparrow pretended to stumble, catching herself on one of their arms. "Sorry about that," she said, slurring her words. "I think my friends and I partied a little too much."

The two guards smiled at each other, relaxing their stances.

"It looks like you did," the one on the left said.

Sparrow pushed herself straight, swaying slightly. "Think we could use the ladies' room to freshen up a little?"

"Sorry. Nobody's allowed inside. Counselor's orders."

Joining Sparrow's play, I ran my fingers down the other guard's bicep. "Are you sure we couldn't come inside for just a minute? We brought our own party supplies."

He licked his lips and glanced over my shoulder to where Cinder and Onyx were standing. "Who are they?"

"Just two more girls looking for a good time."

"One of them looks pretty big."

Cinder quickly came forward, her hips swaying outrageously. "Maybe you could find a couple more friends to join the party?" She winked, leaning into Sparrow's guard, and whispered, "Or not."

The guard looked at his companion and raised an eyebrow. "We really can't let you in. But that doesn't mean we can't party out here."

"Right." The seraph in front of me wrapped an arm around my waist, pulling me toward him.

In two steps, Onyx was on them, slamming the guard in front of me against the wall while he closed his arm around the second guard's neck until the seraph passed out and slumped to the ground.

Sparrow shrugged. "That'll work too."

The minute we stepped inside the doors, I realized she was right.

In a lot of ways, the cavernous room looked like the arrival platform in Hell, with circles, arrows, and signs directing the departing humans onto the train. Unfortunately, there were at least a dozen people between us and the Stygian. Some of them were humans carrying tools and metal tablets that looked like the one the Counselor had been using. But more than half were fully armed seraphs. None of them had noticed us yet, but they would as soon as we started forward.

"Tell me that some of them are moving pictures like the one in the prison cell," Onyx growled.

Sparrow shook her head. "They are all real, and they'll all attack as soon as they see what you're trying to do. Even with four of us, there's no way we can fight them off. And there are more below. I told you this is one of the most secure buildings in Judgment."

Cinder glanced back outside the doors, where the two guards lay on the ground. "It's not too late to go back."

I intentionally willed my fangs and talons to come out, everything zooming into sharp focus as my vision turned red. "Never. We might not make it to the Stygian, but I'm not going down without a fight."

"Hang on." Onyx pointed to a large pulsating ball that glowed the same white as our auras. "What's that?"

"The generator," Sparrow said. "It provides the power to the Stygian Transit—along with half the city."

Onyx nodded. "Right. One of the humans in Hell had some memories of that. He said it used the same power as the swords and that if I plunged an angel-fire blade into it—"

Sparrow's eyes went wide. "You'd blow up the whole station. But then you wouldn't have any power to launch the train."

"We wouldn't need any power if it was already launched," Onyx said. "Gravity would take it from there."

He looked quickly around, then turned to face the three of us. "I'm going to cut through the cage surrounding the generator."

I grabbed his arm. "They'll be on you in a second."

He nodded. "That's what I'm counting on. The minute they converge on me, you head for the train. We never managed to get the full designs when we were planning our attack, but from what we learned, it's pretty straightforward. Turn on the power, shift it to forward, and push the power lever all the way up."

"There's no way you'll make it back through the guards to the train by yourself," I said. "I'm coming with you. Cinder can start the train."

"No." Onyx grabbed my hands. "I told you before. Everything I've done has been for you. I can't do this unless

I know you're safe. Besides, Cinder needs someone to help her get to the train in case any of the guards stay back."

I turned to Sparrow. But she was already shaking her head.

"I'm sorry. I can't go back to Hell. I just can't. And I can do more good here. But I might be able to buy you some time." She turned to Onyx. "Thank you for believing in us humans when you had no reason to. If you make it back and any of the team is still alive . . ."

"I'll tell them you made it. That all of their sacrifices were worth it," he said. "And that they didn't get sent to Hell because they were evil."

She wiped her eyes, then ran to the doors and threw them open. "Attackers outside the building!" she screamed, pointing to the guards on the ground. "Help! They're trying to get in."

Instantly, the seraphs turned and raced toward her, barely noticing us as they rushed past.

"Go," Onyx said, pushing me toward the train.

I wanted to stay and help him, but he was right. Two of the guards had stayed back, protecting the Stygian.

The minute Onyx sliced through the cage protecting the generator, one of the guards pulled out their sword and raced toward him. The second paused, as though unsure of what to do.

Howling with fury, I attacked.

He reached for his sword, but before he could draw it, I was on him, growling and slashing. Fueled by the extra power of the artificial aura, I felt my talons rip through the muscles of his arm, and his head snapped back as I drove him into the side of the Stygian.

Cinder pushed on the front doors, and they slid open.

I was worried there might be more guards inside, but the train seemed to be empty.

Beside me, Cinder lunged to the control panel. She pushed a button, and the floor rumbled under our feet as lights sprang on. A mechanical voice echoed through the car. "Take your seats."

A red arrow next to the power button had an *R* on one side, an *F* on the other, and an *N* at the top. Cinder turned the arrow to the right, and the train jerked forward slightly.

"Prepare for departure," the voice said as the train doors slid closed silently.

Cinder reached for the third control, a lever with a series of lines that grew progressively bigger from the bottom to the top.

"Wait," I shouted, going to the windows. "Onyx isn't here yet."

Outside, something flashed white, and an ear-splitting screech filled the air.

"Sorry," Cinder said, "but he told us not to." She yanked the lever all the way up. The train lurched forward, throwing both of us off our feet.

"No!" I screamed, pulling myself back up to the window. Outside, a pair of seraphs flew backward through the air as Onyx plowed into them.

"Stop the train! He's out there."

Onyx slammed his fist into the face of another seraph. "Turn off the power," I yelled.

"It's not working," Cinder said, pounding the button. "Once the train starts moving, I don't think you can stop it."

Onyx was past the last of the guards running toward the train, but he wasn't going to make it.

Racing to the back, I could see him inches away, trying to keep up as he reached desperately for the doors. I pulled out my angel-fire sword, slashing at the windows and doors. Glass shattered and metal peeled away under my blade.

Just before the platform ended, I reached through the

jagged opening. Onyx grabbed my hand and jumped. For a second, I thought he was going to pull me out instead of me pulling him in. I planted both my hooves against the wall, yanked, and we both fell back onto the floor of the train.

"You did it!" He grinned, pushing himself up off me. Dark blood dripped from his chest and onto the floor, but he seemed okay.

Behind us, an enormous explosion shook the train so hard, I thought we were going to be thrown off the tracks.

"*You* did it!" I exclaimed.

We both hurried to the windows to get a better look, but there was too much dust and debris in the air.

Onyx blinked. "I guess that worked."

"Um, guys," Cinder called from the front of the train. "You might want to come up here."

Onyx wrapped an arm around my shoulder for support, and the two of us limped slowly to the front of the train. Outside, the desert flew by so quickly, it was little more than a blur. Ahead of us, the outer wall of Hell was coming up fast.

"You might want to slow down," Onyx said. "We're coming in too hot!"

"Super observant," Cinder said, licking her lips and slashing her tail. "Only one problem."

She pushed the lever up and down, but nothing happened. She slammed the power button over and over, but we kept moving faster and faster. "Whatever you did back there must have broken the controls."

"What do we do?" I asked.

Onyx pointed to the leather straps on the seats behind us. "Buckle in!"

Quickly, we ran to the back of the train and strapped ourselves into the last row of seats. With no way to stop it, we watched in horror as the Immigration Station grew closer and closer. On top of the platform, I could see demons scurrying around, unsure of what was happening.

"Get out of the way!" I screamed.

At the last second, they seemed to realize we weren't going to stop and dove for cover.

"Hold on," Onyx said, wrapping his arms around me.

The last thing I heard was the sound of tearing metal and exploding rock. Then everything went black.

CHAPTER 39

*Welcome to Hell, all ye damned and demented.
Please keep moving. Welcome to Hell, all ye
damned and demented. Please keep moving . . .*

For what seemed like hours, I drifted in and out of consciousness. At one point, I thought I heard Onyx calling my name. I tried to reach out to him, but I couldn't move my arms. My entire body felt wrapped in a coffin so tight that it kept me from even turning my head. I thought I opened my eyes, but I wasn't sure because everything remained black.

The only thing that let me know I was alive was the welcome message echoing over and over somewhere outside my suffocating cocoon of metal and rock.

Later, I thought I heard my parents screaming and crying, but that might have just been my imagination.

It wasn't until I felt hands pulling my arms and the pain scorching through my body that I finally came completely awake.

I thought I was on the arrival platform, but it was hard to tell because everything around me was reduced to piles of rock and dust.

"Blaze!" a voice cried, and I turned to see Onyx surrounded by at least a dozen spear-wielding efreets. He was covered in blood, and one of his eyes was nearly swollen shut. But instead of getting him to the infirmary, the guards had him wrapped in chains.

"Are you okay?" he asked.

I nodded, and a bolt of agony shot through my neck. "I think so." I tried to look around, but every time I moved my head, the ache was almost unbearable. "What about Cinder?"

"I feel like I've been boiled in lava," she called, waving weakly from a stretcher nearby. "But I'm pretty sure I'm still alive."

"Not for long," a harsh voice crackled, and a shadow dropped over my face. I looked up to see a devil hovering above me. "Get her up."

Hands yanked me to my feet, and I couldn't help screaming in agony. It felt like I was being ripped in two.

I tried to push the people holding me away, but my arms flopped weakly at my sides. Where was I? Everything looked wrong. To my left, I saw what remained of the arrival platform, crumpled train cars sticking up like broken fingers. Even though it was still night, the streets below were crowded with both demons and humans, all trying to get a better look at what was happening.

Glancing up, I recognized the beam Onyx and I had used to swing to the roof of the Immigration Station. But that didn't make any sense because the Immigration Station was nowhere to be seen. Unless . . .

On the ground to my left, I spotted bits of colored glass amongst the wreckage. The stained-glass windows. I was *in* the Immigration Station. Or at least where it had been. Other than a few pieces of the outer walls, there was nothing left of the building. The Stygian must have plowed straight into it.

Realizing where I was and what had happened, I turned back to the crowd below to warn them while I still could.

"It's all a lie!" I screamed. "The seraphs aren't really angels, and the humans aren't—"

A fist slammed into my face, shocking me into silence.

The devil leaned so close that I had to blink against its hot breath. "You have made a grave mistake."

"You're the one who's mistaken," I gasped. It felt like my jaw was broken, and every word was agony, but I refused to give in. "I know the truth, and I'm going to tell everyone."

He clamped a scaly hand to my face, squeezing until dots floated in front of my eyes. "You won't live long enough to tell anyone anything. By the end of this day, you and every single person you care about or even know will have your heads mounted on the outer wall."

He turned to the guards. "Take her away!"

I waited for the guards to drag me off, but they weren't moving. They weren't even listening. Every one of them had turned in the other direction, their eyes looking up. Down in the streets, a soft murmur quickly grew into shouts of surprise, confusion, and terror as humans and demons pointed toward the top of Hell.

Moving my neck was torment, but I managed to raise my head just enough to see a jagged pie-shaped break in what I now knew was the top of the man-made dome covering the city just to the right of the mountain of Judgment, where the tracks of the Stygian originated. The explosion in the train station had broken off just enough of the ceiling to reveal a sliver of the real sky outside.

As we all watched, the opening turned from black to purple, and then a bright blue shade that had never existed in our world. Just over the edge, a fiery yellow ball glowing even brighter than the seraphs' auras appeared.

"Judgment is coming to punish us!" a Dae' Ceal mother screamed, grabbing her child and backing away.

"It's the volcano," a human cried in a panicked voice. "It's erupting."

The volcano was nowhere near the opening in the dome, but in their shock, no one seemed to notice—or care. Humans and demons alike ran in terror, screaming and trampling each other.

With the devil distracted, I jerked away from his grip and raced to the edge of the platform. "It's not the seraphs, and it's not the volcano," I screamed, trying to make my voice heard above the noise of the crowd. "It's called the sun. It's rising in the real sky outside! We've been trapped down here for years, but you don't have to be afraid."

Looking down into the crowd, I spotted my mother and father staring up at me in shock. "Tell everyone!" I yelled. "Before they seal it back up. The real world is outside. It's just been hidden from us."

"Kill her!" the devil shrieked, and hoofbeats came toward me across the broken rock of what remained of the platform.

He was raising his fist to strike me down when the tip of a flaming spear ripped through his chest.

For a moment, he could only stare down at the blood spurting from his body in wonder. He clutched the tip of the spear, opened his mouth, then stumbled off the edge of rock into the street below.

Onyx grabbed my arm with one hand while supporting Cinder with the other. The efreets who had been guarding him ran away in terror, their weapons lying at their feet. It was one of their spears that Onyx had driven through the devil's chest.

"Come on," he said. "We have to go. Things are going to get crazy."

CHAPTER 40

A door slammed shut, and Onyx and I looked up quickly from the table where we'd been studying maps and notes along with several other demons and nearly a dozen humans.

Cinder pushed aside the blanket hanging across the entrance to block any light from reaching the door and shook her head. Her face was still bruised, but the stitches the human doctor had put in her cheek were barely visible, and she seemed to be moving her arms freely. A benefit of being a demon—or as I knew now, a freak.

"Riots still going on?" I asked, standing to look her over and make sure she was okay.

"Worse than ever," Cinder said. "You'd think that discovering we're trapped here would make the demons turn against our leaders. But we're attacking each other instead." She glanced at the humans around the table, her tail swishing anxiously. "Along with the humes—I mean humans."

"No one spotted you?" Onyx asked.

"No one spotted anyone," she said. "I don't think they're even looking for us." She grimaced at me and shook her head. "Stop staring at me like you're my mother and get me something to drink."

Violence, the human who'd taken Sparrow's place as the leader of the underground human resistance, shuffled the papers in front of him and cleared his throat. "You said your kind would revolt."

"They will," I said, handing Cinder her drink. "The truth of what's really happening here is getting out. We just have to give them time."

Onyx grunted, thudding back into his chair. "They won't. Right now, they're rioting because they're afraid. But the workers up above are already busy closing the crack in the dome. Once the fear of the unknown goes away, the demons are going to forget about what they saw. The devils will get control, Judgment will fix the train, and things will go right back to how they were."

"You can't know that!" I shouted, slamming my fist on the table. "You told me once that everyone—demons and humans alike—deserve something better. Have you given up on that belief? More of them are joining us every day."

Cinder slouched against the wall, sipping the drink I'd given her. "Joining us for what? Judgment's still up there, and we're still down here. Even if we did manage to start a rebellion, what would be the point?"

"The point?" I asked, spreading my arms wide. "Look around you. We've been lied to, cheated, imprisoned, used by the people of Judgment because of something no one living here had anything to do with. Maybe our ancestors did break their oath to remain peaceful. Maybe they did make mistakes. But why should we have to pay the price?"

"Blaze," Onyx began, but I shook my head.

"No!" I shouted, looking at all the members of the committee gathered around the table. "I'm not giving up. I'm not going to let the smug bureaucrats up there tell me that we don't deserve to be free. Did it ever occur to them that if our kind hadn't broken their oath, none of them would even be alive?"

Violence rubbed his bearded cheek. "We agree with

everything you're saying. But the truth is, we don't have any more time. The devils are getting the guards back together. They're killing some of our messengers and locking the rest up to torture them for information."

I dropped back into my chair and looked at Cinder, silently asking the same question I had since we went into hiding. Once again, she simply shook her head. "No one's seen any of our families. Violence is right, they might be locked up. But the truth is, they're probably all dead."

"We have to make a decision," Violence said, rubbing his beard. "If the demons' riot isn't going to turn into a revolt, we have no choice but to go ahead with the plan." He turned to Agony, the woman to his left. "Do you have all the supplies gathered?"

"As many as we could get our hands on," she said. "The demons destroyed several of our caches, and a group of humans lit their own neighborhood on fire even though they were the only ones there. Another group attacked a band of demon guards. It wasn't pretty. We aren't going to get nearly as many of them to go with us as I would have liked."

I knew what they were talking about, and I understood why they felt they had to do it, but the idea of running away, leaving things to go back to how they were before, made me sick. "I know Hell isn't what we thought it was. But it's still our home. Our people. Humans and demons alike. Wouldn't you rather stay and change things from the inside? If we can only convince everyone here that Judgment is the real enemy, not each other—"

"That's not going to happen," Cinder said, changing her colors to match the wall behind her. "If you saw what was going on for yourself, you'd understand. Most of the demons don't want to hear the truth. They just want to get back to the way things were."

"To murdering humans, you mean."

"We aren't giving up," Onyx said. "We're just relocating our battle to somewhere safer than here. Judgment will pay for what they did to us."

"Fine," I said, digging my talons into the wooden table. "We run. But don't think it's going to be any easier out there. The desert is just as deadly as it's always been."

Onyx took my hand, his steady breathing calming my racing heart. "We've been through the Outer Circles of Hell once. It will be easier this time."

"Maybe," I said. Yes, we'd made it before. But that was with Visala's help. And even then, we'd nearly died. Father *had*. What made Onyx think it would be any different? And even if we managed to get through safely, Judgment would be waiting. "The only reason we made it out of the dome was because we had the codes. Do you really think the people running things up there are just going to let us out through their tunnels again?"

"We aren't going out through Judgment." Onyx turned to the map and tapped a spot three quarters of the way to the other side of the dome from where we'd gone the first time. "There are a series of maintenance hatches all around the outside of the city."

Cinder leaned in for a closer look. "We have to assume they'll all be guarded."

"They are," Violence said. "But what they don't know is that we have help from the outside. The demons down here may want things to go back to normal. But there are a lot of humans up top who don't."

I looked from Violence to Onyx, realizing there was something he hadn't told me. "Sparrow?" I asked. "Have you been in contact with her?"

Onyx nodded slowly, his hand squeezing mine. "But there's someone else too."

Violence slid a piece of paper across the table.

Turning it over, my heart began to race again, and my fingers trembled. It was a note, written in shaky print. The paper had been folded many times, and the ink was smudged. But I could still read it.

I'm sorry for lying to you before. I hope I can make up, at least a little, for all the mistakes I've made. But know that I'll never lie to you again. This fight is far from over.

It was signed, *Your favorite seraph, Visala.*

Onyx met my eyes and nodded. "He's alive."

The End

As a kid, Tyler H. Jolley always had a knack for storytelling. When he grew bored of old fables, he created his own exciting and unique worlds. Many years later, he still had so many new ideas and stories swirling in his head, but with nowhere to share it. That's when he put his pencil to paper and let the creative juices flow.

His debut novel, *Extracted*, came out in 2013 and swiftly became an Amazon Best Seller and Spencer Hill Press Best Seller. *Prodigal and Riven*, the second and third books in The Lost Imperials series were released in May of 2015.

After a brief hiatus he restructured and returned to writing. His Adventurous Ali series has received much praise. To date, he's released four in the series.

When he's not writing, you can find him at his orthodontic practice, mountain biking, or on the hunt for the perfect doughnut.